Ken N Kamoche was born and raised in Kenya. He was educated at the University of Nairobi and the University of Oxford. He is a management academic, occasional newspaper columnist and writer of fiction. Ken's collection of short stories, *A Fragile Hope* (Salt, 2007), was shortlisted for the Commonwealth First Book Award. After travelling frequently to Asia, Ken took up a job in Hong Kong in 1998 supposedly for two years. The two years soon turned into ten, involved extensive travel up and down China, and ultimately inspired this novel.

Ken N Kamoche

BLACK GHOSTS

AUSTIN MACAULEY PUBLISHERS™
LONDON * CAMBRIDGE * NEW YORK * SHARJAH

A CIP catalogue record for this title is available from the British Library.

ISBN 9781398407824 (Paperback)
ISBN 9781398415003 (ePub e-book)

www.austinmacauley.com

First Published (2021)
Austin Macauley Publishers Ltd
25 Canada Square
Canary Wharf
London
E14 5LQ

I am grateful to Thomas Abonyo, 'Chairman' Phinias Sichongwe and Philip Snow for their excellent insights on China, and to the many friends I met who aided and challenged my understanding of the region.

Part 1

The First Step

I STOOD IN FRONT OF Mrs Chevo, the deputy head, my hands wrapped around my schoolbag, and stared at the scholarship application forms as though they were tainted.

"The Chinese ones are the only ones left," she informed me, with a consolatory half-smile. "You must remember, Dan, that every opportunity is a blessing. And as you might recall from your history lessons, Chairman Mao taught his people that every journey starts with a single step. This is your first step." Her voice was soft and reassuring, like that of my mother explaining why I needed to take my bitterroot cough mixture when I was a child.

I couldn't see how going to study in China could possibly be a blessing. It felt more like a punishment, like being banished away from home, being sent on exile. In school, we liked to make jokes about this mysterious land where everyone dressed in the same drab, monochromatic outfits, walked around unsmiling, quoting from Mao's Red Book at every opportunity.

"The Chinese have always been our friends," declared Mrs Chevo, her voice assuming a less placatory edge. "Why can't we work together? They supported the struggle, as you, no doubt, know."

I knew that all right. When Zimbabwean freedom fighters waged war against the Ian Smith regime, China was one of the few non-African countries that supported us militarily. And during our six years of independence, President Mugabe pursued a Marxist-Leninist ideology, strengthening ties with China.

China hadn't been my first choice. I went about the task of filling in the scholarship forms as if I was being coerced into it, half-hoping I would be turned down. My class teacher made my nomination late, as though it were an afterthought. Since the day he caught me smoking and instigated my suspension from school for a week, he had always viewed me as a troublemaker. His attitude to me never improved after the smoking incident. It was as though his own son had let him down. But I was the top student in the class, so he had no choice but to nominate me for the few scholarships available to graduating high school students.

I reflected on the deputy head's wisdom for a moment. If I was awarded the scholarship, I would be an unwilling participant in the magnanimity borne of a political dalliance. I had to start believing that going to China was, in fact, at the very least, a blessing in disguise. My class teacher was getting his own back for all the grief he believed I had caused him. If only he knew how I had suffered to get that education, waking up at 4.30 a.m. every morning to study for an hour before helping Mother tend her crops, then having to run five miles to school. Weekends, I had to help Father on the tobacco farm and still find a few hours in the day to study and do my homework. Although Brian Walter didn't approve of children working on the farm, the overseers allowed us, so we could make some extra cash for the family. I had to get those 'A' grades. Every time I dozed away on a book late in the night by the faint yellow light of the paraffin lantern, every morning when the cocks crowed to coax me away from my warm blankets, I heard the voice of my father in my head. *There'll be time enough to sleep when you're old.* I truly believe he meant, 'when you're dead' but didn't want to scare me.

Word came seven months later. I was headed for China. The farthest I had ever been from Ndambu village was Harare, our capital city, on school field trips.

The head teacher was right. There was no way I was going to turn down this scholarship, even though I had earned a place at a local university.

Mother saw it as a leap in the dark. For several days, she wouldn't let me out of her sight, as though afraid I would fly away without saying goodbye. She fussed over me, prevailing upon me to eat more and more, carefully scanning the post and asking if there were scholarships from other countries. After all, my cousin had gone to Canada the previous year. The pictures she sent conveyed a world that was magical in its colours and images, just like a dream. Students throwing snowballs at each other, clad in heavy winter jackets. Pine trees stooped down in half-hearted defiance against the weather. It was like a Christmas card bursting into life right in front of my eyes. This was the world I knew my mother willed for me.

We had no pictures of China. No one knew what the country looked like, besides the black-and-white pictures I had seen in history and geography text books that portrayed emperors with beards that reached down to the belly, peasants bent double in rice paddies, rebellions and hangings.

Mother took me to the church and together, we prayed for wisdom and blessings. Then she sought out the fortune-teller, who also doubled up as a traditional healer, and implored him to commune with the spirits of our ancestors and beg them to protect me from harm as I embarked on this journey into the unknown. Only after both the pastor and the healer had declared that my journey to the East was free from danger, did Mother breathe easier. Even so, she wore a mournful expression, as though she had already lost a son, until the day I flew to China.

As we walked back home from the fortune-teller's hut on the edge of Ndambu village, my mother and I stopped by the dam we call Lake Ndambu to take a rest. We had been walking for almost an hour, taking longer because Mother stopped every few minutes to chat to people along the dusty village path, regaling them with news about her illustrious son's academic exploits. I accepted their kind wishes and words of advice, although I couldn't help noticing that some of them were puzzled by my choice of destination. The surface of the dam was calm and serene as usual, belying its treacherous depth, which had claimed two schoolchildren earlier in the year. We sat on a rock in quiet contemplation, my mind racked with worries and the anxiety of the journey ahead.

I pointed out the African fish eagle to Mother. But she had already spotted it.

"I've been watching him, son," she said. "And wondering what his message to you might be."

"Message for me?" I gasped. "Haven't we had enough messages from the healer?"

"Don't be impertinent," she chided me. "That bird has a message for whoever spots him. You see how patiently he perches on top of that tree, seeing tiny ripples in the water that are invisible to you and me? He knows what he wants and will wait all day if he has to. When you return with all your education, you can perch on the highest branches, higher than your father and I could ever reach. See the symmetry of that eagle, the white head and tail, the black wings that let him fly like a shadow. His lesson for you is to wait patiently for the right chance and then spring into action, and your blessings will come to you. Just you wait and see."

"I don't think we have all day to watch an eagle, Mother. What about dinner?"

Mother was exhausted. She needed to rest.

"It's not easy for me to see you leave, son," she said. "But I've had to accept there's a reason for it. It is God's will. I know now that it's your education that will change our lives."

"I'll work hard, Mother."

She went on as if she hadn't heard me. "It will be a different kind of struggle, not the fighting and suffering we've endured all our lives. Education, such a wonderful gift. If only I were young like you. Young people are fortunate today, even young girls. They can go to school and stay there, drinking from the cup of wisdom, until they are truly ready for womanhood and motherhood. How things have changed, my son. But, no, I shouldn't speak like that, like someone choking on regret."

Mother often started to lament about the past then cut herself short, as though to protect your innocent ears from the hardships of the past, the opportunities denied.

"Don't worry, Mother," I whispered, in an effort to reassure and cheer her. "I'll not disappoint you."

"I know. And just like that beautiful bird up on the gum tree, I know you'll be clever enough to recognise the opportunity when it comes."

"What opportunity, Mother?"

She adjusted her headscarf and rubbed my shoulder but didn't say a word. Sometimes she answered questions merely by holding or rubbing your shoulder, leaving you struggling to understand the unspoken answer.

I didn't see the eagle until his feet hit the surface of the water. It happened so fast. Next thing I knew, he was dragging a fish along the surface of the water. He couldn't raise it. It was too big. But he held on, his gigantic wings flapping wildly. I held my breath. For a moment, I thought he would let go and look for something smaller. I had seen eagles hunt before and fly off with their catch. I had never seen one struggle so desperately to hang on to its dinner.

For weeks thereafter, I couldn't get this incident out of my mind.

Father had mixed feelings. I showed him the offer letter when he returned from the tobacco fields one evening.

He didn't smile. He didn't frown. He sat on an upturned wheelbarrow, smoking a roll-up, wearing his thinking look. That's what my siblings and I called it. Eyes half-closed in quiet contemplation, the smoke drifting in gusts from his nostrils, like the exhaust from the tractor he treated as though it were his own treasured possession. He read the letter several times, careful not to miss anything.

"America would have been better," intoned my father. "At least we know where it is."

Did we really? It was as far away as China. But Father was right, in a way. America couldn't have been all that different from the Canada we knew from my cousin's pictures and postcards, with its snow-covered Christmas trees, skyscrapers, farmers in red crash helmets and bright orange jackets driving enormous combine harvesters through wheat farms, smiling chubby-faced children with lollipops in their mouths.

The martial arts films Brian Walker organised once a month in the cow pen were Father's only window into the East. Shaven monks in Shaolin temples going through their dazzling kung fu routine.

"What do they eat there?" said Father.

"Rice, I think."

I hoped they had meat, too, so that at least a better diet would compensate for my going away from home. We didn't have meat very often. But I wasn't optimistic. My school friends were adamant that there were no cows in China. And if the kung fu films were anything to go by, the risk of my turning vegetarian was all too real, as my cousin Chipinduka so ominously pointed out.

I cast my gaze around the farm, to the tobacco crop that went all the way to the distant horizon, beyond the eucalyptus trees at the top of the hill. I would miss this land. I would miss the songs of the birds, the giant eagles that ruled the skies, the smell of grass after a downpour, perhaps even the thick smell of manure that forced its way up your nostrils as if trying to choke you.

"Go and study hard," said Father, folding the offer letter and handing it back to me with a smile of encouragement. "Perhaps when you return, things will have changed."

He went on smoking in silence, reverting to his thinking look.

"How will things have changed, Father?" My question rang superfluous in the serene evening breeze, for I knew exactly what Father meant.

"The land, son." The patience in his voice made me look up in surprise. "Perhaps the Chinese will teach you some new farming techniques. We'll need them, when things change. Agriculture will be a good subject for you. The Chinese work on farms like us. So, China could be right for you, after all. Think about it that way, son. The land. It's our life."

13

That wasn't the way he normally spoke about 'the dream', as he called it. Usually, it was in a tone that might have conveyed the inevitability of rains as dark clouds gathered above. It had been a dream for many years. Ever since Robert Mugabe became our president in 1980, Father had been waiting to own a piece of the farm we live on. Most of the farming land in the country was owned by white farmers. We lived as landless squatters ever since the British first landed here. For seven years after independence, Father waited, like the duplicitous Jacob in the Old Testament, forced to serve the treacherous uncle Laban for seven years for pretty Rachel, only to have the older, ugly Leah foisted on him, and then have to serve another seven years before earning his reward! Father lived for the day when Brian Walter would hand over the farm to his African workers. Many politicians had promised us that it would happen, as surely as day followed night. The bright light of independence would shine upon the dark night of our troubled history, and the war veterans would be the proud owners of the land they had risked their lives for.

So far, Walter and his family had shown no signs of returning to Britain, the land of their forefathers. If anything, every year they entrenched themselves even more firmly into this land, which Father believed was for them but a temporary abode. They extended the land under cultivation, laid out the unending green carpet of the tobacco crop over more and more of the undulating hills, and reared more cattle. They created a private game park in which herds of antelope, wildebeest, and gazelle roamed free, and crocodiles poked their snouts from a man-made lake. It was their playground, as much as it was the animals', a stretch of private jungle, which they loved to inspect on horseback and on a horse-driven carriage when the children were too young to ride horses by themselves.

I wanted to share my father's optimism but I found it hard to believe that the Walters would willingly give up this paradise for the uncertainties of faraway, cold Britain, which they only knew from the occasional visit.

I glanced at the majestic, red, brick-roofed Walter residence in the distant horizon, partly hidden behind a thick hedge and tall jacaranda trees. We could only admire the majestic mansion from a distance. The only time we got close was on Christmas day, when Mrs Walter invited all the farm kids for chocolate biscuits, jam tarts, and juicy red strawberries laid out on gazelle-skin coffee tables guarded by a stern servant in white gloves, so we wouldn't fight and scramble for the goodies. But first, we had to amuse her by singing Christmas carols while she sat on a high-backed leather chair, drinking white wine, flanked by her three children, two boys in blue suits and red bowties and a daughter in liveried dress and red ribbons in her blonde hair. Then we would dash off to church, stuffing our faces and screaming our solemn gratitude to God and Madam Walter.

Watching my father roll up another cigarette with unprocessed tobacco, I felt as though my imminent departure now served as the missing link, the final hurdle before the land reverted back to the squatters and farm workers.

My chest heaved with emotion, as though bracing itself to soak up the weight of expectations Father so effortlessly placed on my shoulders.

But the image that filled my mind at that moment was not one of me studying to be a top-notch farmer. It was that of an eagle chugging an oversized tilapia across the dam.

A Book and a Rice Bowl

THE CLASS FALLS SILENT AS the professor wanders in. Sweeping a disapproving glance across the lecture hall, he places his book on the desk and a bowl next to it. He has a grim expression on his face, as if he has just received some bad news and has to endure the class before rushing off to deal with some emergency. Much later, we realise he's always like that, unsmiling, stern, and thoughtful. Like all middle-aged Chinese men, his grey trousers are pulled right up above the waist and belted across the protruding belly. I've never understood why they make trousers that way, why they don't belt them up at the waist.

I'm finally ready for my first engineering class after studying Chinese for a year.

I watch the professor closely, ready to partake of the blessing that my school deputy head promised. I think of my mother, proudly announcing to mesmerised neighbours, "That son of mine, he speaks Chinese through the nose, like white people." They would rub her shoulders and shake with laughter.

It will be a long time before my family reaps the fruits of my labour. So far, all I can do is send some funds from my grant.

My friends and I occupy the seats right at the back. The three of us are the only black people in the class; in fact, the only foreigners. The American and European students who attended the Putonghua language course with us have already left. They have no use for a degree taught in Chinese. What good would it do them? I quickly banish the thought. Thinking like that makes me wonder what good it will do *us*.

There's Kabinga from Rwanda on my right. He's tall and skinny with a bit of a stoop, and he wears his hair in short dreadlocks that look like stunted spikes. He's always scratching his goatee and shaking his head, especially when he's bored or when he thinks others are speaking nonsense. He speaks rapidly, as if he's afraid someone will steal his thoughts before he has uttered them. When I first met him, he shocked me by saying that he had no real interest in being an engineer. He's determined to be a businessman, and to prove how serious he is, he spends a lot of time doing deals with foreign diplomats and rich Chinese. Sometimes we call him Chin Chin, after the Chinese word for money, qian. On his right is Diallo, from Guinea. He's shorter than Kabinga and I, but sturdier, like a wrestler. He keeps his hair short and tidy. He's soft-spoken and always maintains a studied, calm demeanour. He likes to suck his lips in, nodding his head, as if to weigh the wisdom of what he's just about to say. We've nicknamed him the Enlightened One, or simply Zen, for his amazing knowledge of everything Chinese.

Zen explains the tension and exchanges of abuse between African and Chinese male students as cultural misunderstandings, an expression which cropped up in a Chinese culture and civilisation class last year. For him, the solution is to learn as much as we can about each other.

Kabinga takes a blunter view. As far as he's concerned, the locals hate us because we're black. It's as simple as that. To be fair, we've endured enough hostility to give Kabinga the edge over Diallo in explaining our predicament.

"What's he carrying a bowl for? Christ!" hisses Kabinga, turning to face me.

I shrug my shoulders.

As this is the first lesson, the professor devotes a lot of time to announcements. Standing just behind a painting of Taoist immortals playing flutes against a backdrop of blue smoke, he introduces himself as Professor Sheng Zuyi. After explaining that he's the subject head, he proceeds to lay down the law. Attendance is compulsory; lateness and absence will not be tolerated; students must read and memorise the class notes every week and must be ready for quizzes and tests at any time. Then he picks up the bowl and a pair of chopsticks and pretends to slurp food into his mouth, saying, "I'll give you the education you need to be good engineers, and your duty is to eat and digest it."

The three of us exchange glances, wondering if we missed something in the language. Before any of us can whisper something crude, Professor Sheng says, "What I have said is rule number one." He stretches to his full height, points at the bowl, rubs his belly. "You consume the knowledge like rice from your benevolent father." He casts a stern gaze across the class, the expression on his face reminiscent of that of the university president when he made his welcome speech and left no doubt in our minds that he was conveying decrees from the highest echelons of the Communist Party.

Kabinga shakes his head, his scrunched face a mask of shocked disbelief. Diallo smiles benevolently, as if he has just been promised he'll get his degree without breaking a sweat. The Chinese students are busy writing down everything the professor says, hardly looking up in case they miss a single word. Perhaps they think they'll be tested on the rules.

At the end of the class, Professor Sheng grabs his book and white bowl and heads straight to the cafeteria for lunch. There's already a queue snaking its way through the door at the main cafeteria across the square outside our lab.

We cycle back to the hostel to prepare our lunch. The foreign students' hostel is in a secluded part of campus, separated from the north-wing classroom blocks by a public square and cluster of pine and magnolia trees. It is a good ten-minute walk to the locals' hostels and a fifteen-minute walk to the science labs. But we like the quiet and serene neighbourhood, which is free of traffic noise and allows us to think we have our own little oasis of leisure.

When we first came to Nanjing, we ate at the various cafeterias on campus, but after a while, we could no longer endure the smells. Mastering the skill of eating with chopsticks taxed even the most determined in the first few weeks, especially when you were famished and it took forever to eat. The food itself was good: it was either rice or noodles, and a variety of vegetable and pork dishes cooked in excessive amounts of soya sauce that turned everything black. The offending smell came from the oil, which infects the air and can be heard sizzling furiously in the kitchen. Then there's the smell of fried bean curd, or tofu, which reminds you of a gas leak in the chemistry laboratory. The smell lingers in the air and clings stubbornly to the walls and furniture. They can never get rid of it, no matter how much they wash and scrub.

We normally buy groceries at the wet market in the Cai Chang shopping area, across the road from the main entrance to South Nanjing University. Old women with shawls around their heads and black gumboots on their feet wrap your vegetables in old newspapers, grinning at you and exchanging comments with each other as if you're not there. *They speak the language! How clever. And just look at their nice jackets.* They ask you where you're from and if you like the motherland. Visits to the wet market are a great way to practise the language. They sell everything from fish, eel, and frogs that squat at the bottom of water tanks, to live chickens that crouch in hatches making low cooing sounds, terrified of their imminent demise. The pork hangs on hooks or lies strewn on bloodied tables. Beef is rare, and when you find it, it comes in narrow, wizened black stripes. You have to take the butcher's word that it is beef.

In the winter, they sell goat meat. The Chinese believe it keeps you warm. They cook it in boiling water like a soup. To keep extra warm, some eat dog meat, but you can't find it at the wet market. Kabinga asks for it sometimes, but only to watch the shocked faces. One day, after seeing a man clutching a puppy with its legs tied together with bits of string, I asked a Chinese student where they sell dog meat. He laughed and said it was a secret, not to be discussed with 'guests'.

We live mostly on chicken. It is cheaper to buy a whole chicken and have it chopped up so that you can select a few pieces to cook every other day. We always argue with the butchers because they insist on weighing the chicken with its head and feet, parts we don't eat. They can sell the feet, but there's not much anyone can do with chicken heads.

A strong wind blows through the trees that are already shedding their leaves, an early sign of autumn. By winter, most of these trees will be standing naked, exposed to snow and freezing temperatures, swaying in the blustery winds but with nowhere to go. You can't help feeling sorry for them. The leaves that remain have shrunk to shrivelled-up, spiky, orange and yellow petals, which hang precariously on branches that look brittle and lifeless, just like on the Qing dynasty pictures on the corridors in the department and the etchings on blue porcelain and bamboo tea sets displayed in glass cabinets in the lobby.

In the lawn outside our hostel, the only flowers still standing are the dull yellow chrysanthemums. They add some welcome colour to our drab grey four-storey building, which reminds you of a hospital. An old woman is weeding the lawn. She is wearing green gloves and a black, broad-rimmed hat fringed with cotton tassels. As usual, she stops her work to look at us, her darkened face expressionless. As she watches the *hei gui*, the black ghosts or black devils, casting a shadow over her flowers, the soft eyes speak of voiceless yet innocent curiosity. What does she tell her grandchildren about us? Does she wonder, like someone once asked me, if the blackness can wash off if you scrub hard enough? Watching her bent over reminds me of women tilling the fields in Ndambu, with only a faded, threadbare headscarf to protect them against the searing heat. Even they stop to watch when Walter walks past, though they've seen him all their lives.

Conscious of the woman's blank stare, I tighten my jacket and run up the steps into the lobby. The elderly guard at the reception stirs from his midday siesta and, seeing it's only us, promptly shuts his eyes again. We take the stairs to the kitchenette on the second floor, where we're met by the appetising smells of fried fish and boiling rice as my neighbours prepare lunch.

As we take our seats at one of the two small round tables and tuck into our leftovers from yesterday, the talk is all about our first class with Professor Sheng. It was my turn to cook last night. We either take it in turns or cook together. My specialty is fried chicken stuffed with garlic and garnished with chopped parsley, fresh coriander and green onions. Kabinga says he has no time for such elaborate art, as he calls it. He prefers something more practical, like beef, which he stews with potatoes and a variety of vegetables and lethal-looking green peppers, all thrown in to create a unique blend of spicy flavours. It takes so little work and effort, yet it's one of our favourites. It so reminds us of home. Diallo likes to experiment with things like duck and pigeon, and thick mushrooms that remind you of African thatched hats. He says he wants to live and eat like the locals. Once, he suggested snake, but we wouldn't hear of it. We settled on eel, which turned out to be soft and tender but with little treacherous spiky bones. Diallo couldn't stop teasing us for what he called our hypocrisy. "Eel is a water snake," he declared. Kabinga insisted it was just a long, ugly fish. Diallo has recently started to make sadza using wheat semolina. It's much stickier than the real thing but makes for a nice change from the ubiquitous boiled rice.

The chicken drumsticks are soft and feathery, very unlike the tough, tasty chicken I remember from home. We've found that using garlic and soya sauce improves the taste and makes the experience so much more enjoyable. It is a habit we picked up from eating in the cafeteria last year. But we use the soya sauce sparingly, while at the cafeteria they serve you a bowl of dark soya sauce with bits of meat and vegetables thrown in for good measure. The one good thing we all agree on is the automatic rice cooker that warns you when the rice is ready. Neither of us had ever seen one before, and our earlier efforts at boiling rice were both hilarious and embarrassing, and often ended up with a lumpy, soggy mess that closely resembled corn sadza. When you used too much water, you ended up with viscous congee.

Kabinga is still reeling from what he calls the professor's patronising tone.

"Eat education, my foot!" he mutters. "What I want to eat is a goat rib, *mes amis*." He stares at his chicken leg, as if willing it to metamorphose into a sizzling, roast goat rib dripping with fat. At times like this, it is difficult to get him to focus on anything else. He curses under his breath and, with a murderous look, tears the meat out of the chicken leg with his bare fingers, glares at us as if daring us to challenge his unorthodox table manners, and gobbles up the soft meat, swallowing it almost without bothering to chew it. I urge him to take it easy and enjoy his lunch.

"It's my food, Eggman." That's the nickname the Chinese have given me, because my name Dan translates into egg in Chinese. Kabinga breathes noisily through the mouth. The way he sits hunched over his plate, glaring at the two of us, he reminds you of an injured rhino that hasn't had a meal all week. "You might have cooked it, but it's on my plate now, so it's my bloody chicken, and I'll devour it any way I like."

I put my hands up in mock surrender.

"Not promising," mutters Diallo, licking his fingers. "Not very promising."

"Not promising what?" Kabinga shoots back.

Diallo thoughtfully ignores Kabinga and keeps licking his fingers, making sucking, appreciative noises.

"You're a good man to have around the kitchen, Eggman. *Tres bien.*"

I nod and keep my eyes on Kabinga, who is struggling to keep a lid on his temper, and just about succeeding in not repeating his question in case the hostility consumes him. I turn to Diallo and ask him what he means.

"Well, this doesn't look like a promising start to our degree programme, Chin Chin, does it?" His face exudes a remarkable placidness, as though he was remarking on an unexpected turn of good weather.

"What doesn't, eh?" Kabinga's lips are trembling, as if he's mouthing soundless words. "Are you accusing me of something?"

Diallo scoops the last of his rice into his mouth and chews with great deliberation, like a condemned man savouring his last meal.

"Come on, people. Let's clear up. I have work to do."

"No, Eggman. Wait," says Kabinga. Then, pointing a sauce-covered finger at Diallo, he says, "I want him to explain himself. The *Enlightened One.*"

Diallo and I laugh at the stinging sarcasm, which only enrages Kabinga.

"*D'accord,*" says Diallo. "It's like this. Why get so worked up about the professor's choice of words? I think we all know what he means. He talks like a schoolteacher. Maybe that's the way professors here talk."

Kabinga licks the sauce off his fingers with furious impatience before responding.

"Do not be naïve, *mon ami*." His eyes are still gleaming with anger. "Can't you see this is just a sign of the patronising shit we'll get from now on? Learning the language was a honeymoon. All that nice stuff about a 5000-year-old culture, comradeship to our poor black African brothers from the Dark Continent. Do you know a bus driver once told someone to give up his seat for me, saying they should welcome the dear comrades? You should have seen the poor man's face. He's staring at this scary-looking *hei gui* and thinking, *I'm giving up my seat for a gorilla*? I enjoyed it, you know why? It's the kind of rare niceness you get once in a blue moon. Show the black ghosts we're friendly here, before the real China hits you, man. And it starts now, believe you me."

"I wonder," I say. "If the professor is patronising towards everyone, why should it bother me?"

Kabinga has that look he had in the class when Professor Sheng laid down the law — a look of intense irritation and disbelief.

"You lot just don't get it, do you?" he mutters. I shake my head.

"You might think he was talking to the whole class," says Kabinga, chin jutting out in fierce determination, "but he was actually talking to the three of us, the foolish Africans who don't understand anything."

"Be serious, my friend," says Diallo, in a calm and benevolent tone.

"Just don't say I didn't warn you!"

Diallo and I remain silent as Kabinga grabs our empty plates and washes them, making irritated grunting sounds and frequently firing venomous glances in our direction. He seems to be just as angry with us as he is with the tap, which squirts the water out with noisy gurgling sounds, like a drunk vomiting in a gutter.

"Listen to that!" he yells. "They can't even do their plumbing right!"

After a few minutes, Diallo announces he's going for a siesta, just like the Chinese at this time of day.

"He's become Chinese now," says Kabinga dismissively after Diallo's gone. "Siesta, huh! Is he a kid or what, eh?"

Anxious to change the subject, I mention that I need a haircut and ask Kabinga if he knows someone who can do a good job. We usually cut each other's hair. The local barbers don't know how to handle our hair. Kabinga says if I want to try a local, there's a new barber on Nanning Lu in Cai Chang, but he has no idea what the man is like.

"I can take you there if you like," he says dryly, as if he's offering me dog meat knowing very well I won't touch it.

"Let's do it." I grab my jacket.

"What, now?"

"It's the only time I've got, Chin Chin, before the 3 o'clock class."

"Your hair doesn't look that long," he protests. In the end, he agrees to accompany me because he wants to enjoy the rare autumn sun, in spite of the strong wind that tears into your face and leaves your eyes smarting.

We leave our bicycles, which we call flying horses, chained just inside the university main gate, behind the majestic white buildings fronted by a gigantic clock tower and the university logo. Workers are putting up decorations to commemorate the forthcoming mid-autumn festival. It was one of the first Chinese festivals we experienced on arrival here last year, which we celebrated with mooncakes and pomelo fruits that took ages to peel off the thick, spongy rind, and enjoyed watching fire dragon dances in the public square in Cai Chang. If it's too cold this time, I'll probably not bother to see the festivities this autumn.

The air is filled with that very unique smell of streets and old Chinese buildings, a mixture of deep-fried foodstuffs and uncollected garbage, enriched with the smell of burning coal and exhaust fumes from trucks and buses. There are hardly any saloon cars. Everyone rides bicycles, young and old. Sometimes you find an entire family balanced precariously on a bicycle.

The barbershop is really just a shack, cleverly created out of the empty space between Wang's noodle shop and a shop that sells Chinese medical products. Boxes of gnarled roots and dried herbs at the pharmacy sit in boxes, encroaching on the barber's narrow entrance. Some of them have dozens of roots sticking out of them like an octopus. Others are thick, round, and shrivelled up at the narrow ends, and remind you of aborted foetuses preserved in formaldehyde. A few resemble the roots Mother buys from a traditional healer back in Ndambu village. A middle-aged woman in a white coat measures out doses of dried herbs, inserting them into little paper packets on which she scribbles, eyes peering under her glasses.

We find the barber dozing on a wooden chair, a smouldering cigarette dangling on his lips. The place reeks of the popular but cheap tobacco that makes your stomach churn. The small, elderly man jumps to his feet when we approach, and starts to wave us to the small bench in front of a cracked mirror. He cheerfully tells us his name is Xiao Lui. I opt for the seat close to the door, where the sweet smell from the joss sticks burning in the pharmacy entrance can waft through to me. Xiao Lui seems to read my mind, for he promptly squeezes his cigarette against a plastic ashtray and saves the wobbly butt on a table cluttered with combs and scissors. He feels the texture of my hair with one finger, a bemused look on his face. He says he has never come across such hair before. Kabinga rolls his eyes with his trademark I-told-you-so shrug.

The whole experience turns out to be a hilarious adventure for all of us, including a middle-aged customer who maintains a running commentary directed at Xiao Lui, as if he were reporting from the scene of a crime. His thinning hair is long and unkempt, and he keeps running a hand through it, as if he'll miss what's left of it when it's gone. He carefully selects a comb and runs it through his hair while he waits, never once keeping his mouth shut.

Xiao Lui runs a fine-toothed comb through my hair before realising he can't negotiate the thick tufts that way. In any case, I find it too painful and stop him. He doesn't have a long-toothed comb, so Kabinga and I teach him how to pluck small sections with the inappropriate comb, tentatively, after a quick spray of water to soften it. After that, it is much easier, but Xiao Lui first experiments by holding tufts of hair with his fingers before we urge him to use a comb and then trim carefully over the top.

The commentator picks up a tuft of hair from the floor and examines it carefully, as if it's a rare treasure, commenting loudly about its colour, its surprisingly soft texture.

"Wah!" he gasps, eyes open wide with shock. "I had expected it to be tough and thick like wool. And heavy, eh?"

"The man is nuts!" mutters Kabinga.

I shrug, unconcerned. The man can pick up all the hair on the floor and keep it as a souvenir for all I care. To my surprise, Kabinga picks up a clump of hair and tells the commentator that in our country, it takes a basketful of hair to buy a wife. The man glares at him in disbelief.

"Ask my friend here."

"Yeah. Once you find a girl you like, you start collecting hair."

"It could take years," says Kabinga. "That's where friends and family come in."

Xiao Lui stops trimming and stares at us, before cackling with laughter.

"And have you two started to collect hair?" asks the commentator.

"I did," says Kabinga. "Then I had to come to China, so I stopped."

"Why stop? You're not going to marry the girl?"

"Now that I'm here, I'm afraid I might marry a Chinese girl. I don't think her family will want the hair."

They both burst out laughing, exposing cigarette-blackened teeth.

"What about you?" Xiao Lui asks me.

"In my village, they're still keeping their hair. It's half a basket now. In two years, we'll be ready."

"So you need to save this," says the commentator, a tone of concern creeping into his voice. "It's going to waste, eh? Keep it."

"It's no use. Once you're away from home, you're not allowed to save it."

"That's true," adds Kabinga. "When you're away, the hair is tainted, dirty, and unclean." He spits the words out with obvious disdain. The commentator glances at the hair in his hands, scowls as if suddenly realising he's holding a crawly worm, throws it to the floor, and surreptitiously rubs his hand on his trousers.

When Xiao Lui finishes, he says he may have to charge me more because I put him through more work than normal. We insist that he needs to pay us for teaching him a new skill.

"Look at it this way," says Kabinga. "We can get you all the Africans in Nanjing. Think about all that money. You'll be richest barber in the city."

"Ai! I don't know," says Xiao Lui, scratching his head. "That's a lot of work. I'm just an old man."

Kabinga sucks his lips in, struggling to contain his disappointment.

"Don't you want to make more money?" asks Kabinga. The commentator lights a cigarette, quiet now and looking puzzled by the direction the discussion is taking.

Worry lines crease Xiao Lui's forehead. He coughs, hawks long and hard, then shoots a stream of yellow phlegm into the street, as if to signal what he thinks of Kabinga's question. He offers to waive the charge, saying he's worried we're not satisfied he's done a good job. But I insist on paying and we agree that in future, if the haircuts are particularly bad, we'll get discounts. As we leave, the commentator is lamenting about all that hair going to waste when it could get you a wife.

25

White Card

LIVING HERE FEELS LIKE BEING locked up in a box. There's no news about home, or anywhere for that matter. It is like being in prison, completely cut off from the rest of the world. It makes you long for anything that would remind you of home, anything at all, from the even greenness of the tobacco plantations on the undulating hills and the rhythmic humming of sweat-drained farmers toiling away, to the songs of the birds that announce the break of day.

There's little of interest in the local newspapers, or even the foreign ones, which are mostly from approved communist countries, like East Germany and Albania, supplied here in translation. They are mind numbing in their praise for the revered leaders, the glorious things the Communist Party does for the comrades, the showcasing of model citizens living in harmony and coming together to build party offices, and the scathing condemnation of western imperialism. Sometimes we get news from people who have recently visited their embassies in Beijing, but by the time you get it, it's no longer news.

One Sunday afternoon, Kabinga announces there's a new shop not too far from campus that sells foreign newspapers. Looking for it will give me some welcome respite from my Spartan room, the hard, narrow bed, the desk littered with books and notes. From my window, the day looks sunny and inviting, but it's only teasing you.

Diallo says he wants to revise for next week's exams. I wish him well. I was up till 2 a.m. last night, revising. There's still so much more to cover, notes to memorise, equations to work out. Kabinga says the exams are just a meaningless test.

"Out to impress the professor, eh?" teases Kabinga. Diallo waves us away to ward off an argument and returns to his book, but Kabinga is undeterred. "So what is it, you want to get your degree before everyone else?"

"He's busy, Chin Chin. We'll bring him the news if we find any."

"Eggman, relax," says Kabinga, angrily. "The man doesn't need a spokesman. He can talk for himself."

Diallo flashes his forgiving, benevolent smile that leaves Kabinga hissing with frustration and invites us to sit on the bed. He gets up from his neat and tidy study desk and stands behind the door.

"So what is this now?" demands Kabinga. "We're getting a lecture on good manners? Get on with it then, Professor Sheng."

I nudge him in the ribs to shut him up.

"Okay, it's like this," says Diallo, in a voice so low we have to lean forward. "A bush rat and a chameleon set off on a journey to find a mythical pot of spirit food that never went empty, no matter how much you ate from it. The rat could eat anything on the way, and there was plenty to eat: lizards, insects, worms, small snakes…"

"*Excusez-moi, professeur!*" Kabinga cuts in. "Perhaps you misunderstood. When I said I was going to look for newspapers, I wasn't looking to read some stupid kids' story. It's news I'm looking for, man. What's with the Intifada? What's Reagan going on about the Berlin Wall? Will Jesse Jackson win this time? How's the struggle in Soweto, man? News! Right, Eggman?"

I shrug and wait for Diallo to explain himself. Diallo goes on, unfazed. His calmness leaves me speechless.

"The chameleon could only eat flies. There weren't many. So he had to be patient, he had to conserve his energy. He had never been on a journey like this one before. A lot of chameleons back home were counting on that pot."

Kabinga gets up and angrily zips up his jacket. He waves Diallo out of the way and holds the door open.

"I don't like people calling me a rat, Diallo," he mutters. "That's not what I am, man."

"Wait for the end of the story, guys," urges a cheerful Diallo. "You'll love this."

"Next time, Zen." I pat him on the shoulder and rush to catch up with Kabinga, who is taking the steps two at a time.

We walk in silence through the main public square in Cai Chang, shoulders hunched in a vain effort to beat the wind. We stop to watch elderly people dancing to Chinese opera music beside a small lake with a green pagoda set within it. A man playing a guitar accompanies the music on a cassette player. The dancers' movements are graceful and measured. They're always practicing whenever we pass through here in the afternoon. A short distance away, another group is practicing tai chi under the watchful gaze of a stone lion.

The buildings exude the same somnolent, monotonous greyness that reminds me of my parents' fading black-and-white pictures from the fifties and sixties. There are no decorations in sight, no colour on the shop fronts. You feel as if you're walking past warehouses whose defining character is anonymity. When we pass the bike repair shops on Shungli Lu and cross to the shopping section of Nanning Lu, Kabinga decides he's hungry. I readily agree. Something hot sounds like a very good idea in this cold. As we get into Wang's noodle shop, we exchange greetings with Xiao Lui who, as usual, is dozing away with a cigarette on his lips. Watching Xiao Lui rouse himself like a man emerging out of a nightmare, Wang shakes his head despondently, like a father who has given up on a profligate son.

Wang is the only trader we know who goes out of his way to interact with foreigners. He always wants to know where each student is from, what their country is like, and what he can import from their countries. The locals call him by his full name, Wang Bin. When he introduces himself to foreigners, he shakes hands with a great flourish, and says in English, "Call me Wang. Is enough." He says it with a knowing look, puffing on a cigarette, head slightly bent, a sly smile playing on his lips. Today, his hair is slicked back and shiny, which makes him look like the brokers at the Travel Café. It is a look that doesn't sit well with his officious grey Mao suit. The only concession he makes to the weather is the green scarf around his neck.

His wife sits behind a small counter by the door, hardly ever looking up, never acknowledging a greeting, perpetually playing tapes of someone Wang refers to as Theresa Tang, whose music reminds me of heart-warming, happy chants in Sunday school. Kabinga thinks she's conceited. I think she maintains silence to show deference to her husband, who prowls around the shop and the pavement outside like a lion staking out his territory. She's quiet, unassuming, unsmiling, like a shadow, almost invisible as she flits between the tables collecting dishes. We've nicknamed her Wang's Shadow. No one knows her name. The way she carries on, so unobtrusively, it is easy to imagine she doesn't have one.

Wang's noodle shop is small and cramped. It boasts cracked, wobbly wooden furniture and bright red decorations of Chinese calligraphy that glare down at you demanding to be read and admired as you slurp down your rice noodles. The area around the counter is decorated with prints of Ming dynasty maidens sipping tea in elegant flower gardens adorned with fountains and artificial lakes. Next to the door, there is a miniature red shrine, beside which Wang's Shadow places offerings of fruits, burning candles, and joss sticks.

Every day, the noodle shop looks more and more like a travel agency. One wall is now completely plastered with postcards and posters of Egyptian pyramids, lions on the Serengeti plains, Kenyan long-distance runners, traditional dancers from Senegal, the New York skyline, Le Tour Eiffel, the San Francisco bridge, Big Ben and red, double-decker buses on a London street, the Sydney Opera House and harbour. Wang calls it his international window to the world.

The screaming redness of the calligraphy on the walls speaks of good luck and unending wealth, and is as demanding of attention as Wang himself, who stands at the entrance enticing potential customers with promises of 'today's special', giving you no chance to ignore him.

The special is invariably the same thing, noodles with spicy preserved vegetables and a generous flavouring of light soya sauce. It's a recipe he says he learned on a trip to Sichuan and made it his own.

It is 3 p.m., and we're the only customers at this time. We both opt for the special, which today is a little spicier than normal. The ground red chili floats on oily globules on top of the soup, and you have to accompany each mouthful with a gulp of water. Kabinga claims the water just makes the chili more treacherous and orders a bottle of Tsingtao beer.

"Today, I've made it quite special for you," says Wang, grinning, a cigarette stuck between his teeth. "The pork was braised in Chinese rice wine."

We thank him for this innovativeness and invite him to share our beer. This is just the cue he was waiting for. Pointing at the postcards and posters, he declares that his dream is to see the world and do business with every country there is. We're used to his fantasies, so we ignore him and concentrate on the food. The pork is long and tough, and takes patience and a special skill to bite chunks off while holding it with your chopsticks without it slipping back into the bowl.

For the next fifteen minutes, Wang regales us with heart-wrenching stories about the hardships and poverty they endured before things started to improve a few years ago. We think he tells us these stories to prove to us how resilient the

Chinese are and to silence those who like to complain about empty shelves in shops, the drab clothes and limited choice in food.

"Enjoy the meat, my friends," says Wang, with a wistful turn of voice. "Only fifteen years ago, I had to make do with half a kilo of pork a month, and a bowl of rice a day. When I was a boy, you could see people starving to death. Sometimes when I see what we have, it seems like a dream. Meat and vegetables. Fruits. It is truly glorious to be rich. Poverty is a terrible thing. You don't ever want to have to endure it."

Watching Wang's tormented features and listening to his woeful tales makes you pause and savour the spiciness just a little bit more, stoically ignoring the havoc it's causing your taste buds.

"You're doing well, Wang," says Kabinga, "running this noodle shop. Not many people can afford to run a private business. You must be one of those *wanyuanhu* who earn ten thousand a year."

Wang breaks into a laugh and looks at Kabinga with what looks like admiration.

"I'm impressed, Kabinga," he says, patting Kabinga on the back. "You understand China so well. You'll thrive here. Oh yes, you will."

Unmoved by the praise, Kabinga pointedly repeats his question.

"Me and my family, *wanyuanhu*? It would have been a dream. No, I should say it was a dream. Ten years ago, our neighbours made it to this class. They reared hundreds of chickens and pigs. They did all kinds of home repair work for neighbours, ran stalls in the market. Everyone looked up to them. They were a model family. They got a medal from the local party bureau. The *People's Daily* wrote about them. It was truly a dream come true, to see what you could achieve with hard work. For me, my friends, it was different. Farming was not in our blood. Years ago, my father worked in a steel mill. When the whole country started making steel, he was made head of a village steel furnace. We were truly proud of this wonderful achievement, until we were made to give up our pots and pans, and his bicycle."

"Give them up for what?" I ask.

"To make steel," explains Wang patiently. "Every village had to make steel. But the loss of our treasured possessions was difficult to bear. I was just a youth at the time, who cared only about his studies and dreamed of joining Father at the steel mill. But that loss taught me a lesson I've never forgotten, my friends. That's why I say: Enjoy the meat and spicy condiments when you have them.

But better still: Be sure you know how and where to get them because you never know when they might no longer be within your grasp."

"It's surprising," says Kabinga, frowning. "Such a big country, and fertile too, yet there's all this poverty. This starvation you talk about, Wang, to me it sounds crazy. I can understand starvation in poor countries ravaged by civil war or, like, where they've got deserts. Rains fail, crops die. But here?"

Wang inhales deeply, a questioning look creeping into his eyes. He's weighing his words, retreating to that wariness and reticence, locals take refuge in when personal opinions threaten to disturb the harmony of general chitchat. Even with all the talk of the country opening up, you never know what words might reach the party local branch or the Campus Youth League. Wang knows he has nothing to fear from us, but Kabinga's questions make him uneasy. Kabinga doesn't know when to give face.

"It's complicated," says Wang, forcing a smile. "The good thing is, everything's changing. Comrade Deng has a wonderful philosophy. Those who take their chances will live like kings."

"And you, Wang, will you live like a king?"

"Ah, Kabinga, this noodle shop you see here is the first seedling that became a forest, conquering the hills and valleys. There is no other way for Wang." A manic determination suffuses his face, and for an instant, he's transformed into an unscrupulous moneylender demanding his money back. He jumps to his feet and approaches his international window. Arms raised as if in prayer, he declares, "This, my friends, is me. This wall is Wang."

Kabinga's jaw drops.

After Wang leaves to interest a new customer in his regular special, Kabinga spends the next ten minutes lamenting about Diallo's "foolishness". I let him talk. My late nights studying this week are taking their toll, and I'm still reflecting on Wang's tales of hardships and perseverance. I ask Kabinga why he's so blasé about the exams.

"Exams here are nothing, Eggman," he says. "So long as you memorise stuff, you should be just fine."

"But, calculations…?"

"You know the equations small-small, nothing to worry about." I can't relate to his self-assuredness. The material is not hard, that's true. But there's always that nagging worry that you might misunderstand a word, or write the wrong character, and end up getting it wrong. And every day, you learn some new

31

technical word that never came up in the language lessons. Most of us are hoping for a little leniency during these first exams.

Wang wanders around the tables, wiping imaginary specks of dust, looking for a break in our conversation so he can come and continue reminiscing. But we've both had enough of the past. What we need is news about the present. On our way out, he asks when our holidays are starting.

"We don't have holidays," says Kabinga. "They work us like slaves here."

"Hard work is good," says Wang. "That's how you succeed. I remember when you first came here last year and spoke no Chinese. You worked hard, now you're just like us."

"Of course, we're jungwok yahn!" Chinese people. The cold breeze cuts off our laughter as we step outside.

"Come and drink tonight!" Wang calls out. "Bring some more tapes and play your music."

"We've got exams next week," I inform him. "When we're done, we'll come and have a real party."

We make our way down the main street outside the university, hoping to locate the newsagent on Shenyuan Lu. After rounding a hill at the top of the road, we come face to face with the Qin Huai River in all its slow, majestic serenity. Red pavilions with classical bell-shaped roofs sit placidly along the banks of the river, separated by clusters of bamboo trees and carefully manicured gardens, in which elderly people are practicing tai chi, oblivious of the cold. Further up the river, a low-rise housing district takes shape. A cloud of dust hovers in the sky like a mist, partly obscuring the cranes and trucks. Dust and construction noises pervade the city. There's almost a desperate urgency to flatten the ancient buildings and hutongs and replace them with housing blocks to accommodate farmers fleeing the infertile land for the promise of riches in the city, coming to partake of Wang's dream.

After wandering the streets for half an hour, we decide to head back to Cai Chang, to the Travel Café on Bao Ling Lu. The Travel Café is the only place near the university that remotely resembles a bar. It is where foreigners congregate to exchange news about home, read old magazines and newspapers, and change money over a beer. If you want a bar, you have to go to the hotels downtown, but they are too far away and don't quite have the feel of a bar to them. They are more like conference function rooms with their square tables, high-backed chairs, and solemn-looking staff, who glide silently like shadows between the tables, delivering drinks on painted trays.

In the dusty, grime-covered residential neighbourhood on the edge of Cai Chang, people stream out of their houses to witness the rare spectacle of black ghosts prowling their hutong. A dozen men and women follow us from a distance, pointing, whispering, careful not to get too close in case the black ghosts cast a spell of bad luck. We walk hurriedly, dodging ruddy-faced toddlers crawling on the cobbled street, free-range chickens scuttling about, and mangy dogs barking needlessly while retreating backwards. To lose the staring mob, we take a shortcut through the industrial area of Paoting, where we take cover behind the ancient trucks parked along the roads by the factories that are spewing blue smoke into the sky.

We walk past groups of workers too concerned with getting home on time to bother us. This is the part of China I like, where being ignored is the best welcome you can get. Where you can fade unobtrusively into the drab surroundings, walking along littered pavements, with the noises of buses and trucks in the air, your nose accosted by a mixture of cigarette smoke and the smoke billowing from exhaust fumes and factories. That's when you feel like just another inconspicuous urban peasant.

The first time a group of people followed me, I thought they were going to attack. Now, I just ignore them and walk on, blocking my ears to the calls of *hei gui*, but the feeling still lingers that they see you as an animal, a mad dog that needs to be shooed off the streets from a safe distance. Kabinga puts it down to communism. Right now, he's struggling to control his anger by focusing all this energy on a cigarette.

The Travel Café is in a dilapidated low-rise across the road from the noisy Hangjiang bus terminal that is full of jaded-looking travellers and hawkers rushing about selling cigarettes, dried snacks, small round dumplings, and fish balls in sets of three held together in sharpened skewers. The smell of exhaust fumes and steamed snacks hovers in the air, defying the wind.

We find a scratched and wobbly table towards the back, next to the broker who goes by the name of Dallas Joe, or DJ. DJ is drinking straight from a large bottle of beer, poring over an old Readers Digest. He comes to greet us and yells at a waiter not to keep us waiting. DJ speaks reasonably good English, compared to the other brokers. He's wearing dark sunglasses and the omnipresent brown cowboy boots an American student sold him last year.

Like the other brokers who operate from the Travel Café, DJ makes a living by changing money illegally and procuring bus and train tickets and anything else that has been rationed out of existence. He dreams of going to America, to Texas in particular, where he'll run a ranch so big, he'll be inspecting it on horseback. When he first met us, he was disappointed to discover we were not American.

"Oh, I think is my first chance meet niggers, buddy," he said, shaking his head with disappointment. "You dancing like Michael Jackson? Thriller! I love it! Niggers, they're so great."

Kabinga shot back, telling him never to use that word again.

"Oh, shit man! So you Negro, buddy? Is better?" DJ asked, eyes filled with perplexity.

The fact that we're African hasn't stopped him asking us to teach him what he calls ghetto jive. He likes to show off his knowledge of the world, though he has probably never even left Jiangsu province. Everything he knows he has learned from talking to foreigners.

There are very few other people here. It's only 5 p.m. A couple of European visiting students have buried their heads in last month's foreign newspapers. The news is all about the Chernobyl nuclear disaster and how a tragedy like that could never happen here because the people have embraced discipline at work. A curvaceous blonde woman sits near the door, a backpack with a rolled-up mattress leaning against the wall behind her. She's surrounded by three leering brokers, all-anxious to impress her with their halting English, filling the room with explosive laughter. Their table is a forest of green Tsingtao beer bottles. Two other hangers-on have abandoned their conversation to feast their gaze on the woman. Their eyes are glued to her mango-shaped breasts that are visible through a skimpy cotton top. One of them notices Kabinga eyeing them with barely concealed disgust and points him out to his friends. They mutter under their breath, point their fingers in our direction and spit on the floor in unison.

After placing our orders, we turn to see Cristina walk through the door. She's a Swedish language student who also teaches English at the Foreign Language Institute. She is almost six-foot tall, fine-toned like a swimmer, and her blue eyes and blonde hair that reaches down to her waist never fail to turn heads. She's wearing jeans and a loose-fitting, off-white blouse she says she bought in India. It is made of very light cotton, and when she walks in the wind, the hem lifts up to reveal two silver rings on her belly button. Today she has tied two ends of the blouse together in a knot. She's not wearing a bra. She stops to chat with the two language students, and then wanders across to our table. Kabinga rises to kiss her on both cheeks. I follow suit, somehow feeling obliged to do so. The two of them have been having an on-off relationship for some months now. When she's not around, he calls her "my sweet blonde bitch". He only seeks her out when he's desperate for feminine company. Cristina has something of a reputation. If you invite her to your room, amuse her with good music, jokes, beer, and some good quality joints, she'll reciprocate in kind.

Cristina announces she'll soon be leaving China. She watches Kabinga's face closely for a reaction.

"You're having a great time here," I point out. "The locals love you. They follow you around like a queen bee. Why leave?"

"That's the problem, you see," she says, frowning. "This is a nonsense life. They make you feel like animal in zoo. Thirty people follow you down the street like they've nothing to do. It's stupid. Sometimes they want to touch your skin and hair as if you're a cat or something. Disgusting!"

"I don't understand what you're complaining about," mutters Kabinga. "They follow you with loving eyes, darling, salivating at the sight of a white goddess with blond hair, long legs, and tight arse. When they follow me, they want to see if I'll swing onto a tree. We're living such different lives, it's unbelievable. Like two tribes separated by a ridge. You and your fellow white people are kings and queens here. You'll never get this adulation in Sweden. Enjoy it while you're here."

"I don't need it," she snaps. "I'm learning Chinese for two years now. It's enough."

"So what will you do?"

"Go back to uni, I suppose."

"Hey Cristina, do you think I could apply for your teaching job when you leave?"

Kabinga stares at me as if I'm out of my mind.

"You? Teach English to the Chinese?"

"Of course he can," says Cristina, playfully pinching him on the cheek. "He speaks English much better than me. Taught by colonial British, you know?"

"You're right about that, sweetheart," says Kabinga. "And he can probably make a pretty good teacher. But do you imagine they would let him, a *hei gui*?

35

In fact, I bet a Communist Albanian or Bulgarian who barely spoke the language would stand a better chance."

Cristina looks at us with pity.

When our second round arrives, DJ leans across and furtively asks if we need anything.

"Just newspapers," says Kabinga. "And you can't really help us with that, can you?"

"No new supplies, buddy," says DJ, pointing at the pile of old magazines and newspapers on the shelves. He insists on speaking English even when you reply in Chinese. He's the only broker who does that. The others have gradually shifted from broken English to rapid bursts of Chinese over the year as our Chinese got better.

"I can't believe it," says Kabinga, almost as if he's spitting the words out. "A simple newspaper, man, that's all I ask for." He pauses for breath. "It's a small-small favour, man, you know?"

"Hey, buddy, you wanna change money?" says DJ, ignoring him.

I shake my head. I have all the local money I need for now. Sometimes I wonder whether this policy of having parallel currencies is a way to create employment for the self-styled brokers. Wherever you go, people come up to you offering to change money. Foreigners are only allowed to use foreign exchange certificates, FECs, not renminbi, 'the people's money', which is also known as RMB. It's the best evidence we have that we don't qualify as 'the people' or, in fact, people at all. If you use RMB for example on campus, you have to show a Yellow Card, which keeps a record of all your expenditures. RMB expenditures cannot exceed your grant, a policy supposed to prevent illegal money changing. But that doesn't stop brokers from thriving. In fact, they have helped to make the lives of enterprising foreign students rather comfortable, especially by helping to facilitate the White Card deals. We often complain about the restrictions on the kind of money we can use. But these inconveniences, which force you to pay more than the true price for whatever you buy because the exchange rate is always skewed against you, are more than compensated for by the White Card.

The White Card allows foreigners, including students and a few privileged locals, to import things like fridges, washing machines, TVs, and even cars for their own use, duty free. If you don't need these luxuries or can't afford them, there are plenty of enterprising students willing to buy this magic certificate off you and import things for rich Chinese. A rich man can cover your travel expenses and hotel accommodation in a five-star hotel in Hong Kong so you can shop for him. I know of at least two African students who have abandoned their studies and moved into suites at downtown hotels so they can meet these rich clients directly, rather than have to rely on connections through people like DJ, who insist on charging a fee. The clients are mostly government officials and party cadres, who've made a fortune through bribes. Unfortunately for this wealthy elite, the law doesn't allow them to hold foreign currency or import the luxuries they so badly need. But this doesn't stop them buying US dollars in the black market.

Kabinga clinks bottles with DJ and tells him, "When I need to play in your junior league, I'll let you know. I've moved on, small-small, you know?" He utters the "small-small" so quickly it sounds like "so-so".

DJ grins to cover his embarrassment. When he hears talk like this, he knows he has lost a customer. It's been happening a lot, lately, as more students trade on their White Cards, moving into what they call the big league.

"The other thing I got for you, buddy. What you say?"

"Yeah?" Kabinga is surprised DJ is still lurking about.

"Hey, I got best shit this part of town, dude. Gotta see to believe, buddy."

Kabinga whistles and clinks bottles again. "Now you're talking," he whispers, scratching his goatee. Cristina smiles with anticipation.

"You play ball? Ten minutes, buddy, yeah?"

Kabinga gives him the thumbs up. DJ walks out into the street, licking his lips.

"Crazy bastard," mutters Kabinga, before announcing, "I'm off to Beijing next week, man."

I ask why. Cristina's face falls. In the past, when Kabinga ignored her, she would sidle up to him and hold his hand or kiss him in the middle of a sentence, which embarrassed him into silence. Nowadays she prefers to smoke and drink in a silent sulk, watching the bar for more interesting company. Sometimes she pushes notes under his door, even when she knows he's inside. Lately, she's been writing to ask why he doesn't move with her to Sweden. Kabinga tears up the notes angrily and bins them immediately, often unread.

"A chance came up to buy wheels. Wheels so posh you'd kill for them. I've been looking out for this deal for a long time. I've finally got my chance. Some embassy guy."

"Chin Chin, you're crazy. You've got enough money to buy a car?"

He laughs at my naivety.

"I'm buying it for a local bigwig, man. I've set it up so he finances the deal. I buy it and effectively sell it to him small-small, you get?"

"Wow!" I gaze at him in amazement. I don't know when he gets the time to set up deals like that.

"You're gonna be rich, eh?" says Cristina, massaging his back, a look of admiration suffusing her face.

Kabinga beams with pleasure and says, "Nothing's stopping me, babe." The smile on his face fades away, to be replaced by a determined look that hardens his features much like a broker figuring out exchange rates, bent on extracting the best deal from a hapless customer.

"China's not right for you," says Cristina, shaking her head ruefully. "You need to be in a place where you can be who you are."

"Wow, babe, that's deep. You hear that, my brother? And what country would that be, my darling?"

"Anywhere but a communist state. And, sorry, but forget Africa, by the way. Try Europe, where you can make money legally without going through all these troubles. The communists could really mess you if they find out what you guys do, you know?"

She peers into his face, worry etched around her blue eyes. Kabinga runs a hand through her hair to assure her he can take care of himself. I watch him with envy, knowing that I could never be this blasé, sadly aware that even if these opportunities were to present themselves to me, I wouldn't know how to proceed.

I try to hide the sense of impotence with a brave smile as I say, "There's a lot we can learn from you, man."

"Sure, Eggman, any time." His laughter leaves me a little ill at ease. I look into his eyes but can't detect the sarcasm I sensed in his tone. Maybe he really means it. Maybe he's truly flattered. Cristina edges closer to him and takes his hand. But he ignores her and addresses me. "A guy I know in Shanghai has been doing this car deal all year. He's now moved out of campus into his own place. That's my target, Eggman. It's straightforward, and the beauty of it is you can't lose, even on old wheels. The rich guys will pay through the nose to get what they want. I'm looking to net no less than six grand."

"US?"

"What do you think, the people's money?" He bursts into laughter. "There are people here who're swimming in money, Eggman. Guy in Shanghai tells me the client will pay up to half the value of the wheels as commission, man."

"They're that desperate?"

"What choice do they have? The way I see it, communism is the best thing that ever happened to us foreign devils. The worst situation you can be in is to have loads of money and nothing to spend it on, because the communists say you can't spend, and the bloody shops are empty. It's a perfect setting."

When DJ returns, he hands Kabinga a small package. Kabinga pays and proceeds to roll a joint while DJ opens the window wider. Instinctively, I keep an eye on the door. No one is bothered by the smell of burnt leaves. No one even notices. Everyone smokes cigarettes that smell just as bad. It makes the Travel Café look and smell like a burning bush, with each brand of cigarette adding its own foul, pungent flavour. I've tried to get used to it, but whenever people light up a joint in a place like this, my stomach turns, and I hold my breath, afraid I'll throw up. Then there's the thought of cops storming the bar and arresting us. But no one else is troubled by this, least of all Kabinga and Cristina, who pass the joint back and forth without a care in the world, occasionally kissing. When they finish, Cristina excuses herself, saying she has to teach a class that evening.

"Forget the class, babe," urges Kabinga. "You're too high. Stay here and have fun."

"It's not a problem, I'll be fine," says Cristina, touching up her makeup.

"I pity the poor students," says Kabinga.

Two hours later, as we leave the Café, I can't get the thought of selling cars out of my mind. I've never put my White Card to much use. It is tempting, but it's a grey area, and the risk remains a worry. I envy people like Kabinga, who can pull this off without blinking an eye. If they deported me, I don't know how I could face my parents. My brother and sister are in secondary school, and I have to send part of my grant to help with their school fees. Could this be my chance? Am I that eagle perched on the top branches of a eucalyptus tree, watching out for the giveaway ripple beneath the deceptively calm surface of the water? A shudder runs through my spine, shaking me out of my reverie.

I see them first and nudge Kabinga. Three young boys, not older than fifteen, standing at a street market, grab a banana each and start waving them at us, making faces and sticking their tongues out. They're across the street from us.

People stand around giggling, pointing at us. Some have got off their bicycles and are mimicking the boys, laughing and whistling, shouting *hei gui*!

I feel a rush of blood in my temple, which turns into a slow throbbing sound, like someone tapping my head with slow deliberation at first, then gradually raising the tempo until the head is about to explode.

Kabinga is rooted to the spot, but only momentarily. The next thing I know, he's rushing across the street, dodging a mad cascade of bicycles, and has his hands around the throat of one of the boys. He lifts the boy up until he's got him standing on his toes. He's yelling abuse, which comes out in mangled Chinese. I grab his shoulders and drag him away. With a huff, he lets go of the petrified youth and together we shove our way through the crowd on the busy pavement. It's all over in a matter of seconds, long enough for both of us to realise we could be expelled from the university and deported for this, but not long enough for the passersby to turn from curious observers to a hostile mob. We're both seething with anger when we turn a corner and the campus comes into view in the distance ahead of us.

"Madness!" mutters Kabinga. "Total madness, you hear? I don't think I can stand this bullshit anymore, Eggman." The words come out in a rapid salvo. "This bloody Nanjing town is fucked up. Totally!"

"So what place is better? You plan to relocate? Shanghai maybe?"

"If you think it's any better there, you're dreaming. I'm going to leave this country, man," he declares, with such a grim look of determination I dare not contradict him.

"And your degree?"

"What! I can study anywhere. I don't need this shit!" He clears his throat and spits into the street, just like a local.

"You've spent a year learning the language."

"It doesn't matter. I can still use it. I'm leaving, man. Do you know last week, a group of guys followed me down the street, chanting 'Kunta Kinte, Kunta Kinte', waving their arms like monkeys? I could have broken their necks. I'm getting out of here. You just wait, once I've made enough money, I'm out."

"It's only abuse, man. You should ignore it."

"What! Don't be ridiculous, Eggman."

"Look, you can't go around picking fights. You could get yourself deported."

"Ha! As if that's the end of me. The only reason I manage to keep my cool is 'cause most of these guys aren't exactly the regular Bruce Lee, flying-kick, karate-chop wizards you see in kung fu movies."

"That's what I mean, Chin Chin. If there's any fighting going on, it's just words, nothing more."

"You're deluding yourself."

He knows I'm only trying to calm him down. Whether the abuse is just words or not, it makes you long for the heartfelt greetings and friendly conversations you encountered along the dirt roads back in Ndambu, where no one stared at you as though you had shit rolling down your legs.

"I tell you, Eggman, one day these little fights will get out of hand small-small, and someone will get very hurt. You mark my words."

He sounds so sure of it I remain silent, as though not talking about it will ensure it never happens. But neither of us can ignore the ominous silence that follows his words.

I'll Go With You

IT'S CHINESE NEW YEAR. THE university comes to a virtual standstill during the one-month break. The only people around campus are foreign students, who have nowhere to go and who can't get over the thought of another New Year celebration at the end of January.

As soon as it gets dark, the rumble of fireworks begins in earnest. They sound like gunshots. Sometimes you can see the multi-coloured light shows brightening up the night sky in the distance. But they're nothing compared to the explosions that mark the end of the Year of the Tiger and usher in the Year of the Rabbit. Diallo and I can't wait to enjoy the fun, even if it means standing in the freezing drizzle, waiting an hour for the show to start. Kabinga declares the whole thing a charade and only agrees to go after we promise to buy the beers at Wang's noodle shop later.

Fortified with beer and wrapped up in several layers of clothing, we join the crowds that mill around the Temple Lantern Fair in the public square at Cai Chang, where red dragons and lion dancers kick off the show alongside giant lanterns mounted along the streets. Bright, red plum blossoms, the only flowers that have defied the winter, sway gently as if to mock the wind. I can't resist touching them to be sure they're real and not plastic adornments planted by the authorities to add to the glamour.

The symbol of the rabbit is everywhere, on large paintings draped across the walls of the buildings and food stalls, the dancers' and children's costumes. Firecrackers keep going off, drowning out the music from a band playing Chinese classical instruments. Their music is perky, cracking with jerky movements that sound almost jittery, like a rabbit hopping about on dry leaves.

"Ah, *mes amis*. Here are the snacks the Youth League asked us to try," says Diallo, leading us through a gap in the barely penetrable throng to the food stalls. Laid out on the tables are trays of pastries, dumplings, and sweets. Others are steaming away on coal-heated portable drums, the flavours and warmth acting like a magnet on shivering passersby. The air fills with the noise of traders announcing their specials. We had been warned to avoid the unhygienic hawkers who ply their trade in dimly lit alleys and only buy food from traders with official numbered badges, even though they are more expensive.

Diallo and I take our chances and savour the sweet stickiness of *tang yuan*, the balls of glutinous rice in red bean soup, and *jiaozi*, the cream-coloured steamed pastries with savoury fillings.

I can't get enough of the *tang yuan* with peanut and sesame filling, even though they stick to the roof of your mouth and require vigorous tongue action to dislodge them. Kabinga won't touch them, claiming he doesn't take orders on what to eat from communists. He walks around stiffly, refusing even to sniff the sweet-smelling taro and turnip cakes a grinning hawker thrusts into our faces.

Then it starts to snow, a few flakes drifting in the wind at first, which quickly get heavier and thicker, as if the clouds themselves are splintering and crashing down under their own weight. Children run around collecting the snow in their hands, squealing with sheer delight. Within minutes, a thick layer blankets the rooftops and droops over the pine-shaped cedar trees, as if to smother them so they'll stop them swaying petulantly in the wind. With all the people milling around, the snow on the ground quickly turns into brown sludge. I take my gloves off to feel the cold softness and see it melt on my hands. I wish my family could see this. If only someone had brought a camera. I would have made a beautiful postcard to rival those my cousin sends from Canada.

A lump of snow hits the back of my head, followed by a burst of laughter. I quickly turn around, wincing as a sharp coldness begins to drip down my nape. The first face I notice is that of an old lady gazing up at me, a toothless ear-to-ear grin forcing her eyes shut. Diallo glances around, hands half raised to ward off stray snowballs. Kabinga is staring boldly around him, as if daring anyone to throw a snowball at him. I smile at the grinning woman and clean the snow off my neck. That's when I notice a teenage boy standing next to the old lady, holding her elbow protectively. He waves at me and says, "How's going? America?"

"Africa." His eyes brighten up. He adjusts his glasses and leans forward. "Snow in Africa?" An image of undulating hills covered in tobacco and orchards flashes through my mind.

"No, not in my country."

He seems disappointed, and laughs uneasily, revealing cracked, uneven teeth.

"Sorry, no English to speak."

"Your English is good. Learning at school?"

"Ah, how you say? Middle school. Is difficult." We both laugh. When I switch to Putonghua, he and his grandmother stare at me in shock. He's even more surprised when I tell him I study engineering. He says he's graduating from high school this year and his dream is to be an engineer. Switching back to halting English, he points at his chest and declares, "Build bridge, ah…road, factory. China car. Yes…"

We're interrupted by flying snowballs.

All around us, children and adults are laughing, waving their hands to catch the snowflakes, hurling lumps of snow through the air, exploding deafening firecrackers wrapped in long, vibrant paper tubes. Diallo and I follow suit, and for a few minutes lose ourselves in the exuberance, at one with the jovial crowd, shouting *gong xi fa cai* New Year greetings like everyone else, and feeling the warmth creep back into your skin and fire up your entire being.

Kabinga stands apart from it all, furiously smoking his cigarette, a look of disdain on his face, like a sulking sentry assigned to a raucous children's party as a punishment.

The explosions start without warning. A phantasmagoria of thunderous explosions lights up the night sky and keeps us mesmerised for half an hour. Like an audience at a boxing match, we shout with glee and clap hands after every ear-splitting blast.

When it's all over and the applause dies, the teenage boy says to me, "Africa, have fireworks?"

"Every day," says Kabinga dismissively before I can reply. The young man makes a sudden jump backwards, as if someone has thrust a snake in his face. Then seeing the ominous look on Kabinga's face, laughs uneasily as he leads his grandmother away.

When the students return to campus, they talk excitedly about the little red packets of money they received from relatives. One morning, as we wait for the class to start, Han Wei shows us a colourful little packet. Han Wei is a thin, quiet fellow who always sucks his cheeks in and forms an 'o' with his lips whenever he's about to say something, as if he's inhaling a gust of air or getting ready to whistle, hence his nickname, The Whistle. Lai Guiguo sits beside him. He doesn't say much but always hovers on the edges of our conversations with Han Wei, responding with a brief cackle at the jokes, frowning at Kabinga's irreverent comments, and generally glancing at Han Wei first as though to seek approval for his response.

"Did you get much money, then?" I ask Han Wei.

"*Hong bao* is not about the amount," he explains. "It's for good luck for young, unmarried people. So you can't expect much." Lai Guiguo nods in agreement.

"Over the years, maybe you can save the money to buy a wife?" Kabinga asks. "Maybe the real plan is to get unmarried men to save the money to buy a wife?"

"They give it to girls, too," Diallo points out. "So, are you suggesting girls buy husbands?"

Han Wei's lips form a circular shape and his laughter comes out as a series of breathy ho ho hos. Lai Guiguo covers his mouth with both hands, muffling guffaws that leave his eyes watery.

"Dowry, my friend," says Kabinga after the laughter dies down. "It's an Asian thing, isn't it? The wife brings money and gold. That's fantastic. I want to marry a Chinese woman." Turning to Han Wei and Guiguo, he says, "Where we come from, men have to pay for a wife. Cows and goats, man. But in Dan's country, they collect sacks of hair."

"Noo…" says Han Wei, giving me a look that demands an explanation for this uncivilised behaviour.

"Next time you're in his room, check under his bed. Every time we have a haircut, we save the hair for him."

To change the subject I ask Han Wei why the packets must be red.

"Red is for good luck, good fortune, joy."

"I know. But why not green? Green is for health and prosperity, isn't it?"

Han Wei runs a hand through his prematurely greying hair and shrugs, then says, "Historically, they've always been red. It's just the way it is." Lai Guiguo watches him, wondering if perhaps he shouldn't chip in with a supportive argument.

"Why not white?" asks Kabinga. "You like white people, right?"

"No! No!" Han Wei looks utterly horrified. His voice is a hushed whisper. "You can't give lucky money like that."

"Why not?"

"No," says Lai Guiguo, with a simple wave of a hand that has such an ominous finality to it that everyone watches him, willing him to say more, wondering what can be so abominable as to draw him from his hermitic silence.

"Don't you know?" chides Diallo, without looking up from his book. "White is for death and mourning, Chin Chin. And they're not allowed to mention it at this time of year." Both Han Wei and Lai Guiguo nod with appreciation, but the hardness in their eyes says they would love nothing more than a change of subject.

"And black?"

Diallo puts his book away, clears his throat and stretches a hand out in his now familiar lecturer pose. Han Wei glances at the door in the hope that the real professor's arrival will rescue him from the impending delivery. But for now, we're stuck with Zen.

"Do you know the classic Yi Jing?"

Kabinga and I exchange puzzled glances.

"I know," says Han Wei, cautiously. "Ancient Chinese culture, symbols, line arrangements to explain change and balance in opposites, like yin and yang, you know? I had to study it in school. How do you know about it?"

"Well, I've been reading it. It's also known as the Book of Changes."

"Man, you read everything," says Kabinga, wearily. "Where do you get the time? Or rather, what the hell for?"

"What for? To learn about the Chinese, I suppose," says Diallo, with a mysterious smile. His brow creases with wrinkles as he announces in a conspiratorial voice: "It says in Yi Jing that black was the colour of heaven."

We all stare at him in silence, as if he has uttered an unforgivable blasphemy. Han Wei's face remains inscrutable, but I can sense a struggle going on within. Lai Guiguo nibbles at his lower lip, eyes trained on Han Wei, as if urging him to bring this whole charade to an end.

"Well, in that case," says Kabinga expansively, "I want my money in a black box. Make it heavenly, please!"

"Here's the thing," says Diallo, both hands now outstretched, like a lawyer making his final appeal to the jury. "As Han Wei will confirm, it was normal in ancient China to worship colours. Now, because the northern sky was black for long periods, they believed that's where Tian Di, the heavenly emperor, lived. So, the black colour was worshipped for years, my friends, longer than. Any. Other. Colour."

"Wow!" exclaims Kabinga. "And does it say at what point black became evil?"

As if on cue, the professor breezes into the class, calling out, "Attention!"

*

Diallo comes around to ask if I'm going to the African party. He's got his guitar with him and is wearing a colourful scarf around his neck. He has recently formed a band that plays at the parties, warming the revellers up for the deejay. They usually come on again at the end, for those who haven't wandered off with some girl, often playing to an empty hall. I ask him what the shawl is for.

"This, *mon frère*, is a traditional minority scarf," he explains, showing off the red, finely embroidered great wall designs of silk on cotton. "I believe it's from the Bai minority tribe of Hunnan. One thing you might not realise, Eggman, is that China is like Africa. You might imagine they're all the same, all speaking the people's language. But some of these minority tribes are so different it's like comparing Swahili and Hausa. The majority Han would like to have us believe they're all just one big happy family. Not so, my friend."

"You're really turning Chinese, eh?"

"We have no choice, if we're to survive here. We're the new minority tribe. The black Chinese. Look, we live here, Eggman. We need to understand these people and learn to fit in, right?" I nod, thinking it would be nice if they tried to understand us too.

"We are fitting in, Zen, aren't we? We speak their language, eat their food, breathe their dirty air, date their lovely girls. Argue with their men. Do we have to wear their costumes, too?"

"This, my friend, makes me feel closer."

"Right, like taking siesta after lunch?"

"Don't make fun, Eggman. I'm serious. And talking of dating, is your little girl coming?" he asks.

"She has to study tonight. And by the way, she's not my girl. Well, not yet."

"Not yet? How many times do you have to do her before she becomes your girl? Or haven't you?"

"We only just met, Zen. Still trying to get to know each other."

I met Lin, or Linda, as she prefers to call herself, at an African party a few weeks ago. I first noticed her sitting with two other girls, expectantly waiting to be asked to dance. But as usual, there were more women than men and the three of them had been stalling for a while. I had danced with a few girls myself and was just settling down to catch my breath and enjoy a beer when I caught her eye and the warm smile. In the dim light, at first, I thought we were acquainted, or that she was smiling at someone behind me. Then I thought perhaps she was a classmate. But on closer inspection, I couldn't place her.

Figuring I had nothing to lose, I asked her to dance. She eagerly accepted, as if to spite all those wretched people who had ignored her all night. That's when I realised how small she was; petite really, with a sweet round face, which broke into an easy smile. I wanted to wrap that smile in my hands and pin it on my walls so I could seek it out for inspiration when assignments got the better of me. We threw ourselves into the rocking, sweaty throng with gusto, seamlessly weaving into the waves of the Congolese kwassa kwassa dance. With a mesmerised smile, Linda watched me shake my hips, lowering myself to her level, my swaying arms protectively within inches of her slim waist. She followed suit, but gave up, giggling, and I took the opportunity to hold her waist ostensibly to steady her. A look of alarm crept into her eyes, and I let go, fearing she would stomp away. When that song ended she said she wanted to rest. I cursed myself and led her to the lobby outside the dance hall, where it was quieter. She let me do most of the talking and responded to questions with either a nod or shy smile. A lot of the girls behave like that. It tires me after a while, but with this girl, the silences intrigued me. Perhaps it was that calm patience in her eyes that seemed to say this small talk is all very well, but could I please get to the point.

Tonight, I'm not planning on staying out late. I need to do some reading for a seminar next week. But when Diallo says I should move on and meet new girls if I'm not sure about this Linda, I decide to ask her out. This time, I'll tell her I like her. I'll compliment her on her beautiful silky hair and smooth flawless skin. They like that. This time, I'll hold her when Freddie Jackson comes on and sing the lyrics in her ear.

"She looks good for you, Eggman," says Diallo as we walk to Linda's hostel. "And you know, you're the kind of guy who needs a girlfriend, so don't let her slip through your fingers, like you've done so many times before."

"What are you talking about?"

"Come on, Eggman, there was that tall Beijing girl last year. Everyone could see she liked you, everyone except you. Back then, all you talked about was studying, studying, learning Chinese, man. Now you've got all the Chinese you'll ever need. Put it to use, man."

I remain silent, recalling how I danced with Qiao, held her tight through all the ballads, and then at the end, as the floor cleared, she stood before me, buttoning her jacket, waiting for me to say something. Recalling how the close embrace had stirred my loins, my heartbeat quickened and my mouth went dry. I took a hurried gulp of my beer and some ended up on my jacket. Qiao's hands flew to her mouth to muffle an embarrassed giggle. I laughed it off uneasily, while a rush of ideas filled my head. *Ask her to walk with you, ask her to meet you tomorrow, ask her where her hostel is.* But none of these ideas translated into words. Her friends came to drag her away, but she lingered, and I dithered, rooted to the spot like a tree. And then she was gone. Diallo was watching from the bar, shaking his head, pitying me. The following weekend, she came in with Idriss, the tall Gambian with a reputation as a foul-mouthed womaniser. Diallo said I had made the right decision not to pursue her. I knew he was just trying to console me, but I hated myself, and her, and Idriss. When they split up only weeks later, she stopped coming to the parties. Idriss was already dating someone else.

Diallo has no interest in having a girlfriend. He says he doesn't like the way they cling on to you, stifling you, creating trouble, preventing you from having fun. His style is to pick them up at parties and drop them shortly afterwards, before glue starts oozing out of their hands.

The security guard at Linda's hostel says she's not in her room. I leave a note, asking her to meet me at the party. But I'm afraid if she sees it too late, she might not bother.

"A note's the best one can do," says Diallo. "Let's hope for the best."

A queue of men, mostly visiting students and Africans from other universities, waits to enter the function hall in the basement of the student entertainment block, a short walk from our own hostel. What makes the parties here so popular is the music, which some students bring in through contacts at their embassies.

The irresistible urgency of soukous music already has people tapping their feet in rhythm, raring to throw themselves into the fray. But the bouncers, Sunny and Idriss, aren't letting anyone in. Idriss announces that the hall is full to capacity. He stands at almost seven-feet-tall, a giant amongst the Chinese. He's stocky, like a heavyweight boxer, and loves to wear shirts with the sleeves torn off to show off his biceps, which shine as if they've been oiled. The dark glasses complete the intimidating demeanour. The thought of his bulky frame, all sweaty and stinky, lying panting on top of my Qiao makes me want to throw up.

Girls are allowed in without question, which makes the Chinese guys mumble about the unfairness of it all. Some of the guys are grumbling that they're discriminated against because they are Chinese. Idriss yells at them to fuck off if they can't wait. His words are met with whistles and peals of laughter. A few weeks ago, when Idriss hurled similar insults, they nearly came to blows. Things only calmed down when security guards armed with batons intervened and threatened to shut down the party if Idriss didn't apologise. Idriss insisted he had nothing to apologise for. The standoff lasted half an hour. The guards only agreed to go away when the party committee gave them a crate of beer.

"Calm down, guys," Diallo tells the bouncers, "otherwise, I'm not playing my guitar tonight."

"You're too late, anyway," yells Idriss. "You should have curtain-raised. Who's going to listen to you after this fantastic music?"

"You'd better get in, anyway," says Sunny, ushering us in, "and start tuning your guitar." The sarcasm in his voice provokes laughter in the queue. Idriss pulls a face but moves aside to let us through.

I see Han Wei approaching and beckon him to join us.

"Hey, you!" exclaims Idriss. "Where do you think you're going?"

"He's with us, man," says Diallo. "Auditioning for the band."

"Shower comrades want to play African music now!" mutters Idriss in English, doubling up with laughter as he ushers Han Wei in, reluctantly.

Han Wei either doesn't understand or chooses to ignore the insult. "Shower comrade" is the nickname for Chinese students who befriend us so they can use the much better facilities in the foreign students' hostel, especially showers, as we have bathrooms on each corridor and the water there is always hot, unlike in their hostels. They live six or eight to a room and have six coupons a month for hot showers, which they take in communal bathrooms in a separate building from their hostels. Shower friendship is how a lot of girls end up dating foreign devils.

Grumbling noises follow us through the door, where we plunge straight into the frantic sounds of Ali Farka Toure's guitar blaring from giant speakers in the corners. It makes you feel as though the music is at once being blasted at you and sucking you into the hall with the strong, heart-thumping rhythms. There's nowhere to hide except the dance floor.

We buy some beers from the makeshift bar and stand watching the action.

"By the way, thanks," says Han Wei. "For letting me in."

"That's all right. Maybe you can get us into the next Chinese party."

"No problem. But I doubt you'll like it. They're quite different."

"I'm curious, actually. When is the next one?"

"I'll find out."

"Let me know, too," says Diallo. "I've only seen one from a distance. Girls dressed up in fancy costumes, dancing mostly with their hands. Colourful and symmetrical. Almost militaristic."

"Um, well-organised," says Han Wei cautiously, not sure whether to take Diallo's words as compliment or criticism. "Perhaps you saw some festival variety show."

"Probably. With dragon dances and things. All red and gold. I could probably spice things up with some strong African rhythms on my guitar."

Han Wei stares at him, lips curled in a shocked "o", as if Diallo just volunteered to join a dragon dance in a raffia outfit and spirit mask.

"That wouldn't work?" I ask him.

"No, it would be very strange. The songs they play, they have a special style, special meaning. Each instrument has a role because of the special sound it makes. The two-string fiddle we call *erhu,* the *xiao* flute, Chinese drums. If you added African guitar music, people might not understand what the sound means."

"What a pity," says Diallo, feigning disappointment. "I always thought music could unite people."

"It can," protests Han Wei. "But it depends."

"Look, guys, this cross-cultural mumbo-jumbo is all very nice, but there are plenty of pretty babes sitting here bored," says Diallo. "We're neglecting our duties."

Han Wei opts to remain standing against the wall, nursing his beer, while I wander away to greet my friends, occasionally keeping an eye out for Linda. Like an amateur actor preparing for his debut stage appearance, I prepare myself mentally for the things I'll say to her, the opportunities to look out for. It has been a long time since I had a girl in my room, a long time since I watched a girl undress under the cover of darkness then slip under the duvet, and then humped away to the sound of *Temptations* on a creaky cassette, while she held tight and uttered words they didn't teach in the language class.

Linda shows up at 9 p.m. I'm in the middle of a discussion on politics with Kabinga and some European students when I spot her coming through the door. Her round face glows in the psychedelic lights, like a moon emerging from behind rain clouds. She's wearing her hair in a bob that bounces with every step she makes. I approach her, my heart heaving with anticipation, replaying all over again the things I want to say to her tonight.

We exchange greetings the Chinese way, without handshakes. I ask if she wants a beer. She prefers a soda. I also order a small plate of steamed *xiaolongbao* dumplings for her. We find a free bench in the lobby, where I spend the next hour entertaining her with stories about Zimbabwe. She has most likely heard unflattering things about Africa all her life. All this will change tonight. Once she knows about me and where I come from, she'll hopefully drop that questioning look. She'll have the answers she craves.

Her soft drink stands on the bench between us like a beacon marking a boundary between us, the plate of dumplings trapped in both her hands like a treasured memento. Occasionally she eats one, bending over it and taking slow bites to prevent the succulent meat, soup, and red vinegar spilling onto her dark-blue dress. Her sips of the drink are equally dainty and measured. I keep my eyes on her sweet, round face, the high cheekbones and ready smile that make her face radiate with an inner warmth. I long for that moment when I'll cup her face with both hands and watch her close her eyes as I lean to kiss her.

My beer has long gone flat, but I dare not break my momentum by getting the next round just yet. If I could freeze this moment in time for the ten minutes it will take to queue at the makeshift bar, I would. But I can't take that risk. After a while, I begin to feel like a lecturer, giving lessons to an obedient and patient student who knows better than to question her master. But my own voice wearies me; my throat is parched from talking above the blaring music. I've done the romantic sunsets, the undulating tobacco hills, the music of the birds at the crack of dawn. Why won't she say something? Her eyebrows arch when I tell her about shops that sell everything you would ever want, even small shops in the village, without the need for ration coupons.

"It sounds like heaven", she declares, with childlike fascination.

I laugh. "No, not heaven, but it's a country with a future. There's so much optimism now. My parents lived like slaves. Now we're free, Linda, you see? It's like when you wake up from a nightmare and see the sun shining outside, and you know this is going to be a beautiful bright day. That's how I feel about Zimbabwe."

"I'll go with you."

"Go where? To my country?"

"That's what you want, Dan." Something tightens in my belly. How can she know what I want?

"Linda, I…"

"I understand what you're telling me. And I know how you feel…China can't be your home. We won't be happy here."

"Wait, Linda, please…" My hand reaches out to hold hers but she gasps and looks up in alarm. I search desperately for words to explain myself.

"We'll go, Dan, when we graduate. Your country truly sounds like heaven. I know we struggle much here, but what I've learned from you…it makes me…"

"Linda, please…" I glance around the lobby to see if any of the Chinese students and officials we believe act as spies have heard her.

All those words she kept in check, all those things I willed her to say are now coming out all wrong. She has found her elusive voice as surely as I've lost mine.

"My country is not right for you," I blurt out. "They wouldn't know how to receive you."

She starts to tremble, biting her lips to control the sobs. She can't cry here, in front of all these people and whatever spies that are lurking about. I stand up to shield her from the stares and gently try to lead her to the door.

She quickly recovers her composure, deposits the plate of dumplings on my lap and hisses between clenched teeth, "Your heart is not pure." A knife plunged through my guts couldn't have hurt more than the scorn in her eyes. Before I can find a comforting word, she springs to her feet and stumbles out of the door.

I slump back onto the bench, stunned, like a boxer reeling from the shock of a knockout. A half-eaten dumpling drooling red vinegar grins sardonically at me. When I gather the strength to rise, I head for the door, all too painfully aware of the curious eyes that follow me across the lobby. And the regret that eats away stubbornly in my mind as I stumble into the darkness is: I didn't even ask her to dance.

Back at the hostel, I find Lai Guiguo waiting in the lobby, reading a book. He has a small rucksack on the floor.

"Dan, good to see you," he says, in English. The elderly security guard watches him keenly. "Can you help me?"

I nod. I just want to get to my room. I sign him in and explain to the elderly security guard that he's coming in to study with me. Up on my floor, I lead him to the bathroom and return to my room to reflect on the Linda fiasco.

Five minutes later, I hear a commotion coming from the direction of the bathroom and step out to investigate. The security guard, mad with rage, is waving Lai Guiguo's towel in the air, threatening to throw it out of the window and report him to the Youth League. Lai Guiguo is covering his nakedness with his rucksack, begging the old man to let him dry himself. His body is covered in soapsuds.

"What you're doing is wrong!" cries the old man. "Taking a shower in the foreign ghosts' bathroom is against the rules, and yet you do it behind my back! You think I'm a stupid old man. You don't give me face!"

"At least let him finish his shower," I plead with the old man, whose face is puffed up and red with fury.

"No! You two think I'm just a foolish old man. You don't give me face! Sneaking behind me like this; it's wrong."

"All right, old man. He'll promise he'll never sneak behind you again like this. Just let him finish his shower."

"He must give me face!" insists the old man.

"Wait just one minute." I rush to a neighbour's room and borrow some cigarettes for the guard.

Lai Guiguo apologises and the old man lets him dry himself, while he paces about, inhaling deeply, his face still contorted with anger. In that single instant when Lai Guiguo and I make brief eye contact, I know that the future of shower comradeship will never be the same again. Not for the two of us. It's gone, just like Linda.

Two men are waiting outside my door. I've never seen them before, but from their Mao suits and thick woollen tunics, they're from either Student Affairs or the Youth League, two security units that no one can tell apart. They both have a reputation for investigating complaints with ruthlessness and have been known to engineer at least one dismissal from the university. The two men are stocky and seem to be carrying briefcases hidden in their jackets. Their eyes are narrowed as though to better scan my guilt of whatever I'm to be accused of, and one of them is smoking nonstop, blowing the smoke out of the corner of his mouth onto his shoulder. The other one keeps running a hand through thinning hair, giving me a sideways look.

"We're following up on an incident at the party," the heavy smoker announces, talking through his smoke. "We understand a girl was insulted. Can you tell us anything about this?"

The exchange brings curious onlookers out of their rooms and into the corridor. Some are in pyjamas, others come out holding books or a cigarette. They stand by their doors, watching in silence, as if waiting for the intruders to attack before tearing them to pieces. Seeing them stand in silent solidarity emboldens me to demand why they're asking me. Linda would never have reported our little incident. She would have had to face tough questioning about her own morals and would have been reprimanded severely.

"Why don't you ask the girl? If anyone harmed her she would complain, wouldn't she?"

"We were hoping you would save us the trouble by talking honestly with us."

"You're misinformed. People had fun. They drank, danced, and talked. We don't insult each other at our parties."

They know that without Linda's cooperation, there's little they can do. When they're gone, a few of my neighbours join me to dissect the incident. I listen to them condemn the harassment, but my mind is elsewhere. I can't erase from my head the way Linda's lips quivered as she fought off the tears. No amount of intimidation by the campus police will dislodge that image from my mind or unnerve me the way her parting words did. I kick my feet, rendered totally mute by my anger. *You stupid idiot!* Such a sweet darling. Gone now. Just like Qiao.

Lai Ying

WE HAVE A TEST COMING up next week. I've paid close attention to the lecturer's hints about what sections of the textbook to memorise, but this material on quantum electrodynamics is barely digestible.

I've spent two hours in the library desperately trying to make sense of convoluted descriptions of how charged particles interact by emitting and absorbing photons. There are more than a few unfamiliar Chinese characters on this page alone. Sometimes I ignore the really arcane ones or try to guess their meaning from the context, but this time, I'm like a boat bogged down by treacherous water hyacinth on Lake Ndambu.

That's when I notice the beautiful girl sitting opposite me, casually leafing through her notes. I watch her secretly above my book and notice how her black hair falls like a veil, partly obscuring her face. Everyone swears that long, glossy hair looks sexier, but there's something unique about this girl's hair, which dips just below her ears, accentuating the round shape of her head, skirting and forming a neat curve around the high cheekbones, like a face caught between black brackets, and a fringe that comes to within an inch of her eyebrows. She reminds me of the adverts I used to see back home of models leaning against Japanese cars. You didn't know if they were advertising the cars or the pretty girls.

Her cheeks glow in the light that shines through the roof-high windows. In my desperation to understand how light particles transmit electromagnetic forces, I had completely ignored her, unaware she was emitting sensuous photons that raised the temperature around our table. Her mango-shaped breasts point straight at me through a loose blouse that woefully fails to conceal their stubborn firmness.

She sucks in her lower lip. Her small nose twitches in concentration. She's probably revising for a test too, memorising a passage her professor decreed to be critical. Her lips move as if she's miming or reading aloud. I lean forward to catch the sound of her voice. Perhaps she's not memorising her notes. Perhaps she's saying something to me, whispering a secret message for my ears only. Her lips curl around the soundless message, one minute forming the shape of some word, the next minute offering a kiss. I don't care what the message is. All I need is the kiss. I close my eyes to receive the kiss I deserve. Her luscious lips rest on mine in a moment of intense communion. My hands slip through the short hair and wrap themselves around her head in an embrace that will last forever. Her breasts close in on my bare heaving chest.

I open my eyes to see her packing her notes to leave. I leap to my feet, in the process knocking my book to the floor. She looks up at me. Those lips. Just as I imagined them. They curl up into a smile that infuses me with warmth yet renders me mute. I stand like a fool before her.

"*Ni hao?*" Her voice is little more than a whisper, a gentle question that so effortlessly softens the questioning look in the eyes. My response sounds like a croak in comparison.

After she explains the elusive characters, the conversation veers to more down-to-earth topics. The usual: Where do you come from, how long have you been here, what do you study? After two and a half years of this repertoire, I try not to make my well-rehearsed answers sound too jaded. Her warm, friendly manner makes it so much easier. More importantly, I'm anxious not to repeat the Linda fiasco, which still gnaws at me after all these months.

She tells me her name is Lai Ying. Her tongue dances when she says it, as though she cherishes the sound of her name. I repeat her name a few times, to see if it gives me the same type of pleasure.

"You're funny," she says. "Do you always repeat things?"

"Only when I want to memorise them."

"You need to memorise my name? Why?"

"So I won't forget it, Lai Ying. Chinese names aren't always easy to remember."

"They're easy, actually. Mostly just two syllables, Lai…Ying."

"If I don't memorise, I have to find something to associate the name with. Right now, I can only think of star light, because you've shone like a star on my ignorance, and now I have to find the connection between that and your name."

She laughs, covering her mouth with her hand and glancing over her shoulder self-consciously. But there are no library assistants around and most people have gone to afternoon classes or afternoon tea. I wish she wouldn't hide her lips while laughing.

"How many syllables does your name have?" she asks.

"Let's see, *Chi-pon-da*. Three."

"That's such a long name." She covers her mouth again, looking genuinely shocked. "And that's just your surname?"

"Yeah. I think you'd better call me Dan. It's much easier to remember."

She starts to laugh again, her shoulders pulled back somewhat. My gaze drops immediately to the breasts, which for the briefest of moments jut out, straining against the blouse, drawing me into another reverie. Her voice, this time low and breathy, almost husky, rouses and arouses in equal measure.

"Sorry, it's just that the name reminds me of—"

"I know, an egg. People call me Eggman."

"Can I call you that?"

"If you like. When you see me, think egg."

"An African egg," she says, smiling. I reflect on her words. What does it mean, that I'm brown on the outside and white and yellow inside?

We spend the next ten minutes chatting. Lai Ying speaks with a rare confidence, looking me straight in the eye, yet losing none of that quaint demureness so typical of well-mannered local girls. She says she's studying international relations and some of her courses are taught in English. Eventually she has to leave for her class. My eyes have just a few more minutes to feast upon her smiling face, her finely carved shoulders, to visualise the real shape of the breasts tucked away behind the silent modesty of the flowing blouse.

When she walks past the light streaming down the high windows, her legs are visible through the thin cotton dress. I watch her breathlessly, willing her to turn around and blow me a kiss, or at least to smile. As if reading my thoughts, she turns briefly, and waves. I blow her a kiss, not caring who is watching. But I can't tell if she's smiling, because of the dazzling light which forces me to keep my gaze on her legs. I can hardly concentrate on photons and electromagnetic forces after that.

A week later, when I meet Lai Ying by chance outside the library, I ask her to sit with me so we can have a proper chat.

"You mean the chat we had before wasn't proper?"

Before I can answer, she pinches my elbow and starts to walk toward the benches in the square. I hope she's not planning to sit in the open. Walking in the spring humidity is like wading through a fog of moisture-laden air. I constantly have to take a half-mast. The half-mast, which was first popularised by Diallo, involves washing the top of your torso at the washbasin, especially the armpits, neck, and face whenever you come in from the sizzling heat outside and don't have time for a proper shower. Fortunately, Lai Ying leads the way to the small lake behind the library, where trees provide a welcome shelter from the oppressive sun and a mild breeze help keep my skin cool.

The lake is called Ming Zhu, Democracy Lake. Here students are allowed to say anything with no fear of upsetting the authorities. When I first heard about it, I expected to find students holding rallies, waving clenched fists in the air, yelling slogans, or at least huddled together animatedly discussing politics. I've seen nothing of the sort. Democracy Lake is better known as a quiet spot for dating couples. As Diallo puts it, democracy in this country only exists between lovers. That this sweet girl I met only last week wants us to have a quiet chat here makes my chest heave with anticipation.

Today she's wearing a long blue skirt that reaches well below her knees, and a white, short-sleeved top buttoned up all the way to the neck that accentuates her breasts lovingly. An appreciative warmth spreads through me, and I'm thinking how sweet of her to dress like that, as if she knew she was going to meet me.

I lean back on the bench and listen to the sound of her voice provide the accompanying lyrics to the symphony of the chirruping and screeching of crickets and cicadas. The gentle roll of her words is like the calm Qin Huai River on its silent journey across the city, washing away the memories of past blunders, regrets, and torments, and offering promises that I strain to catch in Lai Ying's monologue.

When she says she has friends amongst the European and American language students, I ask if she knows any Africans.

"No, you're the first one." The almost triumphant tone makes my heart leap. She makes it sound like something unique, like a rare achievement no one would have expected of her.

"That's a privilege for me, Lai Ying."

"Really! Maybe just a coincidence?"

"No. It's more than that. It's an honour, really. But also a...a challenge."

"How's that a challenge?" There's a hint of alarm in her voice.

"It means I have to make a good impression, Lai Ying. Be on my best behaviour."

"You're funny," she says, staring at the birds that have perched on a low branch and appear to be playing a game, chasing each other, one minute gliding to the ground and pecking about on the wet pockmarked concrete. "Sparrows," she whispers, careful not to disturb the birds. "Playful. So cute."

I nod. Playful, yes. Calling out for attention, so unlike the stealthy fish eagles back home. In my subconscious, I see one of the sparrows morph into an eagle, the eyes trained on me in a concentrated stare, as if watching for the giveaway ripple beneath the calm surface of our budding romance. The next minute, the sparrows waft away with a sudden flutter of wings above us and back across the lake, violently shaking me back into consciousness.

Lai Ying has a faraway look in her eyes. Her voice is tinged with regret as she says, "It's hard to believe we once tried to exterminate them." I barely hear her voice, which is faint and distant. I rub my eyes to clear my mind of the image of the eagle which still looms before me.

"Birds? Why?"

She casts a wary look around. There are only three other couples, and they're out of earshot. What could she be thinking? Does she too see an eagle poised to strike?

"No one talks about these things," she whispers. "Well, it's Democracy Lake anyway. In the late fifties, it was decided to kill sparrows because they were thought to be destroying food stocks and causing starvation. My father tells me how as a teenager, he spent hours up on trees strangling birds, smashing their eggs. They killed thousands of birds every day. Sheer madness."

I've heard of Chairman Mao's bizarre projects, like getting villagers to produce steel and build roads and bridges with their bare hands. She's right, this one sounds like sheer madness. Diseases must have spread, with no birds to feed on insects.

"Locusts invaded and, encountering no birds, ate everything in their path. Millions died. Big men got it so wrong." I look into her eyes, wondering why she's telling me all this with such frightening candour, yet she barely knows me.

But there's something I don't understand. Mao did all these things, yet he's still so revered. I say to Lai Ying, "I thought Sun Yat-sen would be more respected, and now, with Deng's reforms, you'd think he's achieving more. But it's Mao's face on the money."

"Chairman Mao is the founder of the nation." If I had heard this from anyone else, I would have known they were just repeating a long-memorised school refrain. But something about the way she whispers it, as though she were commenting on the weather, makes me wonder how much more irreverent she'll get. "That's what we're taught. We've got to appreciate the good things, Dan. What about Africa?"

Where do I start? The civil wars, the frequent military coups, the floods and starvation. This hardly seems the time, place, and audience. As Lai Ying says, we need to appreciate the good.

"We have many problems in Africa, Lai Ying. But in my country, we have only hope now, after a long history of darkness."

"You're so lucky. In the West, they complain all the time. They believe in freedom of expression." She laughs, and yet I can't help but think she's laughing at her own people for believing otherwise. It's the way she shrugs, the wistful way she casts the sentiment, as if it needed to be made, to neutralise the implied criticisms earlier. "They'll never say a good thing about their leaders. You know, I lived in Canada for two years."

I try not to show my surprise. It's not easy for the Chinese to leave the country. Lai Ying explains that her mother's family were landowners and business people. Some of them had emigrated to Canada on two previous occasions to save their skins. First, during the 1949 Communist Revolution, and then sixteen years later to escape the Cultural Revolution. Instinctively, I know she's a Shanghai girl. It's her confident manner, the ease with which she speaks to a foreigner like me, and the suggestion of old money in the ladylike grooming, the clothes that look too bright and foreign for the local shops.

I listen to the pained voice as she talks about the way her family's properties were appropriated by a rival group that enjoyed the protection of what she calls big men.

"It affected Mother deeply," she says.

"Where are they now, your family?"

"They're still in Shanghai, but it's just a matter of time before they emigrate. Mother's not happy there. Too many sad memories. Lai Mui, my sister, is indifferent. She says she can live anywhere. She even talks about Hong Kong and Singapore."

"What made you come to study in Nanjing?" I ask her.

"I wanted a challenge," she replies without hesitation. "Living on my own. You?"

"The scholarship said I had to come here. At least you get to choose your subject. Though there's no guarantee you'll get what you want."

"You like your subject?"

"It's all right. Father wanted me to study agriculture because he thinks it's more useful. Luckily for me they don't offer it on this campus."

She looks up in surprise. "Luckily? Maybe for your father it's not very lucky. It means you can't help him."

"Oh I can, in other ways. They look up to me, the whole family."

"I see. So you're like Chinese people."

I nod. I've heard other students say similar things, about having to support their parents. Visiting students from the west don't have this burden. I ask her if she plans to return to Canada, and she says she'll probably end up working in Guangdong Province.

"Guangdong? What's special about it?"

"There are lots of industries there. Plenty of jobs. My father's always telling me about Huizhou, his hometown in Guangdong. But I've never been there."

"Perhaps you'll rebuild your family business?"

"I don't think so," she says, frowning. "I'm not all that interested in business. What my people lost, it's like a different world to me. I don't feel the loss because I didn't really experience it myself. No one talks about these things. It's like it happened to another family."

"That's sad. But it's also you, your life, and it makes me want to know more."

"More about my family?"

"For now, more about you. It's wonderful talking to you. I want to...you know, spend more time, talking to you, Lai Ying."

She bites her lower lip, perhaps to mask the uncharacteristic coquettishness that suddenly infects her.

"You're funny," she whispers.

"Lai Ying, you know what I want to do? I want to hold your hand and play with your fingers, and count them one by one."

She smiles. I'm pleased to see there's not even a hint of alarm in her eyes, just a quiet playfulness when she says, "You don't need to count them, Dan. I can tell you how many they are."

She holds up her hands across her lips and says, "All right, count."

Like an obedient pupil, I do as I'm told. Then I place my hands on my lap and ask her to count. She counts to ten, looking straight into my eyes. Only then does she look at my hands. She studies the old scars and callouses in silence, like a nurse examining a wound, then asks what happened.

"Playing dangerous games as a kid, falling off trees." She flinches. "It's part of growing up. Lai Ying, we never shook hands when we first met. I would like to do that. It's important."

"I understand. At the right time." I lean back with a sigh of contentment. I know she means it.

"You're different, Lai Ying."

She glances at me, eyes wide open with surprise, as if she has received an unexpected compliment.

"Really? In what way?"

"You talk about things. Politics. Family. Important things."

She laughs, a light cackling laugh that sounds like musical notes bouncing off her tongue before floating away and fading seamlessly in the warm, humid air.

"I talk too much, you mean?"

"I wouldn't say that. It's just that you can talk freely about things. Most Chinese I know don't."

"Who are your Chinese friends?"

I think for a moment. Apart from a couple of girls I've dated in the past, who indeed are my Chinese friends? With classmates, the talk is mostly about work. Except perhaps Han Wei and Lai Guiguo. Some people think they're spies for the police-like Student Affairs or the Youth League to ensure no one badmouths the Communist Party or exhibits what they call imperialist immoral practices. Others dismiss them as mere shower comrades. At least they're prepared to spend time with us, laughing at our jokes, listening to us reminisce about our lives back in Africa.

Lai Ying asks if my friends talk about themselves.

"Never. I don't even know whether Han Wei and Lai Guiguo have siblings, or what their parents do."

"Have you tried asking them?"

"Not really. But after getting enough evasive answers, surprised looks, or silence, you learn to mind your own business. They talk about their studies and future plans. Never about themselves, their families. Where they live. How they live. And you'll never get them to talk about the past or politics."

She nods and falls into a thoughtful silence.

"And your friends?" I ask her.

Her friends fall into well-defined groups: roommates, classmates, and her many friends in Shanghai, like her old schoolmates. I surmise that they're mostly female. She says her best friend is a girl called Mei Ning, who prefers her nickname Minnie. Minnie is from Hubei, and just like Lai Ying, came here to enjoy freedom away from home.

"What about boys?" I ask.

"You mean boyfriend?" She says, chuckling.

"I don't mean to—"

"It's all right, Dan. I met a Japanese student last year. Smart guy. He knew so much about art and films. He wants to be a film director." She falls silent, perhaps ruminating on some forgotten emotion.

"What about Chinese boys?"

"Nice to their girlfriends. Polite. But they behave as if they're being watched, as if someone is going to grade their behaviour like an exam. They're too traditional for me."

"I'm traditional, too."

"No, not in the Chinese way. You're more open. It makes for a nice change." I feel something take flight in me, a swelling in my chest. She smiles, but when our eyes meet she looks away, perhaps afraid she's the one who's too open this time.

The sound of music reaches us. It's coming from a social hall across the lake. We approach and watch through the windows. There are about twenty girls in colourful red and yellow costumes, dancing in two rows, swishing their ankle-length skirts, slicing the air with graceful movements of their hands, fingers executing their own rapid turns and swirls, as if engaged in their own esoteric dance. I could watch this all day, just for the symmetry, the precise coordination, the synchronised head movements and alternating flashes of smiles and pouts, and the way they make it all look so easy, yet it must have taken hours to get the movements right.

The music is coming from a cassette player on the floor. Lai Ying explains that they're practicing for some end of term celebration.

"It's the legend of Hua Mulan," says Lai Ying in a sombre voice. "She joined the army to save her father from going to war. Listen to the words."

As the singers sway from side to side, their mesmerising voices rising and falling with the rhythmic beat of galloping horses, you can almost see the brave girl in a man's armour criss-crossing the countryside

We watch the dance in silence. Lai Ying sings along, in a low, soft voice, lolling her head to the music, so utterly captivated she's become Hua Mulan, lost in the mountains.

The music transports me back to Ndambu. As children, we believed that when a memory from the past haunts you, someone is thinking about you. Could the sparrow-turned-eagle be a message from Mother, reminding me of her expectations, perhaps signalling this girl is the one, or warning me not to be hasty? Lai Ying walks as if in a trance, still humming to the music. Not wanting to break the spell, I walk beside her, one soundless footstep after another. The nearness of her stirs a valiant soldier within me when our arms brush against each other in the esoteric code of Mulan's secret admirer. If it had been dark, I would have risked putting an arm around her waist and said to hell with the bloody campus police. If we had been on a deserted path in Ndambu, I would have held her hand and drawn her close to me, felt the softness of her breasts against my agitated chest, sang along with her, made up the verses as we went along. Like the female and male hare in the legend of Hua Mulan, no one seeing us from a distance would have been able to tell the difference. No one would have cared, not in our own little world anyway.

Only weeks later, when we start dating 'small-small' as Kabinga puts it, does Lai Ying tell me why the legend of Hua Mulan so mesmerised her. Even so, she tells it laconically, with little detail, only to say that she wished she had been around to save her father from being taken away for 're-education' to wean him off his bourgeois property-owning ways. The urge to know more gnaws at me, but I feel as though I've already been let in on a privileged secret. To ask for more would be greedy. Maybe later, she'll oblige. When she's ready. No more stupid blunders, I promise myself. I'll take lessons from the boys if I have to.

My Silly Egg

AN OMINOUS SILENCE HOVERS OVER the department. Anxious students mill around waiting for a late afternoon lecture, chatting in low tones. I exchange greetings with a few classmates. They resemble a motley crew of factory workers in their dull brown, black, and blue cotton clothes. A girl in a red top and blue skirt stands out like a model amongst peasants.

The lecture room itself is locked and the door secured with an imposing padlock. There's no notice of a cancellation of class. As far as I know, we have one more week of lectures before the summer exams.

Neither Diallo nor Kabinga have arrived. I seek out Han Wei to ask him if he knows anything. I find him sitting alone on a bench down the corridor, reading his notes, his face a mask of concentration. I sit next to him and ask him what he knows.

"You don't know what's going on?" I shake my head. "About Professor Sheng, no idea?"

"What, is he ill?"

He points at the classmates who are now getting agitated. The class is ten minutes late. "They live in hope. But what good is that when your ears are blocked?"

"What do you mean, Han Wei? I don't understand you."

"Many people don't understand," he says simply. "I'll tell you what I know, but you must promise me something in return."

"What do you want?"

"Your corduroy trousers, Eggman. How much would you sell them for?"

I look closely into his eyes to see if this is a joke. He stares right back, his face as hard as steel.

"That pair you wear when it's cold. How much?"

"Forget it, Han Wei, I'm not selling my clothes. Not in—"

"I know, I know," he interrupts, raising a placatory hand. "Not in a country with strange rationing, where you don't know when the next supplies will arrive."

"You don't need to buy clothes from me. You're just fine."

Han Wei is one of the few male students who dress in colour, as they say. He dons orange, yellow, and white shirts, blue trousers, colours that most people can only admire from a distance as they make do with the drab grey, black, and green comrade uniform. Reality is just like the pictures that come in black and white, and shades of grey.

There's a small group of enterprising students who buy things like clothes, shoes, cameras, and radios from foreigners and sell them to locals for a profit, but I had not expected Han Wei to be one of them. Now I know why he usually brings a dark rucksack along before riding off immediately after the Friday afternoon class.

"So, you're a trader, Han Wei? I'm impressed."

"People need things, and they can't find them. I try to solve this problem."

I listen attentively as he talks about the frustrations of people who've made money but find nothing to spend it on. He complains about foreigners who show off their leather jackets, cowboy boots, and blue jeans. I feel the urge to tell him they're not showing off but simply wearing their clothes. Yet his ideas get me thinking. Why should he serve as my middleman when I could sell directly to willing customers? Problem is, I need the clothes I have. If only there was some way to bring supplies in. But that would be riskier than the White Card deal, which already has a paying customer as a starting point. How can I trust Han Wei, someone I know so little about, with his small, penetrative eyes, sharp knees that just like clenched fists into the fabric of his blue imitation jeans, and a nose that twitches with every drag on a pungent cigarette? He looks more at home as a broker at the Travel Café than a student.

"You have anything you don't need?" He says. I shake my head. "I envy you, Dan. You have good chances many of us can only dream of. Good money, nice clothes, excellent hostel. It's a good foundation."

Struggling hard to contain my frustration, I once again ask him about Professor Sheng.

He looks disoriented, and for a moment simply stares at the classmates, some of whom are walking away.

"Maybe he was reported," he says simply.

"What do you mean?"

"I heard that students complained about a professor."

"Complained? About what? To whom?"

"That's all I know," protests Han Wei. He's hiding something, the way he crosses his legs and arms, as if to lock the secrets deep in a place accessible only by invitation. He definitely has that look: keep away, foreigner, this is a private problem for the locals.

I excuse myself and go in search of my friends, wondering what Professor Sheng could have done wrong. I remember Wang saying something about professors being purged for teaching counter-revolutionary ideas. But Wang was at university twenty years ago. I've always found Professor Sheng very understanding and willing to explain things privately after class, while the lesson is still fresh on your mind, while other professors ask you to book appointments to see them in their hallowed offices later, when you no longer remember what arcane topic had troubled you.

The mystery deepens into the following week. Diallo and I are at the department finding out about the summer lecture programme when two men dressed in the Mao suits and grey jackets of the campus police stop outside Professor Sheng's door. The man with thinning hair and a cigarette on his lips looks a lot like the one who once questioned me following the incident with Linda. Without knocking, they push the door open and barge in. Except for the two of us, the corridor is quiet and dark. To save energy, the lights are always off, making the corridor look deserted. We approach on tiptoe and try to make sense of the angry exchange coming from within. Minutes later, the door swings open and Professor Sheng is bundled out, collapsing into us. Instinctively, we hold on to him to stop him crashing into the wall.

"Get away from here, black devils!"

Thinning Hair's furious tone and belligerent manner silences us into shocked immobility. Professor Sheng, who has recovered his balance and is straightening his shirt, pleads with the man to be calm.

"These are just students," he says. "They've done no wrong."

"Are you following us?" Thinning Hair barks into my face.

My chest burning with indignation, I shake my head, too shocked to talk back. Diallo grabs my elbow and pulls me away.

"You're the people always causing problems here. We never had this trouble before you came!"

"Let them go," says Professor Sheng. Without warning, Thinning Hair lands a resounding slap on the professor's face, sending him reeling into the wall. Then he pulls out a baton and starts waving it threateningly in our faces.

We turn and walk away as the other man leads Professor Sheng away in the opposite direction, prodding his ribs with his baton.

Two days later, Professor Sheng comes to class with a black eye and a bandage on his hand. We take our seats at the back, watching him closely. He avoids making eye contact and carries on the class as though it's the most natural thing in the world to teach with bruises and bandages. The story is dissected at Wang's noodle shop late into the night. Some people say it's the beginning of a new purge and expect to see it escalate into serious trouble. When we mention it to Wang, he doesn't seem surprised at all. He must have learned the details from the Chinese students. He informs us that students complained that some professors are too hard on them and are more lenient to foreign students when it comes to tests. Kabinga dismisses the claims as nonsense and jealousy.

"Some of these guys can't believe we're smarter than them," he declares. "Smarter than them, small-small."

Wang incurs his wrath by saying it's not unusual to be more sympathetic to foreigners because of language difficulties.

"Nonsense!" exclaims Kabinga. "Language problems in the first year I can understand. Not anymore, Wang Bin. Do we sound like we have language problems to you?"

"No, not to me, my friend." Wang assumes a conciliatory tone. Alienating customers can't be good for business.

"So, what exactly did Professor Sheng do?" says Diallo. "Whom did he favour?"

We look at each other as if to identify the guilty party.

"This is ridiculous," snaps Kabinga. "No one needs a witch hunt. What's your problem, Zen man?"

"Chin Chin, why do you speak as if out of guilt?" says Diallo. "Do you fear you've benefited from some misplaced leniency?"

"*Ta made!*" curses Kabinga, jumping to his feet and throwing his cigarette angrily to the ground. He shakes a fist in my face, exclaiming, "Jesus, man! What's the matter with your friend?"

"My friend?"

"Yeah! What exactly is his problem?"

"But you can ask him yourself, Chin Chin."

Diallo leans back on his chair, watching Kabinga with a slightly triumphant half-smile, like a torturer who knows just where to poke and stab. As usual, Kabinga expects me to ward off the attacks on his behalf in the mistaken belief that I wield some magical influence over the Enlightened One. It is a belief I find both amusing and annoying, especially when I have no idea what Diallo is driving at. It is not inconceivable that someone has had to come to Kabinga's help, given the frequency of his White Card absences and his blasé attitude towards studying and exams. He would never admit to it, of course, and if he has struck a deal with some professor, it wouldn't surprise me. But Professor Sheng?

Wang assumes the role of peacemaker, urging Kabinga to calm down. Looking nervously at the customers who are staring disdainfully at us, he orders his wife to bring us another round of beers. I don't know why he bothers. He has seen enough of these exchanges to know they'll never amount to anything. And the locals are by now accustomed to seeing heated exchanges amongst us, often in a language they don't understand. Kabinga insists on paying for the beers, angering Wang who says it's a matter of honour for having offered. While they're still arguing, Diallo walks up to the counter and pays Wang's wife. Suitably disarmed, Wang and Kabinga settle down to drink in silence, like a couple of enemies mollified into confronting the futility of their hostilities.

When I next see Lai Ying, I ask her what she knows about professors getting into trouble. We're sitting on our regular bench at Democracy Lake, watching a white girl – most probably a language student – feeding biscuits to the ducks. She breaks one biscuit after another and casts a spray of crumbs onto their fluttering feathers. Two local girls approach to watch the action but run away giggling when a daring hungry duck waddles towards them.

I expect Lai Ying to dismiss the whole story as a bunch of rubbish but her silence unnerves me. Her nose twitches with nervousness. She finger-combs her hair, which she has recently taken to growing long.

We've been spending a lot of time together these last few weeks. And every time I see her, I feel as though yet another piece of a puzzle has fallen into place because I've come to learn so much about her, about China. She talks openly, making full use of the democratic rights the lake offers. While other girls become apologetic when you so much as complain about anything, Lai Ying is not afraid to discuss the failings of her country, for which she makes no apologies. It makes talking to her such a refreshing experience. But there are times when a shadow crosses her face, and I can see some inner torment that she's struggling to overcome, and when that happens, I fear the worst and just let her be. I see the same thing happening when I tell her about Professor Sheng. Perhaps the harassment reminds her of the purges of the past, the "re-education" her father and millions of others endured in the sixties.

"So much happened before," she says in a regretful tone. "Even as recently as ten years ago, when China started to open up. My father knew professors. In the fields where they toiled together. To hear him talk about that period, the madness, the sheer terror. It's just terrible." She blinks rapidly.

"It's all in the past, Lai Ying." I try to comfort her and ward off any tears. "But I have to say I was shocked about the supposed leniency. And when that man struck my teacher, it was bizarre, shameful. Someone I respect, Lai Ying, reduced to nothing…"

"I know, it's like a return to our dark past. Dan, some people are very unhappy about the privileges foreign students have."

The ominous tone makes me start. She and I have never talked about this before. Most of us take it for granted that we need to be compensated for the inconveniences we suffer here.

To hear Lai Ying mention this implied discrimination suddenly makes me realise the enormity of the inequality. Only ten years ago, the country was tearing itself apart in a war against privilege and bourgeois ways. Now it looks as though foreign students are the new face of bourgeois decadence. Is Lai Ying trying to warn me of the possible consequences of a simmering discontent amongst the locals? I ask her what she's heard of the Professor Sheng case.

"Nothing, Dan. All I know is that some students are so unhappy they'll do anything to cause trouble. Be careful, all right?" She peers into my face to make sure I'm listening. When I laugh away her worries, she gets upset and pinches my elbow. "I'm serious Dan. If anything happened to you, I…" her voice drops and she looks away, unable or perhaps unwilling to express how much we've come to mean to each other. When she turns to look at me, the plea in her eyes speaks louder than any words that Democracy Lake could ever solicit out of her. The soft glow of her face reminds me of Linda watching me with patient anticipation.

Throwing caution to the wind, I take her hand and squeeze it. Her hand, soft and smooth, curls itself around my fingers like a stolen embrace. She doesn't glance around to see if anyone's watching. She looks straight into my eyes, as if daring anyone to come between us. My mouth goes dry. The urge to throw my arms around her and hold her close is like a raging storm in my belly. But even as I lose myself in the sun-drenched reverie of an imagined kiss, the limits on democratic amorousness are flashing away like red lights on the edges of my consciousness.

The next two weeks pass like a blur. My every waking moment is filled with images of Lai Ying. I hear her voice in the song of the sparrows that twitter and dance in the lawn outside my window, in the wind that blows through the trees that cherish the hot summer days as much as the girls lounging on benches under them in the main campus square. To escape the prying eyes of friends and campus guards, we spend hours in quiet city parks and popular sites, many of which I've only heard of previously but never visited. We often come back to the hostel, where I cook her semolina sadza, spicy fried chicken wings, and my signature beef stew with tomatoes and sweet potatoes. The sweet potatoes here are yellowish-orange and quickly turn mushy when the stew is stirred, which makes for an excellent gravy. I love it when we cook together. I marinate the meat in garlic and lemon juice, while she steams fish and measures the rice and water with a studied meticulousness, as though she was conducting an experiment. Two measures of water for one measure of rice, she says, dipping a finger and watching carefully for the tell-tale mark. Sometimes she makes rice noodles with sliced pork toppings and fresh coriander, which I find even more appetising than Wang's special because she's just as wary of excessive soya sauce as I am and uses just the right amount.

Lai Ying has opened my eyes to a world that previously drifted past my solitary student existence like the Qin Huai River that cuts through the city, and which I only dared to observe from the banks, unwilling to wet my apprehensive African sensibilities, and discouraged by the overt hostility on the streets. Lai Ying persuades me to wade into the culture, and soon enough, I'm submerged into the delights of Nanjing life like a native, hiking through the lush woods of Purple Mountain, paddling boats on Lake Xuanwu, past hordes of men fishing on the shores, studying exhibits of the victims of Japanese aggression in the Nanjing Memorial Museum, and for the first time, appreciating the gory details of my city's troubled past.

For the first time, I feel truly able to appreciate the rich variety of Chinese cuisine, which Lai Ying and I savour in elegantly decorated teahouses and little overcrowded noodle shops in downtown Xinjiekou. From the fiery Szechuan

Kung pao chicken, *la zi ji* (bony chicken fried with peppers) and tongue-numbing Chengdu hot pot, to northern lamb noodle soup, red bean desserts, and Cantonese dim sum in miniature steamer baskets, and green teas, the flavours of China explode into life on my untutored tongue.

With Lai Ying by my side, riding our flying horses amongst the citizens on wide, unmarked streets, the city becomes my home in a way I would never have imagined possible. We cycle to Li Gun temple to see the famous pagoda and inhale the sweet smells of osmanthus shrubs and trees dotted around the well-manicured gardens. We stop to admire the lake with the jutting head of a dragon lustily watching over red goldfish that scuttle around purple and white floating lotuses. We gaze upon the astounding ceiling-high sculpture of Confucius in Dacheng Palace of Confucius Temple, and relax in a pagoda by the waterfront to watch leisure boats sailing lazily down the river.

In our insatiable quest for tranquil crowd-free adventures, we spend half a day exploring the city walls, where we snake around the Qin Huai River. In a quiet spot under weeping willows, I take Lai Ying's hand and for five minutes, we enjoy the tentative stolen pleasures of walking hand-in-hand. At first, she trembles with nervousness and tries to snatch her hand away, but I hold on tight and we skip away to the sounds of dead leaves cracking beneath our feet, laughing with sheer abandon. I release her hand as we approach the Zhonghua Men, an imposing structure that looks more like a fortified garrison than a gate. With her Russian-made camera, we take pictures of each other posing in line with the dummy guards, who stand at regular intervals holding a lance and a flag under the ivy-draped imposing ramparts. From the top of the ancient city walls, we can see the old red-roof houses stacked up against each other like a sprawling shanty town, and into the distance, where they give way to taller, grey-roofed residential housing blocks.

Our summer of love sees us joining a throng of tourists, walking down a maple-lined avenue and braving the 392 stairs up the hill to Dr Sun Yat-sen's Mausoleum to enjoy breath-taking mountain and forest views that fade solemnly into a distant mist, admiring potted Bonsai and magnolia trees in full bloom, cacti and rose gardens ironically flourishing in perfect harmony. Here more than anywhere else, people who have come to pay homage to the founder of modern China are so intrigued by the sight of me and a group of western tourists that they would rather watch us than feast their gaze on the spectacular views. Lai Ying avoids them and constantly flashes reassuring smiles at me. Every time this happens, I resist the urge to squeeze her hand. Yet, imagining the pain and humiliation she must be enduring but stoically concealing with her humour and warmth draws me closer to her than the physical act of holding hands ever could.

I have never imagined it possible to feel this way about anyone. Sometimes the feeling of Lai Ying worming herself into my being is like a stubborn painless cough stuck in my chest, but every time my chest heaves to release it, it entrenches itself more deeply, and my chest is caught in a series of leaps and bounds. Diallo has taken to teasing me about behaving like a lovesick teenager. The feelings that have consumed me have, thankfully, also made me immune to this sort of jibe.

Sometimes Lai Ying watches me as if looking for a secret signal on my face. There's that self-assured glint in her eyes, as though she doesn't care who is watching us. In those precious moments, there are just the two of us in the whole world, and nothing else matters.

One Sunday morning, we discuss with a blend of amusement and frustration the things we have to do to keep our relationship a secret. It's another steamy and muggy summer day, when the air sits still, stubbornly resistant to any overtures of a cooling wind. My windows yawn open in pointless impotence, and the only respite we have is a small electric fan that does little to cool the air and merely stirs the heat and humidity into a sizzling vindictiveness.

This is the time of year when shower comradeship is most intense, when budding relationships blossom and flourish, before the girls disappear for the summer break. It pains me to realise that Lai Ying will be going away like everyone else, leaving a long hangover of an empty summer ahead of me. Perhaps I'll travel to Shanghai and spend a few weeks there so we can be together.

Lai Ying can't believe I'm not bitter about being called names and mocked on the streets, ignored at the shops, glared at like an odd exhibit in the museums we've been frequenting or an exotic animal in a zoo.

"How can you accept this kind of discrimination?" she cries in exasperation. My response is that if Chinese people walked down the dirt roads in Ndambu, they would certainly be stared at. "But would they be insulted to their face?"

I hesitate. That would be most unlikely. Children might call out "Bruce Lee!" and execute mock karate chops, but it would be good-natured and designed to impress. Adults wouldn't waste their time following them around as if they had nothing better to do. But even though I want to talk to Lai Ying with nothing but absolute honesty, I'm forced to conceal the fact that sometimes, the anger wells up in me to the point that it's all I can do not to pack it in and go home. I keep it bottled in because I can't imagine retreating back to Ndambu village like a coward running away from trouble, an eagle that no longer has the stomach for a hunt.

"There's not much you can do, Lai Ying," I explain, throwing myself on the narrow bed. "When you're used to being called a *hei gui* every day, you can't go around seething with anger. It doesn't get you anywhere. And it's not going to change mentalities."

"You can't simply accept it, Dan." She sits at my desk, watching over me, as if I were a naughty boy refusing to get out of bed and go to school.

"Of course, I hate it. And sometimes I react with anger. But then you ask yourself, does the person calling you *hei gui* really believe you're not human, that you're truly a ghost or a devil?"

"It doesn't matter what they believe. It's unacceptable."

"Sometimes you yell at them that at least you're a friendly devil and they're a rude human. The confusion on their faces is a delight to watch."

"Still, that word is not all right. It's worse than nigger, Dan."

"What should they call us, then?"

"Something like *lao wai*, or *wai guo ren*, the polite names for foreigners."

"No one ever says that, except to old friends. Darling, in China, strangers aren't friends."

I've come to accept that for Lai Ying, tolerating any sort of abuse, racial or otherwise, is not an option. She doesn't hesitate to give verbal assailants an earful until they scamper off, red with embarrassment. Such incidents leave her fuming for days. All along, I've planned to get my degree and go home without a single day's delay. It's hard enough for Father to support my siblings through school. Life will get even tougher when my sister goes to college next year. I need to go back and get a job. I don't know if Lai Ying would understand that. I've told her about my family but never about the money worries. Seeing her gazing at me with that look of a worried nurse now makes me question the wisdom of my dutiful aspirations. With a sigh of exasperation, I push the thought away, persuading myself that it's meaningless to plan that far ahead. A lot can happen in three years.

I ask Lai Ying if she wants something to eat. I have fruits and biscuits. She opts for the former. I peel a pear and cut it neatly into two pieces. I'm about to offer her one piece when her face turns pale, and she folds her arms as if she's not planning to eat after all.

"What's the matter?" I ask her. "Don't you like pears?"

"I like them, but—"

"Not ripe enough?"

"No, it's not that."

"You prefer something else? How about an apple?"

"Thanks, Dan. I'll have an apple. But I should explain. It's bad luck to share a pear. When you say *fenli*, it sounds like, you know, to separate."

I stare at her in disbelief. Of course, the words sound the same. But how could she even make such a connection? As if reading my thoughts, she says, "We're superstitious, Dan. You know that, don't you?"

"So are we, sweetheart."

She pinches my nose and says, "*Ban dan*!" My silly egg! She does that when she's amused at my foolishness. She says *ban dan* is what loving wives call their silly husbands.

We eat our fruits in silence, while I reflect on my unexpected lesson, and realise with dismay that acquiring proficiency in the language does not sufficiently protect a black ghost or any foreign ghost for that matter from these cultural traps that show up at the most unexpected times. Meeting Lai Ying has exposed some of these traps, revealing aspects of the language that have remained inaccessible like a locked safe. Some are obvious, like the overlaps in meaning due to varying tones. In the language and culture classes, they warned us all the time about getting the tone right in order not to cause offense or embarrassment. The number eight is considered auspicious because the word 'ba' sounds like the word for wealth. Four is unlucky because the word 'si' is similar to the word for death. Seven is associated with ghosts, which explains why the gates of hell open in August, the Ghost Month, so ghosts can roam free for a while. Chuan could mean boat, pass, bed, or communicate. Mao could mean cat or hair. It makes you suspect they're deliberately trying to put you off the language and force you to go back to your village where things stayed nice and simple.

"Come on." I reach out for her hand. "I'll give you a massage."

She quickly gets up in a half-crouch – like someone trying to ward off the cold, although it must be thirty degrees Celsius today – and lies face down on the bed. I turn the desk fan a little to direct the faint cool air towards her. Then I peel off her top and trousers and admire the smooth texture of her naked skin. She has a suppressed guilt-tinged smile on her face, as if she's embarrassed about enjoying a stolen moment of pleasure. She loves having a massage. Sometimes she offers to massage me, but the grinding, rolling, rubbing of her fingers and knuckles on my back doesn't give me the pleasure that makes her sigh and purr like a cat when I do it. She says it's good for her health, but I can only take her word for it. I prefer to go for a run or play football with the guys if I'm feeling health-conscious. The only thing I like about a massage is that for Lai Ying and I, it's such a natural precursor to sex.

"You've become like a professional," she says, reaching out to pat my arm lovingly.

"You think I should change my career?"

"Oh no! You're so funny. I love the way you know instinctively exactly when to be firm, when to be gentle. It's wonderful."

Feeling my chest expand, and a heatwave course through me, I kiss her lips, the back of her neck and her shoulders. She squirms with delight before playfully pushes me away, saying, "Massage first, please?"

After half an hour rubbing her neck, back, and legs, I realise she's fallen asleep. Careful not to wake her, I roll her slowly to her side and let her lean against me. Her breath is soft and warm on my neck, her breast flattened like a saucer against my chest.

How could I even contemplate sharing a pear with this sweet angel?

Wang's Den

THE SUMMER HEAT IS LIKE a punishment. The sun beats down on you with a vengeance and an intensity I've never known. Han Wei can't believe it when I complain about the heat and humidity. To him, Africa *is* the whole Sahara Desert. I guess I should be delighted that at least he's heard of the Sahara Desert. They never teach them anything about Africa, in contrast to what I was taught about Asia, from Genghis Khan to Japanese militarism.

The room is perpetually hot and stuffy, and the fan that is supposed to keep you cool can't keep up with the maddening pace at which your overheating body perspires. You have to keep drinking water constantly to pacify the parched throat. In the evening, the temptation to consume vast amounts of beer becomes irresistible.

We desperately miss having a bar nearby since we stopped going to the Travel Café. I was having a drink there some weeks ago with Lai Ying, Diallo, and a couple of Japanese girls. We were having a lot of fun playing card games when a guy walked in, spat at one of the Japanese girls, and yelled that Chinese girls who dated monkeys were an unforgivable shame.

Before either Diallo or I could do anything, one of the Japanese girls emptied her glass of beer on him, cursing him in Japanese, while the other one broke an empty beer bottle on his head. He slumped into a chair, clutching his head, looking more shocked than hurt on realising that the target of his affront wasn't even Chinese. He didn't stop screaming insults even as blood ran down his face, blinding him. Then he rose and tried to slap the girl who had assaulted him. I grabbed his arm and pushed him away, sending him sprawling to the floor. The café owner threw us out, accusing us of giving his bar a bad name. We had to restrain him as he grabbed the Japanese girls by the hair and started to drag them away.

Lai Ying went livid, yelling at him, threatening to smash a chair on his head. I grabbed hold of her to restrain and calm her. My heart heaved with admiration for her bravery, and for the first time ever, I enjoyed the fleeting pleasure and pride of holding my girlfriend in the public glare.

Diallo and I were angrier about being thrown out of the café than having to deal with the racial attack.

"The guy clearly saw what happened," he growled, his face contorted with anger, as he recounted the event to friends that evening. "We were attacked, man. That stupid barman should have protected us. But what does he do? He throws us out, forgetting we've been regular customers all these years. He's crazy!"

I knew Lai Ying would never let me drink there again. And it was clear we had lost the calm, patient, reflective Diallo.

There's nowhere left to drink now, except the square outside the hostel, since Wang's noodle shop has been shut all month. Apart from not being able to drink there, I also miss his noodles, the mysteries of which Lai Ying has pried open for my enjoyment. Thin rice noodles are my favourite. When I first saw them, they reminded me of a bird's nest made from white wire mesh. Now I can't get enough of the soft smooth texture when I scoop them from the salty soup, grind them effortlessly between my teeth and feel them melt on the tongue.

One afternoon, Diallo and I are walking to the wet market in Cai Chang to buy groceries when we notice renovation work on Wang's noodle shop. The whole of the front wall has been knocked down and four men in blue overalls are mixing cement and carrying building materials into the shop in a stained, filthy wheelbarrow.

We are both so engrossed in trying to figure out what the renovation is all about that it takes us a few minutes to realise that Xiao Lui's barbershop is missing. The space the shack previously occupied has now been swallowed up by what looks like an extension of Wang's noodle shop. Why on earth does Wang believe he needs a bigger noodle shop? The old one was hardly ever busy.

When the renovations are completed three weeks later, the old noodle shop is unrecognisable. To our amazement and delight, Wang unveils a bar, complete with a jukebox and giant posters of white people downing bottles of beer, laughing and slapping each other on the back. A neon-lit bilingual sign hangs on the pavement outside the bar. It reads: Wang's Den.

Wang informs us he has been on a trip to Europe and seen the future. And the future is alcohol.

"What this area needs is a bar," he announces with an expansive grin. "And our future will be great, from now on. You have fun, I do good business. Everyone's happy. It will be glorious!"

No one believes he has been to Europe. On what he made in a noodle shop that typically operated at less than full capacity, he would never afford a foreign trip. Unless he has another source of income, which no one is ready to rule out.

Wang's decision to open a bar is the best thing that has happened to our social life in Nanjing. The city comes alive like an explosion of fireworks during Lunar New Year celebrations. He must have paid officials a lot of money for the privilege, and most likely taken some bigwigs on as partners. To launch his bar, he has been distributing fliers around the campus and persuading foreign students to hand out free-drink coupons in the foreign students' hostel. Some scorn the offer, fearing the free drinks are laced with Depo Provera to stop us breeding with local girls.

When we ask Wang about this unusually generous offer, he says he wants Chinese to see that it is all right to sit in a bar and drink beer. But *they* have to pay, which they resent. Wang doesn't expect to make a fortune out of them. They don't have much money, much less to waste on alcohol. A free-drink promotion would be wasted on them. Wang's knowledge of basic marketing is miles ahead of my university, which doesn't even teach the subject. I offer to distribute some coupons for him. But I need his assurance the drinks are fine.

"I know, Eggman" he says, wearily. "I've heard the rumours. Look at the bottles. They're sealed from the brewery. And I drink the same beer myself."

He proceeds to open a bottle and take a long swig. I watch him wipe the froth from his mouth with the back of his hand before I accept a beer.

"It's a good beer, Wang."

"Listen, Eggman, I've been in the catering business for many years. I know how to treat my customers well, with respect. I know foreigners love their beer, and they have money. Would I try to harm them and in the process harm myself? If your friends come, the Chinese will soon follow suit. Tell your friends they'll be supporting me by drinking here, and in return they'll be taken good care of here. Wang is an honest and serious man. Tell them that."

I don't know why I believe him, perhaps it's the earnestness in his plea, or the fact that he has no hesitation in drinking the beer himself, but I agree to promote his bar for him. Some of my friends are sceptical and demand to know what Wang is doing for me in return. I assure them Wang drinks the beer himself.

I tell them we can make this our own social club, a place that is cleaner and safer than the Travel Café. The strategy works perfectly.

The free-drink promotion is like a two-week Christmas in the middle of summer. Only later do we find out that Wang stole the idea from the Saxon Hotel in Shanghai. That's when it also dawns on us that when Wang said he had been to Europe, he meant the Bund in Shanghai, which is famous for its European-style architecture and Western-style hotels. The final piece falls into place when Kabinga informs us that the Saxon Hotel has a bar called the Emperor's Den, which pioneered free-drink promotion coupons.

Wang has turned the whole of the wall facing the street into a foldable door, so that people walking by can see foreigners consuming alcohol and having fun. Just like in the movies, or Shanghai. All you have to do is hop in and copy what the foreigners do. Wang has a good understanding of his people's need to look enlightened. I first noticed this anxiety to learn foreign ways in the state-owned Bai Huo, the departmental stores in downtown Xinjiekou. If a foreigner picked up an item, say a finely styled utensil, studied it carefully, then walked away, several locals would come and do the exact same thing. Though they're looked down upon, foreigners determine what is fashionable and desirable.

The locals wander past Wang's Den, watching African and Western students quaffing their beers and enjoying themselves. They point with their fingers, giggle, slap each other on the back, like people watching animals fooling around in a zoo. Wang paces about on the pavement like a lion inspecting his hunting grounds, trying to entice the ogling potential victims into his lair, urging them to come in and discover the joys of getting intoxicated, and learn English while they're at it. Wang's own knowledge of English is limited to socially functional words, which he throws about with relish and an affected suavity. *Hello, where you from, goodbye, drink beer, change money, want lady? Is good.*

His wife weaves her way around the room in her green khaki, loose-fitting clothes, wiping tables, taking empty glasses and bottles away, maintaining a cautious silence, as if she's afraid to contradict her husband. She has always been like that, even when they operated a noodle shop. Wang himself has undergone a transformation. Gone are the drab black trousers and Mao shirts. He now dons a suit and tie, has his hair slicked back, and is perpetually chomping on a cigar.

Sometimes we invite our Chinese friends to the bar. They come along, eyes peeled, ready to leg it if necessary. They believe that when black people drink alcohol, trouble will surely follow, just like in the American black-and-white TV shows.

It has taken them a while to gain confidence, and now a few like Han Wei and Lai Guiguo come in of their own accord. By the end of the summer, Wang's Den is so popular that a competitor opens a bar a block down Nanning Lu. But it can't compete with the original. It closes within a month. Some say Wang paid city officials to have it closed. Lai Ying in particular is convinced it's the sort of thing a businessman with *guanxi* would easily resort to. She has refused to come with me to Wang's Den. She only came once, right at the very start, but she couldn't stand the sight of Wang. She believes he was only slightly less loathsome when he ran the noodle shop.

"He's changed now," I remember her whispering that one time. "Can't you see that cunning look in his eyes? I can't trust him, Dan, and you're a fool to keep coming here."

"I just come here to drink," I protested. "I don't care who owns the bar. In any case, it's nicer than the Travel Café."

I think she's being unreasonable. But to avoid unnecessary arguments, I've reduced the frequency of my visits. I only come Friday and Saturday nights, and occasionally on Wednesdays. Diallo says I'm being controlled, an accusation that makes my insides contract, but the truth is that Lai Ying and I are so close now that my life would be turned upside down if we were to split up, especially over something as trivial as how often I go out for a drink, even though I'm willing to sacrifice other things like clothes in order to afford to drink.

One evening, Wang comes to join us and thanks us for supporting his business. I've been in the bar for a few hours with Diallo and Gerbert, an Austrian student who, unlike other western students who only take certificates in Chinese language, chooses to study for a degree course in China. None of us can understand why he's interested in a social studies degree that is mostly Marxist propaganda and Chinese Communist Party history. Gerbert is medium-built, sports a reddish beard that makes him look older than his early twenties. His arms are covered with the same red hair, and you can see some more of it sticking out of the top of his shirt. Behind his back, we call him the Caveman. The Chinese call him Hairy Barbarian. For a while, he dated Cristina before she left the country, and soon after Kabinga had moved out of the hostel into some downtown hotel. Gerbert once walked into the Travel Café and found her kissing Dallas Joe in a corner. Unfazed, he joined them at the table and ordered drinks for them. After that incident, Cristina always boasted that he was the perfect boyfriend because he was so open-minded.

Wang has something on his mind. Perhaps it is the excitement of running a business of this scale for the first time. There's a glint in his eyes, like that of a man who has recently come to an awareness of the scope of his genius. But there's also a sense of relief about him, as though a weight has been lifted off his shoulders. We spend half an hour making small talk before he starts to reminisce about the past.

"You young people can only imagine what life was like in the past," he says, his eyes locked in a faraway look. We order another round and brace ourselves for a blast of a history lesson. "After what we went through, I swore I would never suffer poverty again. I will do whatever I have to do to succeed. The noodle bar was the first step. This bar is the true beginning."

"So what happened, Wang?" asks Diallo. "Was it the inappropriately named Cultural Revolution?"

"Oh, it goes further than that. China went through so much, the Japanese invasion, starvation in communes. We had no food to eat, not even rice. The world thinks of Chinese as rice growers, but when I was a young man, you could find people eating grass, leaves, everything. When they grew rice, they had to pay most of it to the government as tax. I saw the future when I met the first African students to study in China."

Diallo and I exchange glances.

"It's nice to know *hei gwei* will one day rule China," says Diallo, laughing.

"Let's be serious, my friends," says Wang, raising a hand for silence. "I was a student in Beijing in 1960 when they first brought Africans to China. We always believed Africa was backward and poor, suffering under imperialist rule. But these people had better lives than us. They were not happy here, the way the authorities would have wanted them to appreciate the socialist way. It was very confusing for me. There were, of course, foreign students from other Asian countries, from Europe. We were not allowed to mix with foreigners, except in functions supervised by the Communist Youth League. The League recruited me to be an official friend to a student from Tanga...Tangazinia...Nyika, I forget the name. I was told to observe his behaviour and report back to the League leadership. They wanted to know whether our friends accepted the socialist way, or whether they were hanging on to their bourgeois ways."

"You mean you were a spy?" I ask, unable to control my shock.

"The word they used was approved friend, Eggman. But I was not a fool. I took it as an opportunity to learn for myself how to live well. The foreigners had everything we could only dream of: eggs, meat, milk, sugar, biscuits. As an approved friend, I was fortunate enough to eat well even when I lost or ran out of food coupons. I could get extra lengths of cloth from my friend, or his old clothes, which I had to wear beneath my approved blue uniform. Back then, we were only allowed a few square feet of cloth a year. You can imagine how difficult it was to survive the cold winters. Those from Eastern Europe and Asia stayed on, but after a year or two, most of the Africans left. They said they couldn't stand it here, and yet they were living very well. My friend told me they couldn't stand the never-ending lessons on communism, being watched, having no freedom to meet locals. That got me thinking. It made me realise there's another life beyond what we see in China."

Gerbert shakes his head. I ask him what he's thinking.

"Privilege," he spits out disdainfully. "You set up a minority group above everyone else, what do you expect? There will be trouble. It's the same thing now. The way we're treated, the way you scholarship guys get more money than the locals, you think the locals like it? Look into their eyes and you can see some are ready to kill."

"That's rich coming from you," retorts Diallo. "What is a guy like you doing here anyway, in a poor communist country, living it up and making it sound like we're responsible for the hard life the locals live? It's like you'd like to see us go through the same hardships. Crazy! Oh, I'm sorry, it's not crazy. It's called socialism, although if you're in the Communist Party you're exempt and can live like any other bourgeois capitalist, right?"

"I'm only saying it's a shame the locals have to live in cramped rooms, get a low grant they can't live on, coupons that are never enough for anything…"

"And whose fault is that?" I ask. "The Chinese invited us here, we've made our home here. Diallo says we're the minority black Chinese. If they can't support us, few of us will stay, as Wang recalls from his student days."

"It's the imbalance, guys," insists Gerbert, waving his hands in exasperation. "Can't you see? Thing is, how is this whole thing sustainable?"

"I get it," says Diallo. "You're suggesting there'll be a revolution, and the oppressed masses will rise against the spoilt, minority black tribe. You're letting this Marxist ideology get into your head, Gerbert."

Gerbert buries his head in his hands. Our laughter is short-lived, though, when we see the alarm in Wang's eyes. I ask him what the problem is.

"In a way, Gerbert is right," says Wang, to my surprise. "Years ago, I saw some of my fellow classmates coming to the foreigners' hall to beg for food, with no shame. It made them angry, angry with themselves. It made them resent the authorities for the miserable lives we endured. But there was nothing they could do about it. They certainly wouldn't dare kill anyone. We were taught to show respect and hospitality to foreign guests."

"So they could see how wonderful communism was," adds Diallo, with a dismissive wave of the hand. "I bet they were so secluded, they had no idea how bad things really were."

"They were creative, actually," says Wang. "They managed to make friends, secretly, and talked to Chinese. But it was risky for locals. You could get seriously reprimanded, and that was bad for your future."

"What about girls, Wang?" asks Diallo. "Could the guys date Chinese girls?"

Wang pauses for a long, reflective moment.

"As I said, it was risky. I remember one girl in my class. She danced with a foreigner in a party. The Youth League officials warned her to behave herself. She didn't listen. She obviously liked him. A few days later, she was seen coming from the foreign students' hall. They took her away. We never saw her again."

"*Mon dieu!*" exclaims Diallo, holding his beer in both hands, as if afraid they'll take that away, too. "What happened to her?"

"Some people said she was sent to prison. We never found out. Her foreign friend left the country soon after that, racked with guilt."

Listening to Wang makes me realise how much the country has changed. We can bring girls to our rooms, but only until the 11 p.m. curfew, when all guests have to be signed out. Security guards come around knocking on rooms with unaccounted for guests at 11.15 p.m. But there are many ways to beat the system and keep the girl all night. One trick is to sit in the lobby nursing a beer, wait till the security guard goes to the toilet, then rush to his big blue book and sign your visitor out.

Wang's Den has become the centre for striking deals that allow students to get around the state-imposed obstacles to spending money. It's beginning to rival the posh hotel lobbies in Xinjiekou as a rendezvous for wheelers and dealers. Expensive vehicles parked down the street have become a regular spectacle in the evenings, leaving little room for our ubiquitous flying horses.

Wang has assumed the aura of a hero, admired by everyone: foreign students, local, social climbing party cadres, and businessmen alike. In one swell entrepreneurial swoop, he has succeeded in bridging the racial divide created by authorities, who decree what kind of money you use. Money, it turns out, has a mind of its own, irrespective of currency. Whether it's FECs, RMB, or US dollars. Money has become the great liberator. It recognises no politics and knows no barriers. It doesn't care whether you qualify as 'the people' or not.

Lai Ying resents this obsession with the White Card deals. She insists that the businessmen and cadres are cheating us and using us. As someone who's sat by the sidelines and watched the wonders of the White Card pass him by, I'm tempted to give her the benefit of the doubt. But I only have to look at the way people like Kabinga live. At the end of last year, Kabinga moved out of campus to take up a suite at the Embassy International Hotel downtown. He was spending so much time travelling on White Card shopping deals that he had virtually abandoned his studies.

When Diallo and I asked him why he needed to live in a hotel he said, "Listen, guys, living in a rundown student hostel will never make you realise the joys of the good life. You need to see how rich people live, watch them closely, daily, live with them, if you're to understand the need to make serious money."

The former students who are doing business full-time sometimes invite us to their hotels for parties, where they delight in impressing us and making us feel small and poverty-stricken in comparison to their lavish lifestyles. Kabinga has a habit of showing up at our hostel in the latest flashy embassy car he's about to sell, bringing with him crates of beer, saying things like, "If my boys won't come to the party, the party will come to my boys," before exploding into laughter. Then he stands aside smoking a cigar, to let his excited boys get the beer out and cool it in ice water buckets for a serious drinking session in the square, while he holds forth on the joys of good living.

It is at times like this that I look back at the wasted opportunities, the chances that slipped through my fingers, the lessons I never learned. From Kabinga and the White Card brigade to Han Wei and the locals who call themselves traders. Anger builds up in the pit of my stomach and rises like bile to my mouth. What is it they have that emboldens them to take risks and soar above us, while people like myself and Diallo can only watch and talk? The confidence my mother invested in me makes me feel like an imposter. How could she infuse me with a sense of achievement that I've no right to expect, no confidence to hope for?

Could Mother have got it all wrong about the eagle? Did she really know I didn't have it in me and was just consoling me? When does the eagle know when to strike? Will I know the sign when I see it, the same way I knew it was Lai Ying when I first laid eyes on her?

A Rose Is for Love

THE TOPIC NEVER GOES AWAY. One day, as we're walking in Ngong Yuen Park, Lai Ying brings it up again. We arranged to meet here and arrived separately so as to avoid hostile stares. The park is a half hour walk from campus up the bicycle-clogged Zhouzi Lu. The cyclists here are heading to and from Jiangsu Industrial Park, which is being promoted as the research and industrial future of the city.

We come to Ngong Yuen Park when we need privacy in a public place. The lovers who come here are too busy with each other to pay much attention to a mixed-race couple, especially if we don't do anything remotely foolhardy like hold hands.

By the time I arrive here, my shirt is drenched in sweat. It's mid-afternoon and the fierceness of the sun has only started to abate, but the sun here burns with a relentlessness that borders on malice. In my country, July is the coldest month. Here, it's the hottest. It feels as though my life has been turned inside out. Walking around with your shirt stuck on you and sweat dripping down your armpits makes you loathe yourself. Lai Ying never sweats. But I can tell she's hot because her face has turned a pale shade of red and her forehead looks taut, as if an invisible hand is pulling her by the hair. And she's breathing through her mouth. I ask her whether she wants to sit and rest. We find a bench near a fountain where we can rest and listen to the sounds of crickets and the songs of birds and admire the lush vegetation, the ferns and carefully manicured flower gardens, the pagodas and artificial lakes and rivulets.

I stretch my hands out to wet them under the fountain. The water splashes to my face and runs down my chest. It feels like a reward for having crossed an oppressively hot desert.

"You look silly doing that," says Lai Ying.

"I don't care."

"You don't care if people laugh at you?"

I shake my head. As a black ghost, there's nothing unusual about being sneered at. I scoop some water with both hands and throw it over my head. I ask Lai Ying if she wants some. Ignoring her answer, I scoop some water and throw it at her. She stifles a scream and gasps as the cold-water hits her face. She screams at me to behave myself but I throw more water at her, until her face is as wet as mine. The looks on the spectators' faces turn from amusement to shock. I ignore them and help Lai Ying dry her face. She pushes me away playfully and slaps my arm, feigning annoyance.

"You must admit it makes you feel cooler, darling?"

"If I want a cold shower, I know where to get one."

"Come on, relax."

"This is a public place, Dan!" She points furtively at the two couples standing near the fountain, watching us. I wave to them, and shout a greeting. They step back as if someone has thrown a brick at them.

"See you again!" I call out to them. "Bye-bye!" They turn around and walk away hurriedly, as if fleeing a madman.

Lai Ying can't stop laughing.

"Aren't you afraid they might attack you?"

"For greeting them? I don't think so."

"For making them lose face, ban dan!"

"Who asked them to come and gawp?"

There's no one around for miles. I take her hand and play with her fingers. She tries to snatch her hand away, glancing around her, worry etching itself around her face. I hold firm, and crack her knuckles, one by one.

"This is a public place, Dan," she protests.

"I thought you weren't afraid?"

"It's not about being afraid."

"What's it about?"

She doesn't reply. She pouts, the way she always does when she expects me to read her mind, then shrugs with disappointment when she concludes I'm not getting it. I do, but pretend not to. Her coyness is her way of protecting me. I let go of her hand and lean back on the bench, close my eyes, and listen to the sound of the birds. I know she's leaning forward, watching me, trying to read my expressionless face, willing me to open my eyes and look at her. I could sleep here in the sun, like a lazy lizard, basking in the worried vigil of my forbidden girlfriend.

An old man walks up to us holding a basket of red roses. I watch him closely, wondering whether he's mocking me.

"A rose is for love," he declares. "A young beauty will find a smile in her heart, and an old man will find a bowl of rice for tonight."

Glancing at the people who have stopped to watch, Lai Ying tells the hawker we're not interested. She says she prefers pink roses. The man says if we wait, he can get pink ones. I know Lai Ying won't wait. Brushing aside her protests, I buy a red rose and hand it to her. Watching the man's face break into a toothless grin, I can't help smiling. Even Lai Ying somehow overcomes her embarrassment and manages an uneasy smile. We walk away, ignoring the stares and pointed fingers.

Lai Ying raises the subject of White Card deals an hour later, as we leave the park. I'm careful not to annoy her by asking why she's thinking such odd thoughts when we should be savouring the only public acknowledgment of our love that we've ever seen.

"They're the scum of the earth," she says. "These businessmen you and your friends deal with. You don't know how they've made their money."

"You worry too much, sweetheart," I try in vain to reassure her.

"Dan, did your friends come here to study or to do these silly deals?"

"Kabinga's doing very well for himself." I hadn't meant to tell her, but it comes out, anyway.

"Where is he, by the way? I never see him anymore."

Her face turns red when I tell her how Kabinga's living.

"We can go see him sometime."

"Forget it," she says, without hesitation. "I'm not interested."

"Why? He's not doing anything dangerous. And he's still my friend."

"I have a bad feeling about this, Dan. And I hope you're not thinking of following in Kabinga's footsteps. If you do, it would create problems for us."

"What are you saying, Lai Ying?"

"I just don't think things would be the same, that's all."

I recoil at the uncompromising hardness of her tone of voice. But before I can protest, she says goodbye and crosses the street. I watch her walk towards the university. I want to call her back but dare not. My heart heaves with an intense loathing for this society that forces us to walk on opposite sides of the road and the fear that the sign I've been waiting for will now become even more elusive. She's never walked out on me like this before.

Whenever I meet the guys at Wang's Den, White Card deals is all they talk about. And girls. The popularity of Wang's Den has had one unexpected negative outcome: giving relations between foreigners and local women more exposure than they ever had. Everyone passing by the bar can see girls sitting with foreign devils, drinking and smoking, sometimes dancing. In their eyes, Wang's Den has become just as notorious as the Travel Café, if not worse. Wang is having a tough time keeping hostile-looking passersby at bay. Some of them stand on the street, pointing with their fingers, the looks on their faces going from curious to resentful. It is uncomfortable enough drinking in public squares, with people watching you, giggling and mocking you. It's worse now that passersby, both town people and students, have become openly hostile after seeing the wicked things that go on at Wang's Den, the conspicuous boozing, money changing hands, wanton womanising.

"You want to guess what they're thinking?" Diallo asks me one evening, pointing at a group of students watching us from the pavement. They're pretending to be looking for their bicycles so that Wang can't ask them to leave, which he sometimes does when he senses passersby might be making his valued customers feel uneasy.

"Who knows, Zen? Probably disgusted to see people waste money like this."

"And if anyone's to blame for the display of these decadent bourgeois habits on this sacred land, it's people like Deng and Mao, who thought that bringing black ghosts to study here will help achieve world domination."

"I thought they only wanted Africa on their side to strengthen their case against western imperialists and renegade Taiwan?"

"Whatever you say, Eggman. I didn't ask to come here. I had already started my degree in Conakry. A chance came, and I was crazy enough to take it, without thinking."

"Would you stay," I ask him, "if you had to live on what they get?"

He shakes his head, saying, "Thirty yuan? For the hassle and abuse I endure, RMB 120 a month is barely enough compensation, frankly. I take the troubles as a price to pay for an education."

"You could have had a stress-free education in Guinea."

"I use the word education in a very broad sense, *mon ami.*"

I think I could have done without some of the lessons he's implying.

"Have you noticed," continues Diallo, "local guys don't pick up girls for casual relationships. But they don't mind being picked up by white girls on one-year Putonghua language courses. Boys and girls have such different mindsets, right?"

I reflect on Diallo's words. When it comes to women, the local boys look for wife potential. They're more traditional in outlook than us, preferring to take their time to know the girl even before asking her out. She has to have the right pedigree, her people have to be agreeable, the fortune-teller's almanac has to match the moon, stars, and ocean tides with birthdays and find the most auspicious love match. In contrast, the horizons of foreign male students, be they black or white, are somewhat narrower, uncluttered by too much astrological mumbo jumbo, their sexual urges less repressed.

Chinese male students don't hide their disapproval. In the past, one just shrugged and walked away. Now the common reaction is to swap insults and be done with it, or grab the guy by the collar, push him up against a wall and threaten to bite his head off, and then watch him go as limp as a broken twig, then saunter away, cursing you under his breath.

Kabinga makes a rare visit to Wang's Den one Saturday night, accompanied by an American woman he introduces as his babe, Charlene. He describes her simply as a consultant, but doesn't bother to explain what she consults on. No one is particularly bothered, especially when it turns out that she's a recent arrival and doesn't speak Chinese, often our language of choice at Wang's Den. She's tall, almost as tall as him. She exudes a business-like manner in her navy-blue shoulder-padded jacket, her short dark hair and penetrating green eyes that make you feel as though she's committing your face to memory, every little pimple and crease, every little wiry string of facial hair. There's something about her, something both glamorous and sinister. She reminds you of those smooth, gorgeous women you see in James Bond movies, who are just as likely to unhook a bra for you or stick a gun in your face. She's untainted by that easy-going casualness and simplicity of manner of Westerners, who come here to teach English to finance an Asian backpacking adventure.

Wang welcomes Kabinga with an ear-to-ear grin and hearty handshake. You would think they were old friends. Kabinga hands him two bottles of champagne to chill for us and a bottle of Scotch whisky for himself. Eyes gleaming with pleasure, Wang instructs his wife to get fresh glasses for his favourite guest and his friends. Everyone is watching Kabinga as though he's the new town mayor. As soon as they realise who he is, the students crowd around him, anxious to shake his hand, exchange a few words and share a laugh with him, the undisputed guest of honour. Kabinga absorbs the adulation with a nonchalance that comes with associating with party cadres and businessmen accustomed to having flunkies attend to their every whim. He's not the man we once knew, the student who struggled to make sense of scientific formulae and dreaded tests and exams like everyone else. Kabinga has surely crossed over to another side, a side we can only savour vicariously by lapping up his spasmodic largesse, by shaking his hand and hoping for a bit of the magic that has transformed him beyond recognition.

The few Chinese students here watch disinterestedly, wondering what the fuss is all about, perhaps thinking the nattily dressed visitor is some big shot from one of the African embassies. Not even former classmates recognise him. With his short hair, finely trimmed moustache that tapers around his mouth and drops into a two-inch goatee, three-piece grey suit and red tie, he doesn't look anything like the year two engineering dropout. The humidity doesn't bother him, and if it does, he makes sure it doesn't stop him maintaining the well-cultivated image of a suave dealmaker. He passes a box of cigars around and places a crocodile-skin leather wallet on the table. The wallet is so full of US dollar notes it can barely fold. Charlene edges closer to Kabinga and caresses his back as he regales us, for the next hour, with stories of his travels to places like Hong Kong, Seoul, and Tokyo. We listen in awe, wishing we had the guts to cut the sorts of deals that have turned him into a capitalist shark in the communist waters of China.

Diallo asks him about the moustache.

"It's about personality, Zennie boy," he explains, after filling the air around us with a thick pall of cigar smoke, so that his voice sounds like it's zooming down through the clouds from an exalted place above which Chin Chin inhabits with the crème de la crème. "You've got to make the people you deal with respect you small-small, you get? A lot of people look at me and think I'm just a young man. As you know, I look much younger than I am, yeah?" He pauses for effect. He's not disappointed. Everyone at the table cackles with laughter, slapping each other on the back. The laughter sounds mirthful enough, though you can tell by the looks on some of the faces that they feel they have to laugh at the benefactor's jokes. "Well, the rich old geezers don't take you too seriously if they think you're too young. You have to look the part, hence the moustache, and the threads." He pats the lapels of his jacket and twiddles with his silk tie.

We listen, agog, as Kabinga starts to expound on the intricacies of hotel bureaucracy.

"The hotel policy is screwed up," he says, chomping on his cigar, then switches to Putonghua, ignoring Charlene's momentary perplexed frown. "They say you can't bring a Chinese girl in unless you're married, man. You have to show them a bloody marriage certificate. Can you believe that?"

We've never needed to stay in a posh downtown hotel, so this is news to us. Everyone wants to know how he copes, but the questions are hesitant, punctuated with furtive glances at Charlene. They needn't worry. Babe Charlene looks completely at sea, and if she feels at all isolated, she masks it with a defiantly indulgent smile.

"It's easy, man," explains Kabinga, his face suffused with a mischievous grin. "You have two options. You can keep the moral police off your arse with appropriate gifts, preferably, or simply have a certificate made small-small."

"Do you have one, Chin Chin?"

"Have what, man?"

"Um...a marriage certificate?"

Kabinga explodes into laughter, ignoring the question and clinking glasses all around, then leans to kiss Charlene, with what first looks like an apology in his eyes, but quickly turns into a glint of bravado.

He smiles with the confidence of a high-stakes gambler who knows something the house doesn't. The rest of us are part of that clueless house.

Chants, Sticks, and Banners

IT WILL SOON BE CHRISTMAS. In China, Christmas day passes like any other. There's nothing special. No decorations on campus, in the shops, and, I assume, in homes. It will be a cloudy, dull, depressingly cold day. There'll be snow on the streets, on rooftops, and the cold will bite through the layers of clothing, straight to the bone, like it's doing right now.

It's not the weather I'm worried about. Having survived two winters already, I can face this one. All through the winter we've been hearing about the troubles at Hehai University. But I haven't met anyone from that institution to get the full details. Kabinga was dating a girl from there last year, but he's the wrong person to ask. He has no idea what happens in the universities nowadays.

Diallo tells me he met some students from Hehai at the Travel Café some days ago. They told him that the university authorities started to build a concrete wall around the foreign students' hostel ostensibly to improve security. The students saw it as a ruse to keep local female students out and a group of them tore down part of the wall. They kicked it, hammered away with the mallets left behind by the builders. The authorities reacted by docking their grant to cover the damage and angry students promptly stormed the accounts department to demand their money. Local male students placed posters on walls in support of the university's action.

The tension can be felt even as far away as my university. There's already a fence around our hostel, but the gate is never locked, and the security guards never leave the main entrance. At Hehai, they wanted to stop visitors coming in through the back entrance.

In class, we've taken to ignoring each other like sworn enemies, even though, beyond the usual tensions, which we're all accustomed to by now, there's hardly any reason for overt hostility between us. Diallo and I occupy our seats at the back, wrapped in our winter jackets that are zipped up to the chin, taking long, slow breaths, as if bracing ourselves for an attack. Han Wei and Lai Guiguo have abandoned our study group. I've tried to catch their eyes once or twice but to no avail. Last Friday after class, I asked them to join us for a drink at Wang's Den. Avoiding eye contact, they muttered something about having to study and hurried away. I was about to call out to them when Diallo tugged at my elbow and mouthed an inaudible "no".

Winters in Nanjing are unforgiving in the intensity of the cold, which is exacerbated by the strong winds that howl through the cowed, leafless trees. All week, the whole city has been hibernating under a fog you can barely see through.

When it gets like this, people rush past you like shadows, too preoccupied with escaping the freezing weather to pay any attention to black ghosts. It is the only time I can walk the streets with Lai Ying without attracting attention. Unfortunately, she goes to Shanghai the day after her last exams. I accompany her to the station and as usual when we're on a bus, I take a seat behind her. We ride the half hour in silence. Dating couples sit side by side, gazing lovingly into each other's eyes, furtively holding hands, sharing jokes. I have only the back of Lai Ying's head to watch, and she dare not turn to share a smile. I yearn to run a hand through her long, silky hair. A half chance comes when the bus swings wildly around a bend. I reach for the metal-backed front seat and brush my hands against Lai Ying's hair. She glances quickly behind her and her face breaks into an uneasy smile. I offer an elaborate apology and wait for her to turn around and say it's all right, which prompts the middle-aged woman sitting beside me to shoot me a disapproving frown. Lai Ying is too smart to take up the silly game.

We get to the station with only fifteen minutes to spare. We stand on the platform, separated by Lai Ying's suitcase and an unrealisable yearning for a goodbye hug and kiss. She'll be away for three weeks, at a time when studies give way to festivities and never-ending parties. She wasn't planning on being away, but the family opted for a reunion as some will be away during the Lunar New Year, when they traditionally get together. I think of my family, treating themselves to trays of fried chicken and chunks of steaming sadza. It will be a lonely Christmas in Nanjing.

"You can come with me," she says, eyes wide open with a genuine plea.

The idea is tempting. I could find somewhere to stay with foreign students. But we both know there won't be much time for us to meet. She'll be too busy with family commitments. Either that or the part-time job she does during the holidays for a relative who is a bank official.

An ear-splitting whistle announces the train's imminent departure. As I walk Lai Ying into the train, I throw caution to the wind and plant a quick kiss on her lips. She freezes with shock but the smile on her lips slowly brightens up her eyes. A wave of warmth and delight cascades through me. I hold her hands, but she frees herself and clambers up the steps before I land us into trouble. She rolls a window down and waves goodbye, smiling sweetly, her cheeks flushed with undisguised pleasure. Our eyes lock and hold each other, almost as tightly as though we were holding hands. I clasp my hands close to my face, my elbows digging deep into my ribs, like I'm holding her, preventing her from leaving. I blow her a kiss and inhale deeply when she reciprocates. I yearn to feel her breath on my face, to reach out and grab her hand. The train begins to pull out of the station. I walk along the platform, waving to her. As the train picks up speed, so do I, my eyes never once leaving her face. I see the look of alarm on her face, but it's too late. A cleaner's trolley brings me crashing down. When I pick myself up and clear my head, I look up to see the train chugging off into the distance, spewing blue smoke into the sky.

Christmas day brings with it the excruciatingly cold weather we've been dreading. But it also brings with it the madness and mayhem no one would have expected. I'm woken up at the crack of dawn by war cries and screams that pierce the morning air with a vulgarity that takes a full five minutes to penetrate the fogs of a hangover from last night's party at Wang's Den. The shouts are coming from the streets and, I realise, from within my hostel. Frantic footsteps rumble down the corridor, followed by banging on the doors and voices yelling:

They're coming! Get out, people! Get out!

I sit up in bed, struggling to make sense of the commotion. Who are *they*? Coming for what?

"Eggman! Eggman! Open this door now!"

Throwing away my duvet, I open the door and find Diallo standing there, his face unwashed and unshaven, eyes filled with terror. Before I can demand an explanation, he pushes his way into the room and starts throwing clothes and jackets at me.

"Get dressed, man, we need to get out. Now!"

"What the hell is going on, Zen? Have you gone mad?"

By now, the yelling in the building is deafening. A crowd of Chinese students is marching down the street, waving clenched fists and crude weapons fashioned from tree branches, road signs, and litterbin covers. That's what it takes to sober me up. In no time, I manage to pull on two pairs of trousers, three pairs of socks, two shirts, a jumper, and a winter jacket. Meanwhile, Diallo is explaining the mayhem, but for the first few moments, I can barely concentrate. I'm thinking, *Gerbert's socialist uprising is finally happening right here on campus. The comrades have come to lynch the bourgeois foreigners.*

"There's been fighting all night at Hehai, Eggman," says Diallo. "They're out to get us."

"How did it start?"

"Who knows? The usual, I guess. A fight at a party. That's not the point. The problem is, it's now spreading through the city. We have to go, Eggman."

"Okay, but, where to?"

"Anywhere, man. Away from here. Beijing. Yeah, Beijing. Our embassy people should help."

"You want to go to Beijing? Now?"

"We're outnumbered here, Eggman. Everyone's talking about Beijing. We've got to get to the station right now." Diallo stares at me as though I'm an imbecile.

I peer down the window again and barely miss a rock that comes flying through, shattering the glass, and landing at my feet. Diallo shrugs his shoulders as if to say, *Am I getting through to you now?*

We race through the lobby. The security guards are nowhere to be seen. Everyone is abandoning the hostel, running around the building to the back exit to avoid the chanting mobs that have gathered at the main entrance, waving banners, yelling battle cries and pelting rocks at the building. There's no time to locate our Flying Horses. The air fills with blood-curdling chants. *Kill the black ghosts! Respect Chinese ladies!*

A shower of rocks comes raining down on us from a side street, catching us unawares. I feel a searing pain in my shoulder, but only for a brief moment, as fear takes over. I run wildly, sidestepping like a tipsy rugby player to dodge the missiles, protecting my head with my hands. With all the clothes on my body, progress is painfully slow. It is like being in one of those nightmares where you are being chased down by a charging rhino but can barely lift your feet. Diallo is a few metres ahead. I hear his scream first. The next moment, he's lying on the wet ground, clutching his head. I recoil on seeing the deep gush on his right temple. The look on his face is that of anger and disbelief. There's no time to stop and dress the wound. I hand him a handkerchief to stop the bleeding and drag him to his feet, urging him to keep moving. In the gathering fog, we can barely see the mobs closing in on us. They're just dull grey nondescript shapes fighting their way through the fog. But their vulgar war cries are all around us, desecrating the crisp morning air. I have a fleeting recollection of Lai Ying wielding a chair over the Travel Café's owner and secretly thank God she's not here to witness our plight.

We take a shortcut through a residential area in southern Cai Chang. Elderly people stand petrified by the screaming, their tai chi exercises frozen into grotesque shapes. There are hardly any lights in the windows, although it must be about 6 a.m. by now. The city is still shrouded in fog and darkness, resembling a scene from a horror film. People walking or cycling to work or waiting at bus stops stare at us and quickly steer clear. They can hear but cannot see our pursuers.

Blinded by his own blood, Diallo can barely see where he is going. He can't even see beyond his nose because of the mists from his heavy breathing. He holds the blood-soaked handkerchief in his hand, his arm too tired to keep it raised to his temple. Having to hold his elbow has slowed us down considerably. At this rate, we'll never make it.

"We have to borrow bikes!" I yell as I frantically search around us.

"I can't ride, Eggman. I can't see where I'm going."

"Wait here, and clean your eyes, Zen."

I spot some bikes chained to a metal railing in a quiet alley. It takes a few seconds to pick the flimsy locks with a key. Meanwhile Diallo cleans the blood off his eyes and face and inspects the neighbourhood, trying to locate an escape route. As we clamber up the bikes, a dozen students waving sticks emerge from the fog, their heads wrapped in towels to ward off the cold, and perhaps to conceal their identity. They are only fifteen metres away. They hurl rocks at us, two of which ricochet off our stolen bikes. Another hits my right leg. Luckily, the impact is cushioned by the multiple layers of clothing.

"Lai Guiguo!" hisses Diallo. Before I can ask what he's talking about, I notice our classmate and shower comrade. Lai Guiguo hurls a rock. Diallo and I freeze. The rock flies harmlessly above us. He raises his hand to throw another missile when he recognises us. Our eyes lock, his jaw drops, his hand drops, in slow motion, to his side. He falls back, quickly lights a cigarette. His comrades advance, with slow, measured steps, waving sticks above their heads in a mock martial arts display, chanting, *Black ghosts die*! A bigger mob appears at the other end of the alley.

"Go, Eggman! Go!"

Terror delivers wings. The next moment, we're cycling with all our might towards Lai Guiguo's group, scattering them, oblivious of the rocks raining down around us, tearing down on the wrong side of the road. I narrowly miss riding into a bus when I turn my head to look at Lai Guiguo's face, which is as inscrutable as ever, only this time, the eyes seem hollow and lifeless.

It takes an hour of hard riding to reach the railway station, our eyes smarting in the cold, blustery winds, dodging mobs that keep appearing at street corners, taking long detours through housing estates. We only stay on the main road when we catch up with a dozen of our fellow students. One of them is being carried on a bicycle, having been beaten senseless. His clothes are covered in blood.

At least a hundred African students are huddled at the railway station, shivering in the cold, teeth cluttering, nerves frayed, empty bellies grumbling. It turns out they're from the various colleges in the city. Some didn't even have a chance to retrieve a jacket or put on an additional pair of trousers. Many are bleeding and limping in pain. The anger is almost palpable.

They've occupied the whole space at the station entrance, which is normally filled with weary waiting passengers and hawkers. Others stand on the street, blocking traffic. Officious police officers and security guards are having a hard time controlling the crowd and maintaining the traffic flow.

Banner-waving and chanting Chinese students are assembling across the street, behind a hastily prepared police cordon, going all the way past the public square and into the bus terminal. There must be at least two thousands of them. Someone informs us they've been coming into the city from universities all over Jiangsu Province. They march up and down the streets, unmindful of the cold, waving banners that read 'Kill black devils', 'Respect our women'.

Listening to the various commentaries, we piece together the events that led up to this confrontation. We learn a lot from Julius, who arrived from Zambia last year. He says he was at the fateful Christmas Eve party at Hehai last night.

"I went through hell, man," says Julius. "You can't imagine how many hours I cycled through the night to get out of there." He relishes the limelight, talking at the top of his voice, his eyes shining like those of the only man privileged to have witnessed the greatest event of the year, or the sole survivor of a brutal massacre.

"How did it actually start?" asks Diallo, who has succeeded in stopping the bleeding with a bandage from a torn shirtsleeve.

"Harmlessly, man. This is what I can't understand. Some brothers refused to register their chicks. Security lost their temper. Pretty soon, the party became a war zone. The few locals who were there later went around spreading rumours that black ghosts had killed two of them and raped a woman at the party. Bloody nonsense. Then things got totally out of hand. Hundreds of them invaded the foreign students' hostel, running amok in the corridors, throwing missiles through the windows, trying to smash down doors. We fought all night. People got hurt, man. I have never seen such craziness in my life!"

Whether it is the anger building up in the pit of my stomach that makes me shiver or the cold air, I cannot tell. Right now, I'm ready to pack my bags and get the hell out of China. Let Father say what he will. How would he feel if he saw this bloodthirsty lot? If this is what it takes to be the modern farmer who saves his family from poverty, I'm not ready for it. The image of an eagle flashes through my mind. But this time, much as I would like to share Mother's view of the patient hunter, I'm the hapless fish who has spotted the king of the skies and knows there'll be no escape. I long for Lai Ying's gentle touch, the tenderness in her eyes when she smiles, anything, even the sharp voice when she lectures me for associating with Wang. Because even when she criticises, it is because, I now realise, she cares, not because she thinks I'm stupid. Right now, I don't care if she thinks I'm stupid. Let her call me anything—*ban dan*, whatever. I can't be the only stupid egg out here. But if I can't have Lai Ying at this moment, let me at least be transported back to the serene hills of my people, the long sunny days in a sea of greenery, the songs of women bent double in the fields, the banter of men discussing politics, and the sight of children chasing after a football fashioned from old plastic bags and strings. How my heart longs for the simplicity of life in Ndambu. But the angry mob neither knows nor cares as they pump clenched fists into the air, demanding that the government reforms the unfair system that discriminates against them in favour of foreigners. Some are demanding that the government stop us dating their women.

"This is fucking unbelievable!" exclaims Diallo. "They expect the government to stop people boning?" A few people look up, eyebrows arched, shocked to see Zen give in to bitterness and foul language. But he's not the only one. As we huddle together arguing about what to do, pacing about to keep warm, the one thing we all share is a deep resentment and regret at having left behind the comfort of our homes and warmth of our families to endure this.

As if to mock us, Lake Xuanwu, which is just visible beyond the mist in the distance, lies peaceful and serene, softly absorbing the dark shadows of the city buildings behind it.

"Listen to that section of the crowd." I point to some guys holding a banner that reads, 'Not offend China lady'. One of them, a guy in a green army jacket, is chanting something through a loudhailer. I nudge Diallo. "Let's get closer. I'm curious."

A contingent of police officers quickly blocks our way and pushes us back.

"I want to hear what they're saying," I plead.

"You can't approach. Stay clear." He's just a young guy. He looks terrified. He has never had to deal with a situation like this in his life. Travellers watch the standoff from a safe distance, scuttling away with their bulky bags, afraid to be contaminated and not sure they can count on the police for protection.

We take a step back, straining our ears. I can only pick out a few words because of all the yelling and screaming and beating of drums.

"What! Listen to that," says Julius, straining to hear above the deafening din. "He's saying we'll never date their women anymore? I wonder how they plan to enforce that. I mean, it's like the women don't have a say in this? These guys have no idea how it works, man." I nod. The word is that Julius is a bit of a womaniser. He knows exactly how it works.

We spend all morning pleading with the police and railway authorities to let us board the train for Beijing. They won't hear of it. A few dozen white students anxious to escape the violence add their voice to our pleas. I spot Gerbert huddled together with some language students. They are arguing with Idriss, who towers above everyone and is wearing his trademark dark glasses even though there's little light coming through the cloudy skies and fog. Occasionally, a cold wind descends upon us, whistling with its own incomprehensible anger, desperate to be heard above the cacophony of rallying calls and vituperation. Those who didn't get a chance to dress appropriately huddle together for warmth, sometimes running on the spot, rubbing their faces and hands. But we're all fighting a losing battle against the weather. My ears have gone sore and no amount of rubbing can take away the fear they'll freeze and drop off.

"It's all you fault," Gerbert says, waving a finger in Idriss's face. "If you guys didn't mess with their women, we wouldn't be here suffering like this."

"What are you talking about?" retorts Idriss. "Messing with their women indeed. I would like to know what that little snake in your trousers has to say about that. And what about your women messing with their men? Bloody hypocrite!"

"Your guys started the fight last night," says Gerbert. "Everyone knows that."

Idriss is fuming, biting his lips, lost for words. At that moment, Sunny comes along and drags him away, saying, "Leave the little shits alone, man. The Chinese follow them around admiring their blond eyes and blue hair or whatever. It's gone into their bloody heads."

I spot Han Wei brandishing a branch in the air and point him out to Diallo. He is surrounded by a group waving banners and calling the police traitors for protecting black ghosts. Han Wei looks so different from the shower comrade who once joined us on group projects, shared jokes and cigarettes, sat with us at Wang's Den, drinking till late, playing card games with the black ghosts that he's now trying to drive out of town. I wave to him, calling out his name.

"Leave The Whistle alone," mutters Diallo. "What do you want to do, set up a group discussion on thermo-bloody-dynamics?"

Remembering our encounter with Lai Guiguo earlier that morning, I shrug and look away in embarrassment. What did I really want to say to him? *Hey, Han Wei, how about a drink at Wang's Den when you're done fighting us?*

Diallo announces he's ready to take them on, even though we're hopelessly outnumbered. We've come to know and respect Zen for his sagacity and musical abilities. Right now, with the murderous look in his eyes, there's nothing wise about his words or musical in his tone of voice. With the bloodied bandage across his eye, he reminds me of pirates from a comic book. He's going around yelling, "These bastards can't fight! Let's take them on!" A dozen or so people take up the chant, waving clenched fists. The cops are getting fidgety, their eyes darting this way and that, hands tightening around their batons.

Julius places an arm across Diallo's shoulder and tries to calm him down.

"No way, man!" Diallo yells back at him, pushing his arm away, his whole body trembling with rage, fiery eyes blazing. "This bullshit must stop now. I'm fed up!"

"Let the police handle it, Zen," someone calls out. Diallo turns to him, his face distorted with anger.

"No one calls me Zen anymore! You hear? *J'en ai assez*! How much longer are we going to take this treatment? Are you men or boys?"

I think of my family, waiting for money from me, believing I'm living a life of luxury. In his last letter, Father said he no longer regrets that I didn't go to America.

I don't even plan to tell my parents about this riot. Mother would ask me to go back home. But then how would I make her dreams come true? Yet a part of me keeps reminding me, I don't belong here.

My head throbs with a rhythmic rumbling pain, like the sound of cows stampeding down a dirt road. The pain I've endured all day spills over, and it's as if an alien force has taken over my entire being. I grab a rock and hurl it at the chanting mob, above the police cordon. People gaze at me in amazement, their faces saying is that really you, Eggman? A shiver runs down my spine, and I feel like a bird about to take to the skies. In no time at all, everyone is throwing whatever they can lay their hands on, yelling, "We've had enough!"

Missiles rain down on us from the Chinese side. Deafening war cries, insults, and whistles reverberate through the air. A group of Chinese students charges through the police lines, pushing past the young and baffled constables. The police try in vain to hold them back. In no time at all, they're upon us. I no longer feel anger, even as I lash out, landing blows, absorbing kicks, barely feeling the pain, yelling at the top of my head. The exhilaration of the mayhem is akin to intoxication. The fighting goes on for at least half an hour before police reinforcements arrive and separate us, clobbering everyone, both foreign and local, until it begins to look as though they are our common enemy.

As the police round us up into military trucks, our foes' message has become distinctly political. They're now chanting antiauthority slogans, accusing the government of discriminating against them in their own country.

The police claim they're taking us away to a military barrack for our own safety. They refuse to let anyone board the trains for Beijing. They drive us past the hordes of Chinese students shouting insults and pelting the vehicles with rocks, unveiling new posters with overtly political demands: 'Bring political reform', 'Justice for Chinese', 'Respect Chinese people rights'.

We sit on wooden benches on the trucks, shivering with cold, empty stomachs rumbling, chests heaving with anger. Someone breaks into song. Bob Marley's *Buffalo Soldier*. Before long, everyone is singing their hearts out, song after song. Even those who don't know the words of the Benga and kwassa kwassa, chant along, if only to keep warm.

We spend three days at the barracks, subsisting on cold rice and vegetables and lukewarm Chinese tea, sleeping on hard, sisal mattresses on the floor with only a couple of thin blankets to ward off the cold that appears to rise like an unseen vapour from the bare concrete floor. Everyone talks about finishing their studies and leaving the country, never to return. Some say they plan to flee the country as soon as we're released.

The hours go slowly, with nothing to do but wait and feel the intense loathing for everything this country stands for, simmer in undisturbed solitude in the pit of your stomach. Nothing happens, except when they take you away to a cold windowless room for interrogation, where they make you sit on the cold floor answering questions about everything you did in the last week, where you went to, whom you talked to, what you talked about, how you ended up at the station. The pain of reliving the entire experience fills your mouth with bile.

When my turn comes, I face three armed officers. Two are ruthless, prodding your ribs with a baton if you don't respond quickly enough, their questions laced with threats of jail and deportation. The third one tries to assure you that if they could only isolate the bad apples, everyone else is free to return to the comfort of their rooms. They are in no hurry. We fear we could be here for weeks. By the third day, weariness, hunger, frustration, and fear have set in. People begin to remember things. Those returning from the interrogation chambers head straight to their mattresses, inhaling deeply on their cigarettes, avoiding eye contact.

No one breaks into song on the way back to the hostels. The three who started the fateful fight have been identified and taken away. In my mind, I draft the letter I'll write to Lai Ying. What future do we have here? Is the ejection we've endured a sign of the rejection I'll face from her family? How will we love in a time of such anger and hatred? And later, if I choose to live and work here, how can I ever hope for acceptance? Will we ever walk the streets together, hand in hand, and share a tender kiss by the shores of Democracy Lake?

I know if it ever happens, it will be in the dead of winter, when there isn't a soul in sight, and the only sound is that of chilly winds howling through leafless trees.

Trojan Girl

ALL WEEK, GLOOM HANGS OVER the city like a fog. The deportation of three students has pacified the locals and brought some calm to the city. But the tension remains.

I've been speaking to Lai Ying on the phone every day. She was hysterical when she heard about the riot and for those three days couldn't reach me. Right now, her pain is more intense than mine. We now have irrefutable evidence that we are in the wrong part of the world. I try in vain to believe my headteacher's words when she introduced me to the Chinese scholarships. *The Chinese have always been our friends.* Where did it go wrong? Or did Mrs Chevo know something we could never fathom?

The Youth League has been trying to mend fences and persuade us that the actions of a few students should not affect China-Africa relations. It's not working well. I know at least two students who've abandoned their studies and returned home. Others are talking of leaving. The mood is bleak. I've thought long and hard about what I need to do. It is tempting to give up and return to Zim, but the thought of having wasted three years here and starting again from scratch is even more disheartening. And I can't be sure I'll secure a place at university there. I content myself with the thought that all it takes is a little patience, if the authorities can guarantee security. Then there's the question of Lai Ying. What would become of us? She says she would love to visit Zim and meet my family when the time is right. We've never talked about her living there. I don't have much choice. For us to be together, I have to bite the bullet and stay put, even though there's little chance things will get better.

The pressure is beginning to show already. For Lai Ying, it is the shame and embarrassment, the debilitating disappointment in the intolerance of her fellow students. I struggle in vain to convince her that it is not her responsibility. She wants to come back but I assure her I'm fine, it is safe now, there are security guards everywhere. Much as I would love to see her, she needs to be with her family. I've waited all my life for someone as caring as her. I can wait another week.

On New Year's Day, when we troop down to Wang's Den to relive the sordid experience, we're shocked to discover the windows smashed, the door broken, and the pavement littered with damaged decorations and broken chairs. The bilingual sign lies broken on the pavement. The walls are covered in graffiti. *Hei Gui Wang. Wang the Black Devil. You bring Shame to the Motherland.* A livid Wang says he's lucky the police got there just as the mob started looting the bar and stopped them from torching the place. But he has been unable to clean up until now as isolated riots have broken spasmodically during the week, usually involving small groups of marauding locals.

"These students are mad," he declares. "They tried to destroy my bar. This is not the Chinese way at all."

He is close to tears. He has paid the price for his generosity to foreign ghosts.

Kabinga pays us a visit one Saturday afternoon and brings several bottles of whisky, to cheer us up small-small, as he puts it.

"I warned you guys, didn't I?" he says, puffing smugly on a cigar. "These people will never accept we're human. Studying here is just bullshit. It's not for me, man. Right now, I just want their money, you know? The buggers need me more than I need them."

The discussion is muted. And mostly one-sided. Kabinga spends an hour making us feel small and miserable, almost implying we brought the racial violence on ourselves. The White Card brigade are the only members of the black minority tribe who have escaped unscathed. Theirs is a parallel universe to ours. Their lives go on. If they have any quarrel with their customers and business associates, they're smart enough to understand their priorities. Not so, for most of the rest of us.

"What would you have done yourself?" someone asks Kabinga.

"Fight!" hisses Kabinga, thrusting a finger into the charged air, eyes filled with fury, the goatee trembling as the angry words gush out of his mouth. "You should have got organised small-small and given them a real war. You let them walk all over you one time, and they'll always screw you!"

Diallo shoots him a fierce look but says nothing. All afternoon, he has been rubbing and scratching the beard he has recently started to grow in protest against our treatment.

We watch Kabinga in silence, heads slightly bowed with the futility of explaining ourselves. No one has the guts to tell him it's all right for him to talk like that when he was safely ensconced in some woman's warm arms in the luxury of his hotel apartment. We drink his whisky in silence, failing to prevent the reunion from degenerating into a reflective, sombre party. The exuberance and the old mood died with the riots. And with it, something in all of us.

Peace only returns to our troubled community at the end of January. Right across the province, university authorities are trying to rein foreign students in. In my university, the Student Affairs department has earned itself the name Campus Gestapo for the zealousness with which they have moved to enforce the new rules. Security men armed with batons and whistles patrol the grounds and sometimes march up and down the corridors, provoking arguments with students who say their privacy is being invaded. They have tightened the curfew rules, insist on a one-boyfriend-one-girlfriend rule, and banned girls from visiting our rooms. Girls are only allowed in the reception area.

But we quickly find ways to go around this. One way is to have a friend who lives on a different floor escort your girlfriend into the building while a few others playfully but physically restrain the elderly security guards until she's delivered safely to your room. When the guards finally make their way to your friend's room, he's only too happy to let them in. Everyone knows they can't inspect the whole building. A guard once reported the matter but when officials from the Campus Gestapo and the Youth League arrived, they found the 'culprit' busy studying. They searched under his bed and in the bathrooms and toilets. Eventually they went away, angry and embarrassed, while some students accused them of thinking we all looked the same.

By far the most daring trick is the Trojan Girl, credited to Julius, which involves smuggling a girl into the building in a TV box or large suitcase. Lai Ying scoffs at the idea when I first suggest it to her. But when she comes back from the long Chinese New Year break, I manage to persuade her it's the only way we can spend a weekend together. If it hadn't been for the riots and the new rules, this would never have been necessary. My only worry is that she'll cough or sneeze as we carry her past the security guards. Julius says it's not a problem.

"These guys are clueless!" he exclaims. "They would believe the sound came from the TV if you told them."

"Aren't they wondering why so many people are buying TVs nowadays?" asks Diallo, pensively.

"Tell them since they don't allow women in here," says Julius, breaking into a laugh, "we need a different sort of entertainment. Problem is, most people find the TVs don't work and take them back, right?"

"It can't go on forever, though," says Diallo, as we let Lai Ying out of the box.

"So what should we do?" says Julius. "Stay in, read books on ancient China, and have siesta?"

"*Merde!*" mutters Diallo. After the riots, he stopped talking about the minority black Chinese tribe and gave up trying to understand the Chinese. We miss the old, thoughtful Diallo, who always saw a positive side to everything. Nowadays, he's prone to angry exchanges and dark moods, which were previously Kabinga's stock in trade.

Lai Ying swears it's the last time she's being smuggled in like that.

"You make me feel like a thing you bought in a shop. It's not right."

She's shaking with anger. For a moment, I begin to doubt the wisdom of smuggling her in. I reach out to hold her. She pushes me away, sits on the edge of the bed, and stubbornly stares out of the window. I wait for her to calm down, and then offer her an apple. She glares at the apple and crosses her hands.

I try to imagine what it must have been like, crouching in a TV box, in a small, dark space, dreading what would happen if the security guards demanded to open the box. Nervously, I take her hand and massage her fingers, fully aware that the wrong word could make her explode.

I keep my eyes averted. I sense her begin to pull her hand away. I hold it firmly and massage the fingers once again. Her breath comes out fast and furious as she struggles to overcome her anger. I kiss her hand then hold it close to my chest. When the storm passes, I draw closer to her and whisper, "The riots changed everything, darling. We have to find new ways to be together."

She pouts and pinches my nose.

"Why can't we wait until the situation improves? Don't you believe the university can protect you?"

I wish I could share her confidence. I pick up the apple and take a bite. She takes my hand and makes me feed her, which I do, feeling a weight lift off my shoulders.

"You can't imagine how I missed you when all those things were happening."

"I asked you to come with me to Shanghai."

"You know I couldn't."

"You could have tried."

She's right. I could have tried harder. What was I afraid of? I'm not used to travelling to strange places. Coming to Nanjing is enough of an insane adventure already.

I wrap my arms around her and promise solemnly, "Anything you want, Lai Ying, I'll try. I'll try really hard."

"*Ban dan*! My truly silly egg."

I'm running out of cash as a substantial part of my student grant ends up in Zimbabwe. The only White Card deal I ever had the guts to get into, which involved a refrigerator, didn't net much for me. After sending half the proceeds to my parents and paying a contact a commission to have the money wired in Hong Kong, there wasn't much left. Kabinga said he was proud of me and wanted to see me get more adventurous. But even as I savoured the rare praise by the biggest of the African entrepreneurial sharks, something told me this wasn't my fish. This wasn't what Mother had in mind.

Recently, I've been subsisting on rice and vegetables, unable to afford meat. Diallo says it helps create an affinity with peasant Chinese in order to spur my creative juices. I have to find another way, perhaps a part-time job to learn in a safe environment. I ask Wang if he needs help. He already has two assistants and a student working for him. He smiles and says he has never forgotten how I helped promote his bar when he was first starting out. The money is not much but at least I can just about maintain my old lifestyle.

Lai Ying is aghast that I should even contemplate working for Wang. She believes a repeat of the violence is quite inconceivable with all the security measures in place. Whatever threat I face now can only come from associating with the likes of Wang. Gradually, I've come to understand that for her, businessmen are a different species from the rest of us, not to be trusted, especially if they have extensive *guanxi* and loads of money. It means they're corrupt beyond redemption. Lai Ying still won't venture into Wang's Den. In fact, right after the riots, she told me she wished the mob had destroyed the bar and stopped Wang dead in his wicked tracks. I thought she meant it as a joke, and started to laugh, but the grim look on her face forced me to ask her to take it easy.

"First he gives you free beer," she says. "Then he employs you so you spend all your nights there. He's just using you, Dan. And you're too stupid to realise it."

I remind her that Wang's bar was targeted because he was generous to foreigners, first giving them free beer as she correctly recalls, and always treating them like real people. But I don't tell her I've borrowed money from him once, although I don't think of it as borrowing, but rather like getting an advance on my wages.

"I have nothing to fear from him, Lai Ying. And we're not children. He can't use us. We drink because we love to drink and socialise. There's not much else to do for fun here, you know."

"I just can't stand the look of that man," she says, a look of disgust spreading like a hue across her face. When I ask why, she says, "That look in his eyes, the way he talks with a cigarette in his mouth. This man looks dangerous, can't you see?"

In his officious Mao jackets or creased grey suit and black shoes that look like monstrous wraps around his feet, to me he's just an entrepreneur struggling to make a living, a hardworking man some way ahead of his time. After the things he told us about his experiences with foreigners in the early sixties, we've come to see him in a new light, as a sort of ally, which was confirmed when the mobs attacked his bar. I have no problem dealing with him.

And I need the job. I need that sweet cash that recognises no politics and turns a blind eye to the lapses of morality that *guanxi* engenders. Most of us understand that simple reality and play the system as best we can, some better than others, with a little help from Wang and the chain-smoking, shifty-eyed brokers at the Travel Café. Except Lai Ying. In that sense, I like to think of her as my conscience, the moral spine in an organic being that, if it had more guts, would squirm and weave its way in the murky waters of a malleable financial system just to survive.

The old confidence we enjoyed as foreigners before the riots begins to return by early spring. But my troubles have only just begun.

Lai Ying is pregnant.

She mentions it to me one morning, just as I'm leaving the laboratory. As soon as I see her face, I know something's amiss. We sit on a bench in the narrow lobby, under the glare of notices and paintings of mythical animals and serene landscapes of ancient dynasties.

"What are we going to do?" I blurt out, after taking a full minute to digest the news. Lai Ying remains uncharacteristically quiet. "Are you sure about this?"

I ask. She rolls her eyes. "I mean, could your period be late, perhaps? Is there some way we can be sure?"

"I *am* sure, Dan."

"Lai Ying, you're all I have here. I can't let any harm come your way. Let's think through this carefully, all right?"

"Dan." She fixes me with a stern stare. "You need to tell me what you want. You can't wait too long. It's already at least a month."

"Okay," I mumble, "I'll think of something."

The following week is the most difficult I've had in China yet. I drink every night, racking my brains for a solution. Alcohol tends to give me a strange clarity. Even through my drunken nights, there's no doubt in my mind that Lai Ying and I love each other. We've been dating forever, we could get married, have the baby, and Lai Ying could resume her studies later.

"You're a dreamer, Eggman," says Diallo, when I confide in him. "Get the medical thing done. I know someone we can talk to."

"I can't bring myself to murder a baby."

"Baby? Don't be melodramatic; it's just a bunch of cells right now."

"Living cells. Whatever it is, it's alive. I can't—"

"Very well, but have you considered the practical reality? Forget the moral philosophy for a second. How do you expect to explain it to Professor Sheng and the communist thought police?"

He has a point. This must never get to our course head, especially coming as it does so soon after the post-riot regulations to protect women. This is surely the end. And how could I face Professor Sheng in his office after the way he was humiliated? I try to picture the look on my father's face when I show up, bent double with shame, without my degree. And Mother, what will she think? Were the prayers and purification rites all in vain?

We have to run away. We'll survive, somehow. I could team up with Kabinga in business. I still have my job at Wang's Den. Lai Ying can always get a job through her family's contacts. They can't all disown her. We'll go far away from here, to Huizhou, her father's hometown. There must be some sympathetic relations there.

I call her hostel one evening when I'm neither working nor drinking at Wang's Den. The security guard says she's not in. But where could she be? She's always in the room by 9.30 p.m. It's already 10 p.m. I insist on talking to at least one of her roommates. The girl who answers says Lai Ying wasn't feeling very well and had to go to hospital earlier that evening. A lump builds up in my throat. Why didn't she call me? Questions flood my mind but I can't find my voice. I rush to Diallo's room but he's not there. Someone in the lobby tells me he saw him heading off in the direction of Wang's Den. I find him there with Julius and three regulars, playing cards and making a huge racket. Diallo is about to urge me to grab a seat when I signal to him and Julius to follow me outside.

"Is she all right?"

"I don't know. She's in hospital. I have to see her."

"Don't be silly, Eggman. You can't go there. First, we must establish what happened."

"I have to see her. I have to know she's all right!"

Diallo's right, it's too risky for me to be seen there. But the thought of waiting makes my heart race and knees tremble. I don't care if they expel me from the university. I must see her.

"Look, Eggman," says Diallo. "Trust me on this. Something happens to her, and you show up, you're finished. I know a guy who can help."

"Yeah," murmurs Julius, nodding his head. "Probably the same guy I'm thinking of. He's supposed to be good."

"The best, apparently," adds Diallo.

"How do I know he'll help, with all this shit between us?"

"Where have you been all month, Eggman? It's all right now. Look, this guy is fine. Everyone uses him."

Diallo doesn't reveal who his contact is. I don't press the point. I don't care who it is. Julius and I wait outside while he goes to make enquiries in one of the hostels. I pace up and down, thinking this would be a good time for a cigarette, even though I haven't smoked since I got caught in high school. Ten minutes later, Diallo returns and says we have to see someone else. He has a name and address scribbled on a piece of paper. Julius smiles when he sees the name. It is Yi Guan, a classmate of his.

Yi Guan's slender frame looks awkward in the heavy navy-blue winter jacket, like a boy dressed up in a man's clothes. He has a small mouth that appears a little bent to his left, as if he once sustained a punch that left him disfigured. He is wearing thick glasses that make his eyes look like marbles. He approaches in tentative steps, as if he's afraid. His face lights up momentarily when Julius greets him with a smile, but he doesn't say much.

We hop on our bikes and ride off in the direction of the hospital. When we get there, an attendant at the door says visiting hours are over. Yi Guan advises us to wait outside. From a distance, we can see him arguing with a nurse in a white coat, who starts to herd him away after a few minutes, waving her arms in apparent exasperation. I take a few steps towards them, determined to pay her and be done with this nonsense, but my friends restrain me. Yi Guan reaches into his pocket and hands over some money. The nurse, still waving her arms about, leads him down the corridor. Fifteen minutes later, Yi Guan returns, looking grim and withdrawn. We wait as he lights a cigarette and gets on his bike. I can hear my heart pounding. I try to peer into his eyes but he keeps his face averted, like someone searching for the courage to admit to a crime.

"Bleeding," he announces, without looking at us. "She noticed bleeding this evening and came here."

"Is she okay?"

"Um…" he glances over his shoulder then looks at his feet, before whispering, "miscarriage." His voice is low and almost timid, as if he's afraid to utter the word. It takes me a few seconds to grasp his meaning.

The silence that follows is short-lived, only a few seconds at most. But in that moment, time stands still, my head spins with a myriad of thoughts. I hold onto my bike so tightly, my hands ache. "They'll keep her for a day or two," Yi Guan says, still avoiding our eyes. "There'll be an investigation, who's responsible for the…um…pregnancy, when, where, a report for her professor, disciplinary hearing by Student Affairs. It could get very serious. But there's another way. I've talked to the doctor. It will be more expensive if they know it's a *hei*…um, foreigner. Better for you not to come back."

The mere thought of Lai Ying lying on the hospital bed, almost lifeless, covered in a pale, striped, orange and white bed sheet, with a single fan buzzing noisily in a room full of dejected-looking patients, is driving me mad.

Two days later, when I see her in the lobby of her hostel, she looks pale, haggard, too withdrawn even for small talk. I gaze into her pained eyes, trying to find something comforting to say, but a crippling emptiness grips my insides with a debilitating force, leaving me mute. I don't even have the energy to worry right now about the danger Lai Ying faces from the authorities. Last year, a girl who did the medical thing with a Cameroonian student was taken away and never returned. Some say she was sent to jail. The Cameroonian student avoided deportation by having to please a lot of officials.

"It's finished, Dan," she says, choosing her words carefully. There are six female and two male students lounging in the lobby, chatting, playing cards, reading. The girls barely notice me. They've seen me here many times before. I recognise two of them. One keeps glancing at me, perhaps to see whether the riots changed me in any way. She has short hair like a boy, but what is more distinctive about her is the permanent grin on her face which reveals large front teeth. She looks like a child gazing with amazement at street entertainers, completely untroubled by any suggestion of self-consciousness. "I was scared. It was very hard, but now I feel I can breathe."

I nod. "I still don't know what to think. Anyway, thank God you're okay."

"It must have been that time," she whispers woefully, nibbling at her fingers. "The two days we spent in your room, not caring. How could we have been so stupid, so reckless, Dan?"

I remember that weekend well. Before, she was always so careful, never agreeing to sex outside her safe days. But not that Trojan girl weekend. It was sheer madness. The riots, the fear, the rules, and the mad urgency to celebrate intimacy and forget the pain, unconcerned with the consequences. We survived the riots, and just when we thought the promise of happiness was within our grasp, the aftermath swings back with full vengeance.

"Dan." Lai Ying fixes a gaze on my face, a look I've never seen before. There's a hardness in her eyes that I find unsettling, but which I put down to the harrowing experience she has just endured. She gets up and takes a seat next to me, her back to everyone else.

"Yes, what is it?"

"I had to do this without you," she whispers. "I hope you can forgive me, my love."

What I thought was a defiant hardness in her eyes turns out to be a blend of fear and regret. I feel the blood pounding in my temple, my heart heaving with every forced breath.

"What are you saying, Lai Ying? There's nothing to forgive…"

"Dan, I wanted to talk to you." Her voice is shaky, faltering; she's about to burst into tears. I glance around us. No one is paying any attention, but I can't risk putting an arm around her. The fact that I dare not comfort her, fills me with rage. "But…I couldn't reach you, at first, then a chance came. I knew you would say no. I had to do it, Dan. I'm so sorry."

I sink back into my seat, breathing hard through my mouth. I can picture them coming for me, escorting me to the airport in handcuffs. I see tears on Lai Ying's face as she struggles to maintain her composure. But they drag her away toward a dark-blue van. This is the end. I know it. I want to stand up and walk out of here, get some air, run into the woods and scream at the top of my head. But the only sound that comes out of my mouth is, "Why?"

Without blinking, without hesitation, Lai Ying says, "What else could we have done? We're students, Dan. We're not married." She has prepared herself well for this exchange. I hope she has prepared for the aftermath, for the investigation that will surely follow. I know she hasn't. There hasn't been time. This is something we must do together.

"We could have…we could have…" The words grind to a halt on my tongue. There's no truth in them. We could not have done whatever it is I imagine we might have. It is inconceivable. We both know it.

"I don't want to hide this from you, Dan. It has happened. It was a medical student. I was assured it would be all right. But it wasn't. There was a complication, that's why I went to hospital. But don't worry, I'm all right now."

"Who was it?"

"It doesn't matter…"

"It does," I insist. She frowns and buries her face in her hands. "I need to know, Lai Ying."

"Yi Guan," she whispers through her fingers, then covers her face. "My friend said he was the best. An expert. Expert indeed."

"That little bastard!"

"Shhh! Control your voice." Startled, curious faces turn in our direction. I ignore them. All I'm thinking now is how I need to get to that shifty, skinny guy with thick glasses and squeeze his neck until his eyes pop out.

"What now? There'll be a lot of trouble, Lai Ying. People will want gifts."

"You wouldn't know what gifts to choose." She chuckles. I stare at her, stunned that she would find any of this funny.

When I ask Diallo, he suggests a bottle of whisky, and says he'll check with his contact, who recommends two cartons of cigarettes as well for the doctor and the medical staff.

"Hopefully this will keep their big mouths shut," says Diallo. "By the way, it's for the best, Eggman, what your girl did. She's really smart, man. Now, we can only hope they let the matter drop. Yi Guan should clean it up, really."

"What! You trust him?"

"He has no choice. He's in pretty serious trouble himself. You two could end up being allies, friends even, after all." He's grinning as he says this. "You should consider working together, at least get your stories right, you know?"

Diallo's words are hard to digest. I know that a meeting with Yi Guan will in all likelihood spark off another round of riots. Right now I just want to get away from here, to the simplicity of life in Ndambu village, to the long, slow days that dragged on, assuring you there would be no nasty surprises.

Eventually, I end up supplying two bottles of whisky and three cartons of cigarettes. One carton is for Diallo's anonymous contact. I also reimburse Yi Guan the payment he made at the hospital, which I do with a heavy heart. He should be paying for the suffering he put Lai Ying through. I consider approaching Kabinga for a loan but change my mind. He'll insist on paying for everything, which I can't accept. I end up borrowing some money from Wang against my wages. Wang doesn't ask what I need it for. The gifts and payment are delivered by Diallo and his still unnamed contact. I can't bear to face Yi Guan.

A few days later, the security guard at my hostel tells me that someone is waiting to see me in the lobby. It is Chen Ning, a short, stocky man from the Campus Gestapo, who is also reputed to be the handler of the spies who watch foreigners. It is said he's a kung fu master, though you would never guess it from the size of him. He's built more like a wrestler, with round, fleshy shoulders that have virtually swallowed his neck. Since the riots, he has been spending a lot of time in our hostel, pacing up and down the corridors, chatting with the guards, making notes surreptitiously in a little notebook.

I find him standing against the wall, smoking a cigarette that fills the lobby with the smell of burnt leaves. But it's not a joint. He wouldn't dare. His eyes dart about beneath bushy hooded eyebrows, never settling on any one spot for more than a few seconds.

It's seven in the morning. There's no one else in the lobby. Outside it's raining, and whenever someone opens the door, a gust of cold air invades the lobby, making me shiver in my shirt and light sweater. Chen Ning declines to take a seat. We remain standing. The two security guards watch us, eyes narrowed in concentration.

"We have a report," says Chen Ning, inhaling deeply on his cigarette. "And it's not good. The investigation is going on. I'm here to ask you a few questions."

I watch him in silence, hating him, hating Yi Guan, the so-called abortion expert, hating the riots and this whole country, burning with desperation to go home. If they want to send me away, that's fine. But I shiver to think what might happen to Lai Ying. Maybe she can come with me to Zim. She'll be safe there. We'll find something for her to do. She can teach Chinese. But who wants to learn Chinese in Africa? Maybe she can start a small business.

"What's this about?" I ask Chen Ning.

"The incident with the girl in hospital. Our country does not condone this sort of behaviour. This is what we expect from immoral, uncouth imperialists in the west. Do you accept your mistake?" He speaks in a slow voice, savouring each word, anxious to get the memorised script right.

"I have nothing to say to you."

"And the girl?"

"You leave her alone! She has done nothing wrong."

"So, you'll accept her punishment?" His brow furrows as if in disbelief, and his lips curl into a smile, which accentuates the sinister look he so effortlessly maintains.

"Tell me what you want from me, Chen Ning, but leave her alone."

"As you wish. Just one more thing. We're aware of the incident in a party a while back. Your record is getting worse."

When he leaves, I walk up with heavy steps to my room, my mind in turmoil. I have to warn Lai Ying. I put on a few more layers of clothing and walk into the rain, my eyes smarting as the howling wind blows the chilly rainwater into my face. Ten minutes later, as I approach her hostel, I see a security van driving off from the car park. I race towards it, shouting Lai Ying's name. I catch a glimpse of her, sandwiched between two Campus Gestapo officials in the back. The van zooms past me, splashing icy water all over me. Then it's gone.

People's Sanctuary

I BARELY NOTICE THE COLD. Or the blustery wind needlessly stirring the fog, the streets that are filling up with people cycling to work or to lectures.

In a daze, I trudge back to my hostel, my heart pounding, my head filled with thoughts of that girl last year and her Cameroonian boyfriend. After changing into drier clothes, I sit down to think. I have to find a way to get Lai Ying released. I hope she had a chance to dress appropriately before they took her away. A shiver rocks my spine when I imagine her lying on a cold floor at the police station, facing a pack of menacing interrogators. A sharp pain throbs in my temple.

I have to prepare myself. It will only be a matter of time before Chen Ning returns. I look into the mirror as I comb my hair. The panicked, sickly face that stares back frightens me. The worry lines etched on the forehead, the patchy two-day stubble, the hollow look, the dry, chafed lips. I throw some water on my face and apply a lip balm. The result is not satisfactory, but at least it won't shock anyone as I walk down the stairs. I obscure my face by pulling the neck scarf right up to the nose and my fleece cap down to my eyebrows.

Diallo is not in his room. He must be in class by now. I cycle towards the lab, certain that I haven't the heart for today's lecture on precision control and sensor technology. Life goes on all around me, totally oblivious of my plight. Flying horses converging outside lecture theatres, greetings and hearty exchanges pierce the chilly air. I wait outside the lab, pacing up and down, struggling to focus, waiting for the class to end.

Diallo and I work through the options, which aren't many. The first thing to do is get Minnie, Lai Ying's best friend, to inform her professor and give a sympathetic account of her condition and troubles before the Campus Gestapo get to him with a twisted version. If he's on her side, perhaps he can appeal on her behalf. He'll need a gift.

"If this thing gets big, Eggman, we'll need a lot of help," says Diallo. "We might need to contact Kabinga."

"I would prefer not to borrow money," I protest. "I'll get an advance from Wang."

"Be realistic, it might take more than a few weeks' wages. Besides, Kabinga knows people."

"The man is hardly ever around."

When we call his hotel, the receptionist, the skinny, sallow-faced but cheerful young woman I remember from our last visit says he's away all week. My heart sinks. I readjust my scarf and together, we walk towards Lai Ying's hostel. I don't know if Minnie lives there but I can't think of anywhere better to start. The search is onerous and frustrating. The security guard doesn't know her English nickname. I should have guessed. Feeling foolish, I try to explain our predicament to the girls passing through the lobby. Some of them know Lai Ying, but they have no idea who this Minnie is. We try two other hostels and spend an hour making futile enquiries. Then we end up back at Lai Ying's hostel and start all over again. We're just about to give up when I notice the short-haired, hare-toothed girl who was staring at Lai Ying and I in the lobby last week. Grinning mysteriously, she tells us how to find Minnie.

Minnie's hostel is in the old wing at the far end of the campus, behind the running track and sports field. When we call on her, she says she's busy and asks us to return after her afternoon nap. It is an agonising wait till 2 p.m.

She comes down to the hostel lobby looking a little dazed. Perhaps she had a nightmare. Her broad face and sharp eyes promise no cooperation and are filled with suspicion. Her lips retain the remnants of fading lipstick. Her hair has been pulled back and tied in a bun, making her forehead look stretched and tight.

"I don't want to talk to you," she says in an angry voice. "Lai Ying warned me about you people. She says you're trouble."

Diallo and I exchange glances. Lai Ying has kept our relationship quite secret. Only a few of her friends know, and Minnie is her only close confidant. Her hostility angers and scares me.

"Minnie, do you realise Lai Ying is in trouble? We're trying to help her."

"What do you mean?" she demands, her face hardening. That is when it strikes me that her friend has not confided in her. "What have you done to her? Do you realise she has been unwell? Why are you troubling her?"

I look around the lobby sharply. There are only two other girls there, reading a newspaper, unconcerned about us. But the two elderly security guards watch us closely.

This is a lost cause. We're wasting our time here. But it's impossible for us to approach Lai Ying's course head ourselves. We hardly know who it is, and we dare not let the person know I'm involved.

"Minnie, we need to talk to you," says Diallo, leaning toward her to humble himself. "This is important. Only you can help Lai Ying."

"What have you done to her?" she shoots back.

"It's not us, Minnie. It's the Campus Gest—"

"The authorities, Minnie," says Diallo, rubbing my back. "There has been a misunderstanding. You need to talk to Lai Ying's professor and ask for help. We can't do that."

Minnie stares at us, her mouth agape. It takes me another ten minutes to explain what I saw that morning and the danger Lai Ying is in before she comprehends and agrees to help. But she's still in shock, and her face is a mask of incredulity.

As we get ready to leave, she slumps into the nearest seat, clasping her hands close to her chest as if in prayer, her eyes fixed on the concrete floor. I tap her shoulder and remind her of what to do.

We make our way to the central university administration block and stop to buy several packets of cigarettes. The Campus Gestapo offices are on the second floor. A surly security officer at the reception demands to know what we want. When I say we're here to see Chen Ning, he says Chen has already gone home.

"We have to speak to someone," I plead, and offer him a packet of cigarettes. He proceeds to light one without delay. Then he looks up at us, scratching the dark pockmarks that dot his forehead.

"Uh-huh! These are good," he says, in a cheerful voice. "What was it you wanted to talk about?" I try not to look at the edges of his mouth, where frothy webs of saliva build up when he speaks.

"A girl was brought here this morning," I inform him. "A classmate. We're afraid she's in some kind of trouble. We want to help her."

"Your friend must have done something terrible to be brought here." He scratches his greying, thinning hair and puffs thoughtfully on his cigarette.

"It's just a misunderstanding," says Diallo. "That's why we need to talk to Chen Ning or someone senior. Can you help us?"

"There was a girl," he says, making a great show of consulting an unwieldy Occurrences Book. "You're right. She was questioned. But she's not here now."

"Do you know where they've taken her?"

With officious deliberation, he turns a few pages, running a wrinkly, tobacco-stained finger from top to bottom, puffs long and hard, then says, "It is hard to tell. It could be anywhere. Chen Ning will be here tomorrow. He can answer your questions."

He closes the book with a note of finality, leans back, and gazes at us expectantly.

"Let's get the hell out of here," says Diallo in English. "There has to be another way."

I rack my brains trying to figure where they could have taken her. My heart sinking, I realise she could be at a police station, detention centre, or prison. It dawns on me that there is nothing we can do if the Campus Gestapo have taken the matter forward. But my mind refuses to accept this possibility.

Wang is our only hope. When we get to the bar, he and his wife are just opening up, dusting tables, checking stock records. There are no other customers.

"It's good to see customers this early," he declares, rubbing his hands with glee. "You'll have the usual?"

"Actually, nothing for now," I inform him in a croaky voice. "We've come to ask for some help."

He hesitates for an instant, then waves us to a table at the back of the bar. The look in his eyes says he has seen it all, whatever it is, but it hardly reassures me. The throbbing in my temple is beginning to turn into a headache. Diallo offers Wang a cigarette.

"It's Lai Ying. She's in trouble."

Wang looks at me calmly, waiting for me to continue. Perhaps he thinks I want to take another advance on my wages.

"It must be serious trouble, Eggman," he says, lighting a cigarette. "You look terrible."

"I wouldn't trouble you otherwise. The money helped, Wang, and I thank you. But the situation has changed. Lai Ying has been in hospital recently. The campus authorities came for her this morning, claiming she had an illegal abortion. We don't know where she is now."

"Are they looking for you, too?"

I nod. "But I'm not worried about myself, Wang. We need to find Lai Ying."

"There's someone we can talk to," he says in a slowly drawn-out voice. "I cannot say he'll help, but he can ask around."

"This person," says Diallo, leaning toward Wang, "is there some way we can help him, show our appreciation? To help speed things up?"

Wang breaks into a laugh.

"There's nothing you can do, my friend."

We stare at him, puzzled.

"Er…why do you say that?" says Diallo.

"He will do this for me. He'll try."

"We don't want to make it difficult for you, Wang," I put in quickly. "I'll do everything I have to. This is very important."

"I understand. Oh, the simplicity of love. What a joyful thing. No, do not worry yourselves about my friend."

"You mean we can't afford it," counters Diallo, smiling to take the edge off.

"It is complicated," says Wang. "Master Kong Fu-zi taught us there are appropriate times and good days for launching attacks with fire."

We study his face intently. His only explanation is a cryptic grin.

In spite of Wang's promise to help, I've no patience to wait. Knowing that Diallo will try to discourage me, I excuse myself and ride my flying horse in the direction of the nearest police station, three miles north of Cai Chang. That's where they take students arrested for causing trouble in campus parties. I approach the building with trepidation. If they know I have something to do with the abortion they'll lock me up, too.

It is already dark when I get there, out of breath, cold sweat dripping down my back. As I approach the entrance to the imposing blue building, the wisdom of coming here begins to elude me. I should at least have told Diallo. If anything happens to me, no one will know where to find me. It is too late now. There's no turning back.

A motley crowd of rural peasants blocks the entrance. They are remonstrating with the uniformed police officers, asking to be allowed to see their friends, who are being held inside. They are all clad in dull brown trousers and oversized jackets. Their faces look haggard, drained, and weather-beaten. They watch me in silence. Ignoring their startled expressions and shameless stares, I push my way past them into the lobby.

The two guards at the front desk watch me with a familiar blend of curiosity and disdain. We spend five minutes arguing about whether I should be there at all. Their chief, who has been watching the exchange in silence from an adjoining office, walks up to me, takes a deep breath as if to inflate himself, rises to his full height, and barks in my face, "Trouble! That's what you people are! And this foolish girl, what is she thinking messing about with your type? She's a renegade!" His nose wriggles constantly, as though he's having trouble breathing.

"No, no, Chief," I plead with him. "She's just a student, and this whole thing is a misunderstanding."

"And where are her own friends, her own people?" He stabs me with a fierce gaze, his eyes filled with venom. "What is a *hei gui* doing here at the people's sanctuary anyway? Could it be, you've come to cause trouble? Was it not your type that caused all that trouble recently, fighting our diligent and illustrious young men? The shame of it! I don't know why they let such barbarians into our country." He spits on the floor, missing my shoes by inches.

"Chief, I'm not here to cause trouble. I come in peace to see a friend." I hand him a packet of cigarettes and watch his face lose its belligerence like a chameleon altering its camouflage, the nose wriggling as he suppresses a smile. "Friends share the little they have and help each other."

He exchanges surprised looks with his partner and says to me with a smile, "What you say is true, *lao wai*." Foreign friend. "But I must warn you, coming here to bring a petition puts some pressure on this institution. I suggest you wait in the Visitors' Lounge. I will speak to someone."

The Visitors' Lounge turns out to be a large, cold waiting room down a poorly lit corridor. An officer leads me there and tells me to find a seat. All the five benches are taken. Those who can't find a seat are either seating or lying on the cold, concrete floor, all of them united in their exhaustion, hunger, and forlornness. Some of the men have bruises and dried blood on their faces and arms. I stand against a wall and search for a free space on the floor. A man is sobbing in a corner, tearing his hair out. The nauseating smell of sweaty, unwashed people mixed with high-tar cigarette smoke hangs in the air like an unspoken curse.

Two women lying on the floor embellish the air with mesmerising, almost musical, wails. One of them is holding a three-year-old girl, who has buried her face in her hands, apparently terrified of the wailing. Suddenly the little girl looks up, sees me, and starts to cry. One of the women walks her to a wall and makes her squat. I'm puzzled; she cannot be urinating because she hasn't pulled down her thick winter trousers. After a little while, the woman leads the child away.

That's when I notice the gap that has been fashioned between the trouser legs, allowing her to relieve herself without having to pull down the trousers. I watch with alarm as the urine trickles down in a yellow rivulet toward the face of a man snoring on the floor. No one else pays any attention. Everyone is preoccupied with their own troubles.

The man who was sobbing and pulling his hair is now sitting quietly on the floor, his arms wrapped around his knees. When he looks up and sees me watching him, he frowns then smiles, revealing two broken front teeth. Two bruises run along his right temple and there is an unsightly weal on his right arm. He beckons me with a lifeless hand. I hesitate. He smiles again, a tired, mirthless smile that is closer to a grimace. I approach and offer a muted greeting.

"I've never seen a foreigner here," he says, shaking his head. His voice is soft, as if he's muttering to himself. There's neither curiosity nor surprise on his face, only the listlessness of a prisoner who hasn't a glimmer of hope. He could be in his mid-thirties, though from his condition, I cannot be certain. He looks like someone who has aged prematurely. "Why are you here?"

I glance around the room. A few people are watching us abstractedly. I squat before saying, "I'm searching for a friend."

He nods and remains silent. A few moments go by. Then I ask him, "And you, why are you here?"

"My wife. She's in there." He jerks a thumb over his shoulder.

"What's there?"

"Women's detention centre, where they're torturing her." His voice is matter-of-fact, devoid of all emotion. "They'll make her lose the baby. We can't afford the fine for daring to have a second child."

I catch my breath and watch him intently, while the reality of the one-child policy dawns on me. I dare not tell this man the real reason I'm here right now.

My head throbs with the thought of Lai Ying lying on a concrete floor, covered in pools of urine. If only the new rules after the riots hadn't forced us to spend a weekend together, would that have made us more careful? Did we lose control by spending so much stolen time together for the first time in our lives? Worrying about how to turn back the arms of the clock merely worsens the pain in my head.

The man covers his head in his arms again, after casting a languid, unseeing gaze around the room. I let my mind wander to a land that could now well be a dream. The tobacco plantations that stretched for miles into the distant horizon.

The mango trees outside our house, which supplied fruits and firewood, and rotten fruits for the Walters' cows. I try in vain to shut out the din and recall the chirping songs of the weaverbirds, the haunting call-and-response barking of dogs in the dead of the night. I yearn to step out into the crisp air after a thunderstorm and behold a rainbow arched against the sky, when the rain capitulated on seeing the sun.

After standing and squatting for close to an hour, I realise I might be here all night. I decide to wait fifteen more minutes before going back to the reception for help. I'm so worried and angry I dare not even notice the hunger pangs rumbling noisily in my stomach.

A shrill scream pierces the air, above the mournful noises and barked orders. Then a man comes tearing through the room, his clothes on fire. In shock and terror, we watch him run around and around in circles, leaping over sleeping bodies, evading the guards who are pursuing him, shouting orders, trying in vain to throw a blanket over him. He rushes back toward the open door and throws himself into the arms of an officer approaching with a baton raised above his head. Together, they go crashing to the floor.

When the bedlam gives way to a shocked silence and the smoke clears, I make my way down the corridor back to the reception. Halfway through, I hear terrified screams and the sound of beatings and angry voices coming from a room marked 'Private'. I quicken my steps, avoiding eye contact with two armed guards patrolling the corridor. At the reception, the officers I had spoken to have been replaced by two new ones. One of them is tall and skinny, with sharp, inquisitive eyes that pore over you under bushy eyebrows. His partner is pudgy and thickset, small eyes buried in a no-nonsense face.

"New shift," says the pudgy man, in harsh, officious tones. His breath reeks of cigarettes.

With an effort, I manage to keep my voice calm and say, "Are there any messages, or any instructions for me?"

"Messages? Instructions? This is a police station, not a post office."

I tremble with indignation as I watch them laugh. The fat man's eyes disappear completely, the multiple chins rolling as though he's chewing on the laughter. I fight the urge to mouth an insult, even in a language they don't understand.

A moment later, I offer them my two remaining packets of cigarettes, explain my mission, and beg them to take me to the women's detention centre. It takes another ten minutes of negotiation before the skinny one agrees to take me there.

LianZhu Women's Detention Centre is located just behind the main block. I sign a visitors' book at the reception and we walk past a group of petitioners keeping quiet vigil in a corridor. The silence is only broken by the intermittent barked order behind closed doors. We stop at a guard post outside a door marked 'Interrogation: Waiting Room 2'.

The guard consults her records and confirms that Lai Ying is being held there.

"Your friend refuses to sign a repentance letter," says the guard, with a shrug.

"Repentance? She has done nothing wrong."

"It's not for you to say."

Dismissing my protestations with the wave of a gloved hand, she opens a hatch on the door and invites me to take a look inside. My heart pounds fast and furious. For the longest moment, I stare into the poorly lit room, unable to make out the silhouettes lying on the floor or seated on a bench. Eventually, with the benefit of the additional light from the hatch, I count seven figures. They all look old or middle-aged, haggard, dishevelled, and utterly despondent. I spot her seated on the floor, her head resting on her knees.

"Lai Ying!" I gasp, not loudly enough to be heard through the door, but I see her shift and look up, casting tired eyes across the room.

"Lai Ying!" I call out, in a shrill voice I barely recognise as my own. She sees me. Her jaw drops. She tries to rise to her feet, but there's no energy in her legs. She collapses to the ground. I start pounding on the door with my fists, screaming her name, insensible to the strong hands that lock my arms behind my back. I'm still screaming as the guards frogmarch me down the corridor.

A Good Student

FOR THREE DAYS, THEY WON'T let me see her. It's all in vain, no matter how earnestly I plead her case and petition both the police and their cousins in officialdom at the Campus Gestapo.

The police have warned me that I risk being arrested if I keep pestering them. The Chief says they're investigating my role in the 'renegade's shameful actions'. All this time, Lai Ying has been languishing at the LianZhu Women's Detention Centre. I've lost my appetite and no longer have the heart or patience for class. I've asked Diallo to tell Professor Sheng that I'm down with the flu, which is plausible enough as there's a bug going around this winter. When I'm not out looking for help, I sit in my room, gazing at the posters on the walls, trying to herd my thoughts into some coherent stream, yet only find myself more deeply mired in bewilderment.

In desperation, I seek out Lai Ying's friend Minnie to ask whether she has talked to Lai Ying's professor. Remembering not to disturb her afternoon nap, I wait at her hostel lobby in case she needs to go for an afternoon class. I wait for half an hour and when I can stand it no longer, I ask the security guard to call her.

"Where is she?" she hisses in my face as soon as she sees me. "What happened?"

"Some authorities," I mutter laconically, careful not to alarm her and get her even more agitated. "They'll release her as soon as they finish their enquiries."

"What enquiries? What is going on?"

Her eyes are glaring with unspoken accusations soaked through with mistrust. The anger I feel renders me mute, and I close my eyes for a few moments, hoping this nightmare will go away, hoping the terror that's tearing my insides will subside and fade away, like a mist, together with this girl who stands before me taunting me as though I were in league with the Campus Gestapo. But when I open my eyes, Minnie is still standing there waiting for me to answer her. What is there to tell her?

"Did you talk to her professor?"

She nods. "He's furious."

"Is he going to help?"

"How can he help when he doesn't even know what's happened?"

"He must have seen the report from the hospital, Minnie. Did he say anything about it?"

"Who am I to question him? You know what you've done. Why can't you do something?"

An intense loathing for her builds up in the pit of my stomach. I demand that she tell me how to find this professor. She hesitates. I insist. She gives me a name, and starts to warn me to be careful what I say and do. I ignore her and dash out of the lobby, pushing past two girls at the door, who scream in shock and fire a stream of coarse invectives at my retreating figure.

I stand before Professor Zhang Dunren, panting for breath, my hands trembling, cold sweat running down my back.

"It's all lies, professor," I repeat for the third time, my voice shaky with despair. "This hospital report was doctored because…because she's my friend. Someone told them…one of those people who masterminded the riots, I know, I heard. He told the doctor, when she was down with the flu, that…that she was friendly with a *hei gui*. That's all it is. Professor, some of these people hate us."

He waves me to a seat, glaring at me above his spectacles, as though I were a mad man speaking gibberish. Running a hand through his grey hair, he says, "You say Lai Ying is your friend?"

"Yes, professor," I reply with some hesitation.

"Mmh. You were friends before the riots earlier in the winter, or you just met?"

"We've been friends a long time, professor."

"She's a good student." He gazes out the window at the students walking through the rain. His voice is low, reflective, almost wistful, which makes my heart race with the fear that something terrible has already happened to Lai Ying. "Diligent, familiar with world affairs. Not the kind of person who is easily led astray."

I can bear the tension no more.

"Professor Zhang—"

"A man came to see me this morning," he announces, ignoring me. "An important official. We spoke at length. This has not been an easy matter. An illustrious student could ruin her life so effortlessly, so needlessly, by succumbing to the charms of a young man like yourself. To what end, I ask, this…this foolish pursuit of ephemeral pleasures and ethereal feelings? When I was your age, we were taught to be responsible adults. The future was in our hands. Not merely your own future, but the future of your people, your country, your party. You cannot imagine the strife and tribulations we endured, the sacrifices we learnt to make. The Japanese war, the Kuomintang running amuck across the country before being driven out. I was your age when this momentous event took place. 1949, the year we established a new nation, sowed the seeds for a new beginning." Pointing a shaky finger in my face, he hisses between his teeth, "The future. The future, young man, must never be toyed with. These troubles today, students fighting each other over trivialities, risking their lives, their future!"

Unable to face him, let alone make sense of what he's talking about, I keep my gaze trained on my shoes, which have worn unevenly on the soles. The office cowers in silence under the weight of the professor's unexpected tirade. I rub my sweaty palms surreptitiously against my jeans and after a few moments' hesitation, venture to break the silence.

"This man who came to see you, professor, what did he say will happen now?"

"You haven't listened to me, have you?"

"I heard every word, professor."

Shaking his head, as though he was dealing with a complete idiot, he says, "Young people today, so foolish, so unconcerned about the world beyond their immediate needs and selfish desires. You are lucky that we Chinese treasure our friendships. Even after all the trouble you've caused and continue to cause us. They told me about your history of messing with our girls, young man. Your record is not good. You do not and cannot fathom how much discussion has gone into this unfortunate affair. You will never know what interventions have been made, what sacrifices have been made for you. Perhaps it is better that way. Mystery serves as a lesson in wariness for the impetuous and impertinent."

"Professor, I don't understand…"

"She is a good student. A good student. We need her back in class. Hopefully she'll be in class tomorrow."

"She's being released today?"

"I have work to do now, young man. Be gone."

I'm about to plead with him to give me a little more time, to tell me a little more. But his head is already buried in a dog-eared brown tome. At the door, I turn around to thank him. He waves me away without looking up. I'm surprised he still wants to work. Most professors knock off straight after the afternoon lessons, which end at 4 p.m. It's already five.

Back at the hostel, I fetch Diallo and ask him to accompany me to the police station. I carry an extra winter jacket and woollen scarf. The guards invite us to wait in the Visitors' Lounge. I decline the offer and tell them we'll wait in the corridor just inside the main entrance. There is only a small group of petitioners this evening. Two hours later, one of the guards advises us to go home, saying no one is ever released after nightfall.

I return to the station on my own the following morning, with an extra jacket, sandwiches, and soft drinks. By lunchtime, Lai Ying has still not been released, and no one is willing to answer my questions. In a panic, it occurs to me that she might not even be here at all. Perhaps they've taken her away and this whole thing is just a charade. Would they lie to the professor? Who is he to them, anyway? Do they owe him any explanation? What did that official say to him? Did I read too much into the professor's enigmatic little speech? The questions and worries are engaged in a mad dance in my head, making me shiver and break into a cold sweat. To rein in the riotous thoughts in my mind and give my hands something to do, I decide to eat one of the sandwiches, but give up halfway through. Lai Ying is probably subsisting on the insipid fare of unwashed cold rice and vermin-ridden vegetables.

The wind howls and shrieks as though in pain, perhaps making its own petition at the People's Sanctuary for some unspecified grievance. The multiple layers of clothing I'm wearing are no match for the cold that treacherously works its way right to the bone.

To avoid attracting too much attention to myself, I move to a food stall across the street from where I can watch the police station, an action which I realise is as ineffectual as it is unnecessary. The police have by now become accustomed to seeing my stooped frame lounging listlessly amongst my fellow habitual, luckless petitioners.

At the food stall, the air is alive and homely with the smell of fish balls and steamed dumplings.

As I sit there sipping my hot Chinese tea and ignoring the vendor's incessant questions about where I come from and what I do, my thoughts drift to my family. School fees are due at the end of this month. I barely have enough to live on before the next disbursement. I close my eyes and rub my temples to heal the headache. It's a trick Lai Ying taught me. It always works for her. It has never worked for me, but I still do it whenever I have a headache. Right now, I feel I need to do it in order to invoke the memories of the happy times we've spent together, to forget the pain we've been through in recent weeks – in fact, way back since the riots.

I watch the police station all afternoon, confident I can't miss her. I've walked around the block and confirmed there is no other public entrance, all along fearing she might have exited through the front. The only time my view is momentarily blocked is when a bus or truck drives past, leaving a cloud of black smoke in its wake. Would that give her enough cover to leave without my noticing?

When it starts to get dark in the late afternoon, I trudge back into the station. The chief is not there. The duty officer says the Detention Centre has already closed for the day. He refuses to answer any more questions and tells me to try the following morning. Worn down by exhaustion and the numbing pain of frustration, I have no heart to press my case.

The following day at the crack of dawn, I'm back at the police station. By now, I barely notice the howling winds or the cold morning air that must be filtered through a scarf so it doesn't condemn you to a coughing fit and freeze your lungs.

The pudgy officer leans towards me. A sly but menacing smile spreads across his face. I recoil as his breath that reeks of cigarettes assaults my nose.

I start to explain that Lai Ying should have been released yesterday after the university's intervention.

"Please, tell me what is happening."

"You foreign friends, huh!" he mutters, the cruel smile reappearing on his face. "Living so well, while we toil and suffer. You think it is right?" I watch him distractedly, wondering what he expects me to say. He nudges his partner, the lanky, skinny man, and says, "Not right. What do you think, Comrade Yang?"

The thin man rolls his eyes under thick eyebrows and shrugs his shoulders, as though he couldn't care less. But then his face lights up and a cackling laugh emanates from his closed mouth, making him sound as though he's breaking wind. On hearing the muted giggles, the pudgy man succumbs to his own special brand of sightless, face-shivering giggles. Without warning, the mirth comes to an abrupt end, and the pudgy man declares, "It is fair for foreign friends to help host friends. Many things foreign friends can buy, easily; many things local friends can only dream of. How do you say you make your friends' dreams come true, *lao wai*?"

"What are you talking about?"

"Ai! *Lao wai,* you are a clever man." His eyes start to narrow again as his face breaks into a cunning grin. "You have education. You must understand the words even as they roll down my peasant tongue."

"Peasant?" I mutter into his face. "You know nothing about peasant life. You're a liar, you just want to cheat me. You—"

"We'll keep it simple," he yells back, the grin now an uncompromising scowl. "You have been working illegally, black man. You break our law, you make our job difficult—"

"Now wait just one minute. I have permission to work."

"We have seen no record. Perhaps the people's court can find one."

I sink onto the bench behind me, clutching my aching head, struggling in vain to block out the sarcastic laughter from my two tormentors. That night, I wake up in a cold sweat. In the nightmare, which remains vivid for hours afterwards, I'm confronted by a giant eagle that speaks Chinese and sounds exactly like Wang. It attacks me with a gigantic claw, towering over me, hissing fire and smoke through a twisted beak. Then, I realise I'm looking into a mirror and the giant eagle is in fact me. A mob from the anti-African riots appears from the shadows and chops off the claws and the beak and starts wrapping up the bird with a monster canopy made up of yuan and American dollar bills. It is at that point that I leap out of bed, choking and coughing, weighed down by a duvet, my heart thumping, a scream in my throat.

It takes me two days to find Kabinga. Although he has been back from Singapore for three days, he is hardly ever in his suite at the Embassy International. He listens in silence before chiding me for not having contacted him sooner. I'm in no mood to offer explanations. It's difficult enough approaching him for help, but the two policemen have left me no choice. And the longer this drags on, the more Lai Ying suffers. Kabinga agrees to meet them and hear their demands. He insists on meeting them by himself.

"Be careful," I warn him. "They could be dangerous. Especially the fat one. Watch out for him."

"They're just corrupt, Eggman," he says, laughing it away. "They don't know how to be dangerous. If they tried anything funny, they could get into a lot of trouble with their bosses. I'll personally see to it."

"What do you think they want?"

"Nothing I can't handle. I know their type, man. Relax, okay?"

"Let me know what it costs, all right? I'll do whatever it takes to cover it, Chin Chin."

"Let me advise you, Eggman," he says, holding me by the shoulders as if to make sure the message sinks in. "Get off your arse and make some money, my friend. Be independent, and none of these people will trouble you. Take it from me."

I free myself and nod my agreement so as to be rid of him. But inside, I'm seething with anger for allowing myself to fall into this trap, for my complete and utter inability to rescue Lai Ying from this hell that I threw her into, for foolishly failing to capitalise on the White Card when I had a chance. There's talk that the system will soon change. I try to console myself with the thought that my time will come. The eagle doesn't just spring at the slightest false sign. He bides his time.

But the bitterness won't leave me.

Kabinga comes to the hostel to see me the following evening.

"It's all settled," he announces, with a knowing grin.

"They'll let her go? When? How soon?"

"Any day now, Eggman. Any day."

When I ask him how much I owe him, he says I've done him a favour already, introducing him to a new set of cops.

"Excellent contacts, Eggman," he whispers, conspiratorially. "You have cops eating out of your hands, my man. No one can touch you."

The following day as I walk into my hostel lobby, the security guard hands me a note. It's a simple, standard, brief phone message. I read it quickly, my heart racing. *I'm back. Lai Ying. Time: 5.15 p.m.* No number provided. I know the number of her hostel by heart. The world around me freezes. There is neither a thought on my mind nor a sound my ears can identify. The voices of people walking past me are like textures of sound sweeping dreamlike past me. The haunting look of Lai Ying collapsing in a heap on the ground the last time I set eyes on her flashes through my mind. With an effort akin to fighting the paralysis that sometimes accompanies a nightmare, I rub my eyes, shake my head and leap back into the biting cold outside.

I head straight to Lai Ying's hostel, taking long, brisk steps across the campus, tearing my way through the fog, and only vaguely conscious of the flying horses hurtling about.

I wait in the lobby, pacing up and down, unable to stand still, the way I recall waiting for my high school results. My palms are sweaty, my throat parched, and only now does it dawn on me how little I've eaten these last two weeks. I force myself to sit on the sofa we've both sat on so many times before, letting the weight of the recent events lift like a vapour. I realise with a sigh of relief how badly it might have ended. Lai Ying could have been banished to some village in the middle of nowhere for re-education, and I could have been on a flight to Zim, taking nothing back with me after three years in China except a language I'll never use there.

Lai Ying comes down ten minutes after I send for her. She's a different person, emaciated, haggard, like the petitioners at the People's Sanctuary. A lump builds in my throat. I rise to greet her, unsure I'll find my voice. Her hair falls across her face like a veil. She makes no effort to push it back as she takes a seat disconsolately next to where I'm standing. I freeze, suddenly unsure what to expect. Is she avoiding facing me? I cast a glance across the half-empty lobby before settling down beside her, willing her to speak, to tell me they didn't hurt her, that's she's glad it's all over, to say how delighted she is to see me.

"Leave me alone, Dan," she mutters through gritted teeth, as if she was telling off a molester.

I recoil at the ferocity of her tone. God, what did they do to her? I reach out to touch her elbow, ignoring the curious stares and the silence that descends on the room like the fog outside. Her face is still turned away from me.

"Lai Ying, what—"

"I don't want to see you again, Dan."

Throwing caution to the wind, I hold her shoulder and force her to face me. She frees herself and buries her face in her hands, her pleas for me to leave her alone getting lost in the sobs that rock her weak body. The urge burns in me to hold her, to steady her, to assure her everything will be all right from now on.

"It is time for you to leave!"

I look up and see two guards standing like oak trees in front of me. In that instant, Lai Ying springs to her feet and starts to walk away. Pushing my way past the surprised guards, I rush ahead of her and block her way.

"Leave me alone, Dan."

"No, not now, Lai Ying. Not this time!"

The guards run towards me, drawing their truncheons and blowing their whistles. I don't know where the courage comes from, but I hold out a hand and order them to stand back. Unaccustomed to being challenged, they freeze, and watch me as though I'm a wild animal about to charge. Keeping my eyes on Lai Ying, my mind focused only on placating her, I drop to my knees and hold my arms out to her. The frustrations of the last few weeks explode inside me like a volcano. My lips tremble. My whole body is shaking. Hot tears roll down my face. All I want is for this pain to go. All I desire is to go back to how things were before, with Lai Ying deep in my heart. She can't leave. This cannot be the end, not after everything we've been through. Not this way. Not here.

"Get up, Dan, please..."

"We can't let them do this to us, Lai Ying."

"Dan, please...don't do this!"

"What about us, Lai Ying? What about our love?"

She leans forward, and tries to raise me by my arms. My knees are stuck to the cold concrete. Nothing can raise me and lead me away, unless I'm reunited with Lai Ying. Slowly, she sinks to the floor before me, still holding my arms. The steely hardness in her eyes gives way to a stream of tears. I hold her tight. Her sobs rock her emaciated body helplessly, her cries dying in my shoulder. After what seems like an eternity, she goes quiet. The storm in me hasn't subsided.

"Lai Ying, it will be all right," I whisper. "Go take a rest and we'll talk tomorrow. It will be fine, I promise you. I love you, Lai Ying."

Without looking at me, she takes a deep breath, rises to her feet, and walks rapidly to the staircase. I'm still on my knees, unable to find the strength to rise, blinded by my tears. While still fighting the daze that has overcome me, I feel strong arms raising me to my feet. The two guards lead me to the door, in slow, deliberate steps, as though I had fallen off my flying horse and broken both ankles. Feeling completely mortified, I whisper my thanks and stumble into the darkness outside.

It is a month before she talks to me. I wait, knowing she won't be rushed. She needs to work this out by herself and come back to me when she's ready. My friends urge me to put my foot down, claim her back or forget her. I seek solace in my much-neglected work. Lai Ying takes longer to rediscover her old cheerfulness. The abortion took a part of her away with it. We never talk about it, but its unspoken presence looms above us, reminding us that we had a chance to put it behind us by breaking free of each other. As long as we remain together, everything that has happened since the riots will remain like a scar on our relationship. The smile is still there, but it is tinged with a lingering wariness, as though she's afraid to cause offense, or attract undue attention. One day, I ask her about Minnie. It's one of the things I meant to ask when I was scuttling around the city trying to locate her and getting nothing but suspicion and loathing from Minnie.

"Does she know now?" I ask, holding her hand. We're in my room, sitting on my bed, side by side. The rules on visitors have gradually died away. Lai Ying rubs my hand, then traces lines around my fingers. I hold her close, her head on my shoulder.

"Yes," she whispers, "and she's not happy."

"I can imagine. Still friends?"

She shrugs her shoulders. It's hard having to keep something like that from a friend, bottling it up because it is too dangerous to talk to anyone. I only told Diallo, Julius, and eventually, Kabinga. Repercussions for her would be unimaginable. She tells me about their falling out, how she tried to make Minnie understand. I listen and comfort her. But words desert me when she tells me Minnie was a friend of Han Wei's and knew about Yi Guan's activities. Questions crowd my mind like bats in a cave, flying nowhere, as blind as the darkest night. Minnie's friendship with my classmate and former shower comrade Han Wei is certainly a surprise, but the thing I can't get my head around is whether Minnie knew something, anything at all, that suggested Yi Guan was a dangerous quark. And yet, Lai Ying was determined to go through with it. How safe is anyone else? They're all just students.

"She says she could have helped me," says Lai Ying with a chuckle. "But how? What could she have done? We'll find our friendship again. It will take time. Minnie knows I had to deal with this by myself. If word got out, about you, you know…"

I wrap my arms around her, as the words trail away. It is better to leave it unsaid.

"Dan, everything changed. When I sat in that cell, waiting to know my fate, do you know what I was thinking of?" I shake my head. "My father, Dan."

I listen with bated breath. The troubles of her family during the Cultural Revolution have always been a taboo topic, sometimes alluded to, but never fully explored.

"When they took him away, the abuse, Dan." Her tremulous voice speaks at once of pain and strength. "The utter savagery, and all because he fell on the wrong side of the ideology. I thought about the riots, too. You and your friends, falling on the wrong side of race politics. I thought of the days you spent at the barracks. I felt united with you in a strange way, as though I was shaken by your fears. It was like I was dreaming your nightmares, even as the horrors of my father's experience haunted me day and night. I cried until I had no more tears. And now I know nothing will shake me again. My father never spoke to us about the troubles. We were left to fill in the details from snatches of conversation. The people who betrayed us, people who worked with my father, worked for him, people he fed and clothed, people he called friends. Is it possible to trust again, Dan? Is it possible to dream of a good life? And those who live by making money and doing business, can they truly be sincere, if they're prone to turn against you so easily?"

I start to respond, to assure her that not everyone is like that, that our lives and our world can only get better now. She listens with a gentle, indulgent smile.

"Dan, can you understand why I worry about people like Wang? Can you? You and your friends faced the wrath of confused young people. Can you imagine what my father and millions of others endured? How would you survive? How would we cope?"

Looking into her eyes, I know we shall never move this boulder aside. The best we can do is climb over it and find our way to the other side, or find a way to skirt around it.

We hold each other tight. Then she sits astride me and begins to peel her clothes off. This is the first time she has ever initiated sex. When I start to unbuckle my belt, she stops me and does it herself. She lowers herself onto me. For a full minute, she doesn't move, then she begins a circular grinding movement, her arms clasped around my shoulders, her moans reverberating across the room, her frantic breaths searing my neck and shoulder. She's completely in charge, right up to the moment when she lifts herself clear and I explode against her soft belly.

From the Sidelines

SPRING BRINGS SOME FAR-FETCHED RUMOURS. A student revolution is brewing in Beijing. It all sounds too bizarre to trouble our battle-fatigued minds. In any case, the sense of solidarity we enjoy as outsiders was strengthened after the riots four months ago.

Beijing is too far away to worry about, and it's not clear anyway what is going on there. We're hearing about students boycotting classes, holding demonstrations, but no one knows for certain what their grievances are. Mostly unconfirmed reports, and whatever bits of patchy news we can get from talking to embassy staff or from people like Kabinga, who have access to news on their travels. Living in China is like being locked up in a dark chamber, unable to see your way through the blanket of ignorance.

Here in Nanjing, local students have started to hold the occasional demonstration to show solidarity with their brethren in the capital, boycotting classes, filling walls with graffiti denouncing their leaders, holding rallies at Democracy Lake.

For the first time ever, the lake is finally living up to its name. We had always believed that young Chinese were humble, obedient, and fearful of authority. With the December riots, something changed them. Wherever they got the courage to confront us, I'll never know, but that courage has remained with them. You see it in the confident, sneering looks, the haughty spring in their steps.

Riots and demonstrations are commonplace in African universities. Here, they are out of place, at least to us foreigners. It's as if the students are experimenting with some little freedom they've finally realised they always had but never savoured. It's a little bit like their earlier cautious forays into Wang's Den. After a while, they realise it's all right to do the things they previously associated with ill-mannered foreign devils.

By the summer, tensions between local and African students have risen again. Everyone expects a repeat of the winter riots. But there's a difference. When

African students gather to drink and talk politics, there's a feeling that we're better equipped psychologically to defend ourselves and fight back if it came to that. They're not going to catch us unawares. We've learned our lesson.

The guys think we should organise ourselves into vigilante groups. There is a lot of talk and planning. But we don't even get a chance.

The news comes in the early hours, in the middle of the summer, catching everyone by surprise. Troops opened fire on students. Military tanks rolled over them. The streets of Beijing are filled with blood. The news spreads quickly, like a bushfire. There is nothing on TV or on the radio. All we're getting are snatches of rumours that rise like flames spurred by a burst of wind, before giving way to a new set of reports, claims, and accusations. The local students pour into the streets, waving placards resurrected from the winter skirmishes. We watch from our windows as they wave clenched fists, shouting anti-government slogans, demanding justice, truth, and democracy. We shake our heads with a mixture of disbelief and envy, thinking how liberating it would be to chant those slogans till our throats are sore, how invigorating it would be to demand our rights with such vehemence.

But this is a cause we can only watch from a distance, which we do for several days as the drama on Tiananmen Square unfolds. Much as we recoil with horror at the massacre in the capital, this can never be our war. We can only watch from the sidelines.

I learn of the locals' views from Lai Ying, who says she has never seen the city, or the country for that matter, so charged.

"What are the students planning to do?" I ask.

"There's nothing anyone can do." Her voice is filled with cold despair. "It's like a hammer has come down on the final nail, Dan. It's all over."

"Do you think the government would have allowed any changes?"

"You see, in China, it's all right to vent our frustrations against outsiders, like in the riots last winter. But when it comes to our own problems, our own leaders, it's a no-no. Life will get even harder for anyone who dares talk democracy and all that kind of nonsense. I just want to finish my degree and start working, Dan."

The sense of urgency in her voice makes me start. Though the troubles haven't touched her directly, they have the same effect on her as the riots did on me. We need to finish our studies and move away from here. But where shall we go? Where will we be safe together?

As troops begin to patrol the streets, the looming revolt fizzles away. The bravado amongst the local students gives way to shock and disbelief, and a chilly, funereal silence hangs over the city long into the hot and humid summer. The enormity of the massacre spares no one, not even the black ghosts, who assemble every night at Wang's Den to analyse the incident, and who, for the first time, find themselves in the unfamiliar role of merely being spectators to an act of violence.

*

The party at Wang's Den, grounds to a halt in the most unexpected way in my final year, three years after Wang opened the doors to a summer of free drinks. I walk into the lobby of our hostel one freezing winter evening and find Kabinga signing up for a room. I barely recognise him. He looks shrivelled up, like a cloth that has been washed and allowed to dry without a proper wringing. He hasn't shaved for days, and the three-piece suit he's wearing sits uncomfortably on his emaciated frame. He says very little as I help him drag two suitcases up one floor to his new room. Sitting heavily on the single bed, he extracts a leather cigar case from a briefcase and, after a couple of deep drags, breaks into a grin, shakes his head, and declares, "They think I'm down. Maybe I am, but, my friend, I'll tell you this, I might be down, but I'm not out. Bastards!"

"What happened to you?"

"Don't worry, Eggman, it will be fine." He slaps me on the shoulder, as if I'm the one who needs comforting. "What we've got to do is think ahead small-small, okay? They've won this battle—"

"Who? What's happened?"

"I said relax, my man, okay? Everything's gonna be just fine." He looks at me with such an intense look of pity I can't help wondering what bizarre calamity has befallen me.

"Whatever you say, Chin Chin," I say, shrugging with resignation.

"Like I said, they've won this round, but they've no idea whom they're messing with. First things first, man. I need to get back to school, to regain student status. It's going to need some work, but the first thing is to talk to Professor Sheng."

I nod my head and say nothing. If Kabinga wants to go back to school after a three-year unexplained absence, things must be dire. If his contacts can no longer help him, he'll need a miracle, and a pretty damn good explanation for Professor Sheng. The rest of us are graduating this year. He dare not see Professor Sheng himself, so I offer to do the honours, armed with two bottles of maotai, the local spirit, and three cartons of cigarettes, courtesy of Kabinga's dwindling funds.

Professor Sheng accepts the gifts but is livid when he learns whom they're from.

"That boy again!" he exclaims with sheer horror. "Do you know what shame that boy has put me through?"

Not wanting to bring his wrath upon my own head, I excuse myself quickly, saying that Kabinga is waiting outside but has a very bad flu and is afraid to transmit the virus, but will present himself as soon as he's feeling better. The professor literally throws me out of his office. It takes one more visit from me and two from Kabinga with a few more placatory gifts before Kabinga is allowed back on the course.

The gifts are supposed to give the professor face, which we presume he lost when Kabinga walked out on his course. To thank me for lying for him, Kabinga promises to take Lai Ying and I on a trip to Hainan Island. But it's obvious he has no money, so I just smile and nod my head.

On my second visit, I vouch for Kabinga that family problems had forced him to abandon his studies, and he has been too embarrassed to come forward for help. This time, the professor doesn't say much. There's something ominous about the pained look on his face, the deep furrows on his forehead, the pockmarks on his cheeks that are beginning to turn black. Recalling the way he was manhandled by the Campus Gestapo, I avoid looking him in the eye. It's only when I'm leaving that it hits me. It was Kabinga he bailed out. That's why he was being punished. Did Diallo know something? Was that why he kept goading Kabinga that evening at Wang's noodle shop? When I ask Diallo, he says he can't be bothered about Chinese history anymore.

Meanwhile, Kabinga is still not disclosing the details of his woes. He just explains it in vague terms about a deal gone sour. The place is rife with rumours, but the most plausible explanation is that he got conned out of his fortune, then he couldn't pay his hotel apartment bill, and they threw him out. Julius claims he's been talking to Chinese business people and has discovered that Kabinga lost US$ 80,000, his savings after four years of mind-boggling deals and a lavish lifestyle. The theory goes that he was conned by a local who promised to help him smuggle the money out of the country.

Kabinga pointedly refuses to show his face at Wang's Den, which leads many to conclude Wang had a hand in his woes. Whenever we're out for a drink, invariably at the new, little, trendy bars that have sprung up in recent months a block down the road, he talks of getting a lawyer and suing someone, but never says who this someone is. But we know he's just venting his anger and frustration. He would have a hard time explaining to a court how he came by so much money.

A jogger finds him lying unconscious on the snow in Ngong Yuen Park, beaten up and left for dead. He spends two months in hospital. Shortly after that, he disappears, without saying goodbye to anyone. One hot evening in May, he's having a quiet drink in the hostel lobby with Diallo and I. He still has bandages across his forehead and on his legs. The next morning, he's nowhere to be seen. No one knows where he's gone to. Some say he has transferred to a university in Xiamen. Others claim he's gone to run a student bar in Nanning. The White Card days are long gone.

*

Wang's Den is deserted, soulless, devoid of atmosphere. Some former regulars have told me to my face that I'm selling out by continuing to work for Wang after what he's supposed to have done to Kabinga. I never felt the need to publicise Lai Ying's problems, and hardly anyone knows I had to work for Wang for two months for free to pay back what I owed him. In any case, no one knows for a fact what really happened to Kabinga, who remained noncommittal right up to the end, when he left town.

One particularly quiet evening, Wang calls me to the small office at the back of the bar.

"Eggman," he says. "You've been a good manager. I thank you for your hard work. But as you know, things have changed. We've had some very good years, but without customers, we're finished. We'll close for some time while I plan the future."

I nod and look straight into his eyes. Could he have done that thing to Kabinga? Was this suave, charming, friendly guy capable of ordering a violent robbery or a murder? He had the opportunity. Over the years, he has helped many of us smuggle US dollars out of the country through a contact in Hong Kong.

With Kabinga's money, he's set for life, if indeed he has taken it. My professor earns about 150 yuan a month. Eighty American big ones would keep him going several hundred years.

Wang's face is a blank mask, that expressionless, placid look the Chinese wear so effortlessly. Not a blink, twitch, not even a furrowed brow. Nothing in his manner suggests he can't wait to get out of town and enjoy his fortune.

"How long, this closure?" I ask.

"Here's your money, Eggman," he says, shrugging. "You can leave early tonight. I'll manage. It's not too busy." It hasn't been busy for months.

"When you reopen, call me, okay?"

I say that just to give him face. I'm waiting for the graduation ceremony. Then it's goodbye Nanjing. Wang nods, avoiding my eyes.

A week later, Wang's Den closes its doors. Wang disappears, just like he did before. But this time, something tells us we've seen the last of him.

*

The graduation ceremony delivers an ebullient atmosphere that we have barely savoured for months, one that peels away the layers of doom and gloom. The whole experience is like a dream. Gone are the dirty jeans, trainers, and sweatshirts, replaced by blazers and ties, gleaming leather shoes, and screaming red academic gowns. Looking at the guys, I didn't even know some of them possessed such fine clothes. Diallo has even shaven off his protest beard for the occasion. When I ask him why, he says, "*Mon ami*, much as I hate what happened, I don't want to remember the negative."

He surprises me by leading me to our old shower comrades, Han Wei and Lai Guiguo, so we can have a picture taken by our unofficial photographer, Julius. Han Wei dons his trademark whistle smile and we all shake hands, like the old friends we used to be.

When Lai Ying and I have our photograph taken next to the serene Democracy Lake, I hold both her hands and draw her close to me, so close I can almost feel her heaving chest, but not close enough for a proper cuddle. Julius affects a cough to warn me of possible danger, but on realising that nothing will snatch this moment from us, not even the once dreaded Campus Gestapo, he quickly takes the picture and demands another pose.

For the two hours it takes to assemble everyone in the People's Hall of Learning, the speeches by the university president, party bosses, and school deans, the lengthy processions as hundreds of graduands are inducted into the community of elite scholars, it is almost as if the recent troubles had never occurred. When Professor Sheng calls out my name and I walk over to shake the seated president's hand and receive my certificate, all the emotions come flooding back: the inscrutable eagle, the missed White Card opportunities, Lai Ying in a TV cardboard box, the riots, the heady nights at Wang's Den. How it had seemed as though the journey would never end. I wipe away the tears and stumble back to my seat. The parties last all night, right across the entire campus. We're all consumed by the carefree exuberance of celebrating success, while wobbling drunkenly on the threshold of a new beginning.

I've no idea where I'll end up. After the riots, I've longed to leave China, but this is now proving difficult. Some of us have decided to stay and find jobs in cities like Shanghai and Guangzhou. Hardly anyone chooses to stay and work in Nanjing. The memories are too bitter. Lai Ying already has a job offer in Shanghai. I can't bear to be apart from her. To be together, I may have to remain in China. We've talked about going abroad. Europe, America. She's not keen on returning to Canada. She says it's too cold and too quiet. I'm not ready to return to Zimbabwe, with empty pockets, and she's not keen to move there either. What would she do there?

I'm prepared to move to Shanghai, but only for a while, so we can work through our options. But Lai Ying has other ideas. Like everyone else, she believes the rumour that Wang has gone to Shanghai. She says that's the only city someone with money would head to. And for that reason, she doesn't want me to go there.

"Dan, you need to make a clean break from him and all that he stands for," she warns me. "If you go to Shanghai and end up meeting again, I know exactly what will happen. I can't accept it."

She persuades me to go to Hong Kong, or Xianggang, as the Chinese call it. She believes foreigners are more welcome in the British colony. She'll go to Shanghai to gain proper experience at the bank for a few months and join me later. It's futile to argue with her when she's this determined. Xianggang sounds like a good compromise. Britain will be handing it back to China in exactly six years. By then, I figure, we'll have moved on. Where to, I've no idea. In the meantime, it will offer me the chances Nanjing didn't. Going by all the things

Kabinga and the White Card brigade said about Hong Kong, I'm confident of that.

Father expects me back in Ndambu village by the end of the year. There is talk that the workers will form a cooperative to buy Walter's farm. Father says he's counting on my knowledge to drive the new venture. I've tried to explain that it's not possible. My degree is not in agriculture. The best I can do to support his dream, is work hard and send him some money for this cooperative. He insists that's not enough. We're not getting anywhere. So I've stopped writing.

Part 2

Kowloon Promenade

HONG KONG IS NOTHING LIKE I expected. Skyscrapers reach to the sky like a forest of glass and concrete structures, casting dark shadows on the traffic-clogged roads that snake their way around unending rows of shops and restaurants. Grand glass and concrete structures preside over decrepit old buildings, with aircon discharge units lurking above windows.

In the glittering malls, the attendants look at you with scorn and ask you not to touch anything if you're not buying. I've learned to avoid them after spending an hour trying out shirts, not finding anything I liked, and being shouted out of a shop by a livid attendant who accused me of wasting her time.

Thousands of pedestrians jostle for space on the narrow pavements. After a while, I begin to miss the wide, empty roads of Nanjing. I can't get used to the excesses of this city: the noise, the congestion on the pavements, overcrowded shops and malls with no space to spare for all the goods on sale. And the language here is different, too. People don't understand when I ask directions in Putonghua. They glare at me, shake their heads, and melt into the crowds. Cantonese sounds hurried and angry, as if they're having arguments.

Lai Ying and I speak on the phone once a week. I don't know how long I can withstand this self-imposed exile. My friends and I exchange postcards sometimes. Keeping in touch while struggling to make sense of a new life and earn a living takes a lot of effort. The more I hear about the new opportunities in cities like Guangzhou, the more I question my decision to come here.

The engineering and construction company I work for is in Tsim Sha Tsui, the busy shopping, business, and tourist heart of Kowloon. But I spend a lot of time on site, mostly in the new towns like Shatin and Tsuen Wan, where our residential projects are mushrooming. Half the staff are expatriate British, the rest are local. The hours are long, the pressure intense. I've been here almost three months now. It took me two months to find this job. The English guys say that's too long. They don't need papers. As Hong Kong is a British colony, they fly into town and bag a job within a week. The construction industry is in boom like never before, like a bonanza. They can't get enough qualified people, or even semi-skilled construction workers.

I've taken a room in Chungking Mansions, the inappropriately named block of affordable inns and flats on Nathan Road. I share a room with three British student backpackers, who tell me they've taken a year out 'to do Asia'. They say they can't get enough of the night scene in Hong Kong and have taken jobs waiting in pubs while they decide where to go next. Bangkok, Manila, Tokyo. I can't afford a room to myself and the money I brought with me is running out. In the three months I've been here, I've not seen any of this nightlife my roommates rave about. I leave work around 8 p.m., sometimes as late as 10 p.m. I usually eat at one of the cramped Indian restaurants in my building, before taking the lift or walking up to the motel on the fourth floor.

As soon as you step into the grimy lobby, you're accosted by a dozen touts, mostly Indian or Pakistani, offering you accommodation. *Guest house*! *Guest house*! *China visa*! *Special price, only for you. No room reservation*? *No problem. I arrange for you*. Budget travellers stand in the long queues for the lifts, tugging oversized suitcases, scanning the China visa and travel package signs on the walls.

Traders push bales of garments and boxes probably full of toys and electronic equipment. Others mill around the forex bureaus, studying the exchange rates prominently displayed on LCD monitors.

A lot of the traders are African or South Asian-looking. They have a perpetual weary look, exhausted as much by the effort of negotiating prices as the much bigger challenge of moving their wares about, on the floor, on their backs, or on their heads, in the case of the tall African women, who trudge about, looking dignified, expressionless, gallantly concealing whatever frustrations they must have endured that day.

The traders truly brighten up this place with their colourful clothes, multiple languages, unrestrained laughter, and smells of sweat, strong deodorants, and ladies' perfumes, which all compete with the smells of spicy food at the food kiosks.

Sometimes, I take long walks along the waterfront, to admire the views of Victoria Harbour and to postpone the return to the cramped shared room with its smells of cigarettes and unwashed clothes. Watching couples walk hand in hand on the waterfront only intensifies my loneliness. I yearn for Lai Ying to come here, where we can hold hands and not give a damn who sees us. We'll sit on a bench and watch the kaleidoscopic lights of Hong Kong Island and let the cool breeze caress our faces. Then we'll kiss, eyes closed, ears hearing only the waves crashing against the embankment.

I take my wallet out to console myself with her photograph. I remember the way I used to trace lines up the arched eyebrows, around the tip of her small pointed nose, and watch the lips come alive with a smile. I place a kiss on the photograph and, after replacing it in the wallet, count the last remaining notes. Forty Hong Kong dollars. Two hundred in my back pocket. A travel agent in my building says he can get me an air ticket with that. But I need to shop around. I walk down the MTR station on Cameron Road to get the train to Mong Kok. This area is always crowded, with people jostling to get through the narrow entrance, clogging up the whole pavement. You can barely breathe. My mind is so wrapped up in the thought of seeing Lai Ying this Christmas that I don't pay heed to the shifty, tattooed individuals pushing up against everyone. It is only when I approach a travel agent that I realise my back pocket is empty. I can't believe I could be so stupid! You hear the warnings all the time. Avoid crowded places, watch out for pickpockets. Why did I bother coming to this wretched Mong Kok? In the end, it has cost me a whole two hundred dollars, for nothing, and the Chungking agent turns out to be cheaper.

The following day, I ask my boss for an advance. I don't let on how desperate my situation is. He says I'll become eligible for staff loans after my three-month probation. If the landlord doesn't give me credit, I don't know what I'll do.

On Friday morning, I've no choice but to vacate the room. I tell my roommates I'll be spending the weekend with friends in Shenzhen. They agree to watch my two suitcases, which contain all my worldly possessions. I pack an extra jacket with me in a small travelling bag, along with toiletries and a change of clothes. At work, I can't find my concentration. I've no idea where I'll spend the weekend. I'm in no hurry to leave the office. I watch with envy as my colleagues leave one by one, to their warm, cosy homes. When my boss asks me what I'm doing over the weekend, I tell him I'll be hunting for a flat.

I'm the last to leave, at 10 p.m. My feet steer me down Nathan Road, toward the only residence they know. But there is nothing for me there. I turn left, into Mody Road and walk towards East Tsim Sha Tsui. I walk with measured steps, watching the wares on display in shops that are still open. Briefcases and suitcases, clothes, golf equipment. Showcased in one general store are oriental ornaments, watches, cameras, and an assortment of plastic sex toys in colourful boxes, emblazoned with explicit photographs of genitalia, alongside cigarette packets and shiny, potbellied Buddhas. The middle-aged woman behind the counter glances at me and quickly returns to her bowl of noodles. I sit on a bench by a water fountain in the open square and take in the nightlife buzzing around me. The smell of steamed fish balls from the open-air food stalls wafts through the air, reminding me that I should eat something. I can't keep putting it off. A queue snakes its way around a Japanese teppanyaki restaurant, where a sign on the wall advertises a 'special deal' of $70 plus one drink. The twenty dollars in my wallet will have to feed me all weekend.

Young men with gelled hair and girls in miniskirts and high heels swagger across the square, laughing with abandon as they seek out the pubs and karaoke parlours. A slim, long-haired woman in high-heeled boots struts past me in languorous, rhythmic slow motion, chewing gum. The stirring in my loins fires my imagination. What would it be like with a true professional? Would she take charge, pin you down on the bed, throw her hair back and launch into a gentle grinding motion? Would she spit out her gum or keep chewing, with that seductive pout? I would reach out from underneath her, hold the pear-shaped breasts, wrap my hands around the tiny waist.

Steady on, Eggman! In frustration, I walk to the nearest food stall and buy a box of siu mei and a can of Carlsberg. I have twelve dollars left.

I spend three nights on the waterfront, sleeping on a bench, being lulled to sleep by the sounds of waves crashing on the embankment. The promenade becomes quieter into the small hours, as lovers leave for the comfort and safety of their beds or the urgency of hourly rooms, and the only people about are elderly men, who drape themselves in blankets and sleep with the tranquillity of well-fed babies. I lie on my bench for a long time, wrapped in several layers, just like we did in the Nanjing winters. I count the stars and ruminate on my years in Asia. My arrival into foggy Beijing one autumn evening and the nightlong train journey to Nanjing, the food you couldn't get used to. How I would give anything for a bowl of tofu and rice right now! Just when I thought my time had come to sample the good life, the fruit of my sweat, with a job at last, this is what it has come to.

Late into the night, I try to persuade myself that this is a temporary setback. The fish that got away, slipped through the eagle's claws. Just three nights here. After all, I am going to be paid on Monday. I will serve this period of purgatory for some unknown crime and return to a well-deserved soft, warm bed in Chungking Mansions. And after saving for a few months, I'll rent a flat and wait for my lovely girlfriend to come home. But the weight of failure doesn't lift, even when I drift in and out of nightmares, unable to adjust to the hardness of the narrow bench, until I wake to songs of seagulls and pigeons. I rub the sleep off my eyes and see, gazing down at me, the angelic smiling face of a teenage girl. She greets me in English and then reaches into a bag slung on her shoulder. I close my eyes, thinking she's going to hand me a leaflet for some beer promotion, an invitation to a meditation group or tai chi class.

"Sir, our charity gives breakfast to homeless people," she says in a sweet voice.

And I know, at that moment, that my humiliation is complete, irreversible. The eagle has fallen from his perch on the gum tree, reduced to clawing the earth for handouts. But even as I fight the tears and tuck into the angel's fried noodles, I know the eagle will soar, yet. He has no choice.

Chacha

FATHER STILL TALKS ABOUT A cooperative. But after all these years, nothing has materialised – not the cooperative, not the farm – for he still works for Brian Walter. And I've heard nothing to suggest that the Walters are selling.

I have my doubts about the whole thing. If Brian Walter sold, would he sell to his farm hands, who don't have the money to run the farm, or to some rich businessman? When I put this question to Father, he says he expects me to play an important role in running the affairs of the farm. He understands that I'm not the expert in agricultural engineering he would have wanted, for which I'm grateful. But that hasn't made him give up on me.

Now he says all I have to do is come up with money to help this venture. That's the hard part. Everything is expensive here, compared to China. The rent alone takes a quarter of my pay. If it weren't for the generous Lunar New Year bonuses, I would never save anything.

After moving out of Chung King mansions, I rent a two-bedroom flat in Sheung Wan, on Hong Kong Island. When I first walk in, it feels like a cage. But it is all I can afford. I am afraid Lai Ying will hate it. It comes furnished. But when Lai Ying finally comes, she says the sofa is too old, and she hates the brown colour. The mattress is too soft. It too has to go. The landlord isn't too pleased about all these unexpected expenditures. Lai Ying stands her ground and threatens to withhold the rent. I'm impressed. I didn't know you could do that.

With Lai Ying by my side, my life feels complete. It is all I have always wanted. At first, it feels strange holding hands in public. I have to remind myself that we're not being watched and will certainly not be arrested and thrown into some People's Sanctuary. Lai Ying gets a sales and marketing job in a bank and, within a year, we're both earning decent salaries, sampling the dining delights Hong Kong has to offer. On weekends, we go hiking, discovering mountains that so remind you of China but are much more readily accessible.

I have stopped listening to my friends' exhortations to return to China. From what I tell them about Hong Kong, they can see they are the ones who need to travel. Diallo in particular has started making inquiries. A year after I arrive here, he takes the plunge, and it does wonders for our social life. We spend hours most Fridays catching up late into the night, discovering the popular drinking dens of Wanchai and Lan Kwai Fong, meeting people from all sorts of countries, who have also come here to chase their dreams.

One day, as Lai Ying and I are walking along a family trail on the Peak, admiring the Indian rubber trees, whose multiple roots and branches form a canopy across the path, I ask Lai Ying how she would feel about living with me for the rest of our lives.

"Are you asking me to marry you?" she says, after a pause.

"Yes, Lai Ying, I am asking you to marry me."

"*Ban dan*," she whispers, over and over again. She hasn't called me 'my silly egg' for ages. "I thought you would never ask." We embrace and kiss, oblivious of fellow hikers. The thought of getting married fills me with a mixture of elation and trepidation, but nothing can stop this from happening. I ask Lai Ying if she's truly ready.

"I should ask *you* if you're ready to be a father," she says, thoughtfully.

"Of course, when the time comes." She's still looking me straight in the eye. Then it hits me. "You mean…? Lai Ying, are you saying…?"

"*Ban dan*, a father who can't find words when he most needs them."

Oh my God! I don't know whether to laugh or cry.

"I'll know for certain soon."

When I inform my family I'm going to marry a Chinese girl, Father writes back to say, "Does that mean you're not coming back?"

If that's his only problem, then it's like I've been let off the hook. There's no word from Mother. Not right away. Father says she consulted the traditional healer and isn't speaking to anyone. I don't like the sound of it and can't bring myself to tell Lai Ying. David, my brother, says he can't understand why I want to marry an Asian woman. Aren't there any African girls in China? I inform him that in all the years I spent there, I probably met only about half a dozen. Maybe African girls don't like studying in China. The few I knew, preferred to date people at the embassies. David and my cousin Chip offer to find me a 'suitable' local girl. I tell them that's not a good idea, and omit to say we're a little pressed for time and Lai Ying's disapproving parents would be even more scandalised if she had the baby out of wedlock.

The wedding takes place one humid spring day in 1993. Lai Ying is resplendent in a snow-white gown, and I in a navy-blue tuxedo. The pregnancy is just beginning to show, if one looks closely. We start with a ceremony at the Marriage Registrar's office at Hong Kong Park. Then we spend hours taking photographs in the picturesque grounds of the park, against a background of fishponds, ferns, and artificial cliffs. The state of euphoria lasts all day, and long after the dinner at a restaurant in Tsim Sha Tsui East, close to where I once slept out under the stars.

It's a small function. Some colleagues from work, various friends we've made here, and a few others like Julius, who fly in from China. Diallo is my best man. Lai Ying's sister Lai Mui flies in from Canada, but her parents stay put. I can't afford the fare for my family. But I'm thankful that even though they've never met her, my parents have come to accept her as a daughter, albeit one from an alien land that might as well be a dream.

Lai Ying protests that her parents are not boycotting the wedding. I want so much to believe her. In the end, I know, she's only trying to make peace. They have never fully accepted me, and could have tried a little harder to make the trip.

It's only later that year when Chacha is born that my in-laws begin to warm towards me. They now have a grandchild, and for the role I played in whatever social elevation this earns them, I have been rewarded with a measure of recognition. But not acceptance. Not yet. Maybe that will come when we finally meet.

When Chacha is born, we are not even allowed to hold her. She's so delicate, and so pale. They say she has a bad case of jaundice and has to stay in hospital for a week. It is painful to watch the yellowish skin, the little limbs that look so frail and helpless, the eyes that look vacant and fill with tears whenever she's awake. Seeing her placed under the infrared light is heart-wrenching. It's as if she wasn't ready to be born. It makes you think of a half-cooked sausage that needs to spend more time on the barbeque. I want to snatch her away and make her bask in the sun, like I once saw them do to a jaundiced new-born in my village.

Like many foreigners, we have thought of going to start a new life elsewhere before Hong Kong is returned to the motherland. The thought of returning to the restrictions and uncertainties of the life we knew before is too scary. But then Hong Kong creeps up on you, like a fog enveloping a weary traveller on a lonely, shadowy road. And before I know it, the vitality and vibrancy of the city holds me hostage, claiming me as one of its own, even as I struggle within my mind to reach beyond the horizon to a far more distant prior life, to maintain some sort of link, no matter how tenuous, with my old life in Ndambu. I find many locals here speak neither English nor Putonghua, which forces me to acquire a working knowledge of Cantonese. Lai Ying's facility with the language helps, too. She learnt it from her father, who is from Guangdong. I now see the wisdom of coming here, where no one stares or follows you around. It's much easier to be part of that miniscule black Chinese tribe Diallo used to rave about, if you want to. Only, it feels a bit too late to be nurturing such dreams, yet this is the first time in our lives that we feel accepted in Asia.

Over time, I've heard less and less about Father's cooperative, but I know the land issue still reigns supreme in his heart. I know I have to be ready for that moment when it comes, for it surely will. Whether it will be the purchase of Brian Walter's land or a small piece of land in Ndambu village on which to build a family home.

The need to go back and visit my family continues to gnaw at me, especially now that I can afford it. Every year I tell myself, *this year it will happen*. Then the work takes charge, and I succumb willingly to this captivity, like a prisoner who sees a chance to break free but is held back by leaden legs and a fear that it's only a trap beckoning. Every year, I plan to work harder until I'm truly ready, so they can see I haven't wasted my time here, so they know I have something to show for the long years in China, in which I foolishly allowed so many opportunities to pass me by. Mother says I should keep working until I'm ready, which is reassuring but at the same time makes the guilt that much harder to bear.

*

I look back over the years in Hong Kong, like a man returning home from a long journey and unable to believe the exotic destinations he has been to. Smash the Bug! That's the name of my firm. After working as a systems analyst and programmer in stuffy, high-pressure IT and construction firms, I'm finally running my own IT business, right now committed to the Y2K bug. It's an unpretentious outfit, operating out of a small office in Central. But the phone never stops ringing, keeping me and my three staff perpetually on our feet. Never in my wildest dreams as a student in Nanjing did I imagine I would make a fortune fixing the millennium bug. We never even used computers back then. And never did I imagine I could afford the rent on the spacious, three-bedroomed flat we rent in Mid-Levels, the upmarket district of Hong Kong Island we moved into last year. As soon as this hectic life slows down a little next year, I plan to invite my parents to visit for a few weeks. They might not like Hong Kong itself. I can imagine how bewildering it will feel to rural folks used to a more sedate lifestyle. But they'll love my home, and they'll meet my family.

The one worry about long working hours, including trips to Macau, Zhuhai, Shenzhen, and Guangzhou, is that I get to spend a lot of time with my assistant Tiffany. Lai Ying doesn't like that at all. She has been getting suspicious with every passing day.

Chacha loves going to play at a picnic site in Jardine's Lookout, which sits in the shadow of the forested hills of Tai Tam Country Park. Her mum suggests we have a picnic and invite some of Chacha's friends, especially Surdar, Chacha's best friend. It's a beautiful, sunny day in the middle of summer, a bit too hot and humid for an early start. The sun would bear down on you like a punishment from the heavens. We head out at five when the tamed sun loses its fierceness as it starts its descent behind The Peak. After a heavy meal prepared in several homesteads, and which includes such delicacies as Lai Ying's Shanghai dumplings and Surdar's mother's lamb curry, we spend a couple of hours playing touch rugby. Children who are too young to grasp the rules run around shrieking with pleasure, clutching barbecued chicken wings and getting in the way of the game.

When we get back home, Chacha can't stop talking about Surdar's country in the mountains. As usual, she sounds like Surdar's echo, quoting every little thing Surdar said. Surdar's parents tell us their daughter does exactly the same thing. Surdar is from Nepal. She and Chacha go to the same school. They're in their first year of primary school, the same one where they attended kindergarten for three years. Since the age of two, the playgroup teachers tried to persuade us that Chacha wasn't responding to the school's structured discipline. Chinese kids were obedient and well-behaved. They did what they were told, no more, no less. Chacha wanted to colour when they were told to sing, to build Lego houses when they were told to eat snacks. The school diagnosed an ailment they called slow development. Lai Ying went along with their 'prescription' for longer hours. I saw it as a ploy to make more money off us. We argued about it endlessly, and in the end, I convinced her it didn't matter. If she had been in my country, she wouldn't have gone to kindergarten till the age of five.

I worry about all these years of schooling for kids so young. Life was so different for me. We spent our childhood playing, climbing trees, eating wild berries, ensnaring and roasting grasshoppers, exploring the farm and forests, swimming in the rivers and dams with a brigade of fellow troublemakers, and learning how to spot the crocodiles lurking beneath the serene surface, and run for cover. Chacha has spent three years learning English and Chinese, playing in an enclosed, air-conditioned space, with plastic toys that are disinfected every day.

Surdar believes her country is on the roof of the world. She says you can stand at the top of Nepal and see the whole world. Just like standing on the roof of her building, where we go to watch the fireworks on New Year's Eve. On a good day, you can see all the way to Kowloon, across the harbour. Most days, the territory is covered in a grey haze. The view is like a 1960s black-and-white photograph taken without a flash on a rainy day in the late evening.

"Surdar says their mountains go up to heaven," says Chacha.

"Heaven? That's pretty high up, baby girl."

"Surdar says no other country goes that high up. Is there, Daddy?"

"Do you mean a country or a mountain?"

"Surdar says her country is also a mountain. Is that possible, Daddy?"

"Yes. Her country is part of the tallest mountain on earth."

"Wah!" Her eyes open wide in astonishment. "Surdar asked if there are mountains in Africa, Daddy."

"There are many, my dear, like Kilimanjaro."

"Is it very high, Daddy, like Surdar's?"

"Yes, Chacha, it's almost as high as Surdar's."

"Wah! Wait till I tell her! She won't believe it; I know she won't believe it."

"Do you believe it, darling?"

"Of course, Daddy!" I lift her up and give her a hug. It's like a gift she gives me, every time she believes something, just because Daddy says it.

"Mountains in Africa are huge, Chacha. Can you imagine?" I spread my arms out as far as they can go.

She spreads her arms out too, little, skinny arms that look frail and waif-like. I lift her up and bounce her a few times. She squeals with laughter. Her mother comes into the living room to see what the racket is all about. She has been working on the computer in the study, writing a proposal for the bank she works for.

"This young lady needs to go to bed now," she announces.

Chacha starts her avoid-the-bed routine, sulking, shaking her head, hands crossed.

"Mummy's right, darling. It's almost nine. You've had a very long day."

She only starts to behave herself after I tell her a story about animals that spoke like people and lived in a village on the slopes of Kilimanjaro. I don't always remember the stories my mother told us, so I often improvise, and hope to make them sound real to her, with all their sounds, smells, magic, and fantasy. Some nights, I read for her. Tonight, it's one of my improvised tales.

Lai Ying and I sit on a rug to watch the evening news. As the new millennium approaches, there is little to cheer us up. A wave of violence has swept through East Timor, barely months after they voted for independence from Indonesia. Gunmen have been running amok in warlord-controlled Somalia, raping women, looting, and burning houses. There has been another school shooting in America. In Pakistan, the military chief has overthrown the government.

It is not all doom and gloom, especially when it comes to the millennium bug. In northern Russia, a religious cult is preparing to hide away in mountain caves to survive the impeding apocalypse, and on the streets of Hong Kong, conmen are having a field day. Some are selling pills to cure the millennium bug. A man is in court for tricking a housewife into having sex with him so she won't catch the millennium bug. Fortune hunters have been searching for ancient relics in Penny's Bay before reclamation work starts for the proposed Disneyland project. As the Asian financial crisis continues to bite, the government assures us that Mickey Mouse will save the Hong Kong economy. Many think it's a joke.

Lai Ying is excited about the thought of such a world-famous amusement and theme park coming so close to home. She tells me how she once travelled from Vancouver to visit Disneyland in California.

"Here, it will be less than an hour away," she says, looking at me expectantly.

"Of course, we'll go, sweetheart, as often as you like." I've never been to an amusement park before. "I'm sure Chacha will love it."

"You'll love all the fun and magic, *lougong*." Since we moved to Hong Kong and started to learn Cantonese, she's taken to calling me "old man", in a sweet, gentle tone of voice that makes my heart flutter. "It will be much bigger than Ocean Park."

We visit Ocean Park at least once a year. Chacha can't get enough of the dolphin show, and this year, we saw the two new pandas, An An and Jia Jia, which look like giant teddy bears. Chacha wanted to reach out and touch them, but they were too shy and stayed hidden away behind bamboo trees most of the time.

I ask Lai Ying what she wants to do this Christmas.

"You're so busy working, I don't think we can go anywhere, *lougong*."

"I know, but I don't want you two to have a boring time just because of my work. We can spend a few days on Lantau Island, perhaps Mui Wo or something, just to get away from the city."

Her face lights up.

"That would be nice. Or maybe Lamma. It's more rural, quieter. Do you remember that resort we stayed at once?"

"Yeah. But the word resort is misleading."

"It wasn't all that bad," she protests, feigning a frown. "You liked it, I remember. It was so convenient for the beach and everything."

"It was nice," I concede. "It's just the way everything here is made out to be more than it really is."

"Come on, this is Asia, you should be used to that by now."

"Of course. Impress everyone. Give everyone face, right?"

"Anyway," she presses on, "there's more choice on Lantau or even Cheung Chau."

"Cheung Chau has a fine beach and great seafood, but I'm not staying at some villa. You don't know if there's a ghost there, honey."

"Don't be so superstitious, *lougong*." She laughs and pinches my nose. "Personally, I think this whole thing about people committing suicide in Cheung Chau villas is exaggerated."

"I'm not taking any chances."

I pour us another glass of red wine and browse channels in search of a movie. I find an old romantic comedy, which captivates Lai Ying. I'm just glad for a rare chance to enjoy this closeness. With the suspicions about what I get up to with my assistant, we're more likely to be arguing than enjoying a pleasant conversation. I place an arm around her shoulders and a wave of desire sweeps through me as she snuggles closer and rests her head on my shoulder.

Encouraged by the warm response, I put our glasses away, dim the light, and position myself behind her to massage her shoulders, working my way down to her slim waist and back to her neck, taking in the faint scent of shampoo, massaging around the curves, imagining I'm a sculptor smoothing the edges and putting the final touches on a goddess. I unhook her bra to better twiddle and rub the small of her back with my thumbs while holding her torso firmly in my hands. She shivers, gives a moan, and sits up when I apply pressure on the ribs, and I have to slip my hands under her armpits to hold her still. After a while, she leans backwards and slumps into my arms, still making appreciative cooing sounds. I manoeuvre my hands into her T-shirt and gently caress her stomach, synchronising my caresses with the rhythmic motions of her slowed breathing. I kiss her ear and blow a warm gust of breath along the ear, cheek, and neck, a ticklish action that always leaves her giggling. Moving upwards, I clasp her breasts and give a tender squeeze. She crosses her arms self-consciously to immobilise my hands, at the same time glancing down the corridor. Her nipples harden like a couple of lemon noses. My heart thumps with furious anticipation.

"She's fast asleep now," I whisper in her ear. "We've never made love in the living room, honey."

She gasps with shock, and mutters. "You're crazy! No, not here."

"Okay, okay." I kiss her and start to caress her breasts again.

"*Lougong?*"

"Yeah?"

"Can I watch this film first?" My face collapses into her shoulders. "Please?"

"All right. Let's watch the film." I pick up the half-empty bottle. "Ready for a top up?"

"Just a little. Thanks."

I fill mine to the brim. We'll be here a long time.

Chicken Treatment

WE HAVE A JOB IN Macau. Tiffany found this client. Hiring her was one of the best decisions I've ever made. She's always finding these clients and helping the business grow. These last seven months, she's been bringing them in faster than we can service them. Not that I'm complaining. The money is good, and no one knows when the next windfall will come. The millennium bug has been a true blessing.

Three days in Guangzhou go very quickly. We're staying at the Sunshine West Hotel. But we hardly spend any time at all at the hotel. Most days, we're up at the crack of dawn and don't get back till after midnight. At times like this, I really miss my family, and can't wait to get back. But I love having Tiffany around. She's fun and witty and really understands the business.

On the day we're due to return to Hong Kong, I suggest we make a detour to Macau. This has now become a well-established routine. It's so much more real and safer than the White Card deals in China years ago. If Kabinga could see me now, he would know who the real moneyman is. It's too bad he disappeared without trace, like a rock that sinks into a lake with neither a splash nor so much as a ripple. He would be proud of me, and thrilled to know his old friend is carrying on where he left off.

Tiffany smiles her knowing smile and says she can't wait. The casino brings out the devil in her. Looking at her, I can't help thinking she has been sent by Satan himself to tempt me with an array of forbidden fruits. I will gladly partake, for to say no would be stupid. She has infected me with this incurable fervour, and in recent months, I can't get away from the roulette and baccarat tables. It starts off as a way to celebrate our good fortune. Then the thrill of winning or merely being part of a collective, public fantasy soon becomes an irresistible drug. There is no way to explain the feeling when you cash in your chips and walk away with a thick wad of crisp notes. I can now begin to understand what Kabinga must have experienced. I think of my parents slaving away for a white man all their lives, knowing their plight will never improve, living only for a dream that they'll inherit the land, and yet here, the chance to free oneself from such want is so real, and yet it can pass you by so easily. It did before. And I know, deep inside, that this will never happen again.

Opportunity is finally knocking on my door. And this time, I am not going to let it slip through my fingers. I yearn to see the admiring, loving looks on Tiffany's face when I do well, and the sheer joy in her eyes when she, too, picks the winning numbers. Even though I don't intend for anything further to happen between us, the warmth she exudes, the softness of her body when she leans against me as though to share our joy by osmosis, is something I look forward to during the long hours in dingy offices. It's the heady mix of Tiffany's sensuality and the chance to explore my financial side, driven by memories of Kabinga's White Card and the shower comrades. For now, though, it all feels so wild that I dare not even confide in Diallo. Not now, anyway, especially given Tiffany's involvement. We don't get to meet as often as we did before, but when we do, it's a struggle to keep a straight face while talking about what one has been up to.

At the beginning, I try to keep it away from Lai Ying. Why am I coming back so late from Macau even when I don't have a job there? The line that I'm just drinking doesn't wash anymore. When Lai Ying comes to the office one day and sees Tiffany, it confirms her worst fears. She simply can't abide that raw sexiness about Tiffany, the haughty, languid eyes presiding over high cheekbones and a naughty pout, the voluptuous figure and excessive confidence that signals to other women that she can take their man at the drop of a hat.

We have planned on having a second child but Lai Ying has recently decided I can't be trusted to be a father again. For now, she's right. I don't know how we could handle all that responsibility in this climate.

Right now, an excuse for coming home late is the least of my worries as Tiff and I settle down at the table and wait for the croupier to throw the dice. The night passes like a blur. The chips pile up; they disappear and pile up again. Dead silence alternates with claps and gasps of disbelief. You're a star in a film of your own creation, with an adoring beautiful girl on your arm, focused only on winning, or winning back what you've lost. It's a drug that takes you from one peak to another, a drug ten times more potent than the alcohol that fuels the proceedings.

I wait for the big one. I can feel it coming. Fate owes me this one, as a reward for the many nights I've spent here, losing my hard-earned cash to the house. I've waited, like the African fish eagle, scanning the surface of the dam for the minutest ripple. Mother prescribed patience. I've waited long enough, given patience my best shot. This is the eagle and White Card, all rolled into one sweet deal. Let it happen, Lord, give me the cards, give me those numbers. Now! Now! Let me see the envious looks on the faces of these people, who've been eyeing my good fortune and stealing looks at Tiffany's cleavage, wondering what such a *leng leui* is doing with someone like me, a mere black ghost. Let it happen. Let this ghost shine.

The collective gasp that comes next knocks me back against my seat, leaving me suspended in a state of shock and disbelief. The reality hits home when I become aware of Tiffany's soft, warm comforting arm around my shoulders and a whiff of her perfume fills my nose like a tonic of smelling salts to revive me.

I trudge from the table, chin buried in my chest, and stumble to the bar. Oblivious of everything and everyone, I knock back two straight whiskies to clear my head. Tiffany's trying desperately to catch my eye. I'm in no mood for chitchat.

"Perhaps we should go, Dan," I hear her plaintive whisper.

"Get yourself a drink, Tiff. We're not done."

She looks up, eyebrows raised, unsettled by the edge in my voice.

"You have no money left," she informs me, superfluously.

"I believe there are ATMs here."

She shakes her head. I look into her eyes. Is she trying to tell me I can't access my own money? She's not my wife; she's not even my girlfriend. The thought of my assistant telling me how to spend my money makes me laugh. But I stop suddenly, on seeing the pained look in her eyes.

"What's up, Tiffany?"

She looks away. Perhaps she's trying to tell me something, something like my wife will find out. But how would Tiffany know it's a problem? Is it a woman's intuition thing? I ignore her and replenish my financial armoury at an ATM in the lobby, silently thanking God for the casino managers' thoughtfulness.

An hour later, the thirty-five thousand is gone. But I'm not finished here yet. I dare not raid the machine again. Lai Ying will surely kill me. There must be another way. I turn to Tiffany.

"If you must keep playing, Dan, I know people…people here."

"What people?"

"They can lend you some money."

I watch her closely. "Friends of yours?"

"You can trust them. They're okay. I've dealt with them before."

It's a quick transaction. In an open corridor that leads to a kitsch shopping mall at the back of the casino. I supply my contact and ID card details. Tiffany verifies. It turns out they're well known to each other. He's a Hong Kong guy. Close-shaven, black leather jacket with bright silver studs on the lapels, gold chain around his neck, resting on a cream silk shirt, a cigarette permanently stuck in his mouth. Tiffany introduces him as Chuck. He gives me an address in Yau Ma Tei, where the loan is to be repaid. The interest computation is confusing and daunting. But I'm not worried. I'm confident I can win back my money and clear the entire debt tonight. We shake hands and head back to the hall.

I emerge from the corridor fifty thousand richer. My heart throbs with elation and a wild eagerness to reclaim my lost fortune. This time, Tiffany's smile awakens a somnolent devil in me. My eyes drop to her cleavage, my heartbeat quickens, and the thought hits me. What would Kabinga have done? Would he have worried about a marriage certificate? Did he really have one made? Supposing she says no, reminds me I'm her boss, how will I face her tomorrow?

Instinctively, I hold her shoulder and aim a thank you peck on her right cheek. She turns to offer the left cheek. Our lips meet, and immediately freeze. Her eyes widen with surprise. Then they close slowly, all the life shifts south to her lips. Her breasts against my abdomen are like a cushion to my sudden fall. My arms close around her waist, and in that instant, nothing else matters except the warm and intoxicating feel of this girl against me.

Moments later, realising we're in the public glare, we shuffle away, avoiding eye contact with each other and whoever happens to be watching. Not even the sweet tenderness of Tiffany's lips or her warm body against mine can erase the feeling of being exposed. I button my jacket and walk stiffly to the gaming hall, not daring to look at Tiffany.

Tonight, nothing's going my way. Something's going to have to change. I feel it in my bones. I see it in the tequila shots, the beer bottles. Like a man floating on a wave in the high seas, unsure which way is land but certain he's going the right way, I stand my ground. This is a temporary setback. My money will come back to me. Chuck bails me out one more time. This time, I don't need

Tiffany. She tries to stop me. But I know exactly where to find my man, Chuck. This time, he's with two other guys in black suits, standing like nightclub bouncers, legs wide apart, one hand in the pocket, the other grasping a cigar. With all the alcohol I've consumed tonight, I feel so energised I could take these guys on single-handedly if they don't oblige. They keep glancing over their shoulders, watching the passersby, not saying a word. Chuck stands sandwiched between their protective broad chests and menacing biceps. Speaking in muted tones, he reminds me of the Yau Ma Tei address. I feel like asking him, what's his problem. Does he think I'm stupid?

Two hours later, everything's gone. I can't find Tiffany.

Tiffany doesn't warn me about the interest. Thinking they're her friends, I take my time sorting out their money. I reckon they'll go easy. I go in to pay half of it, only to discover the debt has skyrocketed. The interest accumulates daily, virtually doubling the debt by the time I go to see them. I can't keep raiding my savings and business accounts. When Lai Ying finds out, she goes crazy, yells till she loses her voice. I've turned her life inside out. Everything she loathed and feared about the likes of Wang has come back to haunt her. How could this have happened?

The harassment has been going on for a month. They start by sending letters to my neighbours, as if that would scare me. What do I care if people think I owe money to loan sharks? The neighbours don't pay my rent. Lai Ying has a slightly different take on it. To her, we've lost face, irreparably, and it's just going to get worse. I have to find some way to get out of this hole.

When I come back home one night after trying hopelessly to win back some of my losses, I find the door locked. The phone is off the hook. Lai Ying's mobile is switched off. It's 3 a.m. There's no point in banging on the door. I get back in the lift. The security guard is dozing, but he looks up sharply when I pass through the gate. I do my best to ignore him. But he's already waving a hand and smiling, with what looks like a mixture of sympathy and surprise. Normally I exchange a few words of Putonghua with him, but tonight I'm in no mood for small talk.

I need to find somewhere to sleep. Diallo is away on a business trip.

I call Charlie. I'm in luck. I hail a taxi and head to his place in Happy Valley. Charlie describes himself as Black British and proud of it. Pressed further, he'll offer that he was born in Ghana. He's good company around the pub – has a lot of opinions and doesn't ask too many questions.

"I really hate to bother you, man, but—"

"Relax," he interrupts. "If this is the sort of time you're going to be crawling back home, you can expect to get your arse locked out."

He's got a towel around his waist. The smell around him is a mixture of alcohol, perfume, warm, damp sheets, and sex.

"I see you're busy. Anyone I know?"

He stifles a laugh.

"Some girl I met at the pub, man," he says in a whisper. "I don't even know her bloody name."

"Just show me to a very dark room. I'll make myself scarce at first light."

"Sure, mate. You know where the kitchen is."

When I finally fall asleep in Charlie's spare room, the only thought on my mind is: I haven't seen Chacha for two days. This has to stop.

Life has become a living nightmare. The phone calls come when you least expect them. Sometimes they're ominously silent. Sometimes they're full of abuse and threats. I get the number changed, but within two days, they track down the unlisted number. Lai Ying has quit her job to watch over Chacha. Whatever penny I make goes straight to them, to the little stationery shop in a back alley in a run-down building that acts as a front for Chuck the loan shark. But there's no let-up.

Lai Ying says we need to move out, maybe even leave Hong Kong altogether, to live with her parents in Canada, or her mother's family in Shanghai. I can't bear the thought of her parents confirming their worst fears about my unsuitability for their daughter. Julius is well established in Shanghai. He could give me some leads on business opportunities and jobs. But I refuse to relocate and insist we can weather the storm. After all, I've paid off most of the debt. But this isn't enough to reassure her.

My White Card is taking shape, like the wonderful dream that comes at the crack of dawn and ends abruptly as the day yawns awake. I should have done it in Nanjing when I had a chance, when I could have snatched my catch and flown back to a safe perch. Now I'm like a flightless eagle being dragged deeper and deeper into the dam by a giant tilapia.

"It's that girl, isn't it!" Lai Ying screams at me one night. "She's behind all this, isn't she – your assistant?"

"My assistant has nothing to do with my money problems, Lai Ying." It takes an effort to keep my voice down. Chacha is in the study playing computer games. I slump into a sofa and start searching for the sports channels on cable.

"You think I don't know what's going on?"

"I've said before, she just works for me. There's nothing more."

"You think I'm stupid?" She's standing a foot away from me, between me and the TV, arms akimbo.

We glare at each other, my chest heaving with anger and frustration.

"Lai Ying, I don't know what you want me to say that I haven't said a hundred times already."

She sighs with resignation. She has completely given up on me, but her unblinking eyes are still gleaming with anger.

"What is the matter with you, Dan? What came over you? You're not the nice, reliable man I married. You've turned into this selfish, uncaring creature. This debt, the loan sharks – can't you see what they're doing to us?" Then her voice drops to a whisper. "Dan, I think you've forgotten Nanjing. I haven't. And I don't think I'm ready to go through all that pain again."

The thought of her lying on a cold floor in the People's Sanctuary brings a throbbing pain to my temple. How could I forget? *No, Lai Ying, we can't go back there, we can't go back to that.* I hold her hand and give a gentle squeeze.

"Look, I'm going to clear this debt in a month or so. Don't worry."

"Don't worry? Do you know what I found in the letter box this morning?"

I don't know. I don't want to know. "Please, move aside a little. I can't see the TV." She snatches her hand away.

"I won't move until I finish what I want to say! I don't need dog shit in this house!"

"Lai Ying, please! Mind your language. Supposing Chacha hears you?"

"What's worse, that she sees it or hears it mentioned?"

"What are you talking about?"

"That's what your business associates put in your letter box. I'm sorry I threw your post away. I couldn't stand the smell. You can watch your stupid TV now."

Seething with rage, I dial Chuck's number. There's no answer. It's all I can do not to smash the phone against the wall. I leave a message saying if he doesn't stop this nonsense, I'll break his balls.

The first thing I do the following day is to withdraw seventy thousand from my savings account and deliver it to Yau Ma Tei. The same people I always see are already here at 8 a.m.: a hard-faced, tight-lipped, middle-aged woman, who takes my money and issues me with a receipt, and a stocky man in a zipped-up, black leather jacket, who doesn't even look up from a tabloid full of pictures of half-naked women, but I can feel his eyes boring into me, making my skin crawl.

"How much more do I owe?" I ask.

"Ask Ah Chuck," says the woman, in an emotionless, matter-of-fact voice. As I start to stomp out of the room, the stocky man jumps to his feet and takes a step towards me. Two more men emerge from the corridor and block the door. They look like regular triad hoodlums with the tattoos on their arms and scruffy T-shirts.

"The money," hisses the stocky man, blowing smoke into my face. "Every dollar, black man."

"You tell Ah Chuck to stop messing with me. He'll get all his money back."

"One week."

"Get out of my way."

I try to push my way past the hoodlums, but before I know it, they've grabbed me by the arms, twisted me around, and I'm on my knees, looking up at the stocky man. Instinctively, I close my eyes as I see him raise his arm. The first punch hits me straight in the belly, knocking the wind out of me. All I remember is the way the window tilts on its side as the dancing walls fizzle away. And then it's quiet, cold, and frightfully dark, like those nights I spent on a bench by the Kowloon waterfront.

We're on the last stretch in fighting the Y2K bug. Three weeks to the end of the year, and the millennium. We've only got a few more clients who haven't achieved compliance yet. The work is keeping me so busy, I never have time to spend at home. I fear I'm becoming a stranger to my own daughter. Lai Ying is already a confirmed stranger. She has taken to cold silences that go for days on end. I dare not even ask what's been pushed into the letterbox anymore.

In the past, I drank for fun. I drank slowly and leisurely, savouring the beer, as though it were a fine wine. Now I drink in a vain attempt to drown this misery, looking over my shoulder for Chuck's hoodlums, gulping the beer down like a man dying of thirst, no longer enjoying the taste, but anxious to get to the next drink, like a chain smoker who lights a new cigarette with the last one.

Lai Ying is still not talking to me on New Year's Eve. But I'm more worried about potential call-outs from clients in case anything goes wrong with their technology. I'm not sure what will happen if they call. I have to take Chacha to see the fireworks show across Victoria Harbour to usher in the New Year.

Lai Mui, Lai Ying's younger sister, joins us with a group of her friends. When I first met her at our wedding, I was amazed at the resemblance. The same gentle facial features, high cheekbones descending into a narrow chin. She's a little shorter than her sister, and with a fuller body. She moved to Hong Kong a few years ago. But now, after breaking up with her American boyfriend of three years, her social life has gone down the drain. She has even talked of leaving Hong Kong, returning to Canada, where she went to university, emigrating to Australia or somewhere. The stress of working as a financial consultant is also getting to her.

"It's all about bringing in new customers," she says, "which for me is exciting, you know, persuading people to let us manage their investments. But it's so hard now, with so many people out of work. And those who have money don't want to pay so-called experts like us to manage it for them."

I nod in recognition. Hong Kong people have a lot of confidence when it comes to managing their own money.

"Times are hard, Lai Mui," I try to comfort her. "I'm not sure how the IT industry will fare after Y2K. What's your firm doing to cope?"

"They're laying people off like mad! But now they've started targeting expatriates, who are perceived as having more money than sense, and are thought to be more scared of what a devalued dollar would do to their precious savings." She laughs. I've always enjoyed her wry humour and her forthright manner. Her sister thinks she's too abrasive.

"With an attitude like that," says Lai Ying, "you need lessons in customer service."

"Oh, I'm nice enough when I need to be," Lai Mui defends herself. "But in my field, you dare not be soft. It's like a jungle, sister."

"And you're all wild animals, chasing the dollar."

"It's not for nothing it's called the rat race, you know."

Lai Ying rolls her eyes and stifles a yawn. They're always having a go at each other. Lai Mui accuses her elder sister of being too soft for the rough and tumble of Hong Kong. Lai Ying believes her sister has contracted that quintessential Hong Kong ailment: greed for money.

"You're like this husband of mine," says Lai Ying, her tone a blend of regret and sarcasm. "All you ever care about is money."

"I don't know how you expect to survive without it," says Lai Mui. "And you're forgetting something, my dear sister, aren't you? Our family has always been in business, though we've all seen better days. You're stuck in the past, but I've moved on."

Lai Ying demands we change the subject, causing laughter all around. For her, the family fortunes or lack thereof belong in an unspoken past. Not so for Lai Mui. But Lai Ying always shuts her little sister up whenever she gets started.

The show goes well, as expected, lighting up the night sky in a riot of colours and explosions. It only lasts twenty minutes, but it leaves Chacha with raptures of delight. For a few moments, Lai Ying and I forget our troubles and hug and kiss like the happy family we were once. We start making our way out just before the fireworks display comes to an end, so we can find a taxi before everyone else, holding Chacha's hands between us.

We're still chatting happily and recalling the explosive sounds of the fireworks display when we get off the lift and walk down the corridor to our flat.

As usual, Chacha runs from the lift and tears down the corridor. She can never wait to get home. But this time, she screams and comes running back. That's when I see the blood dripping down the door and chicken entrails arranged on the doormat, as if in tribute to some deity. Trembling with fury, I lift Chacha up and stride back into the lift which, thankfully, is still waiting, as if it knows we will need to escape the desecration of our home.

Lai Ying grabs my shoulder, her screams echoing through the lift. She extricates Chacha from my hands, pushes me back into the corridor, and scrambles into the lift, frantically hitting the ground-floor button.

So Long Time No See

A WEEK LATER, WHEN I return home from work one evening, something tells me all's not well. It's the silence. It's not the normal silence when people have been out all day, but a deeper, emptier silence when there has been no one all week. A quick look into the shoe rack confirms my worst fears. And it isn't only hers that are missing but Chacha's as well. The study tells a more disturbing story. She has kicked my monitor in and left the hard drive a mangled wreck. I hope Chacha didn't have to watch this. There's a note on the desk, scribbled on a piece of paper in that unique language of hers.

Tkng Chch 2 sf plc. I nd sm spc frm u.

Where does one start looking for a runaway wife and child? Lai Mui says she has no idea, and seems in a hurry to hang up the phone. Every day, my life sinks deeper into a dark abyss. The loneliness is unbearable. Unable to bear it any more, I ask Diallo and Charlie to meet up. We arrange to meet at the Sahara Oasis, the African pub on Knutsford Terrace, the liveliest bar street in Kowloon.

It takes an hour of small talk and several beers before I can muster the courage to pour my heart out. The guys listen attentively, interrupting with the occasional murmur of shock or disbelief. I don't expect any helpful advice. It's too late for that, anyway. But somehow everything seems clearer, with every pint of Carlsberg, though I only pay part attention to their supportive comments and suggestions as to how to deal with Chuck and the gang.

"*Mon ami, mon ami,*" says Diallo, "I can see how you kept your head down. This is not easy. Let me see what I can do, all right? You can't deal with this guy by yourself."

"That's true," says Charlie. "Anything we can do, all right?"

I refuse all offers of help, and it takes a lot of persuading for them to accept that this is a burden I must bear alone.

*

175

The new computer boots up the way I get up nowadays. Devoid of spirit. Unwilling to face another dreadful day. As I watch the monitor rouse itself, with flashes of lights and irritating beeps and grunts, I study with a pained heart the pictures in my study. On my desk is a picture of the family. I'm holding Lai Ying's hand, Chacha on my shoulders. This one was taken in Kowloon Park, on a cool autumn afternoon in 1997, a few months after Hong Kong was handed back to China. Nothing had changed. The air still smelled the same, a mixture of exhaust fumes, cigarette smoke, and fried tofu. People still walked about, briskly, talking business on mobile phones loudly enough for the whole world to hear. Some English people from my old jobs packed their bags and left, fearing that the People's Liberation Army would invade the territory and ram communism down our throats. Chacha was about four. The event didn't mean anything to her. But she enjoyed the celebrations and festive mood that last colonial summer.

There are so many people walking around or seated on benches in this green oasis in the middle of a glass and concrete jungle, it's like a market. It makes you wonder why anyone bothers to come here at all, where the crowds are often as bad as those in the middle of bustling Mong Kok.

Every picture I pick up tells a story. There's this one of Chacha's taken just a few months ago, when Chuck and his hoodlums were still giving me grief. She's grinning from ear to ear, blissfully unaware of the torment Daddy and Mummy were enduring.

In another picture, Chacha's chin is raised and she's biting her index finger. I remember that day well. We were at the children's playground, waiting for her mother. I had just told Chacha, I'll take her on her first trip to Africa. It's our little secret. She was so excited she couldn't stop nodding her head, her little hands trembling across the smile that left her mouth agape. Her mother's not too keen. She says it's not safe there. But there must be ten million little girls living in Africa. How can they all not be safe?

Now, I'm more determined than ever before. When Chacha comes home, we'll do that trip. Africa will no longer be our little secret. From now on, we're going to be a real family, just like Jupiter's. Our neighbour's. No more finger-in-mouth, naughty-smile, nodded secrets.

Another of my daughter's photos sits on the monitor, watching my every move. It was taken on the beach at Shek O. Chacha is emerging from the water, grinning with the childlike innocence that always melts my heart. One hand raised in a victory salute, as if celebrating Daddy's business success. The other adjusting her long curly hair, which is wet and sticky, and pushing it from her face. She's surrounded by black heads bobbing about the water, riding the waves as the cliffs and rocks keep vigil from a distance. There's a glint in Chacha's eye, as if she knows Daddy has finally regained face as his business grows with every passing day.

If only face could bring my family back. If only I still had the money. How the world has changed! The bug is gone and forgotten. The debt is gone but not forgotten. I've gone freelance. And the phone hardly ever rings.

Now, I'm struggling to make ends meet by doing regular IT maintenance work for a small number of clients who have stuck with me after the big Y2K budgets dwindled and everyone swore not to throw such insane amounts of money at IT problems again. Things will have to change, and pretty fast; otherwise, I won't even be able to afford the rent.

When the computer finally boots up, the first thing I do is check email. I scroll up the page in the inbox. This must be the fifth time I've opened her email this evening. It's the first one she has sent in three weeks.

This email is brief, like all her previous ones. All four of them. Why can't she just send me a text message, if she wants to write like this?

Dn, hw R U? Gd lck fdng wk. Chch snds hr lv. L.Y.

I don't mind when she calls me Dn, though I've no idea how I'm supposed to pronounce it, but I wish she would at least spell Chacha's name in full. The way she spells it makes my girl sound like a little puppy.

And it would be so much nicer if she let Chacha talk to me on the phone, instead of relaying these de-vowelled, clipped messages, so my baby can tell me how much she misses her daddy. And how much she hates Shanghai and her school, where everything is taught in Putonghua. I didn't find the language easy myself. Maybe it's easier on a seven-year-old. Come to think of it, when I was her age, it wasn't unusual to speak Shona, Sindebele, and English. Sometimes all in the same sentence.

No, I needn't worry about Chacha's language skills. She picked up a fair bit of Putonghua before she left.

Before she left!

I make it sound like she willingly went away to boarding school or something. Yeah, like before she packed her little Hello Kitty bags and walked out of my life.

If only it had been that easy. If only she had done the packing herself, booked the flight, got onto the Airport Express, and boarded the flight to Shanghai. I would have understood that she was perhaps hoping to search for her roots.

But God knows it didn't happen like that! She didn't pack her own bags. Christ, she didn't have any bags to pack. And I know in my heart that she boarded that plane screaming and shouting. Because she wanted to stay here and be with her daddy. Why else do my insides cramp up like this, and my eyes get so watery I can barely see the screen?

I wander over to the living room and turn on the TV, hoping to catch a late-night game of football. There's nothing but old games, recycled over and over again. I stare at the lights over the city for a moment. From the fifth floor on a hill on Caine Road, we have a panoramic view of Central. During the day, you can even see the lush green vegetation at the Zoological and Botanical Gardens. At this time of night, it's just a sea of blackness, just like the harbour a little further north. Somewhere down there are the drinking dens of Lan Kwai Fong, tempting me out of my self-imposed solitude. But tonight is one of those nights when the reality of Lai Ying's departure gnaws at me, turning the thought of hanging around the pub surrounded by happy smiling faces and raucous laughter into self-inflicted torture.

For many, the night is just starting, especially tonight when they celebrate Tuen Ng, the Dragon Boat Festival. Races were held in the day in elaborately decorated dragon boats to commemorate Qu Yuan, who drowned himself two thousand years ago to protest against corrupt leaders. Adrenaline-fuelled competitors raced to the beat of thunderous drums to scare fish away, while others threw dumplings into the water to keep the fish from eating Qu Yuan's body. One wonders what good it did, given the frequent reports of senior officials in China being executed for graft. Two thousand years, so little change.

I fetch a beer from the fridge. Probably the eighth can of Heineken I've had tonight. It's 2 a.m. While I was still a married man with a loving wife, I would not be sitting in front of the computer, downing one can after another at this time of night. Lai Ying wouldn't hear of it. She always closely watched the eating and drinking habits of her *siu Feijau yahn*, her dear little Africans, as she called

Chacha and I. Now, there's only one little *Feijau yahn* in her life, perhaps in her heart.

They've been gone three months now. And the life of a single man is now catching up with me when I'm least prepared for it. Only now do I realise how much I've come to depend on her. She even picked my shirts and matching ties, accusing me of having no sense of fashion. She replaced my socks before the little holes got too big. I used to be able to do all this myself, but after Lai Ying literally took over my day-to-day life, going back to that life is like relearning an old skill, or coping with hazards I've long learned to avoid. It brings back the frustrations of adapting to life in China, learning the language, coping with the harsh winters, abuse on the streets. I don't know if I could start all over again.

At 3.30 a.m., I log off and throw myself on the bed, too tired and too drunk to take a shower. The walls are spinning around and around, and only stop their mad dance when I flick the bedside lamp off, plunging the room into darkness, sinking through a void filled with the dull buzzing of the aircon.

In the morning, I log on, hoping to hear from Lai Ying. There are two emails. One is from a client saying they won't be needing my services any longer. This is happening too often for my liking. I've already lost half my clients this way in the last four months, and more than half my income. Some are either trying to cut costs or simply going out of business. The news makes me want to shut down the computer and go back to bed to nurse my hangover.

But there's this other email. At first glance, it looks like junk email that has somehow slipped through the antispam filters. I don't recognise the source, and I'm about to delete it when I notice the Chinese character for egg, 'dan', in the subject line. No one calls me Eggman anymore. I can almost hear my heart throbbing as I move the mouse and click.

So long time no see, Eggman. Is friend Wang from Nanjing. Now my business good-good. Wang study English, too; you surprise? Wang remembering old friend. Good old days they say, yes? My friend, soon Wang come to Xianggang. To see you. Very soon.

Pipe Dream

I FORWARD THE EMAIL TO Diallo. I'm anxious to know what he'll make of Wang's re-emergence. He calls me two hours later from a site in Kowloon Bay, where they are building a gigantic shopping mall.

I shouldn't be spending so much time at the Oasis. Apart from the fact that money is low, way too low for my liking, the Oasis is where all my troubles started, the humid spring night when I met Tiffany two years ago. She opened up a whole new world to me. And just as quickly brought it crashing down on me. Like the typhoons that sweep with a vengeance across the region in the summer months, knocking down trees, leaving broken signboards and all manner of debris scattered on the streets. Her extensive connections, *guanxi*, came from her previous job as a journalist for a Chinese magazine. At least that's what it said in her CV. What else she did, I never did find out. But the way she got on with people like Chuck at the casino, I should have seen it coming.

The Oasis brings back all these wretched memories. But where else in Hong Kong would I listen to reggae and African music?

After a quick lunch of spaghetti bolognaise, I spend an hour scheduling jobs for next week. But I won't be seeing this money for weeks to come. Many small firms will stop at nothing to delay payment or even avoid paying altogether. There are two clients I've been chasing for three months now. And it's not even a lot of money, just a few thousand dollars. Yet, I have no choice but to keep servicing them, in the hope that every now and then, they can part with a few hundred.

I walk down the five flights of stairs. It's the only exercise I'm getting nowadays, since a developer saw fit to turn the only basketball court for miles into a dusty construction site, with the promise of yet another grotesque addition to the Hong Kong skyline. The other residents can't understand my behaviour. The stairs are not considered a healthy part of the building. That's where residents dump black bin bags, treading carefully to avoid the cockroaches and holding their noses to avoid the smell of rotten vegetables that hangs in the dank, narrow space. At least the roaches in the building stay on the floor where they belong, unlike their cousins on the street, which fly across your face and straight into an oncoming minibus. I had never seen cockroaches that fly until I came to Asia.

I wave to the security guard in the lobby. He gives me the thumbs up as he holds the door for me. He likes to practice his Putonghua, which he hasn't had much use for since he arrived here from Chengdu as a boy. When I first met him, he couldn't get over the idea of an African speaking Chinese.

Now, he treats me like a nephew from the mainland. That's how I like to kid myself anyway. Behind my back, he probably calls me a *hak gwei*, Cantonese for black ghost or black devil. I prefer the Putonghua, *hei gui*. It sounds like a greeting.

Anastasia and her employer, Beth, are just walking into the building as I'm leaving. Beth's son, Siu Meng, slams his bike into the bougainvillea flowerpots, and when Anastasia tries to help him, he screams and makes as if to kick her. His mother doesn't even bat an eyelid. I hold the door open for them, smile and mutter a greeting. I can feel Beth's penetrating gaze like fingers poking into my face. Anastasia and I avoid eye contact. For the last few months, she has been coming to clean my apartment and iron my clothes. She comes in for three hours on Sunday morning before going to church. Technically, it's illegal. Foreign domestic helpers aren't allowed to moonlight. Anastasia tells me she's supporting an out-of-work husband and six children in school in Manila, and several jobless cousins in the provinces. And I used to think Africans had extended family pressures.

Beth always wears that unsmiling, stern expression on her face, the type that says, "Not now, okay?" I've no idea why she looks at me like that. It's not like I'm trying to get her to invest her life savings in some discredited hedge fund.

Her husband, Jupiter Lee, is more approachable. He runs a trading company. When he first told me his name three years ago, I thought he was joking. But he had a well-rehearsed answer. "When I in school, we study planet. The girl, she name Venus. My friend, he call Pluto. I want big name, strong." He flexed his muscles, grinning with pleasure.

We only ever meet either in the fitness room or in the lift. He always wants to talk about Africa. A few years ago, he took his family to South Africa for

Christmas. It left a lasting impression. Their son Siu Meng has been to Africa. But not my Chacha. When he told me, I wanted to hide in a corner and die.

A few months after I first met him, Jupiter said to me, "We go to the happy hour, one time."

"Sure, Jupiter. Where?"

"Everywhere is okay. Maybe the Lan Kwai Fong. One day is okay?"

"Of course."

We've not done the happy hour yet.

Sometimes Jupiter plays football with Siu Meng at the children's playground. Beth sits on a ledge at the water fountain, watching over them like a hen protecting her chickens from marauding hawks.

Chacha and I used to play on that very spot. Lai Ying would sit on that same ledge, one eye on us, the other on *Next*, her favourite celebrity gossip magazine. Nowadays when I walk by the children's playground, I feel as though I'm trespassing on sacred ground. I walk away quickly to escape the mothers' questioning looks.

Haven't seen your pretty daughter recently. Did she go back to Fei Jau?

I smile and nod my head, pretending I don't understand. That's one good thing about being a foreigner here. When you don't want to be troubled with questions or unwelcome conversation, you can always pretend you don't understand.

Mhou yisi, ngoh msihk gong. Sorry, I don't speak the lingo.

Amidst the throbbing of jackhammers at the construction site, I can almost hear the faint echo of a bouncing ball and Chacha's chirpy laughter as we chased each other around the old court. Whenever I hear the chatter of children, I prick my ears instinctively, half hoping to hear my daughter. I'm always gripped by a sense of panic when I realise I might not recognise her laughter if I hear it.

My phone rings as I'm crossing the road. There's no number on the caller display. It simply reads 'Call'. That means long distance. My hand freezes. I'm momentarily rooted to the spot, as a minibus comes shuttling down the road.

Lai Ying's voice jolts me and propels me out of danger. For a moment, I thought it was Wang. I *wanted* it to be Wang. Since I got that email from him, and replied giving him my number, I've been like a leaf tossed about in the wind, unwilling—no, unable—to decide which way to go. Sometimes I want to hear from Wang. I *yearn* to know why he has contacted me. Sometimes I hope he can't be bothered to call, or that he calls and is diverted to voicemail. Then I can decide whether to call him back or not.

"Hello! Hello!" Lai Ying's voice sounds strained. In the noisy street, I can barely hear her. "Are you there?"

"I am, sweetheart. You all right?"

She sighs with exasperation rather than relief. "Why you don't say anything? You just answer the phone and say nothing?"

"I nearly got ran over by a minibus."

"What! When?"

"Just now, as I was answering the phone. In the middle of the road."

"Why you're walking in the middle of the road? Not so clever, la."

"I was crossing the road. Jesus, Lai Ying, can we change the subject? I could have died just now." I don't like it when she speaks to me in English. We always end up having these stupid misunderstandings. In the past, we always spoke Putonghua, until Chacha was born. We try to give our daughter a multilingual experience: English, Cantonese, and now Putonghua. But we're the ones who need serious work on our communication skills.

"Okay. The other night I call you, but no answer. You're in pub again?"

"Lai Ying, you're not here. What am I supposed to do? I can't go out?"

"You start gambling again?"

"Of course not!" I unbutton my shirt and wipe my face. I can feel drops of sweat crawling down my sides.

"How's Chacha?"

"Fine."

"Can I talk to her?"

"Not here. But she sends her love."

"Nice. What else did she say – that she wants to see Daddy?"

Silence. I can picture the rolling eyes, the don't-start look.

"Why you always want to argue?"

"Argue? I just want to know what my daughter's been saying, darling. When she says she wants to see Daddy, what do you tell her?"

"She didn't say that anymore!" she blurts out. "She knows you're not here."

"And have you explained why she needs to be in Shanghai, away from her home?"

Silence. Sigh. I wait, holding the phone an inch from the ear. It must be about thirty degrees Celsius today, and ninety percent humidity. When it gets like this, talking on a mobile makes the ear hot and sweaty.

"I'm protecting her, Dan. You know that."

"Protecting her from what?"

As I wait to cross the road and head into the MTR, a cockroach crawls out of a crack in a building and joins the sea of human traffic on the pavement. Some people cover their noses with a hand or handkerchief in a vain attempt to keep the pollution out. On seeing the cockroach, a woman in high heels screams and moves away to the relative safety of the middle of the crowd, jostling people about, taking small dainty steps. As soon as the light turns green, the cockroach disappears beneath the brown shoe of an elderly lady who is being led by the hand of a teenage girl in thick, round glasses. I'm tempted to take a final look to see whether the roach has been flattened nice and proper, but I'm now caught in a wave of anxious humanity rushing to cross the street, dodging another wave coming from the opposite direction. I nearly bump into a man with a towel around his head. The towel is drenched in sweat.

"You know the answer to that, Dan."

"Lai Ying, they don't come any more. Why don't you believe that?"

"You always tell lies. I can't believe this."

"Lai Ying, this is not fair." I stand facing the wall inside the station, where no one can hear me, away from the ticket booths. "Okay, I was out gambling back then. But that was back then, sweetheart. Not now. Not anymore. And I always told you where I was."

"You claimed you were working, but you were just gambling and bringing all these problems."

"What do you want me to do to convince you it's all right now? I gave them all their money."

Silence. My heart leaps when I hear her next words.

"Maybe you should come here, Dan." The voice is soft and almost despairing. I picture her massaging her forehead to ease the stress.

"I'll come tomorrow! No, tonight!"

"Not so soon. I mean, to live here." Is that a plea in her voice? "You can find good jobs here. Hong Kong is not safe for us. And now there are no jobs for IT people. Hong Kong is finished."

Live in China? Again? After all these years? What about my work here? My contacts, my clients?

"Let's meet and talk about it properly."

"I'm not ready. What you did…" She's gone. Did she hang up? Did her credit run out? I hurry to the turnstile, feeling empty and worthless.

The Sahara Oasis is already teeming with life when I get there. It's rocking with the heavy rhythmic sounds of Lingala music. There's a couple on the dance floor in the far corner, hands on each other's shoulders, swaying to the hypnotic sounds. This early! That's what I love about the Oasis.

Diallo is sitting at the bar, watching a repeat of an English Premier League match. He's a die-hard Arsenal fan. He talks about the club as though he was one of them, saying things like, "We're home to Liverpool this Saturday; we came from behind to beat West Ham." He's wearing one of his colourful striped shirts, and has grown a moustache since I last saw him. It's a bushy one, drooping mournfully over his upper lip and falling off the edges, completely unsuited for the festive mood in the bar, whose walls have recently been adorned with multicoloured African batiks, interspaced with kettle-sized drum sets, goatskin shields, and wooden masks.

After shaking hands, he demands to know what's going on with 'that old crook' Wang. I squeeze his shoulder to urge calm while I order a pint of Carlsberg.

"You saw the email, Diallo. That's all I know. Thing is, I can't understand why he needs to contact *me*."

"You worked for the guy. You were his buddy, if not his humble servant." He starts to laugh.

"He was on good terms with everyone," I protest lamely. "I wonder who else he has talked to."

"You're the anointed one, *mon ami*. Look, I made some calls today, and no one from the Nanjing era has heard anything. Don't worry, I didn't mention you."

A tremor of mild indignation runs down my spine. Wang has no right to put me in this situation. I can't be seen to be associating with him. The guys would never forgive me, especially those like Julius who accused me of betraying the brothers by remaining "loyal" to Wang until I was fired, as they insisted.

"I bet he has a new job for you, Eggman. But after what he did, how can you get mixed up with the man?"

"Isn't it all mere speculation? I mean, no one has any proof he had anything to do with it."

Diallo eyes me with more pity than disbelief.

"You can protect him all you want, Danny boy. But don't say I didn't warn you."

This discussion is going nowhere. When this happens, it's better to talk about women and sex. Diallo has been urging me to find myself a girlfriend. A girlfriend, for heaven's sake! I haven't encountered the species for a decade! The mere thought of it gives me goose bumps.

Diallo says he's not interested in marriage.

"Life is too short to tie yourself down with one woman," he once told me.

"That means you'll never get married?"

"Man, I'm thirty-two," he declared. "I've not had my fair share of freedom and amusement, yet. Frankly, Dan, I can't understand how you could marry at twenty-six."

Lai Ying got pregnant, a second time. That's why, and he knows it.

He had a long-term relationship with a girl he met in Shanghai after he left Nanjing. The company she was working for sent her to New York for training and she stayed put. He was never the same again. Then he got mixed up with an older French woman who was anxious to settle down, as he explained it to me. Diallo couldn't see how she would be acceptable to his people. He got rid of her by telling her that as a Muslim, he was going to marry four wives as was his entitlement; did she mind? That was the first time I heard him mention his religion.

An hour later, Candy appears. She is a sort of Miss FixIt, like many Chinese girls one meets at the pub. Officially, she's an insurance agent. That's what it says on one of her cards. But she also advises on investments, from Hang Seng Index securities to property. For that, she produces a different card that says she's a member of this and that association, a string of indecipherable acronyms, is regulated by this and that body. She studied in London, and that's where she acquired all those impressive credentials, and that sophisticated, smooth, confident returnee accent.

She's tall, has a small sweet mouth that's always set in a pout, as if she's privy to some naughty gossip and is trying not to laugh. She's been hanging around us for some time now, hoping to turn us into customers. I buy my annual travel insurance through her. But I'm keeping my options open on her other offerings. She sees Diallo as her best prospect. He has been talking to her about life insurance for months. He gets her to work out initial sums assured, premium terms, annual premiums, and bonuses. She's always coming back with new figures, new promotions. Special offers. Just for him. Over his pint of Carlsberg and her bottle of Diamond Black cider with a slice of lemon stuck down the neck of the bottle, they get the calculator out, scan the projected guaranteed and non-guaranteed cash values and death benefits, go over the waivers and exemptions. Then she goes away, to revise the quotes, until the next drinking session.

I know he already has a policy. It's obvious she likes him, the way she sidles up to him, flirtatiously hooks her arm into his, cracks up at his jokes, clinks drinks with him, and smiles so close to his face a kiss looks ever so imminent. But this is probably her way of trying to seduce him to sign on the dotted line and make out a cheque, so she'll improve her numbers, get her commission, be in the running for sales agent of the year. Then maybe she'll let him into her knickers. So far, it's a stalemate.

She also says she comes here to listen to African music, which she first discovered on a vacation in Mauritius. Diallo keeps telling her to go to the *real* Africa, the continent. In fact, he sees Candy as someone who needs to be taught a bit more about the real Africa every time they meet. Tonight he's on a new lesson. The meaning of Chinese names for countries and continents. He dons the expression of a weary teacher and starts ticking names off his fingers.

"Take the Chinese name for Africa. In Cantonese, it's Fei Jau. In Putonghua, Feizhou. Zhou means continent. But what's the meaning of fei?"

"Well." Candy furrows her brow. "The written character actually means negative, or wrong."

"Very good, Candy. Negative as in 'the opposite of'. Hence the negative continent. The non-continent."

"Diallo! You're taking transliteration too literally."

"Candy, sweetheart, if the Chinese wanted to give Africa face, they would have placed that funny little thing—what's it called?—a grass radical, above the character fei, like they did with Feileuhtban. The Philippines is fragrant, pleasant, flourishing. But not Africa. But maybe they're right."

"It's not that simple, Diallo," protests Candy.

"Well, let's see how complex it gets. America is Meiguo in Putonghua. Meihgwok in Cantonese. Beautiful land. Take England, Yingguo, or Yinggwok."

"I know," says Candy, hurriedly. "Ying means brave, hero, blah blah blah..."

"Need I say more? Take any European country and it's the same thing, something nice and desirable." Candy feigns a sulk. Diallo carries on, ignoring her. "Africa is just a non-continent full of black devils, man."

Candy instinctively rubs his shoulder, shaking her head, as if to say, you poor thing, why do you burden your mind with these meaningless problems? Aloud she says, "You have to face the problems you guys create for yourselves. It's no good moaning about what the rest of the world says about you."

"You're right, darling," mutters Diallo, sighing with a sense of resignation. "I mean, look at Dan's country, Zim. From breadbasket of Africa to basket case."

"So much for politics, Diallo," says Candy, before I can find my voice, for which I sigh my gratitude. "Are you guys coming out tomorrow night to commemorate 4th June?"

Diallo pulls a face.

"Commemorate what, man?"

"Come on, Tiananmen, the massacre? The day Chinese troops ploughed through several thousand students and innocent citizens?"

Diallo holds his hand up. "Give me a break, man."

I watch the exchange distractedly. From the shocked look on Candy's reddening face, she can't believe Diallo's irreverence. Watching him rehearse the lesson of the Nanjing riots is like watching the football reruns on the TV in front of us. He considers it his duty to educate whoever he meets.

"Students in Beijing only got the guts to turn against their government because they realised their cousins in Nanjing had already done it, four months previously, and got away with it," he declares.

"And the crackdown," says Candy. "You think it was right?"

"I didn't say that." Candy watches him expectantly. "What I can tell you is that the students miscalculated. Running black ghosts out of the ancient capital was one thing. Demanding democracy and human rights on the streets of the modern capital was, quite frankly, a bit of a pipe dream." His voice is tinged with regret.

Candy looks as if she has received news of a death in the family. She'll have to attend the vigil without us. I have enough problems right now, and frankly I don't want to be reminded of the past, with Wang barging into my life like a devious old flame gate-crashing a wedding party. I have only fifty dollars in my pockets, which is not even enough for another round. Tomorrow night, I plan to see Hamlet.

Give Us a Break, Man

I'LL BE SORRY TO LOSE this flat. It's spacious and airy, blessed with a good view of the harbour, at least on clear days. But most importantly, it's close to my clients, who are mostly in the Sheung Wan, Central, Wanchai corridor. It's also close to the action, close to all the trendy bars of Soho and Lan Kwai Fong.

But it's a bit too far from the Sahara Oasis. And that's where I would have loved to meet Hamlet tonight. The Oasis is in Tsim Sha Tsui, on the other side of the harbour. Hamlet, my property agent, never ventures that far away. He says it's too remote, too quiet, too backward, like China. It's a common refrain you hear from residents of Hong Kong Island. Coming from Chinese people, it shocked me when I first heard it. The dwindling, over-reclaimed Victoria Harbour isn't just a physical divide. It also marks a cultural gulf between two sets of classes.

At the pubs in Lan Kwai Fong, the evening mating season has already started in earnest. The lingering looks of admiration, the scents that unambiguously evoke sex, the casual touch. Skinny local girls with long black hair nurse white wines, smiles permanently etched on their faces. Big-hipped foreign women in skimpy tops, cleavages and ringed belly buttons exposed. They take large swigs of their beers, as if in competition with the men who've rolled back their sleeves, ready to embark on the strenuous manual task of hoisting pints, showing off hairy arms. It is like a carnival out here.

I quickly locate Hamlet, the sun god surrounded by three beaming Venuses and a young man. Their business cards describe them as finance and equity executives. Before I came to Hong Kong, I thought executives were senior managers. These boys and girls can't be older than twenty-five. They power-dress and carry big titles to impress clients. I smile when I remember how I, too, fell for this. While Tiffany's Hong Kong business cards described her as my Executive Assistant, which is what she really was, the ones for China carried the

189

title Executive Senior Manager. They're even crazier there about titles than in Hong Kong.

On a normal night, I would be sizing up these executives and plying them with business cards, assuring them to expect my call in a day or two. You just never know where the next freelance IT job will come from.

But tonight is not a normal night. In fact, I haven't had a normal night for so long I've forgotten what a normal night means. Or a normal day, for that matter. For a start, I didn't think to replenish my wallet with the cards that describe me as an IT Consultant. There is so little of this exalted IT consulting coming my way nowadays that I feel like an imposter handing the cards out.

At 8 p.m., Hamlet's friends excuse themselves and fade away through the party crowd. Before any more angels can cloud Hamlet's horizon, I tell him I need to move house. I need something more down to earth.

"Oh no, you need a downward adjustment, right?" He looks at me with disappointment. If you didn't know him, you would think he was worried that the rent would be lower, and so would his commission. The truth is that he'll need to take me to see apartments in less salubrious parts of town. It's not good for his image.

I nod, trying not to show my embarrassment. If he notices, he's too gracious to say anything, except, "Not to worry. It's the new game in town, man."

He fishes out the mobile, dials a number, and speaks rapidly in Cantonese. After a few minutes, he says we're in luck. I get us another round to celebrate five viewings. Half an hour later, I get a call from Charlie saying I ought to get my arse out to the Pirates' Rice Bowl.

Hamlet is not too keen. It won't be easy to find parking for his oversized Lexus on the narrow overcrowded streets of the Soho. And he's not the kind of guy who'll be caught dead walking the streets of Hong Kong or hopping out of a taxi.

People might think he doesn't own a car.

Charlie is drinking with Diallo, Candy, and a couple I've never met. They stand by the bar, holding their beers like trophies, mobile phones upholstered on the belt. Every now and then, someone flicks the upholster open, draws the ringing or vibrating phone out in one quick motion, and fires off a string of words, struggling to be heard above the noise and music. It's not yet 9 p.m., but they all have that smoothness of manner and mellow face that says their throats have been well and truly irrigated.

Diallo introduces us. The strangers are Alex, a fellow Zimbabwean and Meg, his Chinese girlfriend, who gives me a big smile, as though she's waited a long time to meet her boyfriend's family. Alex is white, medium-built, and dressed in a dark-blue suit. He and I immediately embark on a trip down memory lane, reminiscing about the lives and places we left behind. We're not only from opposite ends of the country, I, West Mashonaland, and he, East Mashonaland, but also from opposite sides of the land and wealth divide. It is never made explicit, but the fact that his family do not live in a city can only mean they are landowners. Ndambu pervades my mind as he talks excitedly about the unending greenery, the clear blue skies and fresh air, how he misses the wide-open spaces and closeness to nature. Meg watches us intently, nodding with recognition. She has heard it all before, and can't get enough of this fascinating landlocked country that has been getting in the news for all the wrong reasons. She is small, a little chubby, has sharp, incisive eyes, smiles a lot, but doesn't say much. She says she's a land economist, working for the Housing Authority. Perhaps they've trained her to be economical with words, too.

Alex and I steer clear of the tensions and troubles that have recently gripped the country, the embarrassing accusations of our government's warmongering in Congo, Rwanda, and faraway Sudan, the old land wounds that have recently been reopened.

Alex says he works for a company called Asia Risk Assessment.

"Due diligence, basically," he says, with a contented smirk. "Mostly in China. You want to know if your business partner is for real? We check him out for you."

"You mean like sniff around bin bags," says Charlie, "emptying lunch boxes and used rubbers?"

Everyone glances at Meg. She doesn't look offended. Only slightly amused. That's a good sign. If she can take this kind of talk, she can be one of the boys. Just like Candy girl.

"Well, it's not quite like that," says Alex, frowning. "But we get close. We can tell you if he's in trouble with the law, if he has a mistress, where she lives, what was the last gift he bought her, whether he had noodles or steamed rice, or—"

"I get it!" Charlie cuts in. "Scan their shit under a microscope. Wow! I was wondering what's that smell about you, Alex?"

Alex's reply is drowned by the laughter. I don't laugh. I'm thinking, maybe this guy can help me locate Lai Ying. A private eye! I'll have to get his card. My mind is racing. They probably have an extensive network in Shanghai. Perhaps all we need is to put a call through. It might cost, though. It will definitely cost. There's only one way to find out. I'm thinking strategies, tactics, costs, paying no attention to Charlie's off-colour jokes. This could be just the break I need.

Charlie's the centre of attention, as is usually the case when he's about. He's a senior executive at a merchant bank. A real executive, unlike the kids I met earlier, who described themselves as aggressive when they probably meant confident. Charlie has been in Hong Kong six years and is proud of the fact that he can't speak a word of Cantonese. He constantly reminds anyone who cares to listen how English language standards have deteriorated since the handover to China three years ago. He has a string of girlfriends, mostly Filipina, and has recently started dating Anastasia, my illegal. Sometimes I wonder when he gets to earn his money. And the way he splashes out on amusement, gadgets, and travel, I don't know when he'll ever retire and start that investment consultancy firm he's always going on about. Diallo dismisses it as just another bar pipe dream.

The next few hours pass the way they always do when we're called to the bar. The talk is all about apartment rentals, the worsening economy, and the unstable Hong Kong dollar. At eleven, Meg excuses herself. She has an early morning meeting. Alex walks her outside to get a taxi and comes back to find Charlie holding forth on the inequities of unfair land distribution in Africa. Our Chinese friends find it all rather confusing, especially since Charlie is so very British, as Candy puts it. They find it easier to understand stocks and bonds, apartment prices and the slump in the property market that has plunged homeowners into negative equity for the last four years.

Alex insists they acquired their land legally. His family have been living in Zimbabwe for three generations. He says they have as much right to the land as the Africans.

Looking at the defiance on his face as he says this makes my chest stiffen. My father has been waiting all his life for a piece of land to call his own, in his own Africa. The wait has been a good two decades since independence, when so much was promised. I was only thirteen at the time. How could I ever forget the celebrations when Mugabe took the reins of the newest independent African state! My father said we were finally going to own the land we tilled. *This has to be our chance now. The white man has screwed us for too long. Less than one percent of the population own seventy percent of the land. Is that fair? Give the war veterans a break, for God's sake! Give us a break, man!*

A dark shadow crosses Alex's face. Or is it my imagination? Everyone is staring at me. Alex's face is only inches from mine. I realise in my drunkenness that I'm literally yelling in his face. I take a step back and reach for my beer.

"Fuck you, man!" Alex growls, eyes blazing. "These people you call war veterans are just hooligans who don't know the first thing about running a farm."

Diallo steps between us. "Easy, guys. Take it easy."

"Hey, can someone please tell me," says Candy. "How did the white people acquire land in Africa? Zimbabwe was a colony, right?"

"They fucking stole it!"

Candy recoils from me, as if I've slapped her across the face. Everyone stares at Alex and me, waiting for the blows to start flying. The landowner's son versus the squatter's son. The gloves are off.

"Without us, that country is going to starve!"

"So what exactly is going on, what's the deal?" ventures Candy, after a safe moment of silence.

"As the man says, a tiny white minority owns virtually all the land, that's the deal," says Diallo, rubbing Candy's shoulder. The hand lingers a tad too long. He's getting close to buying that policy. "You've got a South Africa situation here, but there's no Mandela or Tutu to sort it out, sweetheart."

"You can all bloody well go to hell!"

Alex waves a dismissive hand in our direction, his face creased with a mixture of disgust and impatience, gulps down his drink, zips up his black leather jacket, and stomps away. Damn it! I won't be hiring him after all. I've truly screwed it up.

I watch him stagger away. He nearly crashes into a table with Chinese guys playing *tsai mui* (paper, scissors, and stones) and *sik jong* (dice and cup). One of them reaches out to steady him. Alex shoos him away and ends up on the floor. Two waiters help him to his feet. He turns to shake a fist in the direction of the Chinese guys but ends up crashing into their table, scattering their Blue Girl beers. Two doormen grab hold of him and lead him to the door. I'm surprised they don't hurl him out. The Chinese guys are already yelling into their phones, summoning backup.

Twenty minutes later, I'm ready to call it a day. It's almost 1 a.m. I need to go and see if Lai Ying has emailed me this evening.

Charlie and I finish off our drinks and head down the narrow road. Diallo's alone with Candy. I have a distinct feeling he's not sorry to see us leave. It's that glint in his eye, the casual scratch of the moustache, the warm handshake, and the little push he gives me when we say goodbye.

There are plenty of taxis but Charlie wants to have a smoke and take in the breeze coming from the harbour. The breeze has lost much of its nauseating dead-water smell while winding its way around the skyscrapers in Central, and by the time it gets to where we are, it's down to a gust that caresses the face, urging sobriety. From here, you can almost relive the fantasy of the Hong Kong name, which is derived from the Chinese characters for fragrant harbour, *heung gong*. But the smells that come out of Victoria Harbour nowadays are anything but fragrant. The best way to experience them in their raw obnoxiousness is to take a ride on the Star Ferry. Nothing else captures the essence of Hong Kong than the smells from the dead harbour mixed with those of diesel exhaust fumes.

We sense a commotion coming from one of the little dark alleys off Shelley Street.

"Shit! Triads at work," says Charlie.

Four guys are punching and aiming flying kicks at a figure that seems to be suspended from an invisible rope and is swaying from side to side like a yoyo. The kickboxing practice looks like one of those Chinese martial arts films, elegantly choreographed but without the war cries and drumbeat *thump!* whenever a blow makes contact.

I approach cautiously and take a closer look. I stand back, immobilised by horror. It's Alex, his face all covered in blood.

A force propels me into the alley. Charlie's restraining hand grabs hold of my jacket but I push it away and keep running, straight into a flying kick. I raise my hands in time to protect my chest and my assailant hits the ground.

I'm now face-to-face with the three combatants. Even in the half-light, I can see the venom in their eyes. They hate to see someone spoil their party. They are the guys Alex had a run-in with at the pub. Four of them. The fifth must be the *dai lou* they called on the mobile. Whenever the locals get into a sticky situation, there's always a big brother drinking a few streets away who can be called upon to lend some muscle.

"Okay, guys, that's really enough," I appeal to them, raising a hand.

"Who you, man?" says *Dai Lou*.

"If you don't get away now, I'm calling the police."

They grumble in Cantonese, waving their hands about. Alex is lying in a wretched heap on the road, retching into a hawker's abandoned wicker basket. One of the fighters approaches me, shaking a fist in Alex's direction, complaining about how "my friend" made them lose face in a public place.

I promise them that Alex will apologise, and when he does, they should leave him alone. They consult among themselves and come back demanding an apology. Alex is not moving. And he's not breathing. In terror, I glance up at Charlie.

"He's dead!"

Dai Lou approaches, saying, "*Gao choh, ah*!" You're kidding!

I whip out my phone. "I'm calling the police." I look up to see the five of them take to their heels. Before I finish dialling 999, I turn back to Alex and give one final shake and check his pulse. There's some movement, but this is going to require mouth-to-mouth resuscitation. Charlie is pacing up and down, breathing noisily through the mouth.

"Man, let's call an ambulance and beat it," he says. "You don't want to get mixed up in this triad shit, man."

"We can't just leave." Charlie's voice is beginning to grate on my nerves. "They're going to want to know what the hell happened."

"We don't know shit, man. Who is this guy Alex, anyway? I don't know him from Adam, man."

"He's from my bloody country."

"Oh, I get it. So now you're like bosom buddies, eh? Is this a sort of Zimbabwean thing, like fight, quickly make up, and then you're like brothers in arms?"

"Okay, how about, he's a friend of Diallo's? Does that count?"

Charlie curses and kicks the wall. I extract some tissue from my pocket and wipe Alex's blood-stained mouth and nose. One of his eyelids moves. I stand back, holding my breath. An eye opens and then shuts with a sense of finality.

Charlie jumps. "He's a ghost, man!"

A scornful grin spreads across Alex's face. I leap away.

"It's you again!" he mutters. "Christ, won't you leave me alone?"

Charlie grits his teeth and shakes a fist in Alex's face.

Alex can barely walk. Charlie and I have to help him.

"Careful, that hurts!"

"Shit, man!" says Charlie, punching the air in front of him.

I ask Alex if he needs a doctor.

"What I need is a fucking drink, man," he mutters. "Get me to the pub, for chrissakes."

"Damn right!" hisses Charlie. "After we saved your miserable life, the least you can do is buy us a coupla beers, man."

"No worries, mate," says Alex in a mock Aussie accent. "Let's make that Wanchai, right? How about the Peer Pleasure?"

At this point, we could be going to the moon for all I care. That email from Lai Ying will have to wait, if there's one at all. I have a feeling there isn't one. She's not going to write, is she? And I'm supposed to keep rushing to the inbox like a lovesick teenager.

To hell with it. Tonight, I'm getting seriously drunk.

Unfinished Business

I SPEND THE NEXT TWO weeks viewing properties. Hamlet has been keeping me busy, but I can't find anything I both like and can afford. If I just wanted a small place for myself, I would not be too picky. In fact, a small bachelor pad with a second bedroom for a study would be quite enough, and it's all that I could afford right now.

Since Lai Ying won't tell me where she is, I've been trying to track her down through her emails. The header line syntax leads me to a server in Shanghai. The set of machines she's using are definitely at one location. Julius can help me to locate the cybercafé from the IP addresses through his contacts in the Shanghai IT industry. And then maybe I can go hang around there, hoping she shows up. It sounds like a wild goose chase.

I've emailed her about my plan to move house but she hasn't replied yet. Perhaps moving to a new address will give her some reassurance. Meanwhile, the days drag on, pulling me with them to an unknown destination, like flotsam in the floods.

Diallo has been telling me about an African restaurant in Chung King Mansions. He claims it's a real restaurant, not a dining room in someone's flat, like some of the other eateries I've been to. The food in these eateries is mostly Nigerian egusi with fufu, which comes in Styrofoam lunch boxes. I don't like to eat it at lunchtime because it can literally knock you out for the rest of the afternoon if you're not used to it. It sits like a rock in your belly. The two or three places I know open only for lunch. Diallo says this new place is open for dinner. I call him one evening and tell him I'm ready to check it out.

The junction of Peking and Nathan Roads outside Chungking Mansions is like a market. It's a challenge to weave your way past the hordes of touts inviting you to have a suit made, quick-quick, special price, only for you. Others sidle up to you offering Rolexes. You can have your choice of a genuine fake or a fake fake. No one offers the genuine thing. Up ahead the road, there's a huge Rolex sign hanging across the pavement. Presumably, they sell the genuine thing in there. A constant flow of traders and budget tourists makes its way into the lobby. Those not tugging suitcases and boxes lounge on the pavement outside, watching the human traffic, chatting on mobile phones to their families back home and business contacts in Shamshuipo, Mongkok, and Shenzhen. Comparing prices, following up on orders.

The queue for the lift snakes its way past a convenience store and forex bureau. We'll be here forever. I suggest we walk up the fire escape, which turns out to be a bad idea. The building has been caught in a time warp. The narrow staircase is still as filthy as I remember it nine years ago, when I stayed here. The steps are cracked at the edges, and in some places, there are reddish-brown stains, which look like dried blood. Graffiti drawings of genitals with spiky bits of pubic hair adorn the walls. Cigarette butts, bits of used tissue, and supermarket plastic paper bags litter the floor. In every corner lie piles of big, black garbage bins and discarded furniture. The open windows give some respite to the rotten garbage smells that fill the air.

As we step into the lobby on the fifth floor, a gigantic cockroach dashes ahead of us and disappears behind a mattress and broken chairs stacked against the wall next to the lift. My neck and shoulders stiffen. But it's too late to cry off now. Diallo is unfazed. He eats here all the time.

Inside the eatery, it is reasonably clean, if modest. Before we eat, we wash our hands with warm water delivered in a basin. We are the only customers at this time. I opt for the mouth-watering fish egusi. The egusi stew is slippery on the fingers. Elusive. As if it doesn't want to be eaten, but simply admired, smelled. You have to woo, cajole, and tame it with a chunk of fufu, chasing it around the plate with probing fingers, finally trapping it and delivering it to a waiting mouth before it slips away. We eat in silence, watching a Nigerian movie on DVD. The eatery is owned by a Muslim, so alcohol is out of the question.

Diallo informs me that Nollywood is the third biggest film industry in the world after Bollywood and Hollywood. The film is an unlikely fairy tale. Poor, humble, village girl being pursued by a rich city boy anxious to escape from the predatory city girl his rotund, overbearing parents have chosen for him. Before we leave, the proprietor, whose name is Abubakr, gives us his card and asks us to bring our friends next time.

We make our way through the congested street towards the Oasis. On Carnarvon Road, a familiar figure springs into view. My heartbeat quickens. It can't be her, surely? But it is. The brown hair with red and blonde highlights. The tall, slim figure with hips that push out rebelliously against blue jeans, a few sizes too big for a Chinese girl but just perfect for me. As she and her friend turn to cross the street, I catch a glimpse of her face, the beautiful, ever-smiling lips, high cheekbones, small nose, and large eyes that I once thought were dreamy but later discovered were designed that way so they missed nothing. I nudge Diallo and point up ahead.

"Do you see what I'm seeing? Girl in white top."

"With the funny hair?"

"Don't you recognise her?"

"Not unless I see her face, man. Who is she?"

"Good old Tiff, man." We approach Kimberley Road. They can only be going to the Oasis.

"What! What do you want from her, after the way she fucked you up?"

"I'm curious. Come on. Let's check this out. What do you have to lose?"

"You're crazy, my friend. *Mal à la tête!*"

If it's only the head, that's all right. As long as the rest of me is functioning properly, I'm ready for this long overdue reunion.

"Slow down a bit. Let them settle down and get their drinks."

"What exactly are you planning to say to her?"

"I don't know. Hello? What's up, babe? Something like that. Or how about, 'What the devil do you think you're doing here? Why don't you select a chat-up line for me, man? You're good at these sorts of things.'"

"You're crazy, man."

Tiffany and her friend are seated at a table at the far end of the bar. We locate ourselves near the door, where we can observe them without being seen. I keep an eye on them, waiting for the other girl to go to the washroom. My chance comes an hour and three pints into the evening. Diallo wishes me luck, and remains behind, chatting up two girls who come here several nights a week and spend hours chain-smoking and drinking white wine, giggling and squeezing each other's elbows. They're skinny and always have a washed-out look about them, as if they're on drugs. They've dyed their hair a revolting green. Only foreigners ever talk to them. Diallo is convinced they're lesbians. So he's just making polite conversation.

Tiffany doesn't see me approach until I'm literally hovering above her bob of blonde and red hair. I have long fantasised about breaking her neck. But when she looks up, her shoulders tremble and her face breaks into a grin, and all I want to do is kiss her lips. Like I did that night at the casino after she arranged finance for me. It was a public place. We were happy, drunk, and reckless. Nothing further developed. It was as though that moment ceased to exist merely because we chose not to acknowledge it. *This kiss never took place.* Perhaps the same memory is flashing through her mind, too.

After so many months, small talk has never been so difficult.

"I'm running my own business," she says, with a smile that betrays no anger that she was the first one I let go when my own business started to fall apart. "Boutique. We sell fashion accessories and stuff like that. Fannie is my partner. She studied fashion design in Paris." So that's her name. I missed it altogether when we were introduced. Fannie is wearing a shiny silk top that generously accentuates her breasts, reflecting the varicoloured lights shining from the high walls. She's been smoking nonstop since she sat down. She's good-looking too. But not as beautiful as Tiff. Her chin is much too long, and her wiry hair looks like it has been permed once too often, leaving a barren dryness.

In answer to a question I barely hear, I inform them that I no longer run the IT firm.

"The bug's no more, Tiff. But I still do IT work. It's very slow. After Y2K, we never recovered. Maybe you can offer me a job now."

We laugh. It feels strange to be sitting here with Tiff, drinking and reminiscing about old times. All these months I've blamed her for Lai Ying's departure, it never occurred to me in my wildest dreams that I would ever sit down with her, drinking, laughing together, reliving the exciting times we shared. All this time I've thought about how she set me up with loan sharks, and scared the living daylights out of my wife.

Fannie keeps nodding in apparent recognition. I wonder how much she knows. Does she know about the kiss? Is that why she's looking at me with that mischievous grin forcing a near dimple on her left cheek? I'm drinking faster than necessary. I can't keep my eyes off Tiff. The drink takes charge of my life, reminding me that Lai Ying's gone, that I haven't enjoyed the tenderness of a woman's embrace for about half a year. The sheer length of it doesn't bear thinking about. I shouldn't have to live like this, like a clean-shaven monk or some priest, for heaven's sake! But there's Fannie. I need a diversion.

"Do you girls want to meet my friend?" I ask suddenly, surprising myself. Diallo has expressed no interest in joining us. But he might like this Fannie girl. When I go to fetch him, he says he's not interested. It's his way of showing me how stupid I am to be getting mixed up with Tiff again. I tell him that her friend Fannie wants to meet him.

"Really?"

"She says she wants to practise her French."

I've no idea where that came from. But it works like magic.

"*Bien sur, bien sur, mon ami!*"

They hit it off right away. Which suits me just fine. Diallo doesn't pay much attention to Tiff. He pretends he doesn't even remember her. If she sees through his lies, she's too kind to show it. No one who meets Tiffany ever forgets her. And she knows it.

I sit adjacent to her, our knees touching, which sends a thrill through my alcohol-drenched being. Business is going well, she informs me. For her, the economic recovery couldn't have come at a better time. She was heavily in debt. That much I knew. She mentioned it on one of our trips to China. She always talked a lot, about herself, her interests, her problems. Things I didn't really need to know. I listened though, made appropriate ohs and ahs, offered sympathy when it was called for, and gently steered the conversation to what I hoped were more neutral topics. Things have changed for her. It's all about the money she and Fannie are making. The joy of running her own business for the first time in her life. The economic recovery. She's like a little girl talking about her Christmas presents.

This is the first time I'm hearing anyone praising the so-called economic recovery. I haven't had first-hand experience with it. I've read about it in the papers. But with my clients deserting me or finding reasons not to pay, I've seen no reason to believe it, until now. I gaze into Tiff's excited eyes and bask in the warmth of her laughter, hoping her good fortune will somehow rub off on me. But the only rubbing that's going on is under the table. My left foot has come off its shoe and ended up resting beneath Tiff's right foot, drawing it between my feet, where it's nestled now.

"The stuff we sell will always have a market, Dan," she says. "Girls always need to look good. We do weddings, too. People still get married, every day."

She drones on, oozing charm. If I didn't know her I would have sworn she was trying to sell me something. *You know, Dan, I can get you a very good deal on securities. Friend of mine says securities codes twenty-something this, one-forty-something that will be going up. Top secret. Directors held a meeting. They're about to make an announcement that will shake the market. Now's the time to buy. And horses. This Saturday. Look out for Bruised Lightning this, Breezing Comet that.*

It's not money or tips on hot deals I need right now. Though that would be nice. My hand is now holding hers, playing with the slim, soft fingers.

"Well, Tiff, I'm really happy for you." I repeat my veiled request for a job, though what I really want is the IT account. "If things are as good as you say, you must be expanding, and using IT. That's where I come in, you know?" I pinch myself. Why do I sound so bloody desperate? Perhaps because I *am* desperate. When was the last time I held a woman's hand like this?

"When the time comes, I'll call you. Right now, we're keeping things very simple."

Her smile softens to something akin to the calm surface of a fishpond when the wind abates and the ripples even out before fizzling out altogether.

Something tells me I should raise the matter of the loan sharks and deal with it once and for all. But another voice tells me to hold back. Could she really have been in league with those people, or did she know them because she used them, too? There's only one way to find out. I lean forward, my hand now resting on her knee. Her skin is soft, warm, inviting. Diallo and Fannie are engrossed in a conversation in French.

"They turned me into a slave, Dan!"

I can still hear the anguished voice as I replay the events in the cab back home. My head is spinning. I can barely see where we're going. We drank so much. Good thing Lai Ying's not here to see the state I'm in. It's just like being back in Macau. I can't even recall the precise moment we sneaked out from the Oasis, giggling with the anticipation of mischief. Tiff was in titters all the way in the back of the cab. I had no idea she lived in Happy Valley. Big, airy flat, all by her sweet self. Everything was happening like clockwork. A year too late, though. I assumed I was running the show. But she was. Even remembered the ritual shower before bed. Perhaps she wasn't as drunk as I had assumed. The lovemaking was a blur of frantic activity. Throaty moans, shrieks of pleasure. A creaking bed. Laughter. Classical music on Radio 4.

It's a question of unfinished business, Tiff. That's what it is. Unfinished business, from way back. The words keep rocking about my brain. Like pebbles in an empty can. Unfinished business. Then we start talking. Really talking. Like we never did before. I tell her about my family. Show her pictures of my daughter. I tell her they're not in town. I miss my girl. Terribly. And the wife? She asks, smiling to soften the charge. I'm too drunk to care. But a small voice in my alcohol-soaked head is saying, yes, your honour, I'm guilty as charged. Guilty of cheating on my loving wife. Anything in mitigation? She left me, you know. What am I supposed to do, I'm not a vegetarian monk, am I? Tiff means no harm. Her eyes are soft, tender, benevolent, forgiving. We have problems, Tiff. I guess that's why I'm here with you. She rests her head on my shoulder. We kiss. I'm ready to spend the night here. Does she have a boyfriend? She hesitates. Jesus. Maybe she's married. I have to get the hell out of here.

"He's a married man, Dan," she says, simply, matter of fact. "Don't worry. He wouldn't dare come here at this time of night. He's a great guy. Sweet, generous. The wife's family controls the business. He's stuck, poor man. But he loves me. We take what we can get, Dan."

I guess that explains the flat, and the boutique, most probably. She's a lucky girl. He's lucky too, I think to myself, as I run a hand gently across her firm breasts, from one pointed pink tip to a plunging valley, and back up again. It's going to be tricky seeing her. Very tricky.

Then she starts crying. Slamming fists into my chest. What's the matter, Tiff? She's not paying attention. She's just going on about *them*. How they tricked her. Lent her money. Kept demanding interest. It takes me a while to realise whom she's talking about. *Them*. The loan sharks. Chuck and Co.

"They wouldn't release me." She covers her face with a pillow. "They tried to blackmail me. Saying I went to pick guys up at the casino. *Gweilos*. Black guys. Me, a slut, can you imagine? They filmed me and you, Dan, kissing. That night. Do you know what they made me do?"

I stare at her. "What did you do, Tiff?" My voice is no louder than a whisper. What's the worst they could do to a girl like her? She didn't have a husband and a little child. Would she have been put off by the chicken entrails treatment? She's a brave girl. Acid on her pretty face? Now that would be another matter. That would really screw her up. Why didn't they blackmail me? I wonder. Or were they getting ready for it? Was it going to be the next move after the chicken thing?

"Drugs!" She spits the word out, like a curse. My stomach cramps up. "They forced me. From Guangzhou, through Zhuhai, into Macau."

"Jesus, Tiff. You could've been jailed."

"Just do this thing, they said. Then you're free. I had no choice. Can you imagine how terrified I was? But you, Dan…you looked so, so, calm, easygoing. I just tried to be like you. Pretended I was your girlfriend or something."

"What are you talking about, Tiffany?"

"I'm sorry, Dan. There was no other way."

"What are you saying? What the hell did you do?"

"Cocaine. Heroin. Ketamine. We were together, darling. On a business trip. My bag wasn't enough, I'm so sorry."

"My goodness, Tiffany…" My heart deflates, leaving me with a terrible sinking feeling.

"I was a slave, Dan. Can't you see?"

"I could have gone to jail, for nothing!"

"What was I supposed to do? And do you know what? They wanted to get you to do it. They were going to blackmail you. I begged them not to. They made me do it instead, to cover your debts."

"Shit, man! I paid the bastards—"

"Before you cleared the debt. In any case, there was always interest, Dan. Interest charges never end until they say so."

"Tiffany, um…you were not…you didn't get something from them, an introductory fee?"

"What do you mean?"

"Isn't that the way it works, Tiff? You introduce a client and get a piece of the action, right?"

"Are you out of your mind?" She stares at me, shocked and offended. An embarrassing silence hangs above us.

"So what are you saying?" I try to sound angry, ignoring her reaction to my accusation. "You saved my wretched life, is that what you did, Tiff, after making me a drug trafficker?"

"You gave me a job, Dan, when no one would touch me. I had fucked up my life, my whole damn reputation. Debts. Gambling. I lost everything. I was desperate when I came to you. People knew me in this city, Dan. I was finished. I could have ended it all. Charcoal in a villa in Cheung Chau. It's clichéd, I know, but it works. It's painless. And then you came along. I had no problem running that shit for you, believe me."

As I storm out of the flat, I'm ready to believe anything. I'm ready to believe she could have had me killed. Or that she's making it all up.

But why?

What Were You Thinking?

TIFFANY'S REVELATIONS KEEP ME AWAKE all night. The beer helps too, all the six cans I knock back after getting home.

I rushed out of her flat without trying to find out more. I should have stayed, maybe till morning, shagged her again, after the shock had worn off.

Now, the memories begin to come back, my mind clears like a mist under the soothing gaze of the morning sun. She was good, at once gentle and wild, tantalising and voracious. And I want more, more and more of that action. More of that soft, wet, willing flesh. I want more of those sexy eyes that caressed me through half-closed lids as she rocked beneath me, heels digging into my ears, then bobbed up and down as though reaching for the ceiling, long hair flying in all directions while the moans and cries bounced off the walls, drowning out the sound of the rain that beat furiously against the windows. I don't care whether she's being honest about having saved my life. If she did, then the more reason we should meet again.

My successful fight against any feeling of guilt so far tells me this doesn't change anything with Lai Ying. It certainly doesn't change anything with Chacha. Right now, it's like Tiffany's flowing through my veins, occupying every inch of my body. I'll never forget that look in her eyes when she said those words. *And then you came along.*

So I, too, saved her life. Like she saved mine.

That afternoon, Diallo calls to find out what happened. I can't bring myself to tell him everything. He would never forgive my foolishness.

"But you boned?" It's not a question. The voice is loud and assertive, so matter-of-fact. Like a declaration. *I put it to you that you had carnal knowledge of this woman who destroyed your marriage. How do you plead, guilty or not guilty? Let's see, er, you know, like the US president who smoked pot but didn't inhale? What would be the equivalent in sex?*

"And now I'm hooked, man. It feels like an addiction."

"Stay away, is my advice. That chick is trouble. Can't you see, *mon ami*? Is there a boyfriend?"

"Oh, just a married guy." I say it casually, like it's a minor inconvenience, hoping he won't probe.

"Hey! You're skating on thin ice, my friend."

I need to change the subject. "What about you and that girl—what was her name—Fannie?"

"This is not a matter for the telephone," he says, laughing. He says "telephone" with a French accent, the stress on the third syllable.

"So how come my stuff is okay for the telephone?" I imitate his accent, which sets him splitting his sides with laughter.

"You're a free man, Dan, much as you'd like to deny it. Just use the freedom wisely."

If I am indeed free, I haven't been putting this freedom to much use. Until last night.

"You never did tell me what happened with Candy, by the way."

"We'll bend our elbows again, let the wine flow, then we can talk, *ca va*?"

It's 9 p.m. Lai Mui must be at home at this time. She never goes out on Sunday. She is the only chance I have of getting news about my wife's whereabouts.

This time, I'll beg her if I have to. We last had a meal together a few days after Christmas last year. We met for *yam chah* in a crowded teahouse in Wanchai, the type where you place your order with little old ladies, who push their trolleys of *dim sum* around the narrow spaces between tables, and you're hemmed in between potbellied, chain-smoking, middle-aged men scanning the racing pages of their newspaper and a family standing behind you, waiting for your table as soon as you call *mai dahn!* for the bill. I always loved eating in these sorts of places with their festive atmosphere and informal character. Now I have no one to *yam chah* with. My friends prefer to go out to drink, and when they want to eat, they invariably opt for the cleaner, quieter, and more expensive places in Soho and Central, where they charge you an arm and a leg for a tiny fillet of fish that obviously died of starvation, three baby carrots balanced delicately over a tiny tomato and a piece of lettuce with bobs of brown sauce scattered on the edges of the plate. It looks like modern art. You're almost afraid to eat it. But it's so little you have to stop for a big Mac or pizza slice on the way home.

I take the MTR to Quarry Bay and walk to Lai Mui's apartment block. The thunderstorm warning has been lowered but it's still raining. My mind is tormented by images of Tiffany. I feel like a man searching through dusty boxes in a dark storeroom, not knowing what I'll find. Not knowing what I'm looking for, in fact. Those shapely hips rolling up Carnarvon Road, attracting the attention of copy-watch touts and jaded tourists. The screams she uttered when lost in the throes of ecstasy. When I terminated her contract, she behaved as though she was expecting it, after all the trouble with the loan sharks. I had no idea why she hadn't given her notice. She just shrugged, as if it didn't matter. A shrug that said, *What the heck, I have plans.* I was the one who was tortured by the embarrassment, having got mixed up with an employee even though the amorous seed that was sown by that kiss died a natural death. But I foolishly allowed the closeness to get in the way of business, and more ominously, into my personal life.

The rain comes down in tiny sharp pellets that prick your skin like pins. Everyone scuttles off past me holding umbrellas, or a bag over their head, heads bent as if paying homage to the rain goddess. I never bother to carry an umbrella. By the time I get to Lai Mui's block, I'm soaked to the skin.

The elderly guard dozing in the lobby gives me a quizzical look and stands up to watch me. I'm probably the first black visitor he's seen for ages.

"*Sikh jo fahn meih-ah?*" I greet him. He starts to laugh, self-consciously, and waves his hand. I press the intercom.

Lai Mui sounds shocked. I've never been to her place on my own before.

Little has changed in her flat since we were last here more than a year ago. There's not much furniture. Lai Mui says she likes plenty of space to move around. But she spends most of her time slumped in front of the TV, watching Chinese period dramas. She's watching one such drama now, the type set in some ancient dynasty where women wore colourful gold and red robes, kept their heads bowed whenever they spoke to the men, who invariably had their hair in long ponytails and were prone to erupt into flying kicks at the slightest provocation.

"You all right, Dan? It's very late."

She's in pyjamas, a shawl around her shoulders. She has just had a bath. The smell of bath cream with a hint of lavender lingers in the air. Her hair is tied in a ponytail. Fading orange highlights are still visible. She looks so much like her sister, the high cheekbones, the lips that seem weary of smiling and perpetually ready to pout in frustration. We're both suffering. Maybe we can help each other. Maybe I can introduce her to someone, but who?

In her bathroom, I dry my face and arms with bits of tissue and return to the living room.

"Something to drink?"

I ask what she has. She brings me a can of Budweiser. She only drinks white wine. I wonder what other sad reminders of the soured relationship she's yet to jettison.

"I hate to barge in on you like this, sister."

"You could have called." She says it in a low, almost apologetic voice. She knows if I had said I was coming, she would have said it was too late to visit, she had an early morning appointment. Anything to keep the wayward brother-in-law at bay.

"I'm sorry. This whole thing with your sister. It's driving me crazy."

She sighs, and tightens the shawl around her shoulders. Whenever I call to ask about Lai Ying, the answer is always the same. She doesn't want to get involved in our domestic squabbles. But this isn't just a squabble. Lai Mui is the only one of the family still in town, and she's done a good job of avoiding me. She's happy to talk on the phone, but that's as far as it gets, though even a phone conversation is never guaranteed. Sometimes she doesn't even take my calls, and when I leave messages, she doesn't call me back.

She was so sweet before. When the parents shunned Lai Ying for marrying a black man, Lai Mui was the voice of reason in the family, reminding the parents how they themselves fought for years for acceptance. A conservative middle-ranking civil servant from Guangdong marrying a modern Shanghainese girl, who had lived abroad and talked of joining the family business. They were worlds apart. Lai Ying never told me how they met. Once when I asked, she frowned and refused to answer. I feared the worst. The girls borrowed a leaf from their parents and went farther, dating foreigners. They were free spirits, unconstrained by customs they now find they can barely reconcile with the world they inhabit.

"Dan, you know how stubborn Lai Ying is. She never calls."

I find that hard to believe.

"My sister…"

"Who knows where she could be?"

"She must be with your mother's people? You'll know how to reach them, surely?"

"No." She laughs and adjusts her shawl. "My family's not like that, Dan. All that extended family stuff, like you guys?"

"But, what about Chacha, your niece?"

She sits up, blinking. "Dan, please…"

"You're her favourite auntie, Lai Mui."

"Please, stop…"

"Every time her mother lets her speak to me, she says how's *yee-jai*?"

"Dan…" She buries her face in her hands.

She starts to sob, covering her face with the shawl. I wasn't prepared for this, but now I understand. I thank her for the drink, mumble goodbye and get up to leave.

"Those things you did to her!" she mutters, with a look of disgust that makes me freeze in mid-step. "I mean, what did you expect her to do? What were you thinking?"

"It's not…it wasn't…" I remain immobilised in the glare of her accusatory stare.

"Dan. It's not like she and I didn't talk. Those late nights, all that money you lost. The triads harassing her. How did you expect her to take it? You have no idea what you put my sister through, Dan, no idea at all. And then you come here accusing me of God-knows-what. You have no right."

Her face is as hard as steel, her eyes razor sharp, like twin drills waiting to bore through the guilt buried in my heart.

"Lai Mui, I'm so sorry…"

"You should apologise to your wife. She doesn't deserve this, nor does my favourite niece."

I stumble down the fire escape. It's the only place I'll be alone. I can't bear to face anyone in the lift right now, with the pain ripping my insides apart. Lai Mui's words have shredded my heart to bits, exposing the shame that I had all along assumed was hidden away from view, from Lai Ying's eyes, from my own blinded, blinkered eyes. And this thing with Tiffany. I want to punch the walls until my hands bleed. How can I face Lai Ying? All those denials for something that was just waiting to happen. Did Lai Ying succumb to the inevitability of it even though something in her urged her to trust? Did she truly believe I would eventually let her down, no matter how long it took?

There's only one place in the world that will heal this pain. A bar. A dark, smoke-filled place, where the alcohol flows without let or hindrance and the music is loud enough to burst your eardrums and render you forever deaf to abuse and ridicule.

The security guard downstairs give me a 'that was quick' sort of look. I wave at him and walk into the crisp air. The rain has let up and the air smells cleaner, as if it has been washed by the downpour. It makes my head feel a little lighter. In fact, I imagine I'm thinking more clearly. At least I know now, the Lai Mui option is closed. I have to find another way. I've been drifting for too long, hoping Lai Ying will forgive, understand, and come to her senses. As if I was the wrongly accused victim and she was the vindictive executioner. My chest heaves with anger and guilt, fuelled by the poison of my liaison with Tiffany that now runs through my veins. This has to end. I have to make it happen, even if it means crawling in shame all the way to Shanghai and begging her to give us another chance.

Fifteen minutes later, I'm walking the streets of Wanchai trying to find a suitable regular bar amidst all the girlie bars and strip joints. I'm vaguely aware of excessively made-up *mamasans* prowling the pavements, luring men with drink and membership coupons. Outside the Peer Pleasure, a woman in a miniskirt and knee-length, black boots grabs my hand and starts to pull me toward a red velvet curtain, saying, "Darlin-darlin, one beer for you? No cover charge."

No, darlin-darlin, one beer won't do. Let's say seven, then see how it goes, yeah? I try to free myself but she won't let go. Her colleague blocks my way and shoves a drinks discount coupon in my face. They only let me go when I playfully try to pinch their tits, promising to return.

I end up at the East Meets West, which is as crowded as usual, and living up to its name. It's where foreigners and locals congregate in equal measure, reminding us just how cosmopolitan the pubs in Hong Kong can be. Three giant TV screens hanging down the ceiling are showing the repeat of a match in the just-ended English Premier League season. The sound is turned down so we can hear the Filipino band belting out 'Smoke Gets in Your Eyes', as if to mock the patrons gasping in a fog of cigarette smoke. I order a bottle of Tsingtao and find a spot by the bar where I can drown my sorrows in peace.

Twice, I pull out the mobile and start to dial Tiffany's number. Just a quick call to say hello. *Did you sleep well? An apology for walking away unceremoniously, with misplaced indignation instead of staying on to show my appreciation for your having saved me from drug traffickers.*

It can't happen. Diallo's right about her. But he doesn't know why.

When the band takes a break and some silence momentarily descends on the bar like a lull before another thunderous rock storm, I dial Alex's number. He says he's with Charlie at the Oasis. I can hear snatches of jazzy Zairean Lingala music struggling hard to hold its own in the loud banter.

"I need to talk to you, Alex."

"I'm not having any more of that farm crap from you tonight, man."

"This is important. It's business."

"Business? At this time of night?"

"I wouldn't bother you if my life didn't depend on it, Alex."

"Jesus! You've been in a fight in a dark alley again?"

"Come on, man."

"All right, you'd better get your arse out here then, eh?"

When I get there at midnight, Charlie asks whether I've found an apartment. I tell him I'm still searching.

"If that mate of yours can't help, what's his name, Shylock Wong?"

"Hamlet, actually."

"Yeah, whatever. Look, I can introduce you to an agent. She's good."

"Thanks, Charlie. I'll bear it in mind. I'll give Hamlet another week or so."

Alex is smiling to himself. I ask him what's funny. He starts to tell us how he and Meg look up apartments all the time, even though he has no intention of moving.

"It's like this, how do you get to have sex all over Hong Kong, in every sort of apartment you can think of?"

Charlie watches him with keen anticipation.

"Sex all over Hong Kong?" echoes Charlie. "When can I start?"

"We set up viewings, tell the agent we need a moment to ourselves in one of the rooms, and off we go."

"Jesus!" exclaims Charlie, green with envy. "Why didn't I think of that?"

Alex beams with pride, looking rather pleased with himself.

"With all that experience in quickies," says Charlie, in between bursts of side-splitting laughter, "you could be in contention for the Olympic under-ten-seconds dash. Me, I'm more of a marathon sort of guy." Alex's face is somewhere between half-smile and half-frown.

212

Now that we're on the subject of sex, the night is panning out beautifully. That is until I return from the loo and find the two of them in a heated argument, predictably, about the land issue. This thing is happening six thousand miles away in Africa, but it follows us around like a shadow and just won't go away. I get a beer and watch the exchange from the sidelines.

I'm not getting involved anymore.

"The land belongs to the Africans," declares Charlie. "Everyone knows that."

"What do you know?" growls Alex. "We've all struggled to make that country what it is today. And we're not going down without a fight, you mark my words."

The way this argument is going, I doubt if I'll have a chance to talk to Alex. Charlie turns to me and says, "So, what do you reckon, mate? This really is your fight, innit?"

"I have more important things to worry about right now."

"What! What could be more important than your land, man?"

He's drunk. He knows very well what I'm saying. I ask him to leave me alone. He curses under this breath and turns to talk to the Nepalese barmaid. I see my chance and edge closer to Alex.

"What's up? What's this business?"

I'm not sure how to begin. I've only known him a couple of months. And I can't say we've got on famously.

"Your firm, um…can they, can you help find someone?"

"Meaning what exactly?" The hardness in his voice makes me wince.

"I need to locate someone."

"Locate someone? We don't do missing persons."

This is not getting me very far. "No missing persons. Right."

"Not really our forte, Dan, but for the right price, who knows? Are you looking for someone specific, like a long-lost friend from your Nanjing days, or are you cunningly looking for a piece of arse?"

"You do that?" I ask, to cut short his laughter.

"There are websites for that sort of thing, man."

"It's all right. Not quite what I had in mind."

"What is it then?"

I lean forward, to ensure Charlie doesn't overhear. Charlie's solution to my plight is that I should go to the police and report that my wife kidnapped my child. I'm not ready for all that drama and publicity. I need to handle this my way.

"It's like this: I need to find my family, but I need it done quiet-quiet. My wife, you see, she took my daughter and…well, let's say they went away."

"Bloody hell!" He furrows his brow, squeezing suspicion into his narrowed eyes. "What the hell did you do?"

"It's a long story."

"I bet it is. I never had you down as a wifebeater. Jesus, I didn't even realise you were married, Mister Chiponda."

"They're in Shanghai. That's all I know. But no one can help."

"Police?"

"No, no way. Not in China anyway. It's not like they've disappeared off the face of the earth. They're safe, so the cops won't even listen. She emails sometimes. Occasional phone call, but the number's always blocked."

"Mhh. Text messages?"

I shake my head. "Only email."

Alex nods, and downs his beer. "Intriguing."

"Thing is, can it be done? I mean, just how hard can it get?"

"If we have a picture, some basic personal info, it's just a matter of making some checks. We have the resources, and expertise, if that's what you mean. China might be a big country, but we have what it takes, man. The firm actually started in the US. Like a million years ago. We've been in China seven years now."

The thought of surprising Lai Ying sends a thrill down my spine. I picture myself walking up to her with a bunch of pink roses. I have to be certain she's not exposed to any danger. Supposing some rash, ill-trained agent misheard, or mixed her up with someone who was supposed to get the sulfuric acid facial?

"Is it safe, Alex?"

"Absolutely, man. How long's it been?"

"Six months."

"Is she like, sorry to pry, planning to come back?"

"It's like this. We got into a situation, and she got scared. Says she'll come back when she's sure it's safe. I don't know. I could be waiting forever. Shit, man, I miss them."

Alex's bottle rises to meet mine.

"Let me make some checks at the office and get back to you. It must be awful, man – wife and kid gone."

"You have no idea."

We Make the Plan, Okay?

I BEGIN TO NOTICE CHANGES in Anastasia. She has turned into a morose, unsmiling, and quiet creature. She looks as if she hasn't had enough sleep. Maybe I should stop asking her to work for me so she can rest more on her one day off. She goes about her work as though it were hard labour on a life sentence. Even her hair has lost its glossy shine.

She glides about the apartment, noiselessly. She's been trained to get the job done silently, like a ghost, responding only to instructions. It must be intimidating working under Beth's stern gaze, living under the same roof.

We're afraid people might hear the doorbell, so I leave the door on the latch for Anastasia to let herself in at 7.30 a.m. Sometimes the management office places notices on the board in the lobby reminding people that it's a criminal offence to hire full-time foreign domestic workers for part-time work. If you're lucky, you could get away with a hefty fine. Or end up behind bars.

I ask how things are with Charlie.

"Is all right, sir." There's no emotion in her voice. It's as though we're talking about the weather.

"You see much of him?"

"I'm so busy. Not much time."

Charlie has a short temper, especially when he's drunk. I've seen him get into nasty exchanges with people in the pub. I once found him exchanging abuse with an American in the washrooms at the Pirates' Rice Bowl. They were arguing about the bombing of US embassies in Nairobi and Dar es Salaam. I had to lead him away before they came to blows.

When I ask Charlie what Anastasia's like, he gnashes his teeth and curses, saying he needs to move on. One Sunday morning, Anastasia comes in with dark marks around her eyes and a bandage on her arm. She doesn't want to talk about it. She tries to cover the bandage with her blouse sleeve but I can see it clearly. If she's smart, she'll cut her losses and run.

216

I turn to my computer to finish off a job. Hopefully I can get some work done for an hour before Anastasia comes in to clean the study.

Alex hasn't got back to me. But he has got me thinking. Sometimes I pick up the phone to call him, but hang up before I get to the last digit. It doesn't feel right.

Since there's no place to play basketball, I work out in the fitness room and get to see Jupiter from time to time. He works out every day, late in the afternoon. I only go there once or twice a week. He does miles on the treadmill, and then pumps iron as though he's fighting an enemy trying to smother him. His muscles bulge out, the veins on his arms and neck tremble. His nose twitches like that of a buffalo about to sneeze. He bites his lower lip, eyelids smash into each other, the tongue sticks out. Up goes the weight.

One evening, Jupiter nearly passes out on the treadmill. He loses his step and clutches wildly at the safety belt. He barely manages to hit the emergency button and bring the belt to a stop. He ends up on the carpeted floor with only a few minor bruises on his elbow. I help him sit on a stretching board and fetch him a paper cup of water. He's getting weaker by the day, and his hair is greying. It's hard to believe he's only in his mid-forties, about ten years older than me, yet he looks sixty.

"Maybe I too old for this," he mutters, smiling with embarrassment. "Not enough the energy."

Soon after the incident, he stops doing strenuous exercises and contents himself with lifting light dumbbells. He tells me he no longer plays football with his son, Siu Meng.

"I can teach him a few tricks, if you like."

"No, no. Too much the trouble for you."

"No trouble at all." If only he knew how I miss playing basketball with Chacha!

"All right, thanks. I ask my wife which is the good time."

"Any time."

He doesn't tell me what's ailing him, and I dare not ask. But whatever it is, it is rapidly taking its toll. Sometimes while he's exercising, his wife and son come to fetch him. Beth takes him by the elbow and leads him away, like a naughty boy being rescued from a dangerous game that he foolishly allowed himself to be coaxed into. She glances at whoever happens to be around disapprovingly, as though they're responsible for her husband's troubles.

She never speaks to me, even when she finds us talking. When Beth says it's time to go, Jupiter simply stops whatever he's doing and they leave, like a man under her spell.

When I see the three of them walking away, hand in hand, my heart deflates. I lose interest in working out and head down to the pub, my head filled with terrible thoughts about the things I need to do to Tiffany's friends. I think back to our first meeting. *Have a seat, Miss Ho.* I offered her heung pin tea, the smell of jasmine rose to my nose, but couldn't hold its own against her perfume, which exuded a subtle, warm intimacy. She was the fourth candidate I had interviewed that morning. *My friends call me Tiff*, she said, crossing her legs, casually offering me a glimpse of white knickers. And so she became Tiff, to me. Which made me not merely her employer. But her friend.

And now I dare not call her.

I've found a place I like in North Point. Trouble is, the landlady wants a tenant who can move in right away. My current rental agreement expires at the end of September, in seven weeks' time. I stand to lose a month's deposit of twenty-one thousand, unless I can find a replacement tenant. Hamlet's working on it. But I'm not optimistic. Rents have been coming down lately, yet my landlord stubbornly refuses to drop his rent.

This place I've found has been vacant for months. With no rent coming in, she can't wait too long for me to make up my mind. I try to buy time by urging her to do some redecoration. There's paint peeling off the walls in the kitchen, and some of the tiles on the living room floor are discoloured and badly scratched.

The landlady has agreed to consider doing some renovation work. It should take a few weeks and eat into the second month. I don't mind losing a week but a month's deposit is too much, with my seriously depleted resources. But there's always the chance of someone else making a better offer and moving in immediately. You're never sure until you've paid the deposit and taken possession of the keys.

I decide to visit the neighbourhood one evening to see what it looks like at night. The residential complex is just like any other in the territory, where the buildings are stacked up close to each other, broad at the base and narrowing at the top as if leaning to whisper to each other. In the public playground nearby, a charity is overseeing the donation of bags of rice to the elderly. It is the Hungry Ghosts month, when the Gate to Hell opens and millions of restless spirits are let loose to go in search of food and to exact revenge on those who have wronged them.

Throughout this week, people have been burning fake money in small litterbins on the roadsides and street corners. I stop for a while to watch Buddhist and Taoist worshippers performing rites to placate the spirits by burning candles, joss sticks, and wads of hell money and making offerings of food, complete with chopsticks. The dozens of candles and small fires on the ground light up the entire playground to create a mood which is at once solemn and festive. Other worshippers are burning gift offerings of colourful, papier-mâché objects representing houses, cars, and mobile phones for the dead to use in hell, sending a pall of smoke billowing skywards from red-hot garbage bins. There is nothing like this near my current residence. I walk away with a spring in my step. This place will be fun. I imagine sitting here with my family, watching dragon dances, Chiu Chow opera, children lighting the night up with beautifully crafted chiming lanterns.

My cousin Chipinduka emails to say we should consider selling African music CDs on the Internet. He says he can source the CDs from Harare and South Africa. I'm not that enthusiastic. We would have to sell the CDs in their bucket loads to make any profit that would be worth my while. For Chip, the money would be very good, as he lives in Zimbabwe with a currency that is shrinking by the day. His job at the attorney general's chambers doesn't pay all that well, hence the anxiety to find other ways to make ends meet. I reply to say I'll think about it. But I warn him there are lots of people doing this already. There has to be a better way. My tribulations in Macau have forced me to become wary of moneymaking schemes.

One evening, I find two police cars at my apartment building, their flashing lights casting a blue haze across the podium. The lift opens and spews out five cops and a woman in handcuffs. The woman's face is partly hidden by her shoulder-length hair but I recognise her immediately. It is Jupiter's wife, Beth, eyes as steely as ever. I stand aside and let them pass. Beth's capacity to see right through me leaves me unsettled and angry.

It's in the news the following day. Businesswoman charged with torturing domestic helper. There is talk of beatings with brooms and cooking pans, slaps and blows, and even scorching with a hot iron. She is denied bail. Anastasia is transferred to an undisclosed shelter for battered domestic helpers. My head is spinning. I can't reach Charlie. His office tells me he went to Tokyo last week, and isn't expected back for another week.

Two days later, the paper reports that Anastasia has been charged with molesting a child.

Jupiter has stopped coming to the clubhouse. I wonder who is looking after Siu Meng. Although I've known them, or sort of known them, for years, all I know is they're on the eighth floor, three floors above us. That's the thing about living in Hong Kong. You don't bother to know your neighbours. You get to recognise faces when you see them in the lift, or at the fitness room. But that's as far as it goes. No dinner invitations. No outings to the pub for happy hour. It's so unlike Ndambu, where your neighbours are your friends and relatives.

An email from Lai Ying!

Afrd u wnt 2 tk Chch to Afrc. Nt sf thr!

God, don't let me smash up this monitor.

You have a new message.

I click on the inbox. This one is from Wang.

My friend Eggman, so many thanks for your replying. Now, your country too much problem. For me, problem mean money. Your president he throw white peoples out. Is chance for Chinese. Wang visit your country, we buy farm. Minerals. We make the plan, okay?

I close the inbox and log off. I'm not ready for this.

The following day, around five, I find Jupiter sitting on a bench at the children's playground, a walking stick beside him. He's watching over his son playing football by himself. There's a mournful hollowness about his cheeks, and his smart, light-blue shirt and black trousers look too big for his lean frame. His hair's now almost completely grey. I approach and say hello. He nods.

We sit in silence and watch Siu Meng running around in circles with the ball. The poor thing probably doesn't know it, but his mother's facing a possible two years behind bars. After a few minutes, I get up and ask him to kick the ball to me. He looks at his dad first. For the next half hour, I teach him all the tricks I know. His ball control is not bad at all for an eight-year-old.

We're both sweating. I tell him we need a break. He sits and rolls back his sleeves. That's when I see the marks on his arm. Dark, ungainly scars. I glance at Jupiter, who goes into a coughing fit, the haggard look on his face tinged with embarrassment.

Siu Meng wants to keep playing. But I have to go. When I get up to leave, I see that sad, pleading look in his eyes, and the unspoken question: *Why now? Why must you go now, just when I was starting to enjoy this?* It's the same look Chacha had whenever I told her I was about to leave town on a business trip, and she couldn't grasp why Daddy had to keep going away instead of staying home with her.

Jupiter glances about him, like a man caught in a dark, grimy subway, not knowing which exit is safe. A beleaguered man whose wife is in police custody, awaiting jail, and he's too weak to protect his son from the danger that's closing in on them. I can't help wondering where he was, what he was doing when all that violence was unfolding in his home. I'll never know, unless Jupiter and I do *the happy hour*, and talk, man-to-man. But that's not going to happen now. It's too late. We had a chance, but we didn't take it, and now it's gone. Forever. In a sudden moment much like a light going on in a dark room, my troubles pale in comparison to their problems. But it's a fleeting feeling, gone before I can fully grasp it, and the room is plunged into its habitual darkness. Jupiter still has his son, even though he's too weak to play ball with him.

So much has changed for this family. I saw them walk hand in hand. Together. Like a real family. While my own family remains scattered across two cities. Two countries. One holds only memories from a troubled past, and now, surprisingly, serves as a safe haven for my runaway wife, and is beginning to beckon, with the tantalising promise of a new start. The other is fast disintegrating, ravaged by violence and the threat of famine. In effect, they're both echoes of the past, and we're like ghosts, drifting, about to fall through the cracks that yawn as wide as valleys between mountains, into the empty space between.

Siu Meng is still looking up at me, holding the ball in his hands. I might as well be in jail, like his mum. But unlike his mum, I haven't punished anyone for hurting my child. But I continue to hurt us because of this fear that Lai Ying will cut me out completely from my family. And now Wang is coming to town. My head feels like an overloaded hard disk, overheating, threatening to crash. Images flash by. The past. Lai Ying holding me by the shoulder. *You can't go to Shanghai*, she's crying. *He's there now.*

Why can't I go wherever I like? It's my life, my future, my career.
What about us, Dan? Let's go somewhere else, somewhere neutral.
Neutral? Where on earth is neutral?

I dare not let them see the tears. As I walk away, I reach for the mobile and ask Alex to meet me. He sounds surprised. Maybe it's the tone of my voice. He's not free till next week.

"You're sure about this, Dan?"

"Yeah." How can he even ask?

"We'll do it, man. Easy does it," he says.

If only it was as easy as smashing the bug.

The Family Is Everything

BACK IN MY FLAT, I log on. There's an email from Chipinduka.

It's like this: Your dad's joined a band of merry men who've taken over the farm they work for. They've got land, man. Yes, that same one, the place you were born and bred. They're landowners now. That's what I heard, anyway. We don't know what to make of it. I heard it from a reporter friend of mine who's covering farm invasions in Mashonaland. War veterans, or war vets, as they call them. Man, you take it easy, all right? I'll contact you once I know more.

I read the email several times before it makes sense. Yet every time I read it, I understand it even less. Staring at the monitor in silence, reading the message over and over again, hoping for a revelation doesn't bring me any closer to understanding what on earth could have been going through Father's head. Chipinduka must be mistaken. Perhaps it's a joke. But why would he joke about a thing like that? Trouble is, I have no way of verifying it. They've never had a phone at home. We've always relied on good old-fashioned snail mail.

For about a year now, war vets have been taking over white farms, driving off the farmers. They say their time has come. All those years waiting, after the independence struggle that yielded promises upon promises. I've followed the debate that has been raging on Zim Internet chat rooms. Some people say it was only a matter of time before this happened. The whites, who are less than one percent of the country's population, own virtually all the productive land.

So the idea of a cooperative died? And now Father has gone ahead and taken matters into his own hands. The confusion in my mind leaves my heart searching hopelessly for a clear emotion to hang on to.

I see Father, chanting slogans, sweat dripping down his face. Joining hands with two hundred other farmworkers, marching from the workers' quarters to stake their claim on the stately Walter residence.

How will they decide who'll live in the manor-house? What's happened to Walter and his family? Will they subdivide the farm or run it like a cooperative? Or maybe even sell it? They could share the proceeds and start their own businesses. But what do they know about business?

First, they have to savour this while it lasts. It has to last. It has to work. The alternative is simply unthinkable. This should have happened twenty years ago in a more orderly fashion.

I need a beer. There's not a can in the fridge. I was hoping to stay in tonight and finish debugging some systems for a new client. But now I have no mood to stay in the flat. I'll just have to leave the job running on the computer and deal with it later.

I grab my keys and head down to the Sahara Oasis. I stop at the ATM and check my balance. A few thousand. Three clients owe me at least fifteen thousand. Tomorrow I'm going to go down to their offices to demand payment. They have no right to condemn me to a life of penury just because they need to cut costs. They shouldn't be buying this IT service if they can't afford it. I've been too soft on them. Chuck wouldn't approve of my style.

I make my way to the bar and order a beer, after exchanging greetings with the mostly Nepalese bar staff and two early bird English regulars, who are deep in discussion, hunched over their beers.

I take a seat at the counter and admire the African décor while I wait for my beer. As I sip my Tsingtao, I soak in the atmosphere, allow myself to believe that for just a fleeting moment, I'm back in the land of my people. I must make that trip soon. Since I moved to Asia fifteen years ago, I've only been back once, five years ago. For ten years, my family had been asking: Did I find a pot of gold that kept me in foreign lands all those years? In the meantime, my grandfather died of old age. I never had a chance to say goodbye, or tape-record his stories of colonial rule as I had once promised. He took his secrets to his grave.

Five years ago was the first time since I came to Asia that I could afford an air ticket and gifts for the clan. Of course, I could have taken the free return ticket available upon graduation. But I allowed this option to lapse.

Lai Ying said Chacha was too small to travel. So I went alone. My family knows Lai Ying only from photographs. These last six months, I've come to know her only through her cryptic emails and occasional hurried, strained phone calls. If my father is truly a landowner now, perhaps he can afford to visit us and meet my family, if I manage to get them back here.

I'm so submerged in my thoughts that I barely notice Diallo sidle up to me until he shakes me by the shoulder. He has just returned from a trip to northern China, where the construction company he works for is building an expressway. Diallo likes to regale me with stories about his adventures in China. The sumptuous meals that last for hours and are followed by drinking sessions in which the Chinese pit themselves against professional, battle-hardened drinking girls amidst chants of *"gan be!"* Bottoms up. He loves these parties because this is the only time his colleagues drop their guard and reveal themselves. In recent years, he seems to have forgotten or maybe forgiven the shock of the Nanjing riots and gone back to thinking of himself as the black Chinese tribe.

Tonight I'm not in the mood for his stories, or his latest discovery of some esoteric Chinese fact.

"Why are you so quiet, man?"

What can I tell him? I take a long swig, swallow hard, and let out a long, slow sigh.

"Home, man. It's the situation back home."

He nods. He's been reading the papers.

"Seen the reports? An African country in the Hong Kong papers. Every day. Unbelievable, eh?"

"Man, it's amazing," he says, grinning as if it's an achievement Zimbabwe should be proud of. "Normally the media here act as if Africa doesn't exist, unless you've got famine in Ethiopia or genocide in Rwanda."

"This land thing in Zim, I doubt it would ever make the news if it was just one tribe throwing another off their land."

"Your country's different, man. It's white people we're talking about, and the editors are Brits, aren't they? Maybe they're thinking Zimbabwe today, South Africa next. Now that would be quite a story, *mon ami*. Alors, donc. What's new then?"

"My family are in the thick of it."

"My God! What happened? Are they all right?"

"They're fine. Father's taken over a farm, man."

"Jesus, man!" Diallo scans my face to see whether he's supposed to celebrate or commiserate, grin with pleasure or groan with pain. The blank expression on my face leaves him baffled. "So what happens now, *mon ami*? What are you going to do?"

I want to laugh. I want to leap up on the bar, wave my hands about and laugh until this madness goes away. This whole thing with Lai Ying's disappearance. And my father's activism. But something died, and I dare not even laugh. It would be obscene. Laughter doesn't live in me anymore.

"What's there to do, Diallo?"

"All right. They're safe, your family. They've got land, yeah? It's what everyone wants. So, it's all right?"

"It's perfect," I mutter, frowning.

"So, let's celebrate, man?"

Now, I find my laughter. But it's only a chuckle, which almost chokes me. It lurches out suddenly, without warning. Diallo slaps me on the shoulder, his laughter rocking his bulky frame. We clink glasses and order another round. And another. And before I know it, it's 1 o'clock. And I've acquired a new nickname. As far as Diallo is concerned, I'm a landowner. The landowner.

The following day, I try to call Chip. This is the first time I've ever tried to call him. It costs a fortune to call Africa. It's like calling a different planet, light years away. I wonder if I'll recognise his voice. The connection is so bad, I have to try several times before I get through. And when I do, he doesn't answer.

It must be about 9 a.m., his time. Whatever could he be doing? Chip spends a good deal of his time on the Internet, searching for what he calls investment opportunities. I give up and send him an email instead. Who else can I call? I haven't been in touch with my brother and sister for quite some time. If they're landowners now, perhaps they can afford a mobile and call me.

But they're hardly likely to call. We haven't been getting on very well. They think I should have returned to Zim after my degree, married a local girl, and started a business with the two of them as my business partners. They claim I abandoned them, forgetting how I paid their fees for years.

I need to send Lai Ying an email. But what will I tell her that I haven't already said? I dare not tell her about this thing with my family. It would just worry her, and she would email back about "nt tkg Chch 2 tht crzy dngrs plc, fll of crzy dngrs ppl".

The following Wednesday as I get off the lift, I see Jupiter walking towards the gate. It's the grey hair I notice first. He walks with a stoop, taking one painful step after another, like an old man. He has lost so much weight, I barely recognise him.

I catch up with him and greet him.

"How's Siu Meng?" I ask, not knowing what else to say.

"He's fine, thanks."

"Is he still playing football?"

"Oh, Siu Meng not here, now. Not here."

"I see."

"I going for the walk, Ah Dan. To the Garden. You the go?"

I consider for a moment. It is just down the road to the Zoological and Botanical Gardens, but at the pace he's walking, it will be at least half an hour if we can find a shortcut. I need to visit a furniture shop in Wanchai to see if we'll need anything for the new flat. I have time. I'm not seeing Alex till eight.

We turn right into Caine Road and walk in silence past the boutique furniture shops, music stores, kindergartens, and schools, and into Gleneally, where giant ferns and trees overhang the green-painted iron fence and a tall tree with branches pokes into the windows of the building across the street. The short walk up Gleneally is surprisingly steep, but even more surprising is the way Jupiter walks stoically, pausing only twice to get his breath back. From this point on, there's no traffic, and the air echoes with the noises of a true jungle. It is a little foggy and visibility isn't very good. In fact, it gets worse every year. It's the pollution. Sometimes it is so bad they advise people to stay indoors. I can barely see the skyscrapers of Central. The residential blocks of Mid-Levels stand like sentries behind us, shrouded in fog.

Luckily, it's not too hot. It's actually a reasonably pleasant twenty-six degrees. The weather report says there's a chance of a typhoon in the next day or so.

Jupiter is exhausted, but struggles not to let me notice how he's straining himself.

We wander around, listening to birds singing, watching orangutans from Borneo and Sumatra swinging from pipe to pipe in their iron enclosure, mouse-like Brazilian tamarins listening attentively to the symphony of noises, dozing lesser mouse-deer described on the information board as the world's smallest hoofed mammal, and Chinese porcupine. The last time I brought Chacha, here we spent an afternoon watching the Madagascan black-and-white ruffed lemurs dashing about crazily along the tree trunks, swinging from ropes and screaming at each other, attracting the attention of amused camera-toting onlookers. They are cat-sized but with tiny heads and shiny yellow eyes. I pointed out to Chacha the African tulip tree with bright, orange-red flowers that resemble a flame and make the tree look like it's on fire.

Like students on a school science trip, Jupiter and I stop dutifully to read the inscriptions about the origins of the animals and plants, the dozens of species of conifers, figs, palms, gum trees, ferns, and house plants. We stop to admire the fishtail palm trees that look like overgrown shrubs with their unbranched slender trunks and a yellowish swelling at the base of each leaflet.

The air here is fresh but pregnant with humidity. It's like walking into a steamy bathroom after someone has just had a hot bath and the extractor fan is broken.

Small groups of people amble around, admiring the vegetation, taking pictures. It's hard to believe that this oasis of peace and tranquillity exists just a few hundred metres away from the polluted, congested, and heavily built-up district of Central. The only audible sounds are those of birds singing, crickets chirruping, and a thousand unseen insects buzzing and humming, the occasional cackle from the apes, and children's laughter. Jupiter suggests we sit. We find a bench near the water fountain. We haven't spoken much. We're both lost in our thoughts, about the families we've lost or are in the process of losing.

"Siu Meng now in the Ganahdaaih," says Jupiter, suddenly, with a resoluteness that does not accord with his weak body.

"Oh, I see." But I don't, really. Canada? That's a long way off.

"Is better. He away from the Hong Kong."

"Yes, of course." I nod in agreement. There's no need to expose the little boy to ridicule in school. Whose mummy's in jail? Jail, jail, jail! "I'm sure he'll be fine there." I catch my breath sharply, but not fast enough to retrieve the unfortunate words. Jupiter may be right, but now I'm thinking of Chacha. Taken away to escape Hong Kong, too. Or the Hong Kong, as Jupiter calls this place.

"Everything changing already."

He waves a hand, frowning. There's more resignation than pain in his voice. As if he has come to accept the inevitable. It couldn't have been easy, if the rapid aging he has gone through is any guide.

"Now, he stay with *yee-jai*. Auntie. My sister, she Ganahdaaih people now. Is good, three cousins he play with them."

"I wish him well, Jupiter."

"Thank you." He turns to look in my eyes. "Your girl, and her mother. They all right?" I've never discussed my problems with him. He's never asked. Only once before at the clubhouse, months ago, I mentioned they were in China. No explanations. He probably suspected the worst.

"Yes, they are fine, thanks. My wife thinks it's better to stay in China for now."

"One day, they coming back." He makes it sound like a statement, but it's a question. He looks away, as if he doesn't expect a response, as if he believes he's not entitled to one. He's afraid he's prying. But he also envies me, thinking my family will come back in the near future. It will be a long time before Siu Meng returns to *the* Hong Kong, if at all, and two years before Beth leaves *the* prison. Meanwhile, my daughter remains hidden away in *the* China.

"Yes, one day." But what day will that be?

A child, about three, walks up to the edge of the pond, waving his hands to attract the attention of the turtles swimming gracefully, kicking their legs in gentle yet powerful strokes. The child's mother approaches, videocam catching the action for the family DVD collection.

"We Chinese believe, the family is—how to say—everything," says Jupiter, with a faraway look. He sucks his lips in, like a toothless old man. "I think for the Africa people, is same."

"The family is everything. You're very right."

"Everything," he echoes, nodding to the slight breeze blowing in our faces. In spite of the smile, his face looks weather-beaten, like that of a farmer who spends all day out in the fields, braving the sun, rain, and sleet. The pain of the disintegration of his family is etched across his face.

I regret never having done the happy hour. All that beer consumed with mates who mostly talk about women, money, and now land, and here's this kernel of wisdom from a neighbour I've done my best to ignore. Jupiter's words fill me with shame. Here we are talking about family being everything, and yet I've never met my parents-in-law, and neither has Lai Ying met hers. For some time, it looked as though Lai Ying's parents were getting ready to meet their black son-in-law. And then I went and messed it up with the drinking and gambling. God only knows when we'll ever reconcile.

The woman whisks the boy away. He screams in protest, momentarily shattering the peace, then his screams turn into shrieking laughter. No one looks up. The noise blends in, naturally, as if it was meant to be. Just like the songs of the birds, the growls of the orangutans, the croaking of frogs, and the chirruping and hissing of a thousand and one unseen insects.

Alex arrives and orders a glass of South African Pinotage that's on promotion. He loosens his tie and rolls back his sleeves, as if to prepare for a long session of hard, physical exercise. I don't plan on staying here long. I have two jobs pending that I have to finish tonight. And there's not much cash in my wallet.

Alex is dressed like many of the other people here. Dark suits, white shirts, ties that come in all shapes and colours. We make small talk for fifteen minutes. I still can't believe I'm ready for all this Sherlock Holmes business. The whole thing is unreal, like a movie. But I have no option. Jupiter's words still echo in my ears. The family is everything. As if I didn't know that already.

"Your work going okay?" Alex's voice startles me back to reality.

I nod. What I do nowadays isn't work. I'm scraping the bottom of the barrel, and although it pays the rent and keeps my head above the water, it feels incomplete. It's like living on a dozen snacks a day instead of three square meals and just managing to keep hunger at bay.

"You?"

"Oh, man, it's not looking very good," says Alex, frowning. "It's quiet. Very quiet. In fact, they're talking about laying people off. A couple of guys have already gone; they can sort of see it coming."

"So, are you scared?"

He takes a sip of his red wine and his eyes sweep across the bar, as if wondering what he'll miss here when he's gone.

"I first came to Hong Kong in the early '90s." There's just the slightest suggestion of nostalgia in his voice. "Those were the golden years, man. Life was good. The place was just heaving with opportunities. Speculating on stocks, you could make enough money in one morning to finance a crazy-crazy lifestyle for the next five months. You could make a killing speculating on properties, buying and selling without ever stepping in them, without even knowing where the hell they were, or whether they had been built or not. We were making money and blowing it like there was no tomorrow. It's all changed now."

"I know." I nod with recognition. "My neighbour said something very similar to me this afternoon. Everything changed already."

I was here, too. I did the stocks thing for a while, too, before succumbing to the allure of the gaming tables and joining the hordes of punters on the jetfoil to Macau. It got easier when the world started to worry about the millennium bug. There weren't enough IT experts in Macau. Or anywhere, for that matter. Come to think of it, there aren't enough experts in anything in Macau besides gaming assistants.

"You ask me: Am I scared? I ask myself: What have I got to show for the good old days? Still have a flat. Fully paid, I might add. So, at least I've got a roof over my head. I've lived it up. I got shit savings, man. So, yeah, the future's not looking too fucking bright right now. Seen the unemployment figures lately?"

"Yeah. It's never been this bad in Hong Kong." Almost eight percent out of work. Six years ago, they had full employment, as they say. "And just imagine what'll happen if they drop the peg."

The unstable currency is on everyone's mind. A devaluation would amount to a salary cut if you spend or have investments abroad. This fear intensified in 1997, when currencies in Asia fell like dominoes. The wave started with the Thai baht, then it swept away the South Korean won, or, as I remember someone saying, the won was lost. Next in line was the Malaysian ringgit and the Indonesian rupee. The Hong Kong dollar survives only because they keep it pegged to the American dollar in order to maintain stability, even though many believe a devaluation would be good for the economy. We drink in silence for a few moments, listening to the rapid tinkle-tinkling guitar sounds of an Ali Farka Touré track.

"Look, Alex, I'm ready to go through with this."

"You sure?"

"Whatever it takes to get my family back, man."

He downs his pint and orders another one. Is he hesitating? Why is he acting as though he needs to think about this? I'm the one who should be doing the thinking here, and God knows I've done enough of it. He owes me one, too, after I saved his life from those triad gangster wannabes on the street.

"All right. It's like this, man. My company won't touch it."

"Oh, that's too bad."

"Hold on. Hold on. It's not the kind of job we take on. I checked with the boss. But, hey, I see a niche there, and, uh…"

"What, man?"

"I reckon we can do this, you know, like freelance. I see a chance here. Who knows, I might venture out on my own, the way things are going."

I shake his hand. I don't care who does it, Asia Risk Assessment or Alex Does *The* China Limited. I don't care what it takes. If Alex sees a chance to make a quick buck, and can do a professional job that I *can* afford, that's perfectly fine by me. If he can help me find my family, I'll do it. I'm not paying any more attention to Lai Ying's threats.

"So, what happens next?"

"I'll need details, everything you can tell me. Recent photo. Possible contacts she has in…where was it again?"

"Shanghai."

"Right, Shanghai. I'll need to check out your computer. Well, you're the expert there. You've probably tried to track the source of her emails and so forth, I reckon?"

"I've narrowed it down to a cybercafé." Lai Ying is careful not to email me from her computer at home, if she has one, or from her place of work. I hand Alex a piece of paper with some IP numbers, my wife's name, and phone numbers of a few people I know in Shanghai, including Julius's. "I'll email you her picture later. I've thought about going to check out this cybercafé, hover around, till she shows up. I need to know where she lives so I can see my daughter, which means I might have to follow her. I've got time."

"I bet you do."

I do, really. And what's more, I've no reason not to go. I'm not getting much work done right now. This summer, I've lost half my clients. The only thing that will stop me going is if Alex can guarantee a professional service, and deliver results at an affordable price.

"There's not much I'm doing here, you know?"

"But she'll spot you, and then what? You need a third party, man. Someone she doesn't know. I've got contacts in Shanghai."

"No harm should come to her. Let's be very clear, Alex. I just want an address. I'll do the rest, okay?"

"Our people are professional. The best in the country. They tend to be former cops. Detective officers. Pretty well-connected."

I hope he realises it's my family we're talking about here.

Through the clouds of smoke, I see Diallo's sturdy figure making its way towards us. I try desperately to catch his eye and warn him to keep his big mouth shut. I'm too late.

"*Comment ça va, Monsieur* Landowner!" he calls out, and gives me a big hug. "Getting used to your new status?"

I try to wave him away and struggle to keep a straight face. But inside, I'm boiling. Alex peers at me over his beer. Is he recoiling from me? Perhaps it's just my imagination.

"What's this, man? What's he talking about?"

Before I can answer Alex, Diallo blurts out, "You're looking at your new master, my good man. You'd better buy him a beer, and while you're at it, mine's a Tsingtao." He bursts out laughing. I step on his toes and squeeze twice.

"You talk too much nonsense, Diallo."

Alex is not convinced. He leans over so close I can smell his cologne, in spite of the cigarette smoke. "What's he on about, man?"

"You're talking like you don't know the man, Alex." I push Diallo aside and face Alex. "I can't comment on this crap. It's not important. Are you going to help me or not? This is important."

The suspicion still lurks in his eyes.

"Look, Dan, we've got this shit hovering over us, and you know what? I don't need it, frankly. I don't need it any more than you do. You've got to be honest with me. Your family have overrun a farm, is that what Diallo's saying?"

"It's not my family, man. It's just—"

"Oh, don't split hairs on me, man."

"What does it matter, Alex? I've got a much bigger problem on my hands. The stuff going on back in Zim, Jesus Christ, man, right now, I just want to get my wife and little girl back here with me. If you're not going to help, let's just forget it."

His eyes narrow ominously as he inhales deeply on his cigarette. I turn to talk to Diallo but he's busy chatting up one of the Nepalese barmaids. Alex and I drink in silence, neither willing to continue the discussion, allowing the energetic township jazz of Hugh Masekela to fill the silence between us.

Take a Chance, Eggman

DIALLO CALLS THE FOLLOWING MORNING. He wants to find out what happened. After the fallout with Alex, I had another beer, mumbled goodbye, wandered out into the street, and went back home, to my beloved computer.

"You left all of a sudden, man."

"You were busy."

"I was talking to that babe…Nami, Mina…can never remember her name. She's not too bad, eh?"

I've no idea whom he's talking about. There were three Nepalese girls working in the pub.

"So, what's your plan?" I ask him.

"My plan? With this girl? Oh, man. Just forget it. The way they go on about their traditions, it's a waste of time. Did you know they still do that arranged marriage bullshit?"

I didn't.

"Well, my friend, these girls can muck about with fellow Nepalese boys all they want, but their fathers or uncles or elder brothers have got husbands lined up for them back in some hillside village in Nepal."

His unexpected explosion of laughter makes me cringe. I have too much on my mind to appreciate this sort of joke right now. But after listening to him for a few more minutes, it occurs to me that having a dad decide whom you should marry could have a funny side to it if the loving dad, who was anxious to preserve the family dignity with an arranged marriage and to deliver a virgin to the carefully chosen groom in the village, didn't know you were shagging some ponytailed, single-earring-wearing, chain-smoking guy, who works at a bar down Lockart Road.

It's too early in the day for this kind of talk. I tell Diallo I'll call him later. I need to talk to Lai Mui. I've been thinking about her lately, racked by guilt about the way I upset her. It's foolish to alienate the only family I have for thousands of miles around. I wait till 7 p.m., when she's not likely to be cold-calling potential clients but is still expected to be in the office because the female boss, who is in her late forties, single, and has virtually no social life, works till eight. Even though the staff have nothing to do except forward jokes to each other and make plans about where to have a late dinner, they're expected to give the boss face by just being there.

Lai Mui answers immediately, as though she's expecting to hear from me. That's what I like about people in Hong Kong. They don't like wasting time. In Zim, people will let the phone ring for hours, as if they want you to know how important they are. You can't trouble them any time you like. They'll answer when they feel like it. In Hong Kong, a missed call could mean a lost opportunity, money gone begging.

"Oh, it's you, Dan." Could that be disappointment in her voice? I strain to read her mood above the sound of ringing phones and the muted hum of consultants trying to interest potential clients in new-fangled mutual funds and offshore products.

"Afraid so, sister. How've you been?"

"Busy."

Silence.

"Lai Mui, would you like to meet sometime, you know, for a drink, dinner, or something?"

"Dan, you know, it's just so hectic nowadays…"

"I know, I know. But, Lai Mui, I want to apologise for upsetting you that night."

"It's okay, there's no need."

"Please, I insist. I was out of order, sister. I'm really sorry. I shouldn't make you angry when it's all my fault. I feel awful about it. Have *yam cha* with me, please."

Silence. I hold my breath.

"Okay, Dan. That would be nice."

I sigh with relief, as if I've already been forgiven.

"There's that *dim sum* place we used to go to in Mong Kok, remember?"

"Of course." She chuckles. "It's called the Golden Boat."

"That's the one. They have all those little cute *dim sum* dumplings and things, you know? They're really tasty. *Hou mei-ah*, as Lai Ying loves to say. So tasty. She's always going, *sihk do di, ah*." Eat more. "Sometimes I thought she was trying to fatten me up." Lai Mui chuckles, yielding to the luxury of happy memories. She and Carl often joined us for *yam chah* on Saturday mornings. The place was so popular you had to reserve a table well in advance; otherwise, you would be waiting out on the polluted Argyle Street for hours.

"Let me see if I can get some breathing space, Dan, one of these Saturdays."

"Thanks, sister. I really appreciate. I'll call you in a couple of weeks."

"All right."

"Good luck with the work."

"Dan?" Her voice sounds hesitant, tentative.

"Yeah?"

"Lai Ying called me some days ago. I spoke to her and my niece."

"Really! How are they?"

"They're fine. Chacha speaks such good Putonghua, it's amazing. She sounds such a grown-up – the things she says, the way she talks, about her school, her friends, the new stuff they're learning…"

Lai Mui goes on, excitedly. In my mind, I hear Chacha's voice, as I last heard it months ago. I try to imagine what it must sound like now, translating Lai Mui's words into the voice of a seven-year-old. It's too much, it's too confusing, and yet so wonderful to hear Lai Mui's voice relaying Chacha's words, revealing so much more than my wife ever does.

I spend a couple of hours working out in the fitness room in the afternoon, pumping iron, running on the treadmill. Like a man trying to exorcise demons from his mind. I was half expecting to see Jupiter here. I should remember to exchange cards with him so we can hopefully keep in touch when I move to North Point.

There's hardly anyone in the fitness room. Except for the attendant who sits at the counter poring at a computer screen, there's only one other person, a woman working out on the steps, taking one painful step after another, keeping to the rhythm of the instrumental ambience music coming down from tiny speakers hanging from the ceiling. She's been at it for more than an hour, non-stop. A magazine spread out on the control panel has completely captured her imagination. She hasn't once looked up. That degree of concentration reminds me of Lai Ying, who could spend hours reading magazines. If I look at this woman in profile, with the gaze fixed on the magazine, I could be looking at Lai Ying – the narrow waist, the close-fitting, black outfit and white tennis shoes, the quick intake of breath with the lips sucked in. I can't handle the memories.

I make my way back to the flat, take a shower, and sit at the desk to complete a couple of jobs for clients who have faithfully stuck by me. I'm looking in the fridge to see if there's anything to eat when the phone rings. I grab the half-empty packet of frozen chicken wings, throw them into the kitchen sink, and leave the tap running. With any luck, they'll defrost in half an hour. I pick up the phone. The caller display simply reads 'Call'. Long distance. Could this be Lai Ying? I can almost hear my heart beating with furious anticipation.

"Hello!"

"He-loo!" A male voice. Strong Chinese accent. My heart deflates. I walk back to the kitchen and turn off the tap, trying to figure out who this could be.

"Can I help?"

"Eggman! Is your friend, Wang!" I stop in mid-step, hand clasped tight around the phone. The voice is so loud I have to keep the phone two inches from my ear.

"Wang, how are you?" I wonder why it has taken him so long to call since we exchanged those emails.

I turn the packet to let some water run in so the five or so remaining wings are nicely soaking in the lukewarm water.

"Very fine, my friend. So good I hear your speaking now. So long time."

"Yeah. Nine years, Wang. Where are you now?"

"In this moment, Shenzhen. Have business here."

"I see. How's it going?"

Pause. The connection isn't very good. I move back to the living room and stand by the window, hoping to get a better signal. But the problem isn't here.

"Hello! Hello!" I've lost him. Then his voice comes booming through, this time in Putonghua.

"Sorry, my friend. I'm in a car. We just drove into a basement car park. Can you hear me now?"

"Loud and clear. So, are you coming to Xianggang?"

"I was going to. This week, in fact. But there's been a delay. Problem with the visa. I can't understand these people." His voice changes. He sounds angry, like a man who's been betrayed. "I take care of them, and they treat me like this. Anyway, we'll deal with it, and soon, I'll be in Xianggang. And how're things with you, Eggman? How's your business?"

"Not good, Wang. Not good."

"Ah! It happens. Sometimes good, sometimes not. Life is a cycle. But look, why don't you come to Shenzhen? There are many opportunities here for someone with your knowledge. You could make it big here."

Where would I start? I've thought about it. Shenzhen is all the rage nowadays. But Lai Ying wouldn't hear of it. She says the people there are even more crooked than Hong Kong people.

"I don't know, Wang. I think for now my life is here." My words sound empty. No doubt Wang can sense, it too. Living here without a good, steady income is hard, and painful.

"Eggman, life is about opportunities, timing, being able to take the choices when they present themselves, and acting with precision. You don't know Sun Tzu, perhaps. He was a great military writer whose words I admire. He wrote that the well-timed strike of the falcon shatters its prey. It's all about speed, timing, and precision. I've never allowed myself to stagnate, or to shy away from taking decisive action like a military general, at the right time. If I did, I would still be selling noodles with preserved vegetables in Cai Chang." He bursts out laughing. "You remember the noodle shop, before Wang's Den?"

How could I forget? So much happened there. The White Card. The thing he did, or was supposed to have done, to Kabinga. The memories are indelibly etched on my mind. I wonder how he looks now. Hair probably greying at the temples. Beer belly straining against the trousers belted inches above the belly button.

"I'm sure Shenzhen has a lot to offer, Wang…"

"Listen, my friend. Why don't you come here? Just for a few days. We'll talk about our business plans for Africa. Since your business is a bit slow, I guess you can get away for a while, right? A few days?"

I promise to think about it.

"Take a chance, Eggman, and call me tomorrow, when you decide, all right?"

The chicken breasts haven't defrosted properly, so I decide to get the job done in the microwave, which takes three minutes. When I take them out, they're not only completely defrosted but also cooked on the edges, and look as if they were soaked in a chicken soup cauldron but managed to fly away before they got thoroughly cooked. My dinner tonight consists of boiled rice and chicken wings fried with broccoli. If Lai Ying had been here, we would have had an additional vegetable, something like *bak choi* or *choi saam*, neither of which I particularly like because they're stringy, end up getting lodged between the teeth, and require a protracted period of excavation with one toothpick after another.

After dinner, I stay in to work for a couple more hours. At nine, I'm ready to head out. I'll miss happy hour, which is too bad. They'll be charging an arm and a leg for a drink by the time I get to the pub. I haven't seen Charlie for quite some time. He's always travelling nowadays. I try his number a couple of times. The first time, I get a metallic cackling sound, the type I get when I try to call Zim. He can't be in Africa. The Philippines, or Indonesia perhaps. The second time, I get the busy tone, which transfers me straight to voicemail. I leave a message asking him to call me back. Fifteen minutes later, he sends a text message saying he's in Kuala Lumpur and won't be back in town till next week.

My first stop is the Pirates' Rice Bowl in the Soho. It's a bit quiet this Thursday evening. I take a seat at the bar and order a bottle of Heineken. There are only about six other people propping up the bar. One of them looks familiar. He's an English investment banker. We've spoken once or twice before. Every time I see him, he's busy doing the crossword puzzle in the day's Post. He manages rich people's money during the day and relaxes by testing his word power down the pub at night. We talk for a while when he looks up.

Minutes later, I turn and cast a glance across the room and spot Alex seated in a corner with two girls. He spends a lot of time in this pub. It's like his second home. Not surprising, as he lives only a couple of blocks away. He hasn't seen me yet. I don't want to intrude. I drink by myself for the next hour, with only the hypnotic techno music for company, drawing me into itself, forcing me into an intoxicating trance.

"Oh, my, if it isn't the landowner, chilling out with a beer and reflecting on how his old man's gonna rake it in."

I turn around sharply to see Alex's face leering inches from me. He's drunk out of his mind.

"What's up, Alex?"

"You tell me, my man." He sways from side to side, like a tree in a typhoon, threatening to hit the ground any moment now. I glance at the corner and notice the two girls he was drinking with have gone. They must have sneaked out behind my back, afraid I would try to take over their flats or something. Alex must have put them up to it, with stories about land-snatching war veterans, if the state he's in is anything to go by. What the hell was he drinking? He looked quite normal forty-five minutes ago.

"Grab a seat," I urge him, holding his elbow. "You'll fall."

The waiters watch him in earnest, smelling trouble. What's he going to do now, grab my beer and empty it on my head? The state he's in, he's quite capable of pulling off such a stunt. He's still staring at me, swaying unsteadily as if he was standing on the Star Ferry in choppy waters.

"You people, you…people." He waves a finger inches from my face, standing so close I can smell the breath coming in angry, weary gasps from his open mouth. Whisky or rum. I push his hand away and he almost loses his balance. I quickly grab hold of his shoulder and gently push him down the stool next to mine.

"What's up with you, man? You've completely lost it. How much did you drink?"

He's not paying attention. He summons the barman and orders a tequila, which he downs and quickly orders a bottle of Tsingtao. He grimaces, biting his lips, tapping his temple with his knuckles.

"Did you lose your job or something?"

"Lose my job?" His laughter is coarse and guttural. "Well, well, now that's something I can handle, even with my non-existent savings." He continues to laugh.

If he goes on like this, I'm getting out of here. He looks bent on embarrassing us.

"So…"

"So, what did I lose? What did I fucking lose, apart from my sanity, as you've no doubt noticed?" He looks intently into my eyes, as if wondering whether to share a dirty secret. "My family lost their goddamn land, that's what, all right? Happy now?"

I suddenly realise that the bottle I'm holding is surprisingly cold, as if it has just been fished out of a bucket full of ice. My mind fills up with a riot of confused thoughts. I want to say something to Alex, to ask, *what happened? When did it happen? Is everyone all right?* But those thoughts are hijacked by the image of my father wielding a twig broken from a tree, leading a march on the manor house, while the Walters sit in front of their TV, planning a picnic trip by the lake in their private game park. And the only words I can find are,

"Oh, my God!"

"Maybe I should pray to *your* God," says Alex. "He seems to listen to you."

Does he? I don't know if any god is listening to either of us right now. But I know something that will help. I signal the barman for another round.

Part 3

This Is the Life

I HAVEN'T BEEN TO SHENZHEN in ten months. The last time was when I came here to do a couple of Y2K jobs set up by good old Tiff. They were both small firms – a travel agent and a small independent property agent with four offices in the city.

If I have time, I'll look up some of my old clients. As Wang says, the opportunities in this city are limitless. Now that I'm on my own anyway, there's no reason why I can't come out here every now and then. I've ignored this market because the money isn't very good. I would have to do a lot of trips or set up camp here for several days to make it worth my while. But since I'm struggling to expand my clientele in Hong Kong, I can't afford lengthy absences.

The thing that strikes you when you come to this bustling city is just how much it changes all the time. There are new buildings cropping up all over the place. Residential, office blocks, and hotels. As I walk along a verandah of a long mall to the Shangri-La Hotel, where I'm meeting Wang, I see they've started to cordon off sections of the massive square outside the immigration building and diverting traffic. A long queue of buses and taxis winds its way around the road barriers and bollards that have been planted at regular intervals on the makeshift road. The verandah is just as I remember it, full of people carrying red, blue, and yellow-striped carrier bags, dashing in and out of the railway station, heading to the bus terminal in the mall across the square, or towards the immigration building and Hong Kong. Smiling girls in cheongsams with scandalously long slits stand outside doors holding out menus for restaurants and colourful brochures for massage parlours. Haggard-looking women holding crying babies sit by the walls, bowing nonstop towards a bowl with a few yuan coins.

Wang is not in the lobby, where he had said he would be waiting. He had said 10 a.m. It's 10.15. With a twinge of embarrassment for making such an early start, I order a beer at the lounge bar. Everyone else is drinking coffee. Embarrassment turns to shock when I see the bill. This being China, I was expecting to pay a lot less than I would in Hong Kong. At $35, it's even more expensive than the normal, i.e., non-happy-hour price at the Oasis. Prices used to be reasonable in this town. Oh well, I can't complain. I suppose they're catering for the high-heeled here. From my perch on a high stool, I have an excellent view of the street outside and keep an eye on guests coming and going.

One thing you notice is how almost everyone in China smokes. If the cigarette is not wedged between the lips like a snake's tongue, it's stuck to the hand like an additional, deformed and discoloured, smouldering finger. Virtually all the people waiting in this lobby area and bar are smoking. It's the same everywhere. On the streets, in shops, bars, and restaurants, virtually all the men and increasingly a lot of women are puffing away, as if they need the nicotine to stay alive. They smoke constantly, rapidly, anxious to dispose of a withering, dwindling stub in order to savour the delights of the next new stick. They love their cigarettes so much that they often give beautifully wrapped packages of cigarettes as gifts, especially during the Chinese New Year. They even take gifts of cigarettes to sick people in hospital.

Wang arrives at 10.40 a.m., when I'm halfway through my second beer. I recognise him the moment he steps out of the black Chinese limousine, one of those models favoured by the nouveau riche and which looks like a cross between an oversized 700-series BMW and a Cadillac. He breezes in grinning and hands me his card, which describes him as the chairman of Wang Golden Harvest Holdings. I study his face, which exudes that confidence that comes with the ability to confront any challenge with the combined power of the wallet and *guanxi*.

This is not the Wang I knew, the struggling noodle-shop owner turned ambitious bar proprietor. His dark-grey suit and light-blue silk shirt paint the picture of a man of means. He has put on pounds around the waist and on the face. In fact, everywhere, though it's not the stocky build one notices, but the confident, dignified demeanour one might find in a pilot. Only by looking into his eyes do you see the unmistakable shrewdness of a wheeler and dealer. Those eyes do not know how to smile. Even though the rest of his face is suffused with a joyful grin. He has a lot to tell me, he says, but doesn't want to linger here.

"We'll have plenty of time to drink, Eggman. Let's go play a round or two of golf. What do you say?"

Golf? I couldn't even tell the difference between a golf club and a hockey stick. But I haven't got a choice in the matter. Wang insists on paying my bill and we walk out to the waiting limousine, which I notice is in fact a model of Nissan. We sit in the back. The driver is wearing a black suit and white gloves.

"So you're into golf now, Wang?"

"Eggman, my friend, how can you not be?" He turns to whisper conspiratorially, "It's where we make deals. Contacts. *Guanxi*. I play all the time. It's perfect."

We spend half an hour on the driving range, where Wang teaches me the basics of holding the club and whacking the hell out of the ball. Most of the time, I end up smashing the seven iron into the turf, which sends a dull pain through my wrist. As soon as I start to achieve a bit of consistency, Wang declares I'm ready to hit the green. He tells me the Fragrant Dream Summer Park golf club is owned by friends of his, and that he has a minor interest.

"Everything's taken care of, my friend. *Everything*. We'll just have fun and talk."

"I'm not sure, Wang," I start to protest. "I've never played golf before. I'll slow you down, and lose the balls."

"It's all right. You're doing well. You could be the Hong Kong Tiger Woods. And don't worry about the balls. We have plenty. We'll play nine holes first, then see what happens."

"All right."

"Normally, I would do two rounds. Eighteen holes. Then wrap the game up at the nineteenth hole. But since you're a beginner, we'll take it slow. Just nine holes for now. That will leave you more than enough energy for the tenth."

"Oh. Which one is that?"

Wang bursts out laughing, and doesn't bother to explain.

I had never imagined golf could be so much fun. It looks so boring when you watch it on TV. Almost as boring as darts and snooker. Football and basketball are the only sports I have the patience to watch.

"You have a family now, Eggman?"

"Wife and a daughter." In the past I smiled when I supplied this information. Now, I feel as if I'm talking about how much money I lost at the casino. The realisation that I lost a wife and child at the casino sends a shiver through me, forcing me to steady myself on my thankfully strong driver.

"Very good. You're young, Eggman; you should have more children." He laughs as he says this. I affect a mirthless chuckle, struggling not to betray the anger that's welling up in the pit of my belly.

As it's early September, the humidity has eased off a lot and it's not too hot. In fact, the day is just perfect, like Wang said. Cloudless, clean air, acres of greenery. I can understand why Wang spends so much time here. There's hardly anyone else here at the moment, so my fears of holding people up are unfounded.

Wang has hired a couple of caddies, who tug the clubs along and select the club. It's so confusing. Before I take a shot, I have to practice a swing several times to get the hang of every new club. It takes forever to make each hole. Wang is patient, explaining the fine points of each club: the yardage, the loft, wind speed and direction, not once forgetting to fill me in on what he's been doing all these years.

"Shanghai was like heaven after Wang's Den. People there knew how to have fun. They were advanced, you know. I stayed in the catering business. That was my strength, you know. Then moved to import-export. Not easy, not easy at all, with all the regulations and restrictions. Contacts helped. I've ventured out, now. Hotels, karaokes, mobile phones, electronics, and property. In fact, everything. Wherever there's money to be made, Wang will be there. It's a glorious life, Eggman."

"Impressive, Wang. You've really moved on."

"Oh, it's just a start. The best deals are still ahead, waiting to be harvested. Watch this." He lines up the shot for a putt, relaxes his shoulders, shuffles his legs, shuts one eye, takes a deep breath, making it look as though his life depends on this putt. The concentration is unnerving, it's almost as if he's aiming a gun at a troublesome competitor who has caused him untold grief, but now he has the doomed target in his sights. "I'm going for birdie," he declares, lips hardly moving.

The ball makes a neat curve up the slight incline before veering left and sliding gently towards the hole, as if it knows its way home.

Wang punches the air with a clenched fist. The two caddies clap their hands, gazing with admiration at their hero. I give up keeping my own scores after maintaining an average of 11 above par and the ignominious loss of an average of two balls in each of the first three holes.

"So you've been in Shenzhen for how long now?"

"Three years ago, we moved to Guangdong province. This is the best place for business in China today. I follow the money, Eggman. We have a home in Guangzhou city. That's where most of our business is. But now, I'm spending more time in Shenzhen. Hong Kong is next. Shenzhen is great, but it's tough.

I'm still building *guanxi*. Let me tell you why I thought you and I should meet, Eggman. I see Africa as a great opportunity for us here in China. And the best place to be in order to get into Africa properly is here, where we are right now: Shenzhen and Hong Kong. Like members of a family holding hands and looking into the future together."

The thought of Chinese investing in Africa is news to me. Most wouldn't even know where to start. But Wang has always had an uncanny foresight, since the Nanjing days.

"What kind of business do you have in mind?" I ask him.

"Commodities, my friend. Steel, minerals, oil, agricultural products."

At the end of the round, I'm thoroughly refreshed and raring to go the whole 18 holes. I can't remember the last time I had so much fun.

"Maybe we take a break now," says Wang. "Give your palm a break. If you're not used to this, you could end up with blisters. We'll come back tomorrow." Sounds good to me. Anyway, I'm famished. It's almost half past one.

A business associate of Wang's joins us for lunch at the club. He is introduced as Liu Ming. It turns out he has extensive investment interests in Guangdong province, from property to private schools and telecommunications. They run an electronics business together.

Liu Ming looks like a party bureaucrat who is used to dealing with difficult citizens bombarding him with questions about this and that policy. He dons the placid, all-knowing, tolerant, it's-all-for-the-good-of-the-motherland expression like an extra item of clothing in the winter. It's a must-have when circumstances require it, but can easily be discarded for something more suitable if necessary. Something like the no-nonsense resoluteness suggested by the furrowed brow and concentrated glare while he's thinking. The sports jacket and casual polo shirt look just right for his slight stature. They give him the look of a guy who just wants to get the job done, and won't give you any trouble. If you don't give him any.

The lunch is a long, sumptuous affair. Plenty of food, lots of beer. It surprises me to see these guys drinking so much in the afternoon. They're both red in the face, but it doesn't bother them. Many Chinese men turn crimson after one beer, and that's as much as they're prepared to swallow. But with these two, the redder they get, the more they drink. We're all in a great mood. I can't remember the last time I needed to speak this much Putonghua. It feels like being back in Nanjing, especially when Wang and I reminisce about the good old days, the lengthy drinking sessions at Wang's Den, the occasional fights between Chinese and foreigners. It's good to be here. Golf, fine food, great beer, and fiery maotai. This is the life. As Wang puts it, it's a glorious life.

Spending time with these people almost makes me feel like a regular tycoon. It brings back memories of my own moneymaking merry-go-round, which unfortunately ground to a halt nine months ago, and since then, there has been nothing glorious about my life. But right now, I'm letting go, even if it's just for a few days. There has been too much gloom, too much pain in my life this year, since Lai Ying left. I want a piece of this carefree, hedonistic life again, just for a little while. I want to be reminded of how it felt to have a thick wallet, to enjoy what the world has to offer. And then I'll happily go back to my crappy little life in Hong Kong, like a lizard retreating into a crevice on the rocks after sunning himself for a couple of hours and taunting the scavenging predators prowling with intent. After I've had my fill of the sun, I'll be happy to resume the struggle, the hassle, the chase for elusive clients, the worries over rent money.

Wang is generous, like all Chinese tycoons who have risen from humble origins to the dizzying heights of opulence. He thinks it elevates him in the eyes of lesser mortals to spend money like there's no tomorrow, to distribute largesse and win admiration. And he has acquired an uncanny sense of humour, too. He keeps us entertained with tales about the strange things that go on in the world of business, the jealousies between party bureaucrats and businessmen, the silly games officials play to frustrate business when they feel they've been slighted, like shutting down water and electricity supplies in the middle of an important function, the subtle negotiation styles you must use in order to have your way and maintain harmony, giving each other face. When I look back now, I remember he was always ahead of his time. When other shopkeepers and shop attendants gawped or sneered at foreigners, Wang welcomed them to come in and spend, to teach him about their countries. I can't understand Lai Ying's suspicions. This guy and I could do business together. There are so many opportunities coming up in the course of this discussion. He has truly become the international wall at the old noodle shop. And he's very well connected, he knows everyone, the way he drops names.

I can't understand why his Hong Kong visa hit a snag. Perhaps he has enemies in this city. Is that possible? With his cheerful boisterousness and his ability to give people face, he doesn't look like a man who could have angered anyone. In fact, the more time I spend with him, listen to his theories about international business and his jokes, the more I wonder whether he could have been capable of harming Kabinga.

"You see, Eggman, Africa remains unexplored by Chinese," says Wang. Liu Ming nods sagely as he deftly picks a mouth-watering chunk of lobster from the steaming silver pot. "Everyone here looks at America. Personally I don't trust Americans. They want to dominate China. You think we'll allow them? No!"

"They're wrong," says Liu Ming. "They control the whole world, Europe, Japan, in fact, the whole of Asia. Now, they think they can target China." He shakes his head, unable to believe the naïveté of the Americans. I try to imagine this slightly built chap chasing Yankee transgressors with whatever he can lay his hands on, even a menacing, red lobster claw, like the one he's sucking on right now.

"It won't work. They can't touch us. We have a five-thousand-year-old civilisation, you know." I've heard this once too often. Somewhere along the line, this much vaunted civilisation appears to have stalled, and is now being jump-started with a renewed vengeance. These guys are worried about America controlling the world, but they're just as keen to control it themselves, which I find equally troubling. And as much as they resent American domination, without American customers, their businesses would grind to a halt.

"Chinese businesses are everywhere now, all over Asia," says Wang. "But they don't understand Africa. Yet we've been in contact with Africa since our great seafarer Admiral Zheng He visited the continent at the time of the Ming Dynasty. I think it's time to resume this contact and complete the mission."

"That's true," adds Liu Ming. "Let me give you a small history lesson, Dan. Admiral Zheng He's first expedition through the Indian Ocean took him to Africa a good sixty-five years before Vasco da Gama, and his expeditions continued for more than thirty years. If they had continued, we would have had a very thriving business with Africa today. It's not too late, my friend. We're ready for the task."

He leans back, with a smug expression. I'm intrigued. In school, I was taught about Vasco da Gama, Captain Cook, Magellan, Christopher Columbus, and all those brave fellows who went around discovering new lands, but I never heard of this Chinese admiral.

"With your help, Eggman," says Wang, stretching his arms out in an expansive gesture, "we can pick up where Zheng He left off and finish the work he started."

I smile. The history is fascinating, but I can't help wondering how it would have ended had the expeditions continued. Would the Chinese have gone on to colonise Africa the way Vasco da Gama's descendants and their cousins from all over Europe did? Would they have settled amongst black people? Perhaps they would have built trading ports to export ivory, slaves, and minerals back to China. The Europeans would have found a very different world when they started to settle there four hundred years later. I ask Liu Ming why the expeditions stopped. The smile on his face fades away, to be replaced by something akin to regret.

"This was the failure of our civilisation," he says. "We had wise leaders who supported science, technology, and trade. But sometimes, we had leaders and elite classes who did not. Admiral Zheng He's expeditions were stopped by a powerful faction of scholars who said it was demeaning and vulgar to engage in trade and to interact with…with…other people, foreigners."

Back then, foreigners were described as barbarians. Wang nods solemnly.

"It was very bad," says Wang. "The court faction of scholars crippled our efforts at international trade and business. They banned the building of large ships. We closed ourselves in. But now is the time to open up, Eggman. And we're ready to do it in style, and on a scale that Admiral Zheng He would never have imagined possible when he set sail almost six hundred years ago."

"How exactly do you plan to do this, Wang?" I ask him.

"I want to go to Africa and see for myself what we can do. You see, now, China is developing very fast. We need raw materials. We can invest and get very high returns, because the cost in Africa should be much lower than what we pay for Australian commodities."

"Southern Africa should be a good start. You have Zambia's copper, Angola's oil. Textiles and clothing. My country, as you know, is a bit unstable right now."

"That is not a problem," says Wang, face lighting up, as if this is just the cue he has been waiting for. "Where others see trouble, we see opportunity."

"We've talked to people," says Liu Ming. "Market research. Your country now has some instability, and the West has abandoned you. Now your country needs to work more closely with China."

"The West always insists on self-serving conditions," says Wang. "They stop aid and investment when you have some misunderstandings with politicians. We Chinese never abandon our friends. When the West walks away, that's when we walk in. Hand in hand, we create wealth. Because of the troubles you have, land is very cheap in your country now. Ten years from now, when the country is stable, it will be more valuable than gold. We always take the long view, Eggman, so we're prepared to sacrifice immediate gain for the treasures of the future. It's what we learn from Master Kong Fu-zi."

I always thought Confucius was into ethics, respect, wisdom, and enlightened things like that. I wonder what he would have made of the idea of buying undervalued assets in turbulent economies. Anyway, although Wang's view of Zimbabwe sounds far-fetched, I know he's not too far off the mark. The instability cannot go on forever. Eventually there'll be a change of regime. Investors will rush in to pick up the pieces. Now is the best time to get in, if there can be a safe way to do so.

I explain that we'll have to find well-connected people who can provide protection, or perhaps co-investors who just lack cash.

"Good idea," says Wang, after exchanging glances with Liu Ming. "If the security situation can be taken care of, the way is open for us to move in."

This deal is beginning to take shape nicely. I can feel my heartbeat quickening with anticipation. This might be the time to talk to my cousin Chipinduka about these business plans he's been trying to interest me in all these years. With the financial clout of Wang and his comrades, the risk factor suddenly looks so much less daunting I'm convinced this can work.

Yet, there's this niggling doubt lurking on the edges of my thoroughly alcohol-soaked mind, about the attack on Kabinga. But now, I'm here in Shenzhen, making plans with him. It's impossible to back out now. Suddenly it dawns on me, how foolish I've been, walking into a trap. Is this how they lured Kabinga?

"Together!" thunders a grinning Wang, jolting me out of my reverie. "You, Eggman, and us, we can bring Africa and China together." He leans towards me, holding his glass of maotai, his grinning face inches from mine, and whispers. "You hold the key to Africa, Eggman. It is your destiny."

Before I can find my voice, Liu Ming takes my elbow and says, "You will not regret this decision." He fills my glass with the flaming spirit. "We're going to be the new admirals, my friend, sailing across the seas to the end of the world in search of gold and good fortune. Are you ready to lead us to the land of your people in search of wealth? *Gan be!*"

The words of my headteacher loom in my tortured mind. *The Chinese have always been our friends. Why can't we work together?*

"I know he's ready!" exclaims Wang, holding my other elbow. I glance from one grinning face to the other, feeling like a cornered rat, wondering if I shouldn't get up and flee while I still can. Supposing Lai Ying walked in and found me sandwiched between these two, timidly clutching at my maotai as though it was the glue that held us together?

"Let's drink to Zheng He and the new expedition!" proposes Wang.

"Zheng He! Zheng He! *Gan be!*"

I rub my eyes in a vain attempt to clear my head. Why do they treat me like the anointed one, the one to spearhead this fantasy twenty-first-century Sino-African venture? There must be thousands of other Chinese businessmen in Africa already, and hundreds of Africans all over China.

As if reading my thoughts, Liu Ming says, "This time, it will be special because it is your country. We've studied it in detail, and we're satisfied that's where the future lies. Zimbabwe! *Gan be!*"

"We worked together before, Eggman," says Wang, rubbing my shoulder. "You helped me run the bar, I helped you when things were a little tough, remember?"

I catch my breath sharply. Their narrowed eyes are trained on my face like searchlights. I feel like a new schoolboy caught between two benign bullies blackmailing him into picking pockets on a busy street so they won't beat him.

I think of my dwindling bank balance, the long hours I have to put in servicing a shrinking client base, yet I'm forced to make what Hamlet calls a downward adjustment when I should be moving to bigger and better things.

Wang extracts a packet of seven-inch cigars and a Swiss army knife. He offers the cigars around but Liu Ming and I decline. Liu Ming prefers to smoke American cigarettes. Wang unlocks a screwdriver appendage and drills a hole in one end of the cigar. Then he lights the opposite end, moving the lighter up and down as its flame licks at the cigar. He takes a series of gusty drags, eyes half-closed, then leans back, exhaling with such a look of serenity I'm tempted to smoke one, too.

"Pure joy, glorious joy!" he exclaims. "Gentlemen, you should try this fine Cuban masterpiece. A hundred yuan each. My friend brought them last week. You can't find them in China. You smoke one of these over a period of an hour and a half, about fifteen minutes each time, take a break to savour the pleasure. Anyway, back to business. The question is, Eggman, will you be the contact China needs?"

"I'm the man," I declare with a croaky voice, then clear my throat and say, "There's no looking back."

Gan be!

By the time Wang picks up the bill, we're all well and truly wasted, yet it's only 3.30 p.m. The two of them look at me with a new admiration in their eyes, as if I've signed that billion-dollar deal they've staked their lives on all year. My old life is seeking me out, bottle by bottle, glass by glass. I feel like a man who has served too much time behind bars, and is now desperate to get back to the life of free men, to recapture his past, to make up for lost time. I'm the eagle, spreading his metre-long wings and raring to embark on the hunt of his life.

"Okay, my friends. We'll have massage now," announces Wang. "The massage here is top class. Excellent, you'll see." He reaches out to pinch his back and shoulder. "After that fine exercise, this is what you need to relax the muscles."

"Very good for your health," says Liu Ming. "You must try the strong massage, the girl walking up and down your back."

The way he says it, and the laughter that follows it, it's clear there's going to be more to this massage than just a girl walking all over your back. That's when it hits me. The tenth hole!

Wang leads the way to the massage parlour, which is in the basement, as if it needs to be hidden away from the prying eyes of the uninitiated. Wang and Liu Ming have a spring in their steps. Their faces glow with naughty anticipation. The redness is still there, but now it looks as if it's due less to alcohol than mild embarrassment. No one is making eye contact. At the reception, an attendant leads us to the bathroom. The entire facility is elegant, all marble and mirrored walls. You have the choice of steam or charcoal sauna. There are only a few other customers at this time, two guys sitting in the Jacuzzi. One of them is reading a newspaper, holding it high up to avoid getting it wet in the swirling warm water.

The massage is good, if strenuous. As promised, the girl spends half an hour walking up and down my back, taking tentative steps down my legs and calves, pausing briefly when I take in a sharp breath as pain sears the stiff muscles. Then she brings out the oil, and we enter a gentler and more soothing phase. And, as Wang promised, everything is taken care of. The girl doesn't even ask what I fancy. When she's done with this pinching, kneading, rubbing, and caressing, she dims the light and, in a well-coordinated movement, unzips her bra. Her breasts pop out, happy to be liberated. She drops her skimpy skirt to the floor, peels off the flimsiest of G-strings, and searches in her wicker basket of toiletries for what turns out to be a condom. By this time, I've been sufficiently mellowed and too aroused to care what happens next. I play dumb, watch like an anesthetised patient, fully trusting in the surgeon's deft and well-trained hands. No words are uttered. They would simply get in the way of a routine, well-rehearsed procedure. Something tells me I'm in good hands, with this taciturn, ever-smiling, well-proportioned girl in charge. I close my eyes, so as not to see her mouth, which so reminds me of Lai Ying.

Yes, Admiral Wang, I'm the contact. I'm not looking back. Let's do Africa, man.

Buffer Zone

THE THREE DAYS I SPEND in Shenzhen pass like a blur. When we're not playing golf at the Fragrant Dream Summer Park, we're calling on people, holding meetings, setting up contacts. Putting together this Africa deal. Nothing happens in this country without filling out a mountain of forms and taking people either to lunch or dinner and consuming vast amounts of beer and Chinese spirits.

We're staying at the Grand Sunshine Panorama on Hong Ting Zhong Lu, overlooking the lush greenery of Lychee Park with its flower gardens, tranquil lake, ducks, and lovers.

Wang's wife is in town, too. But she spends most of her time with friends, shopping or playing mahjong. She hasn't changed much. She's still living up to the nickname she didn't know about. Wang's Shadow. As reserved as ever, saying little or nothing, at least in the company of her husband and his business associates.

She hangs onto his every word, nodding at this comment, smiling at that joke, never laughing out loud. A lot of women behave like that here, remaining quiet and reserved when the men talk business. It's like they're serving a period of penitence before letting it rip at mahjong sessions with fellow womenfolk, then coming back to atone for the crimes of raucous banter and squandering the man's hard-earned cash. While Wang morphed into the suave, man-of-the-world creature he always yearned to be back at the noodle shop, his wife has remained stuck in the servile, obsequious cocoon of the eighties. At least her dress sense has improved. Gone are the drab, military-like, green-and-blue, loose-fitting dresses, shirts, trousers, jackets, and scarves women wore day in, day out, and which might have been made in the same factory for the entire country. The implicit Maoist 'peasant' label has now been replaced by well-known and easily recognisable Western brand names. Wang's Shadow is now clad in a smart Burberry suit, smelling of a Chanel fragrance, clutching a Louis Vuitton handbag. At least that's what the LV suggests. Whether it's the real thing doesn't really matter. The story goes that knock-offs are of such good quality nowadays even the legitimate manufacturers cannot tell the difference.

Our deal is slowly taking shape. In addition to Liu Ming, we've got one more partner, Yu Shian, an ex-cop. Yu Shian's eyes are permanently cocked, and dart about as if looking out for danger. He sports a pencil-thin moustache and has completely dispensed with his sense of humour. He's the only one who doesn't laugh at Wang's jokes. He simply smiles or sucks his lips in, with a quick shake of the head, as though he can't believe Wang's irreverence.

We settle down to Tsingtao at the lobby bar in the hotel, discussing the Africa deal. Wang is like a chairman at a committee meeting, spelling out details, drawing out suggestions, piecing it all together. Liu Ming and Yu Shian do what the leader expects, to give him face.

"My friend, Yu Shian, is a man who gets the job done," says Wang. "He checks everything, leaves nothing to chance." With a cop's background, that's hardly a surprise. His ruthlessness in hunting down criminals should come in handy when tracking down debtors in Harare.

"I try my best," says Yu Shian, flicking his tongue across the lips. "But I have to tell you, it's always a struggle."

I find that hard to believe. There's nothing in these guys' lifestyles that suggests struggle. The sumptuous meals, expensive drinks and cigars, the limousines.

"It's about working hard," says Liu Ming, perhaps noticing the look of reservation on my face.

"Hard work, taking risks," adds Yu Shian. "Giving up my safe job with the police to go into business at my age was not easy. But it's paying off, slowly."

"Thank you, my friend, for trusting me," says Wang. "You see, Eggman, in addition to the other raw materials and minerals we've discussed already, we believe the electronics business is the future. Have you heard of coltan?"

I nod. I'm familiar with it from electronics lectures.

"It's very important for all kinds of techno products."

They exchange glances, nodding meaningfully. Wang smirks with self-conscious smugness, as if he's won a bet. Yu Shian has a look of puzzlement, or admiration, as if he can't believe I'm this smart.

"Excellent!" exclaims Wang, slapping my back. "This is the most important input for electronics. We use it for capacitors, mobile phones, laptops, everything. We normally buy from Australia. We got some supplies once or twice from

Africa. From Congo. But the war there has disrupted supplies. And some people in Belgium are trying to persuade the world to boycott minerals from Congo. Westerners always want to mix politics with business. We don't think that's right." He leans over towards me conspiratorially, and lowers his voice. "Now, my friend, is the time for us to get in."

"You mean start buying their minerals or actually go to the Congo?"

He leans back, clasping his hands, grinning mysteriously. Yu Shian is nodding slowly, narrowed eyes peering through the cloud of smoke from his cigar.

"We Chinese never abandon our friends," says Liu Ming, smiling benignly.

"We're not like Westerners," adds Wang, patting my shoulder. "Whatever way is best, we'll do business with people in Congo, and Zimbabwe. First, we go to Zimbabwe and lay the foundation. And this is why I thought it was very important that you meet us. I don't know any Africans here. But you, Eggman, you and me, we go back a long way, back to Wang's Den."

"How can I forget? Your bar was the centre of our social life."

The other two listen in amazement as we reminisce. They're clearly impressed with Wang's credentials as a man who wooed and did business with foreigners at a time when most Chinese were content to stare and mock.

"Our time together was like a lifelong investment. Getting back together now is like seeing the investment mature. Together we can succeed." His partners nod meaningfully, a glint in their eyes.

So far, we haven't discussed exactly what my input into this deal is going to be besides accompanying them to Zim. I'm afraid they'll think it rude to ask. I've kept to supportive, if platitudinous, answers. It can be done. What a wonderful opportunity. Let's go for it.

And no one has talked money yet. Although I'm out of touch with Zim and don't know how this will work out, I see myself as something of a resource person, the man who'll help open doors, make introductions, show how to oil and manoeuvre the bureaucracy. And for my trouble, I expect to be paid a consultant's fees, including my travel expenses. I'm not going to bring this up myself just yet, but I make a mental note to raise it before we depart. These men have been generous, insisting on covering all our entertainment costs, which are obviously charged to business expenses. Occasionally I insist on paying for the drinks. I have face to think about, too.

On Saturday night, we're at a high-class karaoke. It's quite a party. The three have brought their wives. Matronly, taciturn, middle-aged women in fancy Western suits and the mandatory LV handbags. The private room is all marble and silver décor with ceiling-high mirrors on the walls. Our dining table stretches out below silver chandeliers, and the walls are adorned with European impressionist paintings. You wouldn't know you were at a karaoke. It's more like a private dining room. The food is brought in by smiling waitresses in yellow and red cheongsams.

Wang is in his element, expounding on the wonderful business opportunities this great country offers to those brave enough to take the risks. Liu Ming and Yu Shian make the occasional appreciative noise, but are content to let Wang hog the limelight, which he's more than happy to do.

Then they start talking about how China has changed, and how their own lives have improved as a result. Wang talks about how his life has changed so dramatically he can hardly believe he was once a small-time noodle-shop owner, whose dream was to buy a refrigerator, a better-quality iron horse, and English books for his child. Now these people eat in the finest restaurants in the country, play golf every other day, and are driven around in limousines with tinted windows. Their children study in the United States.

Wang turns to me and says, "You know, here in Guangdong, you can get anything, even if it's banned. You can get rare animals that cost a fortune. Is there anything you want to try? Take your chance."

I shake my head. There are already several things on this table that I don't recognise, and I'm making an effort not to keep asking what they've ordered. Sometimes it's better not to know. If you don't recognise it, you stay clear of it. It was never my intention to eat dog, but I did once, on a business trip to Zhuhai. It was a buffet, and I assumed I was helping myself to curried beef, when Tiffany said she didn't realise I liked dog meat. I barely made it to the toilet.

"You go ahead and order whatever you fancy," I tell Wang.

The women smile and beckon the waitress as if they were waiting for just this cue.

"Do they have civet cats in your country?" Wang's wife asks me.

"They do." I sense it wouldn't do to tell her that they smell so awful you would not want to have them come anywhere near you, let alone on your dinner plate. They go ahead and order their cat. I can't even bring myself to look at it when it is delivered on a polished silver tray. Luckily, the drinking has been going on long enough to fuel an urge to sing, and from time to time, someone gets up and belts out a tune in front of the massive screens built into the walls while the rest hum along and applaud enthusiastically when the song is done.

After dinner, a new batch of girls shows up. They're clearly a world apart from the waitresses. They're chic, beautiful, slim, and unbelievably sexy in their white miniskirts, white tank tops and knee-high black boots. Their job is to get clients to drink. They cuddle up next to you, lean forward to expose a tantalising cleavage, fill your glass and theirs with this highly potent maotai, clink glasses and, to cries of *gan be* all around, down their drink with a grin. I struggle to turn my grimace into a grin.

Wang treats us to renditions of one Frank Sinatra song after another. He stands up, waltzes across the room, a cigar and mike in one hand, a scantily clad karaoke girl in the other. After telling us how he did it his way, he launches into an off-key Denver favourite, begging the country roads to take him home, to the place he belongs. West Virginia. The girl on his arm is tall, sexy, sophisticated. Everything his wife is not. She introduces herself as Mui Mui. Little Sister. We've split into two groups. The men sit on one side, drinking with the karaoke girls. The wives sit together, chatting and sipping expensive *bik lo chun* tea.

Wang asks if I like any of the girls.

"It's all on me. Don't worry. Pay bar fine and she's yours."

I shake my head, recalling the encounter at the massage parlour and the guilt which still trails me like a shadow. Wang doesn't press the matter. He's having a lot of fun with this long-legged Mui Mui girl. She has permanently attached herself to him, singing with him, pouring drinks for him, engaging him in unceasing laughter-laden conversation. The wife is unconcerned. I and the other two have each got a girl to sing and drink with. But no one is as daring as Wang.

At 2 a.m., voices croaky with the singing, drinking, and cigar and cigarette smoke, everyone's ready to go home. The limousines are waiting on the podium. Liu Ming and Yu Shian and their wives drive off first. The tall karaoke girl gets into Wang's limousine with us. She's changed out of her bar outfit into high heels, a T-shirt, and a black, leather miniskirt, which is only marginally more modest than the white cotton one she had before. Wang sits in front with the driver. He requests me to sit between the two women. It's not clear what is going on. Confident that neither woman speaks English, I ask Wang, "What's the plan with the girl, my friend?"

"Is okay, Eggman. She come with me."

"With you?" I gasp, not without a pang of jealousy.

"Is okay. Wife no mind."

I struggle to get my mind around this with all that drink.

"She's…she's coming with you?" He nods. "To your room?"

He chuckles, as if he's tiring of explaining something quite elementary to an idiot.

"Eggman, me and wife, many years, we live together. But not same together like man with lady. You understand? She has one baby, and is too hard for her. How to say, trouble, pain in have baby…?"

"Complicated birth?"

"Yes, yes!"

"I'm sorry to hear that. I hope it wasn't too bad."

"Me too. But is too bad." The pain in the voice is so clear, even in a foreign language, his wife looks up sharply. "Later, she needn't man again. Is too trouble. For me, is different. I am man. I need lady."

"Right, of course." I can't think of anything else to say.

"Is serious, Eggman. Many time ago, we talk. Decide we stay together."

"You didn't consider divorce or something?"

He laughs at the simplicity of my solution.

"Divorce is for young people, like you, Eggman." I think about that for a moment.

"Nowadays, it's not just the young people, Wang."

"For us, is different. We are, how you say, tradition. Tradition people. You divorce, people no respect for you. And wife, who take care her? She too old, cannot find man. And we have son, so we think is good he have family. You and wife okay, Eggman?"

"To be honest, we do have some problems, Wang." I don't want to tell him all this, but the words have a momentum of their own, after his shocking candour. "At the moment, we're not living together."

"Marriage always too trouble, Eggman. Your wife, she's the girl in Nanjing?"

"Yeah. She didn't come to the bar much. I'm surprised you remember her."

"Wang remember beautiful lady. And Wang see love also, you and the girl. Good love."

"Yeah," I murmur, my heart filling with pain and regret. "Good love."

"Your wife, where she go now?"

"She's staying with her family. Shanghai."

262

"Maybe you divorce? Is what you thinking?"

Is that how it's going to end up? Or would we stay together like Wang and his shadow, without love, without passion, strangers living under the same roof, doing their best to tolerate each other so as not to upset the delicate family balance and bring shame to the family name? It doesn't bear thinking about. Lai Ying and I aren't even living under the same roof. Perhaps our reputation has already been sullied beyond repair without enduring the shame of a divorce.

"No, Wang. That is not going to happen."

"Many people now divorce, in China also," he continues, as if he hasn't heard me.

"I know," I reply, a little brusquely. Why does he sound like he's trying to urge me to do it, or as if he has some divine revelation that mine is a lost cause? "We're going to make it work. I love my wife. I would never leave her."

"Wish you the good luck, my friend. Is no good, man live alone."

His wife sits on my right, silenced into tradition, gazing at the lights through the window. The pretty young girl on my left smiles whenever I glance in her direction, her exposed thighs glowing in the dim light. I'm the buffer, creating a neutral zone to shield the women from each other. For their man in front. I am, truly, the buffer zone.

"You think is strange," says Wang. "My wife, she can have anything. She spend too much money in mahjong already. And shopping. That is her fun. Wang not stop her. For me, fun is drink and lady. Is better like this, she see the lady I meet. If wife no like the lady, I choose the other one. Many friends, they have lady secret-secret, and wife no like. They have big problem."

"You're a lucky guy, Wang. You can bring a woman back and the old lady's fine? It's unbelievable."

"Is okay. Hotel have, how you say, twin bed."

In the morning, when I go to the restaurant for breakfast, Wang and his wife are already there, tucking into a buffet Chinese meal. Wang is his usual confident self, oozing charm. As if nothing extraordinary happened. Obviously, his wife didn't disapprove of the girl last night. I wonder whether she is also pleased with his ability to pick a winner. She nods briefly when I greet them. I avoid her eyes. But there's nothing to see there anyway. She has a stiff look about her face, as though the skin has been stretched back and knotted in a ponytail at the nape. She remains tight-lipped and expressionless, as if she has witnessed a crime and is too traumatised to utter a word.

Wang is keen to wrap up the details of the deal. We'll fly to Harare in the coming weeks. Or sooner.

"There's no need to waste time, Eggman. I would like you to start contacting people as soon as you return to Hong Kong. I'll join you there hopefully this week, and we'll lay out all the plans once I know whom we're meeting."

I'm not sure whom we'll meet. But it's not a problem. My cousin Chip can deal with that. I'll call him as soon as I get back to Hong Kong. I would call him now but his number is in my email inbox.

Wang keeps saying he's keen to invest in agriculture, which includes buying a farm. There must be hundreds of white farmers wanting to cash out before their farms are expropriated. Wang claims he's not too worried about this happening to him.

"The problem is that white people are colonialists," he announces. "With me, it's purely business. It should work because we will partner with well-connected African investors. What's your opinion, Eggman?"

"It should work. I'll have a contact check everything first, just to be sure. But what I know is that the only people able to buy farms right now are influential politicians."

"Then it's fine." Wang taps the table with a sense of finality. "I've dealt with politicians all my life."

"The ones in Africa might be different, you know?"

"Believe me, they're all the same. You talk to them nicely, they'll treat you like a master. You must always show them you're the master, you have what they need. And they need you more than you need them. If they hesitate, it's because they don't know it yet. So you have to be patient, and teach them to depend on you the way chicks depend on the mother bird to drop bits of worms in their mouths."

"I see." I try to picture politicians in Zim standing in line waiting for Wang to hand out bribes. There are some who would accept a worm in their mouth if you told them it would change into US dollars.

"Remember, Eggman, business is like war," says Wang, his face hardening and his eyes focused on me with a gaze that almost feels like it is pinning me down to my seat. "Sun Tzu taught us that at the start of war, you should be shy like a maiden in order to lower the enemy's defences. Then you have to be as swift as a hare to catch him unprepared."

Wang's words, delivered in the tone of a stern schoolmaster, make me realise just how unprepared I am. If I'm going to go on this trip, I need to arrange some cover for the clients who can't wait. There are other things, like the new flat, and what to do about money when I'm gone. I have to clear this money issue with Wang, but I don't want to discuss it in front of his wife. Later in the day, I mention to him that we'll need to work out some logistics, like travel dates, and how long we expect to be away for.

"It all depends," he says. "It depends on how things go when we're there. If we can identify suitable investments before we leave, then we won't need to be there for very long. We'll have a team of managers come and run things. There'll be other trips later. Our target is to buy at least one farm and two mines. Once our managers arrive, we can focus on ways to set up supplies for the other things we need, like coltan. So I would say about ten days. Is that too long, Eggman?"

"It's about my business, my clients, Wang. I can't be away too long. I have to keep working."

Sensing my real concerns, he says, "See this trip as work, too, Eggman, so don't worry about money. Let me worry about your travel expenses. We're retaining you as a consultant. So you get a fee as well. The details we can discuss in Hong Kong once everything's clearer."

It's much clearer already. I'll just have to talk to Chip and see what specific opportunities he can line up. Then we'll work out an itinerary and fees.

"There's also the contact in Harare, Wang. He'll be working very hard to help us. He's a lawyer, so he'll help with legal documents and that sort of thing, and will link us up with important people."

"That's very good. He'll be our lawyer. If he works well for us, we'll take very good care of him. Can we trust this person?"

"Chipinduka is one of my best friends. We grew up together, and more importantly, he's family. He's my cousin."

He grins and says, "Then he's one of the team already."

This is going to be the best White Card deal of my life. Never mind that it's coming about years after the foreign exchange certificates became history.

But there's that matter of Lai Ying and Chacha. If I go before seeing them, what will I tell my family? They'll have to be content with photographs.

I'm supposed to move into the new flat at the end of the month, which gives me just under a month to get this Africa deal done. It's a tight schedule. But as Wang says, there's no time to waste. We have to leave right away.

True Gweilos

I'LL SOON BE BACK IN Zim. The realisation fills me with a mixture of exhilaration and disquiet. I'm excited to be going back and I can't wait to get my fee and see how this deal turns out. But I still have no idea what my father and the war vets are doing.

The first thing I do when I return to Hong Kong on Sunday evening is call Chip. This time, I manage to get through quicker. After a brief exchange of excited pleasantries, I go straight to the point. I tell him I'm coming home, and more importantly, I want to know what's up with my family.

"Nobody knows," he says, with a sense of frustration. "I haven't seen them. It's a little bit unstable out there at the moment, and frankly, I've been too busy."

"Can't you call someone?"

"The phones there don't work, Danny boy. I see you've been away too long."

"Someone must have a mobile phone, man."

"Bad signals. It's not easy. At least we haven't heard anything since the takeover, which means it can't be all that bad. It would have been all over the news. It's good you're coming, man. And about time, too, Dan. Your mum will be so pleased. You know she always says since you married that Chinese girl, you turned your back on your people. What do they feed you there that keeps you away?"

"It's not the food."

"Whatever it is, I can't wait to see her. And my niece. She's got to be at least eight now?"

"She's seven, and Chip, they're not coming with me."

"What! Just like last time? What's the matter with you? Don't you want us to see the two Chinese babes?"

"It's complicated. This is a business trip. We'll do the family thing later. I'm bringing some Chinese businessmen to look at investment opportunities. And I want you involved, man. Actually I've already roped you in. You'll be their lawyer, and their main contact in Zim, among other things."

I spell out the details, and ask him to locate high-ranking officials who are ready for Chinese money. This is music to his ears. He can't wait to get started. We talk excitedly about potential copper and iron ore mines and farms to look out for, the people to contact, places to visit. Chip also wants me to buy things to sell in Harare, things like car spare parts and a laptop or two. It doesn't sound like a bad idea, if I can find time to go shopping. I can get the computers and accessories easily in Shamshuipo and maybe Mong Kok. I'm not so sure about car spare parts. Chip promises to email me with details within a day. When I hear from him, he's already used his contacts in the legal profession to secure an interview with a senior civil servant in the Ministry of Trade. He tells me this guy can hook us up with well-connected big shots who are eager to play ball.

I email Lai Ying to tell her about my trip. Not too many details, only that I want to see my family and do a bit of business. I remind her that our new home will be ready by the time I get back. I plead with her to call me as soon as possible. I need to hear her voice, and Chacha's.

I spend two days seeing clients and trying to reschedule jobs and appointments. I want to be ready to hit the skies when Wang and the gang roll into town over the weekend.

On Monday night, Wang calls to ask if I can go to Shenzhen the next day. Shenzhen, again?

"Eggman, this is urgent. I need you, and a white man, if you can find one."

"What is it about?"

"You remember our discussion on coltan? Wang Holdings plan to buy a rival electronics company and to assure them we have excellent international connections. I hope we can have some foreigners at the crucial presentation, where we sell the idea to their board of directors. That's why I need you. And a gweilo."

The plan is feasible, if a little bizarre. Alex would fit the bill, but right now it's hard to tell how he'll react, with his family problems. And the way things are going, I shouldn't imagine he'll be in a position to talk about *my* problems. The last time we spoke, he didn't even say whether he had made any effort to help me. He behaved as though I'm to blame for the loss of his land. It looks like a closed chapter. Perhaps going off to Shenzhen together will help take away the animosity. I mention him to Wang, adding that my friend understands some Putonghua.

"No, no, my friend." He sounds agitated. "These people must believe you're true foreigners, not local chaps. I'll tell them you've flown in this week from Africa, where the coltan mines are, and the gweilo has flown in from America. Your company supplies the minerals, and we're in fact buying your company to guarantee supplies. Your friend is coming from Wall Street, with a lot of money. He'll open up new markets for us in America."

I laugh, but Wang sounds dead serious. So we're going in as decoys, imitation investors. The thought of sitting in meetings explaining my investment strategy for a non-existent company takes my breath away.

"What exactly do you expect us to do, Wang?"

"Oh, nothing. Just be there. I'll do all the talking. At some point, I'll ask you both to make some comments about your business interests and plans for the future. Actually, you can say anything you like. You can talk about your childhood, or how much you like Chinese girls. They don't understand English. But to be on the safe side, it's better to talk about your countries. I'll make an appropriate translation, that you're excited about this great opportunity to do business with the wonderful people of China. This kind of thing that will give them face."

"Will they buy it?"

"Leave it to me, Eggman. And, you'll both be compensated for your trouble. We are serious businessmen. You should know that by now. It's very important that we buy this company."

I call Alex right away and ask if there has been any news.

"Very little, man," he murmurs in a mournful voice. "The whole place is coming apart. Phones don't work, but I managed to talk to a cousin in Jo'burg. My parents are on their way to London. My sister's already there, at university. There's nothing left for us in Zim. We've lost everything, man. It's all gone, just like that. I'm just gutted, man."

"But everyone's safe, Alex. No one got hurt, right?"

"Thank God for small mercies. House was torched, as you'd expect. They even shot at the dogs, can you believe that? Luckily, they were too drunk or too stoned to fire straight. The whole thing is just a fucking nightmare!"

I try to find words of consolation but I'm tongue-tied. I try to imagine what might have been going through the minds of my father and the Walter family when they faced each other in the dead of the night, each looking a new, unfamiliar beginning in the eye, with no idea how it will all pan out. Alex says there's nothing left for him and his family, as if to imply it's all up for grabs for the African families that remain behind. I know it's not all that clear-cut, from the news I've been receiving.

"Did you know, Alex, that farmworkers are also being threatened and intimidated, and in some cases thrown off the land together with the farmers? That's the latest I've heard."

"Wouldn't surprise me. Frankly I don't believe that the guys who took our land are our workers. I know them, man, known them all my life. There's a third force at play. But look, right now, I'm just too pissed off, I can't get my head around this. You want to meet for a beer sometime?"

"I was just going to ask you, as it happens. But suddenly I wasn't sure you'd be up for it."

"I know. My folks will be just fine. They'll spring back just as soon as they get to London. We have family there. Look, man, I'm not going to sit in the flat whinging."

"Life goes on. So, how does a trip to Shenzhen grab you?"

"Ha! Not by the tits, I can assure you. What do you have in mind?"

I explain Wang's request and ask if he's interested. He breaks into a hearty laugh, saying it's a bunch of crap.

"The guy is serious, Alex. And he's paying. How do you fancy a day's holiday, a fantastic meal, a round of golf, and possibly a girl thrown in for good measure? And all you have to do is sit in some stupid meeting for a couple of hours in a nice suit, looking like a damn serious Wall Street financier, and coming back a few grand richer?"

"Too good to be true, mate. But, what the hell, it sounds like a laugh. You know what, I'm due for a trip to Shenzhen next week anyway. I can bring it forward and get this out of the way as well."

But tomorrow is too short notice.

"How about Wednesday?"

"I'll just make sure Wang can reschedule."

"Okay. I'll see you later then, yeah? And, Dan, thanks, man."

"No problem."

Wang is happy to reschedule.

"Remember, Eggman, not a word of Putonghua. You're true gweilos."

I reflect on that. If you speak the language, you're no longer foreign? I wish it were that simple. Unfortunately, the colour of your skin pretty much stays the same. And that's what people see, because no one walks around with a banner saying, hey, I speak Chinese, I'm all right, I'm one of you.

I clear immigration and step into the crowded street, where a hundred touts are waiting, offering taxis, watches, mobile phones, massage, ladies. Everything a weary traveller with a loaded wallet could possibly wish for.

Alex had set off early in the morning to get his business sorted out. We meet at the Shangri-La.

"I have a bad feeling about this shit, man," says Alex. Wang's driver approaches, waving.

"What can possibly go wrong? We just sit in a meeting and do nothing except look serious. Surely you can manage that?"

"Can't you see we're being used? Paraded like a couple of monkeys? You know, bring the bloody gweilos to make this Wong wanker look—what?— global, sophisticated?"

"At Asia Risk, don't you get paid all the time to do nothing?"

"Very funny."

"I offered you a job, and what have you done?"

"Now don't start—"

"And his name is Wang, by the way. Better get that right, otherwise you might cost him the deal."

"What do you think is the more dreadful sin: making him lose the deal or making him lose face?"

I remind him not to speak a word of Putonghua, except perhaps *nin hao*, the polite greeting.

"Not a big problem," he says. "It's not like I'm fluent in the language anyway, unlike you old China hand."

We stop at the Grand Sunshine Panorama, where Wang, Liu Ming, and Yu Shian are having a late breakfast, or, knowing these guys, a second breakfast thinly disguised as a business meeting. It turns out that the company we're taking over—we? I'm already thinking like the non-Chinese-speaking investor from Africa—is in Huizhou, about an hour to the north of Shenzhen. We set off in two limousines.

In no time at all, we've left Shenzhen behind and are cruising on a wide expressway that looks like a giant, concrete conveyor belt thrusting its way through docile open spaces that have been cowed by its sheer might into a subservient, silent emptiness.

Out in the open, it's quiet and peaceful. There's nothing but shrubbery and mountains for miles around. This is the China I like, far from the jungle of monstrous glass and concrete structures, from the smells, litter-covered, spittle-stained streets, dust and noises. Goats clamber up the craggy cliffs and hillsides, raising their heads to watch the traffic and sniff the air. In the distance, there are scooped-out quarries exposing their empty clay interiors which have been baked in the sun to a hard, white sheen. They once supplied building materials until they had nothing left to offer. Now they lie abandoned, yawning wearily to the blue skies.

As I watch the countryside unfold, I keep trying to think what it is about Huizhou that's giving me this strange sense of unease, as if I've either been here before, or I've seen pictures of it, yet I can't remember what the pictures were like. Ten minutes before we arrive, it hits me. Lai Ying's father is from this town. My daughter's grandfather was born and raised in these parts. We've never been here before, not even Lai Ying. I once asked her whether she would like to visit her father's hometown. She said she wasn't interested. There's nothing there for her. She doesn't even want to know whatever relatives live there. She's not alone in this. Hong Kong people I know whose parents originated from Guangdong province have no interest in tracing their roots.

Watching the wide expanse of land, the craggy hills and clear blue skies makes me feel as if I'm making a pilgrimage to the land of my own ancestors. I must bring Chacha here sometime. Her mother might not be interested, but Chacha must know that Shanghai is only one part of her Chinese roots. She's not going to be like her mother who has the privilege of being able to fit comfortably and without question into any part of China. For Chacha it's different. It will always be different.

The electronics company is on the outskirts of Huizhou.

"This is one of the nicest cities in Guangdong," Wang informs us. "They have lots of forests and lakes here."

We drive down a tree-lined avenue into some sort of industrial zone. Every company announces its presence in large, red Chinese characters, painted on the white concrete walls. Wang points them out as we zoom past, passing dark, exhaust-spewing delivery trucks and minibuses. Each factory has a high-wire perimeter fence. Where there are concrete fences, they are topped with bits of broken glass. What on earth do they need such tight security for? New Century Electronics is located on a hillside, overlooking a green, sleepy lake. Several men have positioned themselves on its shores, fishing.

The meeting is a staid, Stalinist affair. About twenty executives from this targeted company sit in an expansive meeting room, all clad in dark-grey or black suits. It's the new uniform for corporate, capitalist-communist China, a far cry from the old dull clothes, when communism was unadulterated by Deng Xiaoping's reforms. They are here to listen to Wang convince them why he should take a controlling interest in their company. From what I've gathered, they don't have much say in the matter. They've been losing money hand over fist. A huge injection of capital is what they need, and of course, the prospect of cheap coltan from Congo and new markets in America.

Wang is flanked by his loyal comrades, Liu Ming and Yu Shian, who are observing the audience like school prefects watching out for pupils who don't look like they believe the teacher's promises of free fizzy drinks and congee every morning. Yu Shian looks as if he is committing the entire proceedings to memory, watching every changing expression, every twitch on every apprehensive face. He'll be having a big say as to which managers will be fired after this takeover. Liu Ming maintains a benevolent smile throughout. *Everything will be just fine when we're running the show. You can trust us, we are men of honour*, the face announces.

Alex and I are seated next to Liu Ming, watching the proceedings impassively, trying not to look too bored. From time to time, Wang acknowledges our existence and indicates us with an outstretched arm, talking about the great opportunity we're offering. He refers to us as *lao wai*, old friends. When the twenty suits turn to face us with a mixture of admiration and curiosity, we reciprocate with Liu Ming's friendly corporate smile. When Wang finishes his speech, Liu Ming leads the applause. The chairman and a few other big wigs get up to make speeches to bless the new alliance to loud applause. Alex and I join in the applause and grin dutifully, to show them what a special opportunity it is for us to have such wonderful business partners.

Everyone is talking about how this new alliance will help them destroy the competition, teach the rivals a lesson, set new standards for the entire industry. It's like a declaration of war. The way they look at Alex and I when Wang talks about cheap raw materials and new markets, I almost feel as though I'm a part of this great venture, and not a cheap actor who's expected to play deaf and dumb.

Towards the end, Alex and I get a chance to say a few words in English about the great investment opportunities we're bringing, and how we and our companies are looking forward to doing business with the Chinese. Wang embellishes the 'translation' with his own thoughts about how great Chinese companies like theirs are going to take over the world, and will soon challenge Japanese ones as the leaders in Asia, and how privileged the *lao wai* are to be working with such outstanding business leaders as Wang and his team. By this time, the audience are beaming and turning to smile at each other as if to say, *you see, I told you, our future is going to be in very good hands here.* They've been completely won over.

Wang and the chairman sign some documents amid applause. The deal is done. Then they stand to shake hands and take a hundred photographs. Some of these will no doubt end up in the local papers. I'm surprised the town mayor is not here to witness this historic moment. When I ask Wang, he tells me this is the internal, private agreement. The public one will be held tomorrow, in the head office in Guangzhou. Everyone who is anyone in the province will be there.

A few of the top guys come over to shake hands with us, distributing business cards and grinning so broadly the eyes are almost squeezed shut. The guys who've just been taken over now see themselves as the new masters in the industry. The conquered are now the conquerors, out to tame the competition. This festive, corporate warmongering mood goes on into the lunch specifically laid on to celebrate the new alliance, complete with the ceremonial roast pig, whose eyes are frozen in a vacant, unseeing stare.

The whole experience reminds me of when I first came to China, when I didn't speak the language. It's a weird feeling now. Sitting at lunch with all these dark-suited executives, downing maotai shots. Pretending not to know how to use chopsticks. Pretending I don't understand what they're saying, allowing them to teach me words like *gan be* and *xie xie*, and watching them laugh with glee at the wrong tone. When they make snide remarks about the clumsiness of foreign devils, I have to struggle not to wince. Wang will have to compensate us well for putting us through this charade.

Wang has done a great job of convincing these people they need him and his contacts. Alex and I have even 'learned' some words of Chinese, which we utter to the great amusement of our intoxicated teachers. Wang keeps glancing at our direction, with a look of concern on his face.

"It's all right, Wang," I assure him in English. "We're fine."

"Good. I worry you too much drink, and learn Chinese too quick."

"Don't worry, we're totally in control. Right, Alex?"

"Absolutely. We're…what was that again, true gweilos. Totally clueless."

As we head to the car park, we notice a commotion at the north side of the factory. A dull siren fills the air. Could it be a fire? But there's no smoke, except for the fumes spewing from the four chimneys on the roof. A dozen men in green army fatigues and helmets run past us, carrying batons and plastic shields of the type normally used by riot police.

The chairman and some of his executives usher us to the waiting cars.

"A little trouble," says the chairman. "It's no problem. We'll take care of it. Let's move you gentlemen out of here."

"Is everything all right?" asks Wang, a puzzled frown crossing his face.

"Oh, it's nothing."

A group of men dash out of the building, screaming, waving their hands about. They look skinny, and even from a distance of twenty metres, we can see the terror on their hollowed-out faces. They look like they haven't been fed in weeks. There must be about fifty of them.

The guards are upon them, whacking them with their batons, pushing and dragging them back into the building. But the men fight on. A dozen of them make it out of the building, climb over the fence, and run down the street, blood flowing down their faces. By this time, we've already been huddled into the limousines and are speeding down the drive. The gate opens for the cars, and another dozen men scramble past. The guards chase after them, grab three of them, set upon them with their batons. The rest of the escapees run about in confusion, not knowing which way to go, limping, collapsing in a dejected heap, picking themselves up, and throwing themselves at the passing traffic. Begging motorists to pick them up. Cars swerve to avoid them, wheels screeching. Drivers curse and wave fists through open windows. A minibus stops and some of the escapees jump on. The minibus zooms off before the guards reach it.

We're well out of the city and heading towards Shenzhen before anyone finds his voice.

"Jesus Christ, what was that?" asks Alex, face twisted in shock.

"A little trouble. Not serious. Is okay."

"Workers escaping from the factory? Man, that was some weird shit."

"Is okay." Wang's face is set in a stony expression. "I'll check later."

Clearly, he's just as unsettled as Alex and I, but he dare not criticise his new partners. Not in front of foreign devils. He has to give his partners face. Going by this uncharacteristic quiet thoughtfulness, he's probably more concerned that foreigners saw the shameful act of desertion than whatever reasons might have prompted it.

We travel in silence the rest of the way. When we approach Shenzhen, Wang invites us for a round of golf. Alex declines with no hesitation. He can't wait to get out of here.

I'm in two minds. I could use the exercise. It's a beautiful, bright, sunny afternoon. Though with all that alcohol, it's probably not a great idea to be traipsing across the country swinging golf clubs. On the other hand, the violence at the factory has cast a shadow on the day's festivities. Alex and I will be better off having that drink back in familiar territory.

"Sorry, Wang. I really have to go set up our trip."

He doesn't look disappointed. He can sense it's for the best.

"That's all right. Please, work hard on your contacts. We should leave as soon as possible. Now that we have New Century joining the family, we'll need fresh supplies of coltan urgently."

I nod. I can sense the urgency. Not even this little incident at the factory can hold things up.

"My cousin has been working hard. We've got people ready to show us mines, Wang. And a farm or two."

He grins with the satisfaction of a man accustomed to seeing lackeys deliver. Every single time.

"You know, Eggman, you should consider coming to work for me. This New Century will need new technology, and new management. Think about it. Electronics is your field. I know you're an expert. You would do very well here."

I promise to think about it. Before we get off at the Lowu border crossing, he hands me a white envelope.

"For the good work you both did for us today," he says, smiling.

We shake hands and thank him. I don't open the envelope until we're in the immigration building, filling out the departure cards. Six hundred dollars each. American, not Hong Kong.

"You sure you want this man's money?" I ask Alex, who has still not recovered his composure.

"Don't try to rob me of my hard-earned cash," he says, snatching his share. "What do you really know about these guys you're dealing with?"

"Wang and I go back a long way, man. Nanjing, as I told you."

He frowns. On the train back to Hong Kong, he pulls out the cards which are all in Chinese, which he can barely read. Only Wang's card has some English on the flip side.

"Wang Golden Harvest Holdings. So what exactly is he harvesting?"

"You should know, the name's supposed to be auspicious and all that."

"So he wants you to work for him, eh? I just about got some of that. Join the big, happy family, man. It might not be such a bad idea. He has faith in you. You could rise very quickly. I can just imagine you the general manager or something, bringing all these minerals from Africa. You'd be set for life, man."

"I couldn't live there. There's nothing happening in that town." There wouldn't be much for Lai Ying to do there either.

"Hong Kong's only an hour's drive. You could head out weekends. It's a perfect set up."

I have to admit, the idea does appeal. Maybe this is what I need to be doing, running an electronics factory in China, instead of running around fixing broken computers like some amateur technician.

"Mind you, Dan, there's that little matter of your identity."

"Meaning?"

"You were introduced as a non-Putonghua-speaking black devil straight out of Africa. Remember?"

Oh that! Alex doesn't get it.

"Not a problem, mate. All black devils look the same. Just like white ones, in case you didn't realise it. This should work to our advantage in this case. You see, if anyone suspected I was the same guy, he wouldn't dare ask, 'cause then he would look like he was stereotyping and admitting that Chinese think all black devils look the same."

"Wow!" he exclaims with a wry smile. "I suppose racism has its advantages, yeah?"

"You too could come back with a different identity. Imagine the possibilities. Today, you were a New York financier. Next time, a rich Swiss banker,

Australian mine owner. Whatever suit Wang creates for you, you just wear it, and pocket a few hundred bucks in the process."

"Yeah, the guy's a fucking magician. You have to hand it to him."

"There's more. These guys are modelling themselves on the fifteenth-century seafarer who led expeditions down the Indian Ocean, all the way to Africa. They have a lot of respect for him. Guy called Zheng He."

"What, they see themselves going down in history? Are they nuts?"

"It's funny you should say that."

"Say what?"

"Talk about nuts. The man was a eunuch."

"Bloody hell!" Alex's face puckers up with shock, as if he has been informed he's slated for the next round of castrations. "Oh, I get it: He must have served in the royal court or something. They used to castrate guys so they wouldn't trouble the concubines. What a life, man."

"I looked him up. He was a Muslim. Very rare, back then."

"So, a Muslim eunuch was the greatest trader to have come from these shores? Amazing. Shows there's hope for you and I yet, Dan. But I'm uneasy about the whole thing, man. I should have this guy checked out if I were you," he mumbles, poring over Wang's card. "Yeah, that would be fun. I think I'm gonna check his arse out."

I shrug. He wants to waste his money on a wild goose chase. And he won't even help me locate my family.

A New Beginning

I'M BACK IN HONG KONG. After confirming with Chip that one or two political bigwigs are prepared to meet the Chinese investment delegation, as Chip describes Wang and the gang, I call a travel agent in Shenzhen and reserve a ticket for Shanghai. The ticket is only about a third of the price I would pay if I flew from Hong Kong. I leave tomorrow. I have to try and see my family before I leave for Zim.

I consider for a moment whether to seek Lai Mui's help. But I quickly banish the thought from my mind. That would be too much pressure on her. I don't want to undo the progress I've made reconciling with her. It is better if I try this option after we've had that *yam chah,* then I can observe her more closely and weigh up my chances. That is, if this trip doesn't help.

I get an email from Julius saying he has identified the cybercafé Lai Ying has been using. He says he's had to be nice to many people. It's not cheap activating *guanxi* networks in China, and getting people to reveal confidential information, especially when it involves operating on the edges of the law. I'll need a thick wallet.

The thought of 'accidentally' running into Lai Ying stops my heart for an instant. But only long enough for me to realise that it might not actually happen. I'll just go hang around there and hope she shows up.

Early Thursday morning, I call Wang to tell him I'll be unavailable for several days, possibly until early next week. No specific date has been set for our flight. But he might as well know.

"It's all right, Eggman," he assures me. "I was just going to call and tell you we need to postpone our trip. A few days. A week at most. The little trouble at the factory in Huizhou is in the papers and TV this morning. We have to fix it before we go."

I ask him how bad it is.

"It's not good. Not good to start a new business this way. Bad feng shui, probably. We'll need to have a top geomancer look at it."

"The ones that got away? Can they take action, maybe demand their pay?"

"No. They wouldn't testify. They're illegal, you see. They've gone underground. I can't understand how these people live. They're like rats, Eggman. The ones left behind, they've gone, too. We let them go. If there are no witnesses there can be no case."

"So everything's all right?"

"There's talk of an investigation. It could be embarrassing to us. But we can handle it. Yu Shian has excellent contacts in the police force. We'll clean it up. There are jealous people here who would like to stop us making money, like the person who was interfering with our visas. We found it is the same person behind this recent trouble. We can't have that, Eggman." The voice is low, steely, uncompromising. "What did you say you were going to do? Are you going somewhere?"

"Uh...I'm going to be out of town. Some errands I have to run, Wang, that's all. By the time you've cleaned up this mess at the factory, I'll be ready."

"If you need any help, just tell us. Any trouble? We'll clean it up for a friend."

"It's fine, Wang. Thanks." Clean up the mess with Lai Ying? How exactly would they do that – get Yu Shian to flex his police muscles and have her hauled back to Hong Kong?

The story makes it into the Hong Kong press. I notice it when I buy the paper at my local 7-Eleven as I head out to catch the train to Shenzhen at 10 a.m. Scores of immigrant workers had been forced to work for little or no pay and prevented from leaving the factory. They were often beaten, forced to work up to eighteen hours a day, fed on rice and boiled vegetables, and watched over by armed guards. According to the newspaper report, it was nothing new. People coming into the province from the poor rural interior without the right papers usually end up living like slaves, at the mercy of unscrupulous employers. Business owners usually bribe their way out of trouble. The paper carries another story about a fire that destroyed a factory in Shenzhen yesterday evening. There are no clues. It is not clear if the two stories are related. The police say they suspect arson. Investigations are under way.

The Shenzhen airport is surprisingly smart and clean. I was half expecting the dull, drab buildings I remember seeing at train stations when I was a student. The airport is nothing like that. It's big and airy. Not as big as the Hong Kong one, but well-organised. Smartly dressed attendants and unobtrusive security personnel are on hand to offer help. Clean, shiny glass and smooth concrete everywhere. And the cab drive isn't cheap either, at RMB 130 from the Lo Wu border crossing. I was expecting to pay at most half that.

After landing at the airport in Shanghai, it takes forty minutes to get into the city centre. Julius is still at work when I arrive at 5 p.m. The traffic is unbelievable. When I last came here nine years ago, the streets were crawling with bicycles, like every other Chinese city in the early nineties. There are hardly any bicycles to be seen now. The streets are choking with smoke-spewing cars, buses, and trucks. Even the delivery boys have ditched their bicycles for motorbikes. It's amazing how a city can change so much in a decade. Shanghai is draped in traffic-clogged expressways that sweep across the city like monstrous snakes, winding their way around skyscrapers, resting on giant, concrete pillars. How does anyone ever find their way here?

Julius has reserved a room for me at a small hotel not far from where he lives, in the Hongqiao area. The Sweet Memories Hotel is in a leafy, tree-lined avenue sandwiched between low-rise residential blocks, so that from the sixth floor, I have a partial view of the city lights, which stretch for miles around like a constellation of winking stars. The name reminds one of hourly love motels in the Kowloon Tong district of Hong Kong.

The room is airy and spacious, yet it costs only a few hundred yuan, a fraction of what I would have paid in Hong Kong for something comparable. I'm prepared to spend up to a week here, so I have to watch expenses. I'm carrying cash as I'm not sure whether credit cards are all that widely accepted. Julius says I should expect to use cash in most places. The room is also clean and has a well-stocked fridge, which has a constant buzzing sound loud enough to rival that of the air con. The buzz stops intermittently with an angry cough, as if the fridge is clearing its throat the way people on the streets sputter before shooting a stream of gob on the pavement. It goes silent for several minutes and comes alive again after another coughing bout.

Fifteen minutes after checking in, I head straight to the cybercafé Lai Ying uses. It's called Pointblank and is on Shenyang Lu, a narrow popular bar street off the busy shopping district on Huai Hai Lu. It's a small place tucked away between an antiques shop and a noodle bar. Each of the five computers is located in a booth set on the table. Rock music throbs from two bowl-sized speakers built into the walls. All the five computers are taken, two by white girls with long

280

unkempt hair, rucksacks dumped on the floor, the rest by locals who look like students. I buy a can of beer at the reception and wait. The attendant, who is wearing orange glasses and has red and green highlights in his hair, gives me a number. Three Chinese men are waiting on the sofas near the door, heads buried in comic books. My turn comes forty minutes and three cans of beer later. Lai Ying hasn't shown up. I log on and check my email. There's nothing there of interest. I surf a couple of Zim websites but find nothing new. More farm takeovers, violence, stern decrees by the president. The Zim dollar continues its downward spiral. Two years ago, one US dollar was equivalent to 24 Zimbabwean dollars. The current rate is now around 55, and at the rate it is falling every day, the currency could soon be worth nothing. This is a currency which was worth more than the US dollar when it was first launched in 1980.

Before I leave, I send Lai Ying a message to remind her I'm going to Zim next week. I cross the tree-lined street and locate the bar Julius suggested. It's called the Midwest Bar. Its walls are covered with pictures of American celebrities and memorabilia. The music is Kenny Rogers, Don Williams, and Dolly Parton. A piece of America right in the heart of Shanghai. You can get your fill of American culture here, then walk down to the cybercafé to search for reasons to emigrate, like colleges and jobs.

After a couple of drinks, it becomes painfully clear that this bar doesn't quite appeal. The staff look ridiculous in their white boots and oversized cowboy hats, and red scarves around their necks that cannot be very comfortable in the heat out on the terrace. But it's strategically located. From here, I have a good view of the cybercafé, which is just across the road. I take a seat on the terrace, where I can see people going in and out. If Lai Ying comes along, I can't miss her.

Julius arrives at 7.30, bubbling with energy. He has put on weight since his last visit to Hong Kong some years ago. Most of the weight is around the belly and cheeks. It's not just the beer. He looks like a well-fed man. He's casually dressed in a loose-fitting polo shirt designed to obscure the pot belly, and brown jeans, looking every inch like an IT guy, with a brown briefcase, no doubt full of CDs with all manner of diagnostic software. We're one of a kind.

"So you're on the hunt for a wife, then?" he asks, after ten minutes of small talk. "We're supposed to have moved on, my friend. If anything, you should be hunting for a girlfriend."

"I've got enough of those, Julius."

"I bet you do, you married bachelor."

"I wish." Tiffany flashes through my mind. "Your family okay?"

"My boy is good. He'll soon start going to kindergarten. He's growing like a reed. It seems like yesterday when he was born, and he was yelling his head off so loudly we couldn't sleep."

"And your wife, how is she?"

"Well, well," he mutters, shaking his head. "The wife never stops nagging, but apart from that, everything's fine. After hanging out with you tonight, I'll be expecting fireworks." He starts to laugh, the way a lot of guys do when they complain about their wives. The laughter is mirthless, uncomfortable, as if they regret having got married, or at least having married their wives. "Anyway, it's not like I get to see the old Nanjing gang every night. You have to come and see us before you go."

Julius met his wife when he moved here after Nanjing. She's originally from Hebei, in the north, near Beijing.

"Of course. I would love to, just as soon as I've found my family."

His face changes. Assuming a serious expression, he says, "So, how do you want to do this?"

"If I have to sit here watching that café for a week, I'll do it."

He looks as if he has something on his mind. The way he laughs awkwardly, avoiding eye contact. He wasn't always like this. He looked you straight in the eye, leaning close, as if what he was saying was for your ears only. This time, it's almost as if he's embarrassed for me. Because my wife ran away? Because he knows something I don't? I guess I'll know soon enough.

Julius spends the next hour filling me in on all the exciting things that have been happening in this city since I was last here – the nightclubs and trendy new themed bars dotted around the city. The only problem is that Shanghai is so big you have to spend hours commuting from one end of the city to another if you want to sample its night-time delights.

It is clear that Lai Ying is not visiting the cybercafé tonight. But I'm reluctant to leave just yet, so we stay till nine, then Julius suggests we go explore another part of town. The country music is starting to grate. We get into Julius's Honda Accord, which is parked in a small alley off Shenyang Lu, two blocks away from the Midwest Bar, and drive fifteen minutes to the Amazon Place, a bar decorated with bamboo poles, bamboo leaves, and an assortment of ferns in giant pots that have been arranged in such a way as to evoke a jungle. They are spread over the tables, creating a quiet and intimate ambience. Others are located at intervals on the walls or dangling from the high ceiling, partly obscuring stuffed squirrels, monkeys, civet cats, and koalas that hang from invisible wires or are stuck on bamboo poles. Part of the wall opposite the main entrance is devoted to a mini waterfall decorated with flashy lights and craggy rocks. One section of the bar has five pool tables, but at this time of the night, only two are in use. According to Julius, the regulars start filing in after 11. I haven't come across a bar in Hong Kong that has the space for pool tables, and once we take possession of one table, I hardly notice the time pass.

We reminisce about the good old days, the White Card deals, the difficulties of adjusting to life in this country, and how things have changed so much since the late eighties. The overt hostility is virtually absent now. Shanghai is an extremely cosmopolitan city. Everyone's trying to learn English and associate with foreigners. No one follows foreigners around like before, not even those who just want to admire leggy, blue-eyed blondes. We talk about life at university, where education was geared to memorising what the professor said. Exams were straightforward affairs that did not require much thinking. They would reproduce a passage from the textbook with one or two words missing, and you were required to fill in the blanks. You were examined on what the professor said, and what the professor said passed for education. We were expected to memorise formulae and merely repeat them rather than apply them. Only rarely were you expected to do real calculations, and there were hardly any open-ended questions.

"About a month ago," says Julius, as we start another game of pool, "I picked up a promotional leaflet for a new bar called the Sundowner Blues. They have a live band playing most nights. Rock, R&B, some soul, pop. Everything, even the occasional reggae. Perhaps I'll take you there tomorrow. It's a bit of a drive but it's worth checking out. So, anyway, I've been frequenting this Sundowner Blues place and about a week ago, the most bizarre thing happened. There was a reunion party, some sort of function by old Nanjing students. Someone emailed me an invite and I thought I would check it out. I went there with Luvanga, you remember him?"

Luvanga was a quiet, unassuming Angolan. Good at football, and volleyball, in fact, all sports.

"Did he not get into some sort of trouble with a girl? I never did learn the details."

"Yeah," says Julius with a wry grimace. "She had to have an abortion, which as you remember was nothing new. There were complications. Later she split up with Luvanga and started to date a local. It looks like they got married. So, anyway we ran into them at this reunion party. She had changed a lot, I could barely recognise her, and of course, I didn't know the guy, neither did Luvanga. She and her husband were whispering, looking in our direction. You could sense the tension in the air, man. Anyway, the long and short of it is that in the course of the night, the guy confronts Luvanga and words are exchanged. It was nasty, man, stuff going back all these years."

"What were they arguing about?"

"It turns out that something bad happened. The woman can't have children, and the husband is obviously not too pleased. Luvanga didn't like being confronted and blamed for it. Things only calmed down when the woman herself pulled the husband away, saying that if anyone was to blame, it was herself for being so naïve, and the medical student for his recklessness. She said she's happy she didn't lose her life in the process, that her eyes were opened, like she was facing a new beginning, and starting all over again after having been condemned to death. That was some heavy shit, Dan. Everyone had been drinking, and I don't think this woman was all that sober. She was nursing a glass of white wine, but she was very focused. She knew exactly what she was saying. The guy's face was red. He had had quite a bit. But when she spoke, he changed, his eyes opened wide and it was like he was hearing her voice for the first time. It was pretty weird. He changed from this angry man who was raving mad to a quiet, sober, meek husband, allowing himself to be led away like a child. The animosity was gone."

"And Luvanga, what did he do?" I ask in a low voice, as I remember the pain of my own encounter with the 'medical thing'.

"Not much at the beginning. You know him, quiet fellow. No one knows what's going on in his mind. Then he just lost it, and both were like they had gone mad. But after the woman spoke, it all went very quiet. I thought they were going to shake hands, man. I've never seen anything like that."

"It's bizarre how these things from so long ago crop up when you least expect them."

I resist the temptation to remind Julius that he was all for the 'medical thing' for Lai Ying. The realisation shakes me with a sudden jolt that at this very moment, Lai Ying and I are in the same city, possibly within a few miles of each other, yet we've never been this far apart.

The bar is filling up. We've lost the exclusive right to our pool table, and have to book a game like everyone else by placing a couple of yuan coins on the edge of the table. Everyone here is in their mid-twenties or early thirties, the new Shanghai young social climbers, dressed in designer clothes or smart casual. They look like IT experts, designers, and entrepreneurs. Some are wearing dark sunglasses. Many have come here on oversized motorbikes which are parked outside, as if on display. The girls are in high heels, jeans, and tank tops, armed with designer sunglasses and flashy mobile phones and knocking back colourful cocktails, while the guys sip vodka and tequilas. Most of them, both male and female, have the omnipresent cigarette dangling from the lips or fingers, or smouldering away on ashtrays balanced precariously on the edge of the pool tables. Everyone here exudes a confidence that says they're totally in control, and are wasting no time in taking the chances the city has to offer, including making as much money as possible and acquiring the appurtenances of the lifestyles they always dreamed of and which the modernisation of China is now happily delivering.

"I'm just thinking," says Julius, "looking at all these trendy people, if anyone needed an abortion today, they wouldn't need to take those awful risks like we did before, putting our lives and futures in the hands of student medics. You can probably get it done at a private clinic at the drop of a hat."

"For a fortune, I guess."

"These people have money, man. China is not what it used to be. You ought to spend more time here. I think you would like it. The rough edges of the communist past have been softened, man. Things are much easier here, frankly."

The things Julius says about the new Shanghai keep playing on my mind. There's a certain vibrancy about this city which wasn't here before. The more I see of this city, the more I think it might suit me. But am I ready to relocate and start all over again? First, I have to find my family.

At 1 a.m., I'm ready to go to sleep, which suits Julius. He has a meeting at eight. He drives me back to my hotel in silence, my mind preoccupied with thoughts about how I'll spend the whole of the next day before I go to watch the Pointblank Cybercafé in the evening.

I spend the following morning in my room reading a novel. I've brought three novels and some IT magazines to help kill the time. It is a long, uneventful day, and although I've got the novels to keep me busy, I can barely concentrate as my mind keeps filling up with images of Lai Ying seeing me approach and running away.

In the afternoon, I go shopping in the famous markets along Huatin Lu for designer shirts and shorts, which probably fell off the back of a truck. They look like the genuine thing but are refreshingly cheap. The place is full of tourists, haggling over prices with grinning old ladies, holding up the clothes against their bodies to see if they're the right size. It's a lively atmosphere, with all the chatter, laughter, and music coming from invisible speakers hidden below the stalls. Later I spend a couple of hours relaxing at the peaceful Huangpu Park, reading my novel, and watching people practise tai-chi. An American couple asks me to take a picture of them standing outside the People's Heroes Memorial, which features three enormous rifles stacked up against each other. Bubbling with excitement, they inform me that this is their first trip to China.

"It's not the dark communist state I expected," says the man.

"It's the year 2000," I point out. "You ought to have seen the eighties."

"You've lived here all this time?" She looks at me as though I said I was in jail all these years.

"I lived here for a while in the late eighties. I barely recognise it now."

"Gee!" the woman gushes, hooking her arm into the man's possessively.

At 5 o'clock, I'm back at the Pointblank Cybercafé. The queue today is not as long as yesterday. I only have to wait half an hour. Luckily, I have things to read, including a newspaper I bought this morning, which I've not had a chance to read all day. The paper is surprisingly thin. For a country as big as China, the press doesn't have much to say, certainly not in English.

I have several emails from clients in Hong Kong, requesting appointments. I tell them I'm available probably from Tuesday next week. Any longer than that and I run a real risk of losing them. I've made up my mind to fly back on Tuesday morning, whatever the outcome of this wild goose chase.

Chip has written to say he has spoken on the phone to some powerful contact and will be meeting him next week. This piece of news raises my spirits. Chip must have entertained a lot of people to get this far.

Sometime after 6.30 p.m., I leave the cybercafé and wander around the neighbourhood, watching the office blocks to see if I might spot Lai Ying. There must be a reason why she comes here, either her office is close by or she lives near here. I stop every now and then to see if she might be approaching the café from another direction. Several times, I notice girls who remind me of her, and one or two who, from a distance, look just like her – the slim figure, long hair. The trouble is, a lot of girls look like that. It's like the standard size and shape.

After walking around aimlessly for forty-five minutes, I head to the Midwest Bar, exhausted, my feet aching, my spirits low, and my heart burning with an intense anger. Julius calls to say he's held up at a meeting and doesn't expect to be free until much later. I don't mind drinking on my own tonight. I tell him I'm very tired and won't be staying up late. We arrange to meet tomorrow evening instead. He tells me how to get to a popular pub where Africans hang out. I thank him but I'm in no mood to socialise.

From the terrace at the bar, I watch the cybercafé for an hour while I tuck into an appetising black pepper steak, then take a taxi back to my hotel.

These hours of waiting are beginning to wear me down. The whole exercise is looking increasingly meaningless. But I'm here now, and I'm going through with this all weekend.

This Is Trespass

SATURDAY AFTERNOON FINDS ME DOWN in the dumps. I rotate between the Pointblank Cybercafé and the Midwest Bar. Julius comes to meet me at the bar in the evening. With all the sightseeing I've been doing, I almost feel like a tourist, admiring the temples, taking in the smells from foods stalls in narrow food streets, squeezing my way through crowded shopping streets and market alleys decorated with multicoloured flags and red lanterns, and sculptures of dragons in a variety of postures. But I'm more like a reluctant tourist, forced to do the sights to kill time while waiting to begin my vigil. Tonight I just want to sit and drink, and by 8.15 p.m., I'm ready to find a bar with a bit more life than this somnolent country music.

"Come on," says Julius, beckoning a passing cowboy for the bill. "I want you to meet someone. I've been trying to sound people out, but no one knows anything. Anyway, out of the blue, I got a call just this afternoon from a web host. He didn't say who sent him. All very mysterious. But he referred me to this other guy he's been talking to. Someone we both know, as it turns out."

"Who is this?"

"Patience, my friend. Let's just say, a shower comrade. You remember them, don't you?"

Shower comrade. I've not heard that expression in years. How would a shower comrade help me find Lai Ying?

We get into a beat-up old taxi and squeeze into the tiny space in the back seat, inches from an iron grill that protects the driver from being attacked by unsavoury passengers. The cotton cloth spread across the backseat is smooth, without blemish, as compared to the ones on the two front seats, which are old and tattered. It covers the seat completely, making it impossible to buckle up. The seatbelts lie impotent on their backs.

Julius gives an address. The driver discards his cigarette through the open window and we speed down the narrow bar street, made even narrower tonight by the line of cars parked on either side. Minutes later, we're inching along a jam-packed expressway sandwiched between smoke-belching buses. Thank God for the closed windows, except that the aircon isn't working all that well, and the air in the car is dank and putrid, reminding one of fried tofu in the old college cafeteria and remnants of the driver's cigarette smoke.

In the half-hour drive, Julius brings me up to date with what he calls the incredible job opportunities as American and European companies flood into town. Marketing. IT. Accounting. All you need is Putonghua, English, and a university degree, subject irrelevant. You can be taught to sell anything, recruit new clients. That's all it boils down to here. Selling stuff. Or finding new ways to sell old stuff.

"There's no place like Shanghai," intones Julius, clenched fist slamming into open palm. "This place has everything. The new opportunities out here, there's nothing like it elsewhere. You would do very well here, man."

Here we go again. "I don't know."

"And the cost of living, Dan, well, you've seen it for yourself. The beers we had for example. Eight yuan a bottle. You pay at least four times in Hong Kong. And it's not like you have such a great job right now."

He pumps my fist to soften that last statement. He's right. There's no reason why I shouldn't move here. Except for short business trips, I have never seriously thought of living in China, not after all the things that happened. The riots, the terror, the police investigation, the aftermath of Lai Ying's abortion, the days at the people's sanctuary. But then China sneaked up behind us and swallowed up Hong Kong, and we've ended up living in China, although Hong Kong claims to be semi-autonomous. I ask Julius how he came to live here after all the heartache from our student days.

"You have to move on, man," he says, without hesitation. "That was then. We were simply up against disgruntled students, who didn't represent the mood of the country. And you must remember that after Tiananmen, the students were effectively neutralised, man. All over China."

"You mean the massacre made it safe for foreigners?"

"I don't know about safe. Politically, it all went very quiet. What people care about is making money now that they're allowed to have the good life. The racism hasn't gone. It never will. But it's different now. It's not in your face. You just have to be realistic about things, man. Nanjing is history. If I were you, I would move here like a shot. And what's more, your wife is here."

"I'll find her. And take her back."

"I don't know, man. I don't know." He shakes his head with such a sense of despondence a sinking feeling comes over me. What's left for me in Hong Kong? But shouldn't I first try to get a job off Wang? I hadn't intended to bring up the subject of Wang, at least not just yet, knowing Julius's opinion of the man. But I see a chance to redeem myself, although the thought of it makes me nauseous.

"I'm not hell-bent on Hong Kong, Julius. In fact, there's a chance of a job in Guangdong."

"Really! What would that be?"

"Remember Wang from Nanjing?"

Silence. He stares out the window.

"So it's true, then?" he asks, in a low, deliberate voice. I shoot him a questioning look, my heartbeat quickening with alarm. "The rumours, man. I've heard rumours. It's a small world."

"What did you hear?"

"You're hanging out with that old crook, doing business together. Drinking together. Hey, don't look at me like that, Dan. The talk is that he's your golfing buddy. Word is you're the next Tiger Woods, man. You've been spotted, you see? People talk, two and two together, and all that."

The taxi pulls up outside a commercial building. I'm anxious to know everything. But Julius strides into the building, as if trying to put some distance between us.

"Who saw us?" I demand, as I join him in the lift.

"Oh, it doesn't matter. Anyway I don't know. All I heard is bar talk, you know?"

He's lying. But he's right about one thing. It doesn't matter a jot.

"Well, it's simple, Julius. The man wants business partners. We're heading out to Zim as soon as I get back. And, who knows, he might come up with a job." I laugh to hide my anxiety.

We're on the fourth floor, walking down a busy corridor full of shoppers. All the shops are small enterprises, selling mostly electronic goods and mobile phones. Neon lights and bright Chinese characters adorn the walls. Loud music assaults you from every direction. What would Lai Ying be doing in a place like this? I'm struggling to make a connection with this thing about a shower comrade. After the Nanjing riots, most of us had very little contact with the shower comrades, unless it was unavoidable, like in class. Socially, they ceased to exist.

I've no idea how they got their fair share of showers. The riots took place in the middle of a particularly unforgiving winter.

I didn't expect to find shops open this late. It's almost nine.

"Everything's changed here," explains Julius. "It's going to be just like Hong Kong."

Julius leads the way into a small mobile phone shop at the end of the corridor. A woman sits behind the counter, eating a bowl of noodles. She's mid-thirties, in glasses that make her look like a graduate student. She looks up, surprised to see customers this late in the night.

"Here we are," announces Julius, ushering me in. He addresses the woman. "Is Han Wei here, miss?"

Han Wei? I shoot a puzzled look at Julius. He nods meaningfully and crosses his hands, as if to say, so there you have it. What it is, I've no idea.

"Wait." The woman puts her chopsticks away, disappears behind a curtain of beads and comes back a minute later, followed by a skinny man who is greying prematurely at the temples. His skin looks too pale, unhealthy. He needs to spend more time in the sun. He peers with timid eyes through round glasses, like a doctor looking at a case that is like nothing he recognises from textbooks. But Han Wei The Whistle is not a doctor. As far as I can remember, his only connection with the medical world was his ability to procure abortions through his contacts.

His facility with the medical community wasn't something he advertised. I had known him for a number of years but I had no idea he was doing this. Diallo only revealed this aspect of Han Wei's identity much later. It didn't matter anyway, because many of us had long stopped talking to Han Wei, with the exception of Julius, who started off studying medicine and maintained contact with the medics, and, as I'm finding out now, with Han Wei. But Julius' dream to become a doctor never materialised. Suspecting he would have trouble practicing in other countries with a Chinese degree, he reluctantly switched to engineering.

He and Han Wei shake hands, like old friends, making small talk about business. I watch them in silence, getting increasingly puzzled by this camaraderie. This is not the Han Wei I remember, the shy shower comrade who miraculously transformed himself into a banner-wielding, slogan-chanting, fist-clenching combatant, whom we later discovered had been a ringleader in the anti-African riots. There's nothing about his slender, emaciated frame and jaundiced pale skin to suggest any remnant of that student-activist aggression. What could he possibly know about the whereabouts of Lai Ying?

"I'm sure you remember Han Wei," says Julius. "And his wife."

We shake hands. His hand feels lame, like a child's. He's clearly ill.

"You don't remember me," says the woman, smiling. I smile apologetically.

"I guess we've met…"

"Mei Ning. My friends call me Minnie."

My jaw drops. My mind is a nest of confused thoughts. Minnie. The strained meetings in her student hostel lobby, when Diallo and I begged her to tell us how to find Lai Ying's professor. Now I recognise the broad face with the perpetual uncompromising hardness. But she has changed. The worry lines etched on her brow, the prematurely greying hair. The hardness and suspicion are gone. She looks like someone recuperating from a long illness, only just beginning to savour the joys of good health, but knowing she's not out of the woods yet. I remember her now. The falling out with Lai Ying, and although they reconciled, their friendship was never the same. They didn't keep in touch much after Nanjing. Now that I think about it, I vaguely recall Lai Ying mentioning her marriage to Han Wei. But it didn't register. I didn't want to be reminded of him. And now here I am, with the two of them, and they're supposed to tell me how to find my wife.

"Let's talk in the office," says Han Wei.

He leads us past a beads curtain and a private door behind the cashier's desk to a room which is twice as big as the shop. It is furnished more like a living room than an office, with comfortable leather sofas and a coffee table in place of a desk and chairs. At the far end of the room is an oak shelf, with an assortment of hefty volumes. A wide-screen television set and hi-fi sit majestically in one corner, alongside a drinks' cabinet. The aura of affluence in the office couldn't be further removed from the tacky decorations and garish neon lights that adorn the corridors outside.

"Whisky? Brandy?" Han Wei gestures towards the drinks' cabinet. Minnie walks across the room noiselessly and pours the drinks, then returns to her dinner in the front room. Han Wei extracts a packet of cigars and offers them around.

We take our seats, and then Julius embarks on a monologue about the good old days. Han Wei looks ill at ease, as if he's being praised for an act of heroism he had nothing to do with. He has something on his mind, and is just waiting for

Julius to end his story. After a few sips of brandy, he has already turned red in the face.

Tiring of Julius's reminiscing, I interrupt and ask Han Wei how his business is faring. His face lights up, relieved by the change of subject.

"It has been a struggle," he says, smiling. But the signature "o" on his lips is stretched into an awkward angle by the pale, sagging skin of his sunken cheeks. A series of wrinkles on his forehead bear down on his eyes, narrowing them.

"He has a lot of contacts with African traders," Julius informs me. "Actually he's always worked with Africans."

"Really? How's that?"

"Going back a long way," says Han Wei, with a touch of pride. "Back when some of us helped you guys to find clients for your White Card deals."

"It's more than that, man," says Julius, warming to the subject. "Han Wei was the biggest player of the lot. But no one knew that. I didn't know myself until he told me recently. Han Wei was the quiet, behind the scenes contact man, organising the scouts, as they called themselves."

I grin at the mention of scouts. We knew them as shower comrades, or traders.

"You're too generous, Julius," says Han Wei, embarrassed at the praise. "I was just trying to make some money, helping two communities work together. As you remember, there were many Chinese people with money but they couldn't spend it. Quite a ridiculous situation."

"It must have really helped with your current business."

He winces. Maybe it's the illness that's eating him. Perhaps his extra-sensitive ears picked up a tinge of sarcasm that was quite unintended.

"You know in China, you can't survive without guanxi." He puts on a brave face, to match the defensive tone in his voice. "It's the way it is. It's the way we do business."

"You remember Wang, the Wang's Den chap?" I ask him. "You went there a few times."

He chuckles with recognition. "Of course. Everyone knew Wang Bin. He gave foreigners free beer. We Chinese used to call him Wang Fei Jau." African Wang.

Julius and I laugh. What would Wang have made of that, with all his Africa expedition dreams and Zheng He? Han Wei omits to mention that after the riots, they called him Hei Gui Wang. Black Ghost Wang.

"He's an excellent businessman," says Han Wei, downing his brandy and reaching for the bottle for a refill. "I learned so much from him."

"Are you still in touch?"

He hesitates. But only long enough to take a swig and think. He swallows hard, grimacing, like a patient taking bitter medicine.

"I have kept in touch with many of the businessmen from back then. Including Wang Fei Jau." He nods continuously, like a wise old man defending the veracity of tales that sound increasingly bizarre when sifted through the mists of time. Or in this case, through the thick smoke from his cigar.

"The other day, we were talking about Kabinga," says Julius, turning to me. "Han Wei says he knew him well, and remembers how he accumulated so much money, then lost it all so suddenly." Han Wei nods but remains silent, clearly apprehensive about the direction the discussion is going. "There was something you were going to tell me, Han Wei. What was it?"

Han Wei takes a deep drag on the cigar, eyes half closed. He releases the smoke in a series of rings that chase each other and coalesce into a seamless cloud above his head.

"I'll come to that. Dan is anxious, I'm sure." He glances at me with a plea for patience. I remain tight-lipped. I've waited a long time, I can wait a few minutes to know where to find my wife, if that's what's on his mind. "But first, I should mention something. The people who did Kabinga in, I knew who they were," he announces with a smirk. "They were tough guys. No-nonsense types. Kabinga was lucky they didn't kill him."

Julius and I exchange glances. I quickly down my brandy and pour another one. I hold the glass so tightly I'm afraid it will crack, and the pressure sends a ripple of pain through my knuckles. But I'm barely aware of the pain as I digest Han Wei's revelations.

"One of them was a policeman. Senior guy. I don't know his name. I think he's retired now. A few others were politicians. Middle-ranking party cadres."

"Was the cop known as Yu Shian?" I ask him, trying to sound calm, though my heart is throbbing.

"I don't remember the names," he says, looking away. "It was a long time ago."

Julius is first with the question we're both dying to ask.

"Wang? Was he among them?"

"Oh no!" he looks up, startled. "He didn't even know these people."

"How can you be so sure?"

"I just know, Julius. We knew who was doing what, those of us doing the deals. It was common knowledge. Wang was definitely not in on this attack. Not his style."

I lean back and sigh. Only then do I realise I've been sitting on the edge of my seat. So it's just like I thought. Wang is clean. I've waited for this reassurance for so long that when it comes, it feels like I'm the one being vindicated. Now I can savour the brandy, let the hot liquor burn my tongue before letting it slide down my throat. But even as I reflect on what sounds like a reprieve for Wang, I can't help feeling that Han Wei's denial came too quickly, as if he needed to make it. As if there was a reason he needed to clear Wang's name. But what could that reason be? Why would he want to defend him? I push my doubts to the back burner to listen to Han Wei's now slightly tremulous voice, which is so low we both have to lean forward to hear him.

"The riots. The incident at the railway station. It was not good. I've often thought on it, long and hard. Friends turned against each other. We showed each other no respect. We all lost face. It wasn't good. Were we too young? Did we get caught up in the heat of the moment? When you cast your eyes back over the expanse of time, things become clearer. Much clearer. Perhaps we should have had more money to live on. Life was hard. Perhaps the visitors should have treated our women with more respect. Perhaps we should have understood they were different from us. We wanted serious relationships. They wanted amusement. Perhaps we shouldn't have turned against them with anger and hatred the way we did. Running them out of town. Why am I telling you all this? A few years ago, everything changed. I found my liver is not so good. I've spent a fortune on treatment. It doesn't help. I need a transplant. But we'll never find a donor. I'm on my last days. All these thoughts from the past follow me like a shadow of shame. It doesn't help my health. Neither do the cigars and liquor, I know. Eggman, recently when I got a call asking me to help find your wife, at first, I thought this is none of my business. But Julius and I have been talking. And I've not forgotten the happy times I spent in your parties, in the same study group, doing projects together, drinking together in Wang's Den. Am I going to die with the shame of the past clouding my view? It is not right."

A solemn silence hangs in the air, the type that follows the confessions to a heinous crime after the initial gasps of horror have evaporated. The words I've heard have little connection to the Han Wei I knew. When he starts to cough, his face turns pale, he shakes as if he's having an epileptic fit. I hand him a packet of tissues and ask him if there's anything we can do. He shakes his head. I search his face and see nothing but pain and regret. It is the same regret I feel deep inside, that is buried deep in the foolish stubbornness I have dragged along with me all these years. Julius says he moved on and accepted to live in China, as did many others. Hearing Han Wei speak of his own loss and tribulations makes me realise just how intertwined our struggles were, how Nanjing made our lives crash into each other. I feel my chest heave, my breath slows down to a measured, gentle throb, and I know this country can be my home.

Han Wei clears his throat and fixes his gaze on me. I brace myself for another devastating blast from the past.

"Perhaps this is not important," he says, studying my face for a reaction. "Wang is a good man. He helped many foreigners, but later he lost face when that trouble happened. And he was forced to shut the bar. With my contacts amongst the scouts, I learned a lot. I know that Wang helped you with money, Eggman." I sit back stiffly, holding my breath, my heart filling with a mixture of shock and indignation. What business is it of his? "Your girlfriend was sick in hospital. You didn't tell him why you needed the money. But when he found out what the trouble was, he sent more money to the hospital staff to keep them quiet."

"What!" I gasp. "This had nothing to do with him."

"Wang Fei Jau is that kind of person," says Han Wei, chuckling and ending up coughing. "He'll do anything for a friend."

Julius also stares at him with disbelief, chin buried in his hands. He never said who the contact was. I turn to question him, as recognition now dawns on me.

"Julius, when you and Diallo sent the gifts to the hospital—"

"Yeah, yeah," he interrupts, shrugging. "Han Wei helped us. He knew those people, man."

"The person I remember was that skinny guy. The guy who…who…"

"Yi Guan," offers Han Wei. "He's a respected doctor now."

I steal a glance at Julius and see him wince. He and Yi Guan had been in the same class and talked of working together before Julius was forced to abandon his medical aspirations. I remember wanting to strangle Yi Guan when Lai Ying told me what had happened. I shut my eyes to calm the riot of thoughts in my head. Who knew what, whom did I confide in, did I miss anything? And Minnie? She didn't know anything. Both Lai Ying and Han Wei kept her in the dark.

What could she have done, anyway? Would it have made any difference if she had warned Lai Ying to steer clear of Yi Guan? Anyone could have botched the abortion. They were all a bunch of amateurs, experimenting with life and death.

"You didn't say…Julius, you didn't say your contact was Han Wei."

"It was a long time ago," says Han Wei, needlessly coming to Julius's aid.

"Look man, you two weren't talking," retorts Julius. "If you had known, you'd have said no. Anyway, Diallo understood the whole deal between you two better than I. He made the decision, and I thought it was a realistic one."

I look away, wanting to be anywhere but here.

"They said the Chinese spirits and cigarettes weren't enough," murmurs Han Wei. "I gave them my share of your cigarettes, but they were adamant. If you ask me, they were just plain greedy. Somehow, they found out it was a foreigner with money. Someone must have said something, someone who knew you two were dating. So, I talked to Wang. I'm sorry I went behind your back. But your girlfriend and my girlfriend were friends."

I lean back, struggling to take it all in. But my mind is in chaos, my heart thumps with conflicting emotions. So, in spite of the mess Yi Guan caused, I'm indebted to Han Wei, the shower comrade who turned against us so vehemently, and whom I had never found it in my heart to forgive? And then there's Wang. Is this why he's dragging me along to Zim, to call in a favour? Han Wei's strained voice starts to penetrate my consciousness, forcing me to wade my way out of the fogs of confusion that have almost forced my troubled brain to a grinding halt.

"My wife, Mei Ning, she remembers your wife well," announces Han Wei, then pauses to take a sip of brandy and relight his cigar. "She has guanxi in this city. She'll take us to see her."

Before I can get my breath, he calls out to his wife.

"We're ready," he announces.

From the way he says it, and the matter-of-fact way she nods, as if she had been waiting months for just such a solemn signal, it's clear they're truly ready. Which is more than I can say for myself. After all these months of waiting. And suddenly, this man I haven't seen for ten years is declaring that we're ready to smoke Lai Ying out of her hiding place. I'm filled with revulsion that someone I remember as an enemy could be this privileged, while I've struggled and endured the shame of neglect and rejection for so long.

"But…how did…I don't get it…" I stare at Han Wei, lost for words.

"Perhaps I should explain." He puts his fingers together, both thumbs poking his lips in a pensive, almost supplicant gesture. "We run a chain of cybercafés. I got contacted by…" he shrugs his shoulders, indicating it doesn't matter. "We get lots of calls from the Technology Department, demands to cooperate to locate users accessing prohibited websites. That kind of thing. It's quite common. We have a good contact there. I had no idea who initiated the search. But when Julius and I spoke, I understood everything."

Julius has a blank expression on his face, and is doing his best to hide his perplexity. Only one other person could have taken the search to that level. Alex, and his contacts in this city, which leaves me dumbfounded. He gave me little reason to believe he was going to help.

I remain silent in the back of the grey Mercedes, clutching the bouquet of pink roses I bought at the florist outside the lobby. Julius is equally lost in thought, though I've no idea what he's thinking. Han Wei is at the wheel, speeding down one expressway after another, listening to Minnie talk about her plans for tomorrow. I search in vain for something in her voice that would remind me of our exchange years ago. I keep my gaze focused on the lights of the buildings that line the roads. Fifteen minutes later, we're cruising through a quiet residential neighbourhood.

Minnie turns to speak to me, the first time she has addressed me.

"Lai Ying and I were walking away from class one day, going for lunch on the street outside the university—you remember the Cai Chang area?—when we overheard some people talking about how they dealt with—sorry to use the words—a black ghost. They were arguing about money; money they had been paid. It sounded as though they were cheated. First, they were told to finish him off, then they got word in the last minute to go soft. So they ended up being paid much less. For some reason, Lai Ying concluded it was Wang, or some of his associates. You know she always hated the business networks with all her heart. That incident just made it worse. She was very scared. Scared for you, and your friends. She knew your people, because she was your friend, so she sort of felt closer to them. Yet she couldn't protect them."

I nod as the memories assail me. Lai Ying has never talked about this overheard conversation, perhaps uncertain of my reaction. I sense how helpless she must have felt, unable to do anything to help the foreigners, yet she was dating one.

"It wasn't an easy time," I murmur, out of politeness to Minnie.

"I'm sorry to say this but…" she hesitates. I nod to urge her on. Nothing she says can hurt me now. "The girls who had foreign friends, um, some people didn't take them very seriously." She's trying to be polite. "But this thing that happened to your friend, well, it was a shock. He was just a student, trying to survive, just like Han Wei. Why try to kill someone for that? Why couldn't they just take his money and leave him alone? I could begin to understand Lai Ying's frustration."

I ask her if she and Lai Ying have kept in touch. She hesitates, unsure what Lai Ying might have said.

"From time to time," she says, without turning to look at me. "I knew of her family but never met them. I don't know how I'll face her."

Han Wei squeezes her knee and says it's not a problem. After a moment he adds, "You'll forgive each other. It's what friends do. Anyway, here we are now."

At the entrance to an imposing, modern residential block, the security guard demands to know who we are. I let Han Wei do the talking. He's enraged to be accosted so rudely. He certainly doesn't look like the chauffeur. Not with the smart, dark suit and the cigar dangling from his lips. He shouldn't have to worry. The acrimony is directed at the two black men sitting in the back. The guard obviously has his instructions. That can only confirm we're at the right place.

"We're here to visit a relative," says Han Wei, struggling to maintain his composure. "Your job is to let me sign the visitors' book and open the gate."

"Not this time. And if you don't leave, I'll have to call the police."

Han Wei reaches for a card in his wallet and hands it to the guard.

"Be my guest. Call him."

The guard's manner changes instantaneously. He bows, salutes, and offers apologies, pushing the gate open and bowing again as we drive through.

"Police Chief's card," explains Han Wei, laughing. "It never ceases to amuse me how a mere card can turn a lion into a mouse."

The flat is on the third floor. We stand in the corridor, outside the imposing, brown-panelled door. Minnie steps forward and rings the bell. After a few moments, the door opens. A woman's towelled head pops around the door. There's a freshness about her elderly features that makes her look younger than she is. She's a regular at the spa. And in spite of the interrupted bathroom routine, there's that air of elegance about her that comes so naturally to the old-money types. It's in the haughty, unblinking eyes, the proud nose, the high, northern cheekbones, the finely chiselled lips. I recognise her from photographs. Lai Ying's auntie.

"Who are you people?" she explodes. "And what kind of time is this to come knocking on my door?"

"Sorry to trouble you, auntie," explains Minnie. "We're friends of Lai Ying. Is she asleep yet?"

The auntie sees Julius and I and her face darkens. Sharp creases materialise down her cheeks and on her brow. For a moment, she looks as if she's going to scream.

"She's not here!" she snaps. "And I want you out of here this minute. If you don't leave now, I'll have to call the security, *and* the police, you hear me? This is trespass!"

I have a feeling Han Wei's magic card won't work this time. This woman probably plays mahjong with the mayor's wife. She is livid. She tries to push the door shut, all the time spewing expletives that denude her of the dignity she had brought to the door just a little while ago. Han Wei's foot sticks out and holds the door. The three of them are yelling at the top of their voices, pushing and shoving. I can't stand this. I start walking away down the corridor, ignoring Julius' entreaties to come back, looking for a dustbin to dispose of the bouquet.

"You've come all this way, man. You can't turn back now."

Oh yes, I can. I didn't intend to reunite with my family this way, by fighting my way past Lai Ying's auntie.

"Daddy!"

My heart stops beating. I don't know how I manage to keep my sanity when that sound tears through my brains, searching for assurance that it belonged somewhere in there. Searching for a memory of itself embedded through layers of alien sounds and voices that have in the last eight months threatened to erase it and purge it from the place it rightly belongs. My eyes fill with tears. I can't even see Chacha's face. She's a blur of movement, fighting her way past the enraged, arguing adults to rush into my arms as I sink to my knees to receive her. I don't know how long I remain immobilised in her embrace, but when I look up, I see Lai Ying standing in the door, holding onto her auntie's restraining arm, looking down at me. Her eyes speak of shock and disbelief. No words issue forth from her parted lips. She peers into her auntie's eyes. Her auntie snatches her arm away and scuttles back into the flat, her body shaking with exasperation. I hold a hand out to Lai Ying, begging her with my eyes to forgive and take me back. She stands beside me, hands cupped around her mouth. I tug gently on the soft cotton of her light-blue pyjamas, trying to draw her towards us. That's when she notices the others standing in the corridor. Her shocked gaze settles on Minnie, who is dabbing her eyes with a piece of tissue. Her arms sway to her side, in a gesture of utter incomprehension. Afraid she'll collapse, I raise myself up, gather Chacha in one arm, and wrap the other around my wife, who leans against me, motionless, stiffened by indecision. Minnie approaches, offers trembling hands, her face twitching, muttering soundless entreaties. I avert my gaze and notice the flowers which now lie discarded on the floor, their task of appeasement unfulfilled. I feel Lai Ying's arm snake itself around my waist. Then she offers Minnie a hand, and a calmness settles on her face when she whispers, "I'll call you."

I'll Be Ready for You

SHE HAS CHANGED SO MUCH, Chacha. She's grown so fast. The plaited hair makes her look more African than ever before. And she speaks such good Putonghua. When she tells me about her friends, her school, it looks as though her stay here hasn't been altogether a bad thing. I have missed so much in such a short time. It's as if she's been at boarding school, with no holidays, and not even a vague suggestion as to when they would let her go home.

The night at Lai Ying's auntie's apartment shook us to our very roots. I frequently think about the moment we faced each other, my wife and I. The pain that was so clearly etched in her face spoke of the loss, regret, the time needlessly wasted. And I knew it creased my own face, too. She saw it, because not even the joy of seeing the two of them could have concealed it.

These last two days, there has been so much to talk about, so much to catch up on. Lai Ying is shocked when I explain how Julius and I tracked her down. But I omit much of the detail about the past, and the discussion with Han Wei that left me so unsettled. She can't believe Minnie remembered about her family. With a sense of guilt, I remind her how easy it is to find people in this Internet age.

Every time I go to meet my family, Jupiter's words keep coming back to me. The family is everything. The urge to make up for lost time and lost opportunities is so overwhelming I have to pinch my ear to remind myself that we're actually together after all these months. Chacha watches me closely, as if trying to find the reason I've been away. She asks why I never come to see her. I can't find it in my heart to sadden her with the details. But even as I reassure her that we'll always be together, I hate to tell her I have to return to Hong Kong in a few days' time. I lift her up and walk around holding her, like I did when she was a toddler, but she's much bigger, and I can't carry her for long before my arms start aching. Her high-pitched voice and snatches of laughter fill a void whose depth in my heart I've become conscious of with every passing minute.

Whenever I look into Lai Ying's eyes, and listen to her complaints about the work pressure at the travel agency she works for, I hang onto her every word, making sure I miss nothing, desperate to understand the life she's living now and how I can be a part of it. Her office is only a few blocks away from the Pointblank Cybercafé. The thought that the cybercafé we both used is part of Han Wei's and Wang's empire makes me painfully aware just how easily we're connected, even to those we'd rather forget about.

Yesterday, we went sightseeing. We started at the Jade Buddha temple, with the sitting and declining Buddhas. Thick incense smoke filled the main courtyard and the Grand Hall. The extensively decorated streets outside were lined with hawkers selling all manner of trinkets, souvenirs, and replicas of the Buddhas. It was like being at a carnival, without the music and dance. Later we went to Yuyuan Garden and spent a lovely afternoon admiring the rockery, the perilous peaks, cliffs, caves, and gorges, the ponds and lush vegetation, the pavilion with the splendid roof and window decorations.

Today we're at Renmin Park, the people's park. I persuaded Lai Ying to take the day off so we can spend another day together before I leave tomorrow morning. After lunch, we head into Shanghai Museum, which is located in the park. It is said to be the biggest museum in China. Walking around this gigantic structure is like being in another world, going back in time, visiting new lands. We walk hand in hand, Chacha between us, stopping to read the inscriptions, to admire this African bronze sculpture or that Tang dynasty ceramic treasure and vase. I tighten my grip on Chacha's hand. Walking hand in hand, without inviting any animosity like in the old days, except for the odd stare, is almost like a dream. This is not the China I knew.

"It's truly like a dream," I tell Lai Ying.

"What, you coming to find us?"

"Holding hands in the street. We could never do that."

She laughs. There's a faraway look in her eyes.

Chacha tugs at my hand and demands to know what we're talking about.

"We've come a long way, darling. When your mummy and I first met, we couldn't hold hands in public."

"Oh, I know, Daddy, because you're black and Mummy's Chinese."

"You've grown fast, little lady. What has Mummy been feeding you?"

"Don't you know?" Lai Ying says. "She might have your hair, but she's got—"

"I know, your brains."

"Good boy, you're learning fast."

"I've had to, darling, living on my own."

"*Ban dan!*"

I haven't heard that for a long time. I laugh until Chacha squeezes my hand, and says people are staring. But I don't care if they are. At least there's no hostility in their eyes, only a harmless curiosity. I lift Chacha up and with my free arm squeeze Lai Ying until she pleads with me to let her breathe. I look into her eyes as I plant a gentle kiss on her lips. Her eyes are full of unspoken expectations, and regret, as if she has waited too long for this moment, too long for a kiss to matter. My heart sinks. But then she smiles, pinches my nose, and says we should go.

"It was like you didn't care, Dan," she says in a mournful voice as we sit on a bench in the park, watching people taking pictures. "You saw the things they pushed through the letterbox, under the door. But you were not at home to receive the phone calls. You didn't understand what was happening. You didn't listen to me."

The fear in her eyes is still there, as if she expects the loan sharks to crop up from behind the statues and monuments with buckets of sulfuric acid. I put an arm around her. How could I have so underestimated the likes of Chuck and the gang? The stories I've been reading in the papers, about constant harassment, people disfigured by acid, being attacked with choppers. Just thinking about it makes me shiver.

We wander around the park, taking pictures like every other tourist, chatting in Putonghua, like a regular Chinese family, recreating our past as a happy family, believing we're in Victoria Park in Hong Kong, planning where to eat in the evening. Just like we always did before. It would be easy to believe that everything's back to normal, or that nothing changed after all these months. Yet as Chacha chatters away excitedly about her friends at school, disabusing me of the notion that she has had a terrible time, the gulf between Lai Ying and I is taking much longer to bridge.

"You've lost weight, *lougong*." Lai Ying's voice slices through the thoughts racing through my head. She hasn't called me *lougong* for a long time. The voice is soft, tender, caring, only mildly admonishing.

"I've no time to cook, honey."

"So what do you live on – pizza and beer? That should make you put on weight, if anything."

Chacha snuggles up closer, her eyes trained on my face.

"Come and eat with us, Daddy. Je-je makes such nice dumplings."

"I'm sure the helper makes good dumplings. But I guess your mummy knows a place where they make even better ones."

Lai Ying smiles, with a mixture of embarrassment and fatigue. At least that's how it looks to me. Her auntie is not ready to sit down to eat with me. Though the three of us spend the days together, I end up going back to sleep at the Sweet Memories Hotel.

I hold my wife's hand and remind her about how we met. I don't think I've ever told our daughter this story. She needs to know. And this is as good a time as any. I tell Chacha about the chance meeting in the library. The test I was revising for, the inscrutable Chinese characters coming between me and advanced physics, and how a quiet, unassuming lovely lady came to my rescue. Chacha stares at us with a childlike innocent admiration that makes my heart glow with pleasure.

"It's going to be all right, Lai Ying," I whisper and kiss my wife's hand. "I understand your worries, but everything's changed. Soon we'll have a new flat, a new beginning. Please, tell me you're ready for it."

"Is this new flat nice? What kind of view do we have?"

I explain as much as I can about the new place in North Point. Lai Ying listens with apprehension. She would have wanted to be involved. She hates the thought of being herded to a flat she had no say in choosing. But it can't be helped. She didn't even respond to my emails about it. I fight the urge to remind her of this when the stern look in her eyes warns me that blaming her should be the last thing on my mind. I know she can tell from my tone of voice that if she wanted to be more involved in the decision, all she had to do was talk to me.

"I want to go back to Hong Kong," cries Chacha. "I want to see my friend Surdar. I want to go back to my school. Can we go back, Mummy?"

"Darling, there's no rush. We'll see."

"But what is there to see?" I struggle not to raise my voice. "There's no more trouble. This is a new beginning for us."

"Daddy, I'm afraid of those things. The bad men who did those things on the door."

"They've gone, darling. They're not there anymore."

"So, we can go back? I want to go back, Daddy. Can we go back? Please, Mummy, I want to go home."

"Not yet, darling. Daddy's going away on a trip."

"I'm only going for a few weeks. As soon as I come back, we'll be ready to start all over again, like a real family. You can come back then. I'll be ready for you."

"Where are you going, Daddy?"

"I'm taking some people to Africa. I wish I could take you, but I'm going to work."

"I want to go to Africa. Daddy, you promised." There's that look on her face, just like the one I last saw on little Siu Meng after our football practice. I lift Chacha and place her on my lap. Her eyes are filled with unspoken questions and doubts. I hold her tight and whisper in her ear.

"I know, and I'll keep my promise, baby girl. But this time, I'll be working. I won't have time to look after you or show you around. Next time, it's you, me, and Mummy. We'll have a proper holiday, darling."

"Can we go back to Hong Kong, Mummy, when Daddy returns from his trip?"

Lai Ying smiles, but remains silent. I know what she's thinking. *Daddy has to prove he's changed. We're not taking any chances on him just yet.*

After an early dinner, we visit the majestic Oriental Pearl TV Tower in Pudong. I had wanted to come here during the day, but Lai Ying said the sights are more breathtaking at night. The tower is an imposing structure. It looks like a futuristic, vertical crop circle with its blue and purple spheres held together by giant columns and slanting stanchions. Chacha holds my hand tightly as the double-decker lift shoots skywards, causing a collective gasp from the people whose faces are glued to the glass windows. The city below is a symphony of lights and colours.

From high up on the tower, the boats on Huangpu River look like toys drifting about in the calm waters, leaving behind a trail of froth in the water. The traffic on the roads looks like an infestation of tiny red-and-white ants crawling in hundreds of lines along the city. There is so much we could do up this tower if we lived in Shanghai. There are restaurants, shops, a space city and exhibition hall, recreational palace and sightseeing floor.

When Chacha has had her fill of the sights and delights, we take her home and go out for a drink. Chacha wants to come along but I explain that Mummy and I have to make plans for the future. She rolls her eyes, the way her mum does when she knows you're pulling the wool over her eyes but isn't bothered enough to protest.

We find a small pub at the Bund, where we can see the fascinating lights of the Tower and surrounding buildings. The lights hold a mystery and secrets that I'm hoping will be revealed tonight. Whatever happens, I've made up my mind that Lai Ying is not going back to her auntie's tonight.

"You're coming back to my hotel, honey. I need to spend a night with my wife. I've waited long enough, wouldn't you say?"

The tender, indulgent look in her eyes says she's come prepared to be a wife to her husband because she's prepared to consider forgiving him.

In her T-shirt and jean shorts, she looks just the way she did when we travelled together in the past, when we took weekend breaks to Thailand and Hainan.

If they ask us to show our marriage certificate, I don't know what we'll do. We have no luggage. We're just like a couple of lovers checking into a motel after a night out on the town. Our wedding rings aren't even inscribed with our names. Luckily, they match, two old-fashioned gold rings that no longer glitter like they once did.

The first thing Lai Ying asks when we're alone in the hotel is what exactly I'm going to do on this trip to Africa. I make some Chinese tea for her and get myself a beer. She sits on the bed, propped up against the pillows, holding one pillow protectively against her chest. I sit on the edge of the bed, watching her, trying to convince myself that she's finally back with me, that after all these months, we're back together, and everything is going to be just fine. But I sense our troubles aren't over yet. She might be here with me, but the past still looms between us like a mountain, obstinately, stopping us from reaching out to each other like we did in the past, when we dated in secret.

"I don't have a good feeling about this," she says. "Travelling with that man, Wang. I can't believe you're so blind and so forgetful, after what he did."

My heart sinks.

"I had a very frank discussion with Han Wei. Wang is clean. He had nothing to do with that incident."

"Han Wei would say that, wouldn't he? They're all working together. I wouldn't be surprised if Wang paid Han Wei to lie to the lot of you."

"But why would Wang do that? I'm not all that important to him, am I?"

"It's not just about what he wants from you, it's about face. You all abandoned his bar, and yet he had done so much to befriend you. When it became unfashionable, everyone else stopped going. And don't forget the students who tried to trash his bar a few years earlier, saying he had sold out, gone across to the other side, and become their enemy. Wang lost face, *lougong*. He felt betrayed, and he's not going to forget it that easily. You must be careful."

"I didn't abandon him. I worked for him till the end, till he shut Wang's Den. And *my* friends accused *me* of betrayal. If anything, I believe Wang owes me. You talk of face, darling. I believe I, too, lost face, don't you agree?"

"Anything you say. But I must warn you, Minnie and I talked."

"Did you?"

"Yeah. She helps run her husband's businesses, but she's not keen on it. She doesn't complain to him, because the guy is dying. I wouldn't be surprised if after he's dead she sells everything and goes to America. She's always dreamed of going there, living in a nice bungalow with a garden, where she can grow flowers and watch their son play basketball." She chuckles as she says this, as if she can't believe the naivety of Minnie's dream.

"What did she say?"

"That shop of theirs, that place that supposedly sells electronics, it's just one of many fronts for Wang and his friends. They set Han Wei up in business; he's smart, educated, and has connections in Shanghai. They're bringing in things into the country – cars, wines and spirits, electronics – just like before with the White Card, but this is on a much bigger scale, and they don't need foreign students now. They have politicians and party bureaucrats in their pockets."

"You're saying they're smugglers? Wang, Han Wei, the lot of them?"

"Minnie is afraid. Very afraid. If something happens, they could be in a lot of trouble. She hates this whole thing but can't persuade her husband to get out."

"Sounds familiar. A lot of wives don't like what their husbands do for a living."

"Don't find excuses," she says, frowning. "This is serious, Dan. She's a prisoner."

"But she enjoys the lifestyle, I guess. The things the money can buy."

"Believe me, it's her husband's poor health that keeps her here. Business is not everything. I should know."

"I know, darling. The troubles your family faced."

She goes quiet, and her face stiffens. Then she places her cup on the bedside table and closes her eyes as if to shut out the memories.

"They lost so much," she whispers. I have to lean closer to hear her. A whiff of shampoo fills my nose, making my heart swell with nostalgia. "My mother's family. Almost everything they had built. She never talks about the details, but I know. They had property in this city. Shops, factories. Gone. Ended up in the hands of rival families, people with connections, power. And my father. Taken away for so-called re-education. Five years in the countryside. Working like a slave. Starved almost to death. Betrayed by people he trusted, Dan."

I sit beside her and hold her hand, which feels cold and limp. She opens her eyes and looks at me with a half-smile.

"People don't talk about that period. Shame. Embarrassment."

Tears well up in her eyes. She sucks her lips in and takes a deep breath, struggling to control the sobs that rock her body. I hold her and dry her eyes.

"What does it matter now, *lougong*? It's all in the past."

Her head on my shoulder, we sit in silence for several minutes, listening to the buzzing of the air con and the occasional grunting noises coming from the fridge.

"Yeah, it's in the past," I whisper in her ear.

"But you never learn from the past, *ban dan*, do you?" She pinches my nose.

She has recovered her composure. Her voice has that accusing and disappointed edge again. This is the Lai Ying I'm accustomed to dealing with, though there's a new tenderness, a soft vulnerability in her manner that she kept tucked away before.

"I'll be careful, sweetheart. As long as I can see what's going on, and I'm not being asked to do anything illegal, I'll be fine. I'm just a tour guide. Let me do this trip. I'll come back with good money. God knows I need it. It's a great chance."

"You and your chances," she mutters. "It's like gambling, the way you make decisions."

"Lai Ying, you know so much about what's wrong with me, my poor judgment of people, my stupid business ideas. Yet you run away instead of staying with me and helping me stay out of trouble."

"Dan, you're a man. I expect you to take care of me and your daughter."

She stares at me with that look of frustrated despair she assumes when she's winning an argument. It's at times like this that I realise what a good business manager she would be if only she could agree to work with me. When I first started out, I wanted us to run the business together. She wouldn't hear of it. But she didn't mind working for other people. Her explanation was that she didn't have to care about other people's businesses, and she could always quit if it wasn't going her way.

"It's just that you always know what I should and shouldn't do. I really need you, sweetheart. But all you do is run away. How am I supposed to live if my own wife can't even bear to be with me? How do you think I feel when people ask me where you are, or when you and Chacha are coming back?"

"Why do you worry what other people say, Dan? It's none of their business."

"I don't mean strangers in the lift. I mean my friends, my family. It's their business, honey."

"You should have thought of that last year. Where were your friends and family then? What did they think about you then?"

"I was wrong, Lai Ying. Mother of my child, I swear to you, what you're talking about is all in the past. I've moved on. What shall I do to prove myself? Twelve years we've known each other, Lai Ying. I learnt my lesson. I'm a new person, sweetheart. Can't you sense it?"

I dim the light and start to massage her fingers, one by one, rubbing the palm and then her temple the way she once taught me to relieve her stress. Her perfume draws me toward her like a magnet. The feel of the smooth, silky texture of her hair on my fingers brings back memories and ignites a raging fire in me.

"I missed you, sweetheart."

"You made me angry. You always make me angry." There's no anger in her voice, only a deeply felt disappointment, a sense of having been let down once too often. In the dim light, her eyes look soft and subdued, as if they've been dimmed, too, and cleansed of their anxiety.

I draw her towards me. She tries to push my arm away, pretending to be angrier than she really is. We wrestle each other for a while. She goes through a process of trying to bite my hand to pinching my nose and calling me a very bad boy. It's just like the good old days. If she was really angry, she would go on and on about how I don't care about her feelings, and how stupid I am. Tonight I don't mind being a very bad boy.

It feels like we're on a date, making love for the first time, hesitantly, fumbling with the clothes, handling her with a deliberate tenderness as though it were her first time. In time, the hesitancy gives way to a maddening intensity

I've never before seen in her, the rhythmic upward thrusts of her hips synchronised with my frantic exertions, like a duet in perfect harmony, moans that build to a deafening crescendo. I hold her tight so there is no distance between us, so no one can ever come between us, not even Tiffany, whose surly face flashes through my mind, mocking and taunting, wrenching my heart with guilt.

We drift off to sleep in the silence that envelops the room, a silence that is strangely oblivious to the now subdued buzzing sound from the fridge and the air con.

It's as if the room itself is snoring, gently, without a worry in the world.

Lai Ying is up at the crack of dawn, so she can get ready for work. I watch her dress and do her make up, and it is as if I'm seeing who she really is for the first time. She and Chacha are all I have. All I'll ever need. Jupiter's words come back to haunt me. *Family is everything.*

But what about my mother's eagle, patiently waiting to pounce, or Wang's falcon, knowing just how to shatter the prey? Can there be any room for them any more in this ongoing tussle? I think of Wang and his shadow, crafting a life together for the sake of their son out of the adversity of their sexual incompatibilities, the shock splintering of Jupiter's family in spite of the wisdom he articulated so succinctly. Is the eagle's true wisdom buried somewhere in the midst of all this confusion?

Anxious not to see her leave just yet, I persuade Lai Ying to have the buffet breakfast with me in the lobby restaurant. There are only about half a dozen other people, all dressed in business suits. We have a little of everything, from bacon, fried sausages, and tomatoes on a bed of scrambled eggs to rice congee with salted duck eggs and slices of bamboo shoots. It feels like lunch, which suits me fine because I don't know when I'll next have a proper meal. As we share a plate of fruits, not bothering to find out if there are any inauspicious pears on it, I take Lai Ying's hand and tell her I'll be waiting for her and Chacha when I return from Zimbabwe.

She pinches my nose and makes faces, as if she's playing with a child. My rehabilitation is almost complete. But it's not yet time to celebrate. Yet the urge to test the waters and build on this momentum is irresistible. I lean forward and whisper, "One more thing, sweetheart. It's not nice for Chacha to grow up all by herself."

"What!" A hand flies to her mouth. "She's already grown up, Dan."

311

"You know what I mean. Please, think about it, all right?"

She shakes her head. "Not now. I need time."

I inhale the sweet jasmine flavours of my tea, watching her, wondering what I must do to earn her trust again.

"When are your parents next in town?" I ask her.

"Chinese New Year," she says, eyebrows raised. "Why?"

"I'll meet them. We'll surprise them, darling. We can't go on like this."

She places her hands on my face, and looks at me the way she looked at baby Chacha when she learned to say "mama".

Before I leave Shanghai, I call Han Wei to thank him. It feels weird talking to him like this. The past is behind us now. He keeps coughing and can barely talk. I tell him to take care. His reply is drowned by a coughing fit.

Part 4

So Long a Wait

I CAN'T HELP FEELING I'VE left Shanghai too soon. There's an email from Wang saying they're coming to Hong Kong today and will stay at the Hyatt. He tried to call me but couldn't reach me. We're booked to leave on Friday evening. I spend two days shopping for gifts, packing, and completing some pending jobs, and also showing my guests around Hong Kong. In between visiting clients, I squeeze in visits to the delights and amusements of Ocean Park, where my guests spend a pleasant afternoon watching dancing dolphins and sleeping pandas, the obligatory tram ride to the Peak, where our hopes for panoramic views of the territory are hampered by pollution-induced haze, and have an overpriced lunch at a sea-food restaurant in Sai Kung. They scoff at my naïve suggestion of a trip to the cheap shopping areas of Temple Street and the backstreets of Mong Kok, but my suggestion of a visit to a nightclub in Tsim Sha Tsui East goes down very well. It turns out to be an almost exact replica of our notorious Shenzhen nights, complete with the excesses of gourmet dining, vintage whisky, loud music, and scantily clad hostesses.

I get back home every night long after midnight, exhausted, and fall asleep as soon as I collapse in bed. I try to reach Alex but his office says he's out of town. It's just as well. I'm not sure how to ask him the question that has been troubling me since that discussion with Han Wei. Diallo refuses to come out and meet Wang for a drink. He says he'll pray for me. I've never heard him talk of praying before.

When we go to get the tickets, Wang turns to me and says, "You'll of course, be anxious to spend some time with your family, so here's a suggestion. When we get to Zimbabwe, we'll go straight to business. You can spend a few days with your people first and join us later."

"That suits me."

"All right. The three of us will stop in South Africa for a few days. You go ahead, and meet us in Harare on Wednesday evening."

I check my voicemail just before boarding the South African Airlines flight. Two clients want to schedule a visit. The third message is from Alex. He says I should call him right away. There's an unusual urgency to his voice. When I try his number, all I get is voicemail. I leave him a message asking him to contact me by email. The business class queue moves fast. What on earth does Alex want to talk about so urgently? It can't be helped. He'll have to wait.

We part ways at Johannesburg International Airport. Liu Ming says he's keen to see what the Chinese are doing in this city. The travel agent has set up a detailed itinerary for them, which is just as well, as I've no idea what to recommend. I've never visited this country before. Perhaps on the way back, we can stop here and I can spend a day visiting the city.

I travel onwards by myself to Harare after waiting three hours for my connecting flight. My phone is not going to work here. Luckily, Chip is waiting for me at the airport. He has lost weight and looks ten years older than he is. The furrows on his head have multiplied since I last saw him. His eyes look sunken, like those of a starving man in mourning. He's wearing a dark-blue suit that is a couple of sizes too big for him. The coat hangs loosely over the stooped shoulders. It is unlikely it's the coat that has expanded.

"This is what the life of struggle here does to you," he explains when I ask about the washed-out look. "This crappy job I have with the government pays peanuts. I have to hassle like mad just to make ends meet. We all do, but we're going nowhere fast. And the way things are going, we're looking disaster in the face, Dan. Food shortages are just around the corner. Fuel shortages have started to bite. Nothing works any more. It doesn't look good."

He leads me to the taxi rank, where we hire a ramshackle taxi. He spends five minutes negotiating the fare.

"My car hasn't been on the road for months," he explains. "Crank shaft is gone and there are no spare parts."

This sense of despondency is everywhere. It's in the hungry looks, the weary eyes that have given up hoping, the arms hanging dejectedly by the sides, the shuffling feet heading nowhere, the hordes of hawkers selling an assortment of curios, trinkets, and souvenirs on every street, the high inflation and the wads of currency that was devalued again last month and whose value shrinks by the day. It's in the jaded queues snaking their way out of shops and onto the dusty pavements, like the queues I saw in Nanjing as a student whenever there was a rumour that some state department had released supplies of cloth or cooking oil.

It's in the two dozen cars waiting for limited, rationed supplies of petrol at a gas station, the drivers dozing off in the heat. This is not the country I remember from my last visit. So much has changed for the worse. There's such a sense of loss everywhere it's like coming to a funeral. The soul of the country is dead or dying. I remember the girl many years ago who wanted me to marry her and bring her to what she called my heavenly country. I swallow hard to clear a lump in my throat and end up with a coughing fit, blinded by tears.

"I know how it must look to you," says Chip, slapping my back. "The US dollar now fetches 50 to 70 Zim dollars, depending on where you change it. It's hard to believe that just two years ago, it was only 24, man. It's this meaningless war in the Congo that we're funding and yet can't really afford to. So they just keep printing money. It's not going to get any better so long as Mugabe's in power, believe you me."

In spite of all this surface gloom, the streets themselves have lost none of their old warmth and buzz. The jacaranda- and gum-tree-lined avenues of Harare are as green and alive as ever. The old, colonial, historic buildings stand proud and majestic in spite of the peeling paint and gaping cracks on the walls, unscathed by the political conflagration that is consuming the entire country and pitting wealthy landowners against penniless war veterans and politically connected investors. The Mining Pension Fund Building on Central Avenue is just as stately as I remember it. Driving down wide thoroughfares like Robert Mugabe Road, Nelson Mandela Avenue, and Julius Nyerere Way and seeing the Shona soft-stone carvings being peddled by street hawkers reminds me of the famous collection we visited on school trips to the National Gallery.

"And where is it all headed, Chip? What's going to happen?"

"Look, this had to happen some day; the land had to revert to the people. But it's not going well. The ordinary people, including the innocent farmworkers, are paying the price. I sent word to your family through a friend. I hope they got it; otherwise, they'll think you're a ghost when you show up unannounced. Are you tired, man? Jet lag? Do you want to rest for a while and head home tomorrow?"

I see no reason to hang around the city longer than necessary.

"I only have about four days to spend with my family. My guys will be in town on Wednesday evening."

We head straight to the bus terminal. There are so few buses with engines running you can smell the scent of eucalyptus trees that line the avenue that leads to the terminal. A wheel-less van balanced on rocks and three buses sit morosely side-by-side, waiting for spare parts and repairs. There's a lot of uncertainty and frequently changing information about what routes are available. It takes us two hours to secure tickets and seats, after a lot of jousting and to-ing and fro-ing. I fall asleep as soon as I get on the coach, succumbing to jet lag.

We arrive in Mashonaland Central late in the evening, just as the sun begins to set over the hills in the horizon. The coach chugs down the highway past trees and shrubs that have turned brown and lifeless and are desperate for the rains to restore them to their natural luxuriant green.

An hour into our journey, we stop at a roadblock.

"Foot-and-mouth checkpoint," explains Chip.

The roadblock is manned by four soldiers roasting mealie cobs by the side of the road. The smell rises through the air, reminding me how I've missed this delicious staple. One of the soldiers marches into the coach, inspects our faces closely, his rifle at the ready, cigarette dangling from his lips. A large scar runs down his left cheek. Another stands guard at the door, gnawing furiously at a mealie cob. The other two walk around the vehicle, perhaps checking to see if any cows are strapped to its sides.

"Cattle, anyone?" Thunders the scarred soldier, blowing smoke in an old man's face. "Cattle? Remember it's an offence to move cattle without a permit."

Silence. After pacing up and down the aisle several times, he jumps off the coach and waves us on. Passengers exchange bemused yet haggard glances.

The district is just as I had feared, chaos and gloom, as is Guruwe town, where we change to a local minibus. Every now and then along the way, we encounter fires burning out of control in the countryside.

"It's the so-called war vets," says Chip, in a whisper, after glancing around to ensure no one is listening. "When our supposed leaders realised they were losing control and popularity, they mobilised these gangs to take over white farms. I'm sure you know all about that anyway."

"And the genuine landless? I mean, my father, for instance…?"

"It's more complicated than you think. All you get out there is mere propaganda. Of course, your father is landless, a farmworker, like many others. But what made these guys decide to take over the farms all of a sudden?"

"This is what they always wanted, Chip. To be masters of their own destiny, to own the land they tilled, right?"

"What you don't realise is that most of these guys have no such desire. They've no idea how to run a one-thousand-acre farm themselves. They've literally been hijacked by gangs of unemployed, urban hoodlums. Of course, genuine war vets exist, but who in his right mind would set fire to farms, burning crops, destroying the very country they risked their lives fighting for?"

"Some secret force?"

"Politics, man. Bribe the poor, promise them heaven on earth so they can vote ZANU-PF. Opposition areas that dare resist are simply torched. Having the support of white farmers doesn't do them any favours. Man, they bussed these hoodlums from Harare, promised them money to manage the farms, but when they didn't deliver, these thugs went on rampage."

"Dreadful."

"It gets worse, man. The world out there thinks it's just white farmers being targeted. No way. Black farmers who support the opposition have been slaughtered, and no one says anything about it. Our own people, man!"

I swallow the lump in my throat and struggle to digest Chip's words. Is Chip implying my father and many like him have been hoodwinked?

"Your father, whom I greatly admire and respect and have always considered my favourite uncle, is a man consumed by unbridled and misguided political passion. You'll see him. He's a leader. But I've no idea where he's leading the people to, frankly."

My heart sinks lower as we drive past another raging fire. You would think the farmers were clearing the land and preparing it for planting if it wasn't for the fact that the fires were right in the middle of wheat and tobacco crop. At this rate, this land will be worthless. And there'll be no food to eat.

"Now I see where Wang is coming from. If you take a long-term view and buy now, years down the line, when things go back to normal, you'll be laughing all the way to the bank."

"Question is, when will things go back to normal?"

"Hence the protracted view, Chip."

"But you must also factor in the uncertainty of ownership. You buy now from a fleeing farmer; how do you ensure the gangs won't come after you?"

"This is where your political contacts come in."

He doesn't look convinced, which makes me wonder whether there's any point to all this. "Do you honestly see this whole Chinese thing working, Dan?"

"From what you're saying, and from what I've seen so far, I'm not sure any more. But perhaps that's why I'll never be rich. The difference between me and these Chinese blokes is that they're not likely to be put off by all the negatives. To them, it's simply a business opportunity that requires a calculated risk."

"Come on, Dan," he says, frowning, affecting disappointment. "Are you saying you don't have it in you?"

"I'm saying maybe I can't deal with this level of risk. I'm a businessman, too, you know. Anyway we'll see what they have to say next week. Frankly I don't think they're all that keen on the actual farming right now. It's more about speculating on the land, and selling on in better times. But of course, there's the tobacco. They'll take their chances and grow tobacco for the Chinese smokers, of which there are hundreds of millions."

Chip purses his lips for a moment, thinking, trying to put himself in the shoes of the businessmen. Then he asks, "So how does it work out, this tobacco business in China? Do they grow tobacco?"

I recall my discussions with Wang.

"Millions of tonnes of it. But it's all very centralised, very tightly controlled, the production, distribution and everything, all through the state. Which means if you can bypass the bureaucracy and sneak in your own, much cheaper supplies, you could make a fortune."

"You mean, like…smuggling?"

"That's probably what they're planning, knowing the way they operate. I must warn you, they have a bit of a reputation."

"What exactly?"

"From what I gather, smuggling, corruption, and what have you."

"So what's new?"

"You don't mind?"

"I'm not smuggling with them, or bribing anyone, am I?"

"Okay. So long as you know what—"

"Dan, I've seen more corruption than you can ever imagine. I'm a government lawyer."

"Oh, I'm sure. Look, my wife didn't want me to do this. But I need the cash."

"Don't we all? Hang on to those guys, Danny boy," he says in a coarse whisper. "You could be looking at being set for life, my man."

He makes it sound so easy. He doesn't know the half of it.

Farmer Walter and his family have long gone, and the old manor house is now occupied by a local politician. No one knows where the Walters went to. The war vets can't be bothered. They never knew the family. Some of the farmworkers share their view. Others talk fondly about the family they worked for all their lives, about how the couple cared for them as though they were their own children, even though most of them are much older than Walter and his missus. They talk about the beautiful blonde Rachel and how she grew into a lovely young lady, whom they haven't seen for years ever since she went to university in England, and the young Edward, who used to creep up on them in the farm, frightening them out of their wits by running around firing an air gun, and then they would all collapse with laughter and tell their children in the evening, as if it was all a big adventure. They reminisce with nostalgia about how the two children used to race their bicycles and horses around the farm, screaming their little heads off and sending the workers scampering for cover in the tobacco plantation. It was all so much fun. Now it's all over, they moan, and they have no idea what to make of the new breed of would-be farmers who have invaded the entire countryside.

The one thing that troubles me as soon as we walk into the estate in Ndambu is that there's little evidence of any farming except for some small-scale cultivation of crops for their own use, mealie, cabbages, carrots. The tobacco crop is drying and withering. The farm equipment lies disused and rusting.

None of this gloom takes away the joy of meeting my people, and the three days I spend with them are full of bliss and happiness. My brother has recently moved to South Africa in search of work. No one is sure what he's doing. My sister lives in Mutare, on the border with Mozambique, where she has a clerical job in a school. There's only Father and Mother here.

My father has changed. He has acquired a confidence and aura of leadership I never knew he had. The rest of the workers look up to him. They gaze at him when he speaks, like some sort of messiah. They speak in awed tones about him, as if afraid he'll hear their whispers and set the dogs on them.

I approach Mother with some measure of trepidation, wondering what she expects of a son who chose to live far away from his people, fearing she long gave up on me on discovering I wasn't the eagle she dreamed of. I find it hard to face her, even though she knows nothing of my failures and decadent lifestyle that nearly cost me my family, hoping the modest remittances I send her have at least earned me some reprieve, for redemption is too much to hope for. Even now after so many years, it still amazes me how easily she communicates her acceptance with an indulgent silence, as though she's convinced I could do no wrong, and if I did, I would still be her beloved son. I want so badly to teach that to Chacha. The image of the eagle struggling with an oversized fish fills my mind. And the look on Mother's face at the time, taut, focused, unblinking, as though she lived the eagle's zeal and determination, and in that instant saw her son's destiny. I look into her eyes now, set amidst weary shadows, drained of the light that once shone with unspoken expectations. And now I know. She just wanted her son to excel. But my own fears drove me to the edge.

Looking at her, it is difficult to fathom the depths of her worries and disappointments, the dreams that never came true for her, the current troubles that threaten to diminish her motherly satisfaction of raising three children to adulthood. She has aged. She has a perpetual haggard and weary look about her, and goes about her chores with a mechanical sense of duty devoid of the old warmth. She, like most other women in the community, has borne the brunt of the repercussions of the political upheaval, struggling to put food on the table, while the men constantly whip themselves up to an activist frenzy and celebrate the hollow freedom of being masters of their destiny.

Mother meant no harm. How could she? How can I make her understand I wronged her in my heart without hurting her now? The words come to me with a hesitance only matched by their futility, for Mother requires no explanation. When I start to tell her how hard I've worked so she and Father can be proud of me, she tells me our lives are meant to be a struggle, so we can be better people. Her tone speaks of a pain I'll never know, and simply makes me ashamed of my own self-indulgences.

Her face only lights up with joy when I tell her about her granddaughter. She studies the photographs closely. She can spot the resemblances, and can't stop marvelling at Chacha's long, curly hair, tender eyes, and chubby cheeks.

"Although her mother is a foreigner," she coos, "you can see this is our own little girl. Everything about her is the Chiponda clan. That sweet little round nose presiding over the upturned lip, and those bright eyes with a look of surprise about the edges – it's everyone from your grandmother to your cousin who married some fellow from Namibia."

"That's true, Mother. But Chacha's not really a little girl. She's a big girl now."

I wish I had brought some recent pictures. We'll have to wait until Lai Ying develops the ones we took in Shanghai. I do my best to explain how Chacha has changed since those pictures I sent almost a year ago. That's the easy part. Explaining that they're now in China with Lai Ying's people creates a lump in my throat. Mother doesn't ask why, but I know she fears the worst as she runs a wrinkly finger along the picture, as though she were caressing Chacha. I take simple comfort in the implicit knowledge that she understands that whatever transgression might have divided us was unavoidable but would in time heal. But she's not smiling now. She says, "Maybe in China it is like here, too, for the little one, and her mother."

"How do you mean, Mother?"

"I'm not one to moan, son, and God forgive my ungrateful heart, but you're saying they are alone, without you? It is like when our men were away fighting. Or the mothers left behind when the men toil in the city, never knowing what their little ones are eating."

My shame overwhelms me. Where would I begin? How can I say everything is all right without explaining why it wasn't before? Mother comes to my rescue by asking, "And when is this little princess going to come and spend some time with her people in our ridge?"

"Soon, Mother, soon. We'll start planning it as soon as I get back. But I'm worried about this place, it doesn't look safe enough."

"Don't let all this madness worry you, my son. We wake up every morning and find the day waiting for us. Why shouldn't it wait for Chacha? Listen to what they say on the radio. It is those who are jealous of our freedom that are spreading foolish stories about us. They don't want to see us happy."

Mother and I never discussed politics before. In fact, I cannot remember her discussing politics at all. She left such matters to Father, saying these were the ways of men. I warn her not to believe everything she hears on the radio.

"We believe what we know in our hearts," she says. "Even if the day starts cloudy and stays foggy so you can barely see where you're going, eventually it clears. That's what your father reminds the workers."

"The days are too foggy, Mother. To be honest, I can't see where we're going."

"I know your fear," says Mother in a tremulous voice, for the first time betraying her own doubts. "Sometimes it's so dark. All this tension, high food prices, shortages. And the families scattered about like pieces of a broken clay pot. Where will it end?"

I find Mother's doubts unsettling, now that I realise the earlier confidence was just her way of reassuring me. Her voice cuts through my thoughts. "Tell the little one we are safe, my son. We will always be safe. But remember, son, let me not hear talk of your coming back when everyone else is leaving. Bring your family to see us, but chase your dream where you can. I'm glad you didn't study to be a farmer after all. This kind of life is not for you. You have eaten book well."

"Yes, Mother," I murmur in reply, reluctantly fighting off the silence that my own doubts and trepidation dictate.

Mother's words warm my heart. Years ago before I left Nanjing, when I argued with Father about returning home, I never found out what Mother thought. Later when I came to visit, the issue was long forgotten. Mother didn't raise it, and neither did Father, though I always felt he had not quite forgiven me for going against his wishes.

I know Mother is right. There's nothing for me to do here. As for bringing Chacha to visit, much as I've yearned to do it all these years, I dare not tell Mother I'm not bringing my daughter here until peace returns to this land. How would I explain to my little girl these ghoulish fires, and the war cries and gunshots in the night as rival gangs engage each other? This is not the Africa I've painted for her ever since she was born. The lovely green countryside, the pure air filled with the scent of pine and orchards, and the clear blue skies all pale in comparison to the noises of violence and mayhem, the threat of famine and fuel shortages. The pride that glowed in my heart every time I spoke to Chacha about the beauty of the temperate climate in the high veld and the serene lakes and sleepy mountains gives way to a fear that it will take a miracle to heal this destruction.

Before I set off back to Harare, I draw Father aside for a heart-to-heart talk and beckon Chip to join us. We take a walk around the charred farm, inspecting the damage. In the distance, a section of the tobacco crop is on fire, filling the air with the smell of a million cigarettes. It's nauseating, and impossible to ignore. I ask Father what is the point of all these fires.

"Temporary madness," he says, waving a hand dismissively. "Things will soon get back to normal."

Chip tries to hide a sigh of disbelief with a yawn.

"But who is doing the burning, and why?" I ask. "I really need to know because I can't understand how destroying a farm helps anyone. What will people eat?"

"There has been a lot of confusion, my son. Many people don't quite understand how to handle the changes. People from the city, like your cousin here, think we're old and stupid."

"No, uncle," protests Chip. "I just want peace in this country. But it's very confusing what's happening."

"Can you imagine how much more confusing it is for those of us abroad?"

"It's not easy for anyone," says Father, in a stentorian voice more suited to issuing orders to recalcitrant workers. "I have a tough task, as leader, holding things together here. For some years now, I've been a supervisor, reporting directly to the farm manager. He's gone now, the poor chap, scared out of his wits. He was a slave to the white man. The workers chased him away. Now they don't want to do any work. They resent the fact that the farm has been taken over by war vets. I have to struggle to convince them that we can all work together. But without trust, nothing happens."

"I was really hoping that all those disturbing reports I was hearing are false, that things have truly changed for the better. After waiting so many years."

"We're getting there, my son." There's little conviction in Father's voice. "Every revolution goes through pain. It's the way it is. We fought long and hard to free this country, endured the pain of the struggle from the first *chimurenga* a hundred years ago, when we fought British colonial rule, then the second *chimurenga* against Ian Smith, and we suffered, we shed blood, but it was well worth it. People are saying this is the third *chimurenga*, the struggle for the farmland. There'll be suffering, then things will get better. I worry about your mother; she's losing her faith. But as leader, I must remain strong, for her, for the families here."

Now it begins to make sense. "Was this the right way, Father?"

He shoots a condemning glance at me, as if he can't believe I'm not on his side. His face is a mask of proud determination, like a man whose destiny is finally within his grasp, and nothing will stop him now. Although Father himself never took up arms against the Smith regime, he has paid the price. He endured the harassment in the seventies, the discrimination, and, on one or two occasions, the arrest and beating up for joining protest marches. All his life, he has worked on the land he loved so much, hoping that one day he would reap where he sowed for his own people, on his own land.

He turns to Chip for support. Chip's gaze is fixed stubbornly ahead, at the smoke that has completely obscured the setting sun.

"Do you know how long we've waited for this chance to own land?"

"I know, Father. You talked about it all the time."

"So why the doubt now? Can't you see we're about to get real freedom in this country? That Walter fellow is lucky he complied when ordered to leave. Others have tried to resist and faced the consequences."

"I have a friend in Hong Kong. Alex. His family lost their farm."

Speaking of Alex reminds me that he was trying to reach me. I can't get a signal on my phone here. It will have to wait until I get back to Harare and find some Internet café. I try to push it out of my mind but it looms large in my subconscious, like a police siren screaming out on the streets, fading every now and then behind tall buildings, then re-emerging as the wind changes direction, refusing to be ignored.

"It's a strange world we live in, son. Your friend's family, they were lords and masters in a land in which they're in fact guests. Now the true owners have a chance to own their land. It's the way it goes." He takes a deep breath, as if bringing the matter to a close. Then he adds, as an afterthought, perhaps hoping to reassure me, "You and this Alex, you'll remain friends. You're the new generation. Don't let the politics of your fathers come between you."

"It's not that easy, Father, because it's all tied to Mugabe's politics, too. When I think about this, I wonder where does ZANU-PF end and where does this hunger for land begin, Father?"

"That's a good point," says Chip, in a low whisper. "Remember the parliamentary elections just three months ago? Such a mess. And now we have the presidential election coming up."

"If you're saying we've been bought, you're mistaken. It's more like a coincidence, actually." Father starts to laugh, and stops to roll up a cigarette with raw, dried tobacco. This is one of the advantages of living on a tobacco farm. You never need to buy cigarettes. "We were going to take over the land one way or another. It has been discussed on and off for years now. Our plans for a cooperative didn't go far. Now this chance is upon us. Mugabe himself has spoken for many years, but backed down when foreign governments put pressure on him. He has now decided to show his true colours, and his support is coming just at the right time. It was long overdue, twenty years, to be exact. People say we're being bribed, that all this is just politics to destroy the opposition MDC. Nonsense, I say! People like Brian Walter believed they occupied land that belonged to no one; empty space. Nonsense! Can you go to that China of yours or England and carve out vacant land for yourself, just because no one is living there? That's when you'll discover how quickly you can end up in jail. Just because this is Africa, they think they can treat us like fools. Our time has come."

Father's eyes shine with a grim resoluteness. He smokes furiously, waving his hands about. "This is our land, my dear sons. Let the foreign devils return to their country."

Startled, I look up at the uncompromising, stern expression on Father's sweat-drenched face.

"Foreign devils?"

"Away with them!"

"You know, Father, that's exactly what the Chinese call us. Black devils, white devils. Black ghosts. It seems this world is full of ghosts and devils."

"Do not make jokes about this, my son. This is serious."

We walk back to the workers' camp. There's little to see. I have no wish to get any closer to the burning tobacco. This is the farm I grew up on. It was a beautiful place back then, green rolling hills in the shadow of the mountains to the east and north near the border with Mozambique. Now even the trees we climbed as children have been cut down for firewood, and the whole countryside looks bare, denuded of its serenity and ravaged like a disease by these fires that fill the entire sky with this obscene billowing black smoke.

"I wonder what uncle thinks about your friends," says Chip, after a few moments have passed, and calm returns to Father's face. "The Chinese."

"What Chinese?"

"It's a long story, Father."

From the look of suspicion on his face, this is obviously not the right time to bring this up. I silently curse Chip.

"I have some Chinese businessmen who are interested in buying farms – that is, if there are any farms for sale to...foreigners."

"Foreign devils?" says Chip, suppressing a laugh.

"Are you treating this whole thing like a joke?" demands Father, lighting another roll-up.

"No, Father. These Chinese are quite serious. And to be honest, since no one is doing any work here, perhaps this country needs them. You should see the Chinese at work. They're very diligent, very focused."

"So they want to buy land?" Father has a faraway look in his eyes.

"I need your advice."

Father puffs away thoughtfully as we walk along in silence, past the manor house, which is guarded by armed men in police uniform. The grazing field is deserted and is overrun with bushes and weeds. Parts of it bear the black scars of old fires.

"What happened to all the cattle, Father?"

"The cattle? It's a shame. It couldn't be helped. The war vets needed the land to build their huts, so they asked Walter to take away the cows. He refused, saying he couldn't move them because of the foot-and-mouth outbreak. They didn't want to argue. They set the place on fire, and Walter had to drive his animals away."

There's an unmistakable tinge of regret in Father's voice. He understood the cattle, he knew them well, as though they were his. In fact, there were times you would have thought he treated them as part of his extended family.

"When I was a child, I remember you knew them by their names, Father."

He looks away and walks stiffly, looking straight ahead. When we get to the house at the workers' camp, he waves us away and starts to walk in the opposite direction. Then he calls out, "Tell your Chinese they can come and talk to us. People here need every penny they can lay their hands on."

Father can't stand the idleness; it's like an illness he can't shake off. He has known nothing but work and struggle all his life. Now, with literally nothing to do, he looks like a man wandering through the wilderness, gradually coming to the realisation that he's totally lost but is too embarrassed to admit it.

When I ask Chip what he thinks, he says, "It's not that I have reservations about working with the old man, but I can't see it working, man. For me, it's important to look beyond the current screwed-up regime. When Mugabe's no longer in power, everything that has happened will be reversed, even if it takes decades. Look what's happening in Uganda. Amin chased the Indians away in the seventies. The Museveni government has been welcoming them back, man, two, three decades later. Some of them have even got their old businesses back, the ones that were handed out to Amin's cronies. So where does that leave you if you're deemed to be occupying land acquired illegally?"

"They're passing laws to make it all legitimate, aren't they?"

"Laws can be challenged, and repealed. Your investment, if that's what it is, might not have appreciated sufficiently for you to cash in by the time the changes come. But as you're saying, maybe the Chinese are prepared to take that risk."

"As I said before, that's why we need high-level contacts."

"General Josh Chuma, that's our main man."

"A general, yeah? You're not doing things by half, are you?"

"We're going the whole hog, man." The expression on Chip's face has an uncanny resemblance to Father's. And his eyes shine with anticipation, just like Father's. He grabs hold of my shoulders and stares deep into my eyes, saying, "This is the best break we'll ever get, Danny boy. Your old man has waited long for this land. You and I have no use for land. What the hell would we do with it? We've waited for opportunity. That's what we're just about to get now. It has been a long wait, man."

"Yeah, like an eagle waiting to zoom down on its prey. I know."

"What are you on about?"

I shrug my shoulders.

We walk in silence, watching children playing football in what used to be a cowpen. I calmly inform Chip that Wang will be covering his expenses and a decent lawyer's fee.

His face breaks into a grin that says, *now we're talking.*

A Pretty Tight Deal

WEDNESDAY AFTERNOON SEES US IN Harare. First, we drop my luggage off at the Crowne Plaza Hotel on Park Lane. Chip's mouth hangs open with a mixture of admiration and disbelief as our taxi pulls up at the majestic entrance to the hotel. The uniformed, fawning lackeys, the marble floor, the chrome, glass and wood panelling, the potted plants and life-sized stuffed animals, the crystal chandeliers hanging at least two metres down in the three-storey-high lobby with the red-and-white, diamond-shaped design all conspire to promise grandeur and luxury on a scale unimaginable in the despondent streets outside.

"You're staying in style, man. This puts my small flat in the suburbs to shame."

"Courtesy of the Chinese, Chipo man. Do you imagine I could afford to live here? They've booked us in here for a couple of weeks. So this is my base, when you need to reach me."

My room on the twelfth floor is the size of a normal flat in Hong Kong, made to feel even more spacious by the gleaming mirrors on the walls. A bed that could easily fit in a family of four, propped up with a dozen pillows and embroidered cushions, is separated from what looks like a mini-living room. The luxury surpasses anything I've seen in China and Macau, where I stayed at three-star hotels on business trips. Chip is so completely mesmerised he has lost his voice.

I have a breath-taking view of Harare's Central Park, the Harare Gardens. The luxuriant greenery stretches for miles. You can spot courting couples sauntering hand in hand and families picnicking in the beautiful, manicured lawns. It looks so peaceful, and such a far cry from the fires and mayhem in the countryside, it is almost like being in another country. I can't wait to take a walk there myself, or perhaps go for a run tomorrow morning. It will be wonderful to jog in this low humidity air, which, after coming from Hong Kong, is like walking out of a tiny sauna room and straight into an air-conditioned hall.

As we attack the Zambezi beer in my room, I ask Chip to tell me about this Josh Chuma we're supposed to meet tomorrow. It turns out that he is a retired army general and now a prominent businessman and top ZANU-PF man. He's a behind-the-scenes operative who has been associated with some of the murkier dealings of this government for years.

"To get hold of this bloke," says Chip, "I talked to a former lecturer of mine who is now a judge," he says. "He in turn talked to a politician and God knows who else. When people smell money, they come out of the woodwork faster than you can say Chinese delegation. What I know is that there are definitely these three waiting to rock and roll. The only person who has time to meet us, at least for now, is this General Chuma. The other two opted to remain behind the scenes. It doesn't matter, so long as they're in, pulling the strings, getting things done. I must explain something: Chuma is a bit of a character. There's no proof, it's all hearsay, but he's supposed to have been knee-deep in the Matabeleland troubles in the eighties, you remember…"

"What! A war criminal!"

"Relax, Dan, you and I know it was basically an undeclared civil war. Word is he was with the notorious Fifth Brigade."

"Jesus Christ!"

"You know the story, man. They're linked to the deaths of at least ten thousand. As I said, there's no proof…"

"Hold on, man, what kind of people are you involving me with, Chipo?"

"Easy, man. It's all hearsay. The facts are, Chuma was handsomely rewarded for supposedly helping stabilise the situation, as they say. He's swimming in money. Seaside villas in Cape Town. Kids in finishing schools in Switzerland followed by college in the States, tobacco farms and vineyards in Marondera. Incidentally that's where we're meeting him tomorrow. He has a second farm with a private zoo in Hwange, that sort of thing. He lives the life of the white settler, the life we would all love to sample, just for a little while, at least."

"So why would he need my Chinese?"

"Show me one man who swears he has enough money, Dan. I thought you lived in Hong Kong, where money rules? I bet Chuma's right now thinking how he can use your Chinese, knowing they'll use him if they have half a chance. I've explained that the Chinese are bringing money in, and they need partners. Look at the Zim dollars in your wallet. They're not worth the paper they're printed on, and that's a fact. Everyone's desperate for some hard currency. For Chuma, it's more than that. The man sees a chance to go global. He's not stupid. He knows it's only a matter of time before the West starts imposing economic sanctions and travel bans. They're just waiting to see if our African neighbours will take the lead. The Commonwealth is already making noises about expelling Zim. If that happens, where does it leave the local tycoons with their sacks of worthless Zim dollars? Chuma knows that as soon as there's a new, democratic regime, he and many others could be charged for their involvement in Matabeleland, and I personally don't rule out genocide. The general needs an exit clause. That's what the Chinese partners offer. So, his assets get some protection that way. No future government will want to alienate the much-vaunted foreign investors."

"It sounds pretty neat."

"It gets better, Dan. I can bet my last dollar that the general will not disclose the true value of the farms and mines he's selling, and that he's not going to reveal the true identities of his fellow local partners to the Chinese. All the Chinese will be told is that they're dealing with top-level contacts."

"That should keep them happy enough. That's the way they themselves operate."

"Sure, but that's neither here nor there, Dan. Thing is, if we can broker a deal, man, we're set."

Chip has a stern, uncompromising look on his face. He reminds me of Wang's associate, Yu Shian, the ex-cop who wears his mean, law-enforcement expression like a permanent mask. He has changed. When we were in high school, we used to call him Chipish, a wordplay on sheepish. He was shy and unassuming, prone to being bullied. With the slightly bloodshot eyes and the lips parted in a somewhat mocking smile, there's more wolf than sheep about my cousin. I ask him, "So we have to deal with war criminals in order to make money?"

"Don't go all soft on me, Danny boy. Are you in or not? You've come this far, man. It's too late to chicken out. I've taken two weeks' leave for this. Have you any idea what I've had to do to put this deal together? Do you know what it has cost me to keep people happy and to keep this General Chuma on tenterhooks?"

Chip looks livid, struggling to control his temper, his eyes redder than ever.

"You're saying these are the best contacts we can get?"

"Why go to war with a kitchen knife when a missile launcher's at your disposal? Whatever else these guys do, they're serious about business. I've waited for this opportunity all my life, man. Nothing is stopping us now. We'll put this deal together, get paid a pretty decent fee, and you know what? After this, I'm ready to start afresh. South Africa. Namibia. It's not safe doing business here, man. You've heard about the attacks on foreign businesses?" I nod my head. "NGOs, Western firms, South African – anyone who is deemed to be supporting the opposition, though the only way they figure that out is if anyone makes any sort of complaint against the government. Even the diplomats are now receiving threats, being branded economic saboteurs and blamed for everything. A minister has baptised them foreign devils." He laughs as he gets up to fetch some more beers from the fridge.

"Oh! So that's where it came from?"

"What?"

"My father used that expression, remember?"

"Must have heard it on the radio. That's the new term for foreigners who criticise the regime. Gangs are going around attacking foreign firms, extorting money, claiming they're settling labour disputes to protect exploited workers." He lets out another peal of laughter. "It makes you wonder who's doing the exploiting, man."

I need to check email before we head to the airport to pick up our distinguished investors. I email Lai Ying to tell her I'm all settled and my people are fine. Then I turn to the inbox that has seven messages, mostly clients. Two of them say that if I can't see them this week, they're hiring someone else. Another says they'll no longer be needing my services. They're merging with a bigger firm and will have their IT taken care of. I slump back into my seat, and feel the energy draining from my entire being. It is like being sucked into quicksand and there's nothing I can do to stop myself going under.

It takes an urgent message from Alex to jolt me to my senses. I have to read it several times to understand his meaning.

Checked out your three villains through our contacts as I promised. Nasty piece of work, each one of them. Wouldn't touch them with a bargepole if I were you. Maybe it's too late. Well, if there's dosh to be made, do it and get the hell out, is my advice to you, mate. Hope things work out for you in Zim. There's bugger all for me there now.

I show the message to Chip and explain the context. He's unfazed, though he's anxious to know more about what Wang and the gang do. I tell him everything I know, which isn't much.

"What do you reckon?" I ask him. "It doesn't sound good."

"Sometimes it's better not to know too much," he says evasively. "This Alex isn't really saying anything specific, is he? So we have General Josh Chuma on the one hand, and your Chinese dudes on the other hand. What does that mean – we're caught between the devil and the deep blue sea?"

"What if we are, Chip? It's not too late for me to change my ticket and get the hell out of here, man."

"Don't be a chicken, my friend. Come on, let's go. They should be arriving about now."

Wang and the gang are just getting into the arrivals lounge when we rush in at 6.30 p.m. I introduce Chip as our business consultant and lawyer and explain how he has struggled to arrange a meeting with a top government man and successful investor, just the kind of man they need. They greet each other with hearty handshakes. We're getting off to a very auspicious start. On the way into town, Wang regales us with stories about their experiences in South Africa. They went on a game safari and met with various businessmen courtesy of a contact in Johannesburg. They're in high spirits. Although he's not revealing very much, it is obvious that agreements have been reached, and money has changed hands.

Chip is grinning and beaming, convinced these men will deliver, and nothing can go wrong now. The redness in his eyes has cleared, though the focused determination of a mad scientist is still there, indelibly etched on his furrowed brow. He's like a leopard primed for attack, narrowed eyes trained on a doomed eland, playing the waiting game, just waiting for the wind to change so the prey won't get a whiff of his approach. The concentration both unnerves and strengthens me. He nods his head with patient encouragement as Wang sets out his plans in halting English.

"We see future in Africa," enthuses Wang. "Opportunity, investment, everywhere. South Africa, we there already, meet important people, do business already. Now we in Harare, is next stop. Is very good."

"It's excellent," says Chip. "I've waited a long time to meet the three of you. My cousin has been telling me about you and your exciting business ideas. I've arranged everything here for you."

"Is what I like – people ready for work. No need wasting time. We have dinner. Ready for meeting tomorrow."

After dropping their bags off at the hotel, we're ready for dinner. Chip recommends the Club Capricorn, which is famous for game meat. The Chinese are ecstatic when they see the open braai pit bedecked with enticing ostrich, crocodile, bush tuck, and impala. A broadly smiling waiter with an oversized chef's cap drops by our table intermittently dropping off juicy game steaks and spicy salads on plates that are emptied clean almost as soon as he turns to serve the next table. Our guests tasted similar fare in South Africa and can't get enough of it. They can't believe game meat is served openly here, while in China, they have to order pangolin and civet cats on the sly. Chip explains it's all legal. The animals are raised specifically for food, just like a domestic herd of cattle.

We wash the sumptuous meal down with gallons of Zambezi and Castle beers. Wang orders their best Cognac and Chip receives a timely introduction to the famous practice of *gan be*!

The atmosphere in the club is like a party. The cream of Harare society is here: senior civil servants and politicians, some members of the national cricket team, a top golfer – the only people in the country who can still indulge their palates without leaving a dent in the wallets. The band strikes up a fine groove, sending everyone into a frenzy with their selection of the highly danceable, quick-rhythm songs of Thomas Mapfumo and Oliver Mtukudzi. Chip explains to our guests that Mapfumo's revolutionary music is frowned upon by the authorities and the singer has in fact been living in exile in the US, but his music, mostly sang in Shona, galvanised the resistance ever since Ian Smith declared that the country would never be ruled by an African in his lifetime.

"Mapfumo's song *Pamuromo Chete* dismissed Ian Smith's words as just talk," says Chip. "The people loved it. We call this music *chimurenga*, which means struggle."

"It's like revolution," says Wang to his colleagues. They raise their glasses. *Gan be!*

"People's revolution!"

"Struggle continue," says Wang in English, drunkenly. "Struggle is succeed in business. *Gan be*! Remember Zheng He?"

Zheng He! Gan be!

I have to explain to Chip about their seafaring hero.

When the band takes a break, Wang asks me about the unfamiliar instrument with narrow metal keys mounted on a wooden soundboard, a wire with beads and seashells stuck on a metal plate.

"The mbira dzavadzimu," I explain, with pride. I've always loved the hypnotic sounds of the xylophone-like instrument. "The mystical mbira music has been with us for a thousand years. The Shona people use it for purification and healing or for meditation, and nowadays, you see it played in pop bands like this one."

"Amazing!" exclaims Liu Ming, his crimson face lighting up. "It sounds like an orchestra by itself."

"You could say that. Sometimes they play it inside a calabash—which we call the deze—for more amplification. Then it truly sounds like an orchestra."

We clink glasses, and when the band returns with a hit by the Bhundu Boys, we sing along.

After dinner, Chip announces that at the back of the Club, there is a casino and disco. Not surprisingly, the Chinese opt for the casino, where they spend a couple of hours at the roulette and blackjack tables. Chip and I stand by watching for a while, sipping our beers. I strenuously fight the temptation to get involved. Chip is keen to try his luck, but limits himself to the slot machines. I don't even dare touch them. Noticing my unease, Chip asks me what's wrong.

"I could hold my own with the top players here, man," I explain, feeling my heart uplifted with pride. "I learned my craft in Macau. But that, my friend, was the start of my problems with my wife. I shouldn't even be here. Let's check out the disco."

The disco is heaving with sweaty bodies swaying to hip-hop alternating with African music. We lose ourselves in the music, dancing with a couple of girls who look like college students. Wang and the gang join us after an hour and immediately throw themselves into the thick of it, dancing away like people half their age. Wang is the soul of the party, leading his friends to a group of dancing girls, losing himself in the music, even as the girls stop to gawp in amusement before pairing off with each of the grey-haired Chinese. Why would Alex want to warn me about these guys? All they want to do is have fun and make money. Even Yu Shian has shed his mean-cop look. He is at one with the twenty-year-old girls shaking their booty to the hard, gritty rap music of Snoop Doggy Dog and Dr Dre. Liu Ming's face is set in a permanent grin, suffused with a pastor's benevolent indulgence.

I haven't had so much fun for quite some time. But questions still hover about me like a persistent mosquito buzzing around the ears when I finally get to bed at 3 a.m.

Chip is already waiting at the lobby at 8 the following morning. Wang had asked him to join us for breakfast so we can go over the day's plans. Everyone is looking a bit under the weather after last night's festivities, and trying their best not to show it. A few cups of coffee should do the trick.

The first thing Wang does is to announce he made some excellent contacts in Jo'burg.

"They'll assist us with some of our projects here," he says, with the solemn and confident air of a general setting out a battle plan. "They're white people, and they've asked us to assist some of their brothers in this country." He looks at me almost apologetically, before continuing. "We're businessmen, Eggman. We see an opportunity and exploit it. We're not concerned about the politics, although we know the political situation here is a little delicate."

I translate to Chip, who simply nods, indicating he couldn't care less about the politics either. His face is set in an expression of focused determination, nothing will come between him and this deal. I dare not ask for too much information, partly because I wish to maintain some distance with the deals being cut, and also because I sense somehow that Wang is onto something I would rather not know too much about.

"We'll see the government man this morning," says Wang. "And in the afternoon, we'll attend to some business in—what was that name?"

"Ch-chih-yoh," mumbles Yu Shian.

Chip and I look up in surprise.

"Chinhoyi? That's famous for the caves."

"Yes, caves," confirms Wang. "We'll drive there this afternoon."

"That may not be feasible," says Chip thoughtfully. "Though the distances are not that long, there are roadblocks everywhere."

It is agreed that we'll try anyway. Then Chip announces he has already arranged to rent a luxury van with a driver and bodyguard and is just waiting for payment. An impressed Wang pulls out his wallet and hands me a wad of notes, amounting to three thousand US dollars.

"This should do for now," he says. "A thousand for expenses, like the car rental and other minor expenses. The rest is your fees for now, a thousand each.

We want you both to be comfortable, you've done a lot for us. If you need anything else, just tell me."

Both Yu Shian and Liu Ming grin and nod their heads, smoking contentedly, Liu Ming his beloved Marlboro and Yu Shian a thick cigar. They watch Chip and I pocket our wages, as if to say, *be good boys, there's plenty more where that came from.* Chip bows his gratitude to Wang and accepts a cigar from Yu Shian. At the current exchange rate, this allowance is more than his monthly salary.

A quick phone call and the vehicle is confirmed. It is waiting for us outside at 9.30 a.m. Chip announces we're going to Chuma's farm near Marondera town, about an hour's drive from Harare. Our appointment is at 11, so we have some time to show our guests a bit more of Harare than they saw last night. The driver takes us around Harare Gardens, which is already teeming with joggers; through the main city avenues lined with jacaranda and eucalyptus trees and the low-density suburbs in the north; past the jostling street markets displaying wood and soapstone carvings, oil paintings by unknown masters, woven baskets, and crocheted fabrics under aging buildings badly in need of a coat of paint; and out of the city. We drive through the satellite town of Chitungwize with its sprawling shanties, past beautifully manicured golf courses, game parks, and lakes, yawning into gently rippling wakefulness as the sun begins to warm their tranquil surfaces.

Wang and the gang are enthralled by the views, and captivated by my improvised and sometimes embellished running commentary. Chip jokes that I should take up a job as a tour agent. I still remember my country well enough to get away with the masquerade.

The extensive grapevines on rolling hills announce that we're nearly there. Chip points out Josh Chuma's farm, which is perched on top of a hill surrounded by vineyards. The wind blows in the smell of eucalyptus, pines, and tobacco through the van's open windows. It is markedly cooler in this high, veld region. I explain to the Chinese that the temperate climate here is perfect for orchards, maize, and sheep rearing.

"It looks perfect," says Wang. "We could grow grapes here and export wine to China. Rich Chinese are very keen to sample fine wines nowadays."

Four armed guards are stationed at Chuma's imposing steel gate. They are dressed in army fatigues and are carrying rifles and revolvers. Chip goes out to talk to them. One of them talks into a walkie-talkie for a few minutes while recording the vehicle's licence plate. Another one comes to inspect our passports. Chip is made to sign a visitors' book before they wave us through.

"There has been some trouble around here," Chip whispers in my ears, so the driver and guard won't hear. "Some farms in this region have been taken over, including a black-owned one. He didn't have protection, and more to the point, he was said to be an opposition sympathiser. Several others are earmarked for takeovers, which could happen at any time. You don't have to tell them the details."

In my much-edited translation, I explain that security has been a problem here, just like everywhere else, and farmers need to protect their land. My comments meet with crestfallen faces, so I quickly add that the man we're going to see can guarantee security. The faces thaw immediately. At the end of the long drive, there's another gate, manned by two armed guards. One of them talks into his walkie-talkie, while the other one inspects our identities, records the van's licence plate, and leads us a short distance to the visitors' parking bay. A man in a blue suit and red tie, presumably a butler, leads us into the majestic building and into a lounge decorated with stuffed animals and full-size sandstone carvings of impala, eland, and a leopard. The animals lounge on the carpeted floor, each guarding his territory, partly hidden behind flowerpots and plants that reach almost to the ceiling. The walls are adorned with family pictures, showcasing a plump wife and three sons, one of whom followed the father into the military. We take in the décor and ambience in subdued silence, while a retreating uniformed maid serves tea and chocolate cookies.

Presently our host marches in. He's a big, tall man, at least six-foot-two. He looks every inch the retired army general, with the stiff, confident gait, the black boots that have been polished to a glittering sheen, the close-cropped hair, the thin moustache, the pipe dangling from his lips. He exudes an aura of authority that is undiminished by the casual polo shirt and brown khaki safari trousers.

We rise to shake his hand. He looks as if he's expecting salutes. Chip thanks him deferentially for agreeing to meet us and introduces us. It emerges that he has been to Beijing on government business, as recently as two years ago, before the current troubles, as he calls them, escalated.

"We were courting investors," he elaborates, "as we continue to do, and I can't tell you how glad I am personally that our efforts are beginning to bear fruit, seeing you three gentlemen in Zimbabwe today."

He talks a lot, almost too fast for me to keep up with a comprehensible translation. But a clear picture soon emerges. In a bid to raise scarce foreign exchange, the government has already sold some coal, chromium, and copper mines to Chinese investors.

"But this is classified information, you understand," he warns, placing a finger on his lips. "I'm ready to organise the sale of a copper mine right now as we speak in addition to a tobacco farm. I'm looking at you gentlemen and I know you mean business, to have come all this way from China. Everything is ready. My government is keen to strengthen our relationship with the Chinese. We need foreign exchange, we need arms to support our friends in Congo, and we need to protect our people from saboteurs."

"You've spoken well," says Wang. "And let me also add, especially for the benefit of our two young friends here, that our collaboration goes way back to your country's struggle with imperialists."

"Absolutely!" exclaims the general. "China stood by us in our liberation struggle against racism and oppression."

"War planes, guns, artillery, we always support our friends," says Yu Shian, shaking hands with the general. "No matter the cost. The millions of dollars we put in were well worth it. Your country is now free. Imperialism is a very bad thing. We in China would never support it."

"We shared and continue to share a socialist ideology," adds Wang. "We knew African liberation was inevitable, that's why we supported you. And now we're ready to continue working together, long into the future."

I'm impressed. They have done their homework. The conversation that follows between Yu Shian and the general touches on warfare, military strategies, things I don't even understand, and merely stumble through the translations, improvising where the arcane meanings get the better of me. They are like old friends chatting about their days in some guerrilla war. The general is quite an entertainer too, full of amusing anecdotes and jokes. When he laughs, throwing his head back and his face is ready to explode, his eyes never leave the Chinese. He's sizing them up, and they him. After a while, the general brings out some documents and a set of maps. They are government documents detailing the transfer of ownership of a copper mine and a tobacco farm, with all the government seals. Chip steps in as the investors' lawyer to study the documents. According to the maps, the two items for sale are right here in Mashonaland East. The farm is only a few miles away, on the other side of the hill on which the general's home sits perched like a medieval castle. By the look of it, they'll be virtually neighbours.

The Chinese consult amongst themselves for fifteen minutes. Excusing himself so they can consult in private, the general leads me to an adjoining room, where he questions me about them, how well I know them, what they do. I answer as best I can, leaving out my own fears and suspicions. He lets on that the foreign exchange shortage is beginning to hurt the economy.

"We must find ways to save our country," he says. "If your friends here know other investors out there who are happy to work with us, we could all have a very fruitful relationship."

"I'll keep my eyes open, General. China is growing at a furious rate. If they can be assured of security, they'll be flocking here in droves."

"Tell them it's all right. Do you see any trouble in this country? If the Western press could stop spreading malicious untruths about us, we would be a very prosperous nation. This deal is just the start of a great relationship with our Chinese brothers. I can tell they're ready to spend. I hope you two are being compensated well for your trouble. Don't be shy to ask for the moon. Otherwise, you get nothing."

He looks pleased with himself. I dare not ask him what his percentage is. Chip had mentioned it could be anything from ten to twenty percent, depending on how many hands will be in the pie.

"There's the issue of ownership," says Liu Ming, in a calm, unthreatening voice, as if he's commenting on the salubrious pine-scented veld air.

"Ownership has already reverted to the state," says General Chuma. "The previous owner was fully compensated and has already settled in South Africa. You shouldn't expect any trouble."

"That's reassuring," says Wang. "However, we would appreciate it if you could provide security and help us hire temporary caretakers, while we organise management teams from China to move in. They're ready. Just waiting for word from us. A few days' cover will do. There'll be papers to sort out at this end, too."

"Consider it done," says the general, shaking Wang's hand in a solemn gesture. "Whatever you need, it will all be organised. After lunch, you'll be driven to see both sites. If you don't like what you see, of course the deal is off. But I can assure you there's no better bargain, and I'm speaking as the man in charge of these things. We're offering you eighty percent ownership in each investment; the rest is held in trust for the state. All the documentation is here.

As to the matter of price, your financial input is three hundred thousand US dollars for the farm and 1.2 million for the mine. Half now, the rest in seven days. Prices ascertained by professional evaluators, and confirmed as a bargain. All the paperwork is right here."

"About twelve million RMB," murmurs Yu Shian, after I rumble out a translation.

They exchange expressionless looks, the placidness on their faces belying the rapid calculations going on in the grey matter. My own mind is in overdrive, calculating the general's cut. A conservatively low ten percent kickback works out to a hundred and fifty thousand, which is half the cost of the farm. Each of the three pockets no less than fifty thousand, and that's assuming they're only taking ten percent.

"It's a fantastic price, Wang," the general enthuses, moistening his lips, as though to savour the deal. "You've got yourselves a pretty tight deal. As for the mine, all the production and financial documents are here, fully audited, as you can see. It's operating at less than full capacity, basically because of a lack of capital. And that's why we're offering it to you at such a discount. We're literally giving it away, and the farm, too. If you look closely, you'll see the copper reserves are quite substantial. We're confident you'll provide sufficient demand and will help us earn much-needed foreign exchange."

The Chinese resume their private consultation, occasionally turning to me with questions. Half an hour later, Wang declares they need independent verification of the title deeds through their lawyer. Chip asks the general for permission to make some phone calls on his cell phone. The first call is to his office in the attorney general's chambers. He reels off some numbers from the two sets of documents and waits for the return call. While he's studying the documents, General Chuma calls for a bottle of whisky and announces we'll be ready for lunch soon. A call for Chip comes through twenty minutes later.

Satisfied that everything is in order, Wang signs the transfer documents, witnessed by his lawyer, the unsmiling and grim-faced Chip. He promises to wire the first tranche of the payment twenty-four hours after they've inspected the sites. The ownership documents will be ready for collection from the General's Harare office.

Dumb Tour Agent

CHIP WAS RIGHT. THERE'S NO way we're ever going to make it to Chinhoyi after inspecting the farm and mine. By the time we start heading back to Harare, it is already 6 p.m. The sun is beginning to set, casting a red glow across the farmlands. The rays come peering through pine trees, creating a colourful halo around the trees, forcing you to blink as they shine blindingly through the windscreen. The driver is having a hard time keeping his eyes on the road. The Chinese carry on a muted conversation throughout.

Wang has spent a lot of time on the phone to his office, issuing instructions, confirming bank transfers. They have pulled it off. A management team will fly out this Saturday.

The celebrations go on late into the night. After a couple of hours at the Capricorn Casino, Wang says he wants a change of scene, preferably to a place that has nice girls. Chip recommends the East End Disco at the Bamboo Lodge Hotel, two miles out of town in the Edgevale suburb. The driver and bodyguard look up in surprise but maintain a reverential silence. The hotel itself is on a wide, well-lit avenue, but to get there, we have to drive through narrow, unlit streets in a high-density neighbourhood, where the aging, dilapidated buildings are decorated with political slogans and crude graffiti, and idle youths hang around street corners smoking and listening to rap music on oversized CD players. The nightclub is in a converted warehouse behind the hotel. The car park is littered with an assortment of top-of-the-range luxury Japanese and European models. Attendants in suits and bow ties keep watch and, for a generous tip, promise to keep an eye on your vehicle. There is a queue of smartly dressed young people at the door. Chip leads us to the door and squeezes a wad of notes into the bouncer's hand.

The dance floor alone covers an area as wide as a squash court, and is packed with people of all ages, most of whom are single women in miniskirts, high heels, excessive makeup and fantastic hairdos.

"There's a lot of choice here, man," says Chip superfluously. "If your guys want to take chicks back, they're literally spoilt for choice."

I decide against doing the translation. It's better to wait and see how things pan out. There are all kinds of women here, mostly black and white. But there's a sprinkling of Asians, too, who look Chinese and Filipina. The air is heavy with the smell of warm bodies and a riot of perfumes. We find a table and settle down to some serious drinking. With the loud music, there's not much conversation, unless one shouts in his neighbour's ear. It doesn't take long before four girls make their way to our table, smiling sweetly at our Chinese friends. One of the girls asks if they are from Japan, which makes Wang first scowl with disgust before finding the question so amusing he can't stop laughing. I have to step in with a translation for Yu Shian and Liu Ming, who at first frown with irritation and then join Wang in head-thrown-back laughter. The girls are from South Africa. They keep us company for the next two hours, drinking and dancing. It would have been more fun if I didn't have to translate two conversations, for Liu Ming and Yu Shian. Luckily for me, the two of them aren't all that interested in their admirers, and Chip and I end up chatting up the girls ourselves. Wang holds his own remarkably well. His companion is perched on his lap, one hand holding her glass of white wine, the other caressing Wang's nape and neck.

A commotion at the door makes everyone sit up. The reggae music grinds to a halt and the dance hall is flooded with lights. If they are trying to tell us it's time to leave, they're doing it rather crudely. From our table in the far corner, we can barely see what is happening.

"War vets," mutters Chip, with a look of despair. "At least that's what they claim they are."

A dozen young men pop into view as the partying crowd retreats in fear towards the walls, screaming with terror. The men force their way into the club, wielding machetes and rifles. They are dressed in army fatigues and most of them are wearing trainers, dark glasses, and baseball caps. Chip and I quickly usher our guests to the narrow space behind our sofa, from where we can watch the unfolding drama, kneeling on the cement floor as if in supplication. Wang and his friends look more irritated than frightened, as if they've seen it all before. The intruders have the dance floor to themselves but with their sinister weapons hardly look like they're here to dance, unless it's some esoteric military masquerade.

Their leader, who can't be more than twenty-five, raises a revolver and fires into the ceiling, shattering a strobe light and sending everyone cowering to the floor. He's a tall, thin chap in dark glasses and with an unkempt beard probably designed to make him look older than he really is. His trousers are tacked into knee-high cowboy boots.

"Listen up, people!" growls the cowboy. "We heard there's a disturbance here and we're here to keep the peace." He raises his gun above his head, then waves it in a semicircle, forcing the few people still standing to drop to the floor screaming.

A girl wails and collapses heavily to the ground. Cowboy fires his gun into the ceiling just above her, raining bits of glass and a shower of white plaster all around her.

"What do they want?" asks Wang.

"Who knows? Maybe they'll rob us. Watch your wallets."

They surreptitiously push their thick wallets into their underwear. I silently pray they won't be made to stand up. They'll never be able to fool the cowboy and his gang that they're that generously endowed.

I raise my head a few inches to observe the intruders, who are pacing about impatiently, cocking and uncocking their guns, wiping the machetes against their trouser legs, as though sharpening them in readiness for a bloodbath. Their eyes have a glazed look about them. They've definitely been smoking dope. It will take just the tiniest bit of provocation for them to fire indiscriminately, just as likely out of fear as anything. It is embarrassing to see all these grownups reduced to cowering in terror on the edges of the dance floor, afraid to make eye contact with these thugs, who have usurped the glory of freedom fighters and turned history into a tool of extortion and terror. The fear that initially made my stomach cramp up gives way to anger and resentment, directed first at these thugs, and then at everything around me, including Wang and his schemes.

"What the hell are we doing here, man?" I ask Chip in a stage whisper.

"Scared? Don't be. They can't hurt us."

"How do you know?"

"They're just a bunch of thieves, man." He smiles sardonically as he says it. To Chip, this is all part of the struggle to get the deal done. Right now, I would give anything to be back at the Safari Oasis in Hong Kong, drinking the night away, with no risk of hoodlums invading the place, firing guns above our heads.

Meanwhile, Cowboy demands to see the manager. A middle-aged man steps forward, his eyes trained on the cowboy's gun. He's dressed in a well-pressed, dark-blue suit and blue tie to match. His goatee sticks out defiantly, as if daring the cowboy to do his worst. They face each other.

"I'm here, my friend…"

"I'm not your friend! You're exploiting the workers here. How can you be my friend? You've betrayed the revolution!"

"Revolution? We have a revolution tonight?" The hall goes completely quiet. Everyone expects the intruders to gun the manager down for his insolence. The cowboy seethes with rage, but before he can find his words, the manager puts an arm around his shoulder and says, "Look, my son, we are all for the revolution and we're very pleased you've come here to remind us of our duty. Let's not frighten our distinguished guests. We'll sit in my office and talk this over, all right?" He turns to his staff and shouts, "Hey! Get the roast meat and beers out for our young revolutionaries!"

The cowboy starts to protest and rams his gun into the manager's ribs. But the manager is in his element, cajoling, begging, pleading with the men to leave the dance floor and enjoy a feast in his office.

"You can't exploit us!" yells the cowboy. "You can't cheat us, we're not your workers! You must make compensation through the party…"

"All right! All right!" the manager cuts him short and leads him away, promising the house's best wine. The rest of the gang look both confused at their boss's uncharacteristic docility and excited at the prospect of free food and drink, in addition to the money they had obviously come to collect. The cowboy fires a parting shot into the ceiling, but this time it's met by a collective gasp of exasperation and irritation, like that of adults fed up with a child's attention-seeking antics. He opens his mouth to say something but Bob Marley's Revolution descends on our heads like a clap of thunder.

At the same time, the hall is momentarily plunged into darkness before the psychedelic lights resume their dance routine to reveal a sea of laughing and relieved faces.

"I've not encountered these people before," says Chip, "but I've heard talk about them. They go around extorting money. And that bit about a revolution, man, it's just pathetic."

The Chinese laugh dismissively when I offer an explanation.

"They are just children," says Liu Ming with a benevolent grin. "They have no idea what a revolution is." He's lost in his thoughts. Yu Shian nods thoughtfully to himself, eyes tinged with regret and pain, perhaps also recalling his experiences in their Cultural Revolution.

"These are the people you're calling war veterans?" asks Wang.

"Nonsense," mutters Chip angrily. "See how old they are? These kids were born at independence. Perhaps they were fighting while in their mothers' wombs. They give the real veterans a bad name."

The thugs have destroyed our mood to party. And no one wants to hang around and see whether they'll come back to harass the revellers after exhausting the club's supply of wine. Wang's lady friend is nowhere to be seen.

We set off for Chinhoyi at 9 the following morning. Wang has still not explained exactly what we're going to do there. In answer to my question, he simply says, "Oh, you remember our contacts in Johannesburg? There's someone we need to meet. We need to check on some new investments. You help us to get there, Eggman. How long will it take us?"

Chip says just over an hour, slightly longer if we encounter foot-and-mouth roadblocks.

"Is it another farm, or mine?"

"It could be anything. We'll know soon enough."

I translate for Chip and ask him what he thinks. He shrugs and looks away. Just as long as he gets his lawyer's fee and expenses. But Wang's manner is a little disconcerting today. It tells me it's none of my business what they do, so long as I'm paid to take them there.

"You don't think there could be something sinister?" I ask Chip in Shona. "The thing Alex was trying to warn me about, man? What the hell could they be up to?"

"We're in our own country, Dan. What can they possibly do? What trouble can they possibly get us into, seriously?"

Chip's argument makes sense, but it does little to allay my fears. I resolve to keep a close eye on them, and listen to every word they whisper among themselves. Their faces are as usual inscrutable, especially Liu Ming's, who maintains a bored, patient expression, while Yu Shian's eyes are narrowed to slits, as if to shield them from the glare of the sun, yet we're heading westwards. He could be mistaken for being half-asleep if it wasn't for the perceptive comments he keeps making about the farms we're driving past, and the projected cash flow figures and currency conversions he keeps spewing out. Clearly, he's the financial wizard here, while Wang is the dealmaker. Liu Ming is the hard drive, buzzing away in the background, looking bored half the time, yet revealing just how alert he is every time he reminds them of some minor detail they've overlooked.

We get to Chinhoyi at 10.30 a.m. I haven't been here since a school trip when we visited the limestone caves with a deep, blue pool beneath, which we call the Pool of the Fallen, in honour of fallen freedom fighters, the real ones who fought in the Second *Chimurenga*, rather than the thugs who are now running amok across the country. The first thing we do when we get into the town is find a hotel where we can take some refreshments. We end up at the Chinhoyi Tavern right in the town centre, order tea and biscuits, and wait for Wang to explain his mission. I'm getting nervous about his caginess. I lean towards Chip and tell him that if Wang is not forthcoming, I'll demand an explanation.

"I'm tired of being treated like a dumb tour agent."

"Relax, man. I'm sure he knows what he's doing. He'll talk when he's ready."

I take a deep breath and feel my chest expand with repressed anger. I feel a sudden urge to call Alex and ask him what exactly he unearthed. I've been holding back, hoping Chip is right, that there's nothing to worry about, although I can't explain to myself why I should believe Chip. He hardly knows these people, and whenever he looks at Wang he sees nothing but dollar signs. I'll have to call Alex pretty soon. It's 4 p.m. in Hong Kong. He's probably in a meeting and can't talk.

"We'll meet an important contact today," announces Wang. "And we'll strike a very important deal."

"Who is that?"

"Let us be patient. This will be a nice surprise."

Neither Yu Shian's nor Liu Ming's placid expressions reveal who this mystery person might be. At least Wang is starting to talk, although his evasiveness only raises more questions.

"They're funny, these guys of yours," says Chip. "A little crazy in the head, playing these sorts of games. Are they always like this?"

I shrug my shoulders, then ask Wang what happens next. He says we need to drive out to a farm to meet this mysterious contact.

"We'll meet our important contact, Eggman, but first we need to talk to some gweilos."

"Gweilos?"

"Farmers, businessmen, aspiring politicians," he says, laughing. "They want to be everything. For us, it's strictly business."

"And this mystery contact, is he also into farming, business, and politics?"

"Ha, ha! Not a farmer, certainly not a farmer."

"I think I know, Wang. It's the coltan, right? Coltan from the Congo, for your electronics business."

"You're very smart, Eggman. Coltan is important to us. But we're not going to get it today. It might take a little while. We may have to go to Congo. Let's see what our contact has to say first."

Chip waves a hand for silence. Everyone turns to look at him.

"Okay, it's like this, I'm the lawyer here," he says, in a low, dry voice, devoid of all emotion. "I don't like working under uncertainty, so I want to request that the rest of my fees are paid in advance, right now; otherwise, I'm out. Lawyer's fees and consultancy fees for a week, I'll take six thousand US dollars. A thousand down already, five to go. And as for you, Danny boy, you shouldn't demand a penny less. Don't sell yourself cheap."

The Chinese exchange surprised looks when I translate the relevant bits. I glare at Chip. What the hell is he doing this for? Wang's and Yu Shian's faces are contorted with irritation, which they're struggling to contain. They hate being challenged. Completely nonplussed, they turn to Liu Ming, who nods sagely and continues to stare thoughtfully into space. Wang sighs and then forces a smile.

"Is okay," he says, reaching for his briefcase. His manner has softened. "We work together, and maintain harmony. You're doing a good job, helping us find our way, and negotiate with people here. We appreciate your help, both of you." I translate some of it for Chip, without looking up.

Wang hands each of us a wad of US dollar notes, amounting to five thousand. I have no trouble looking him in the eye as I pick up my dues. But I can't face Chip just yet.

The drive takes half an hour. The main gate at the farm is guarded by half a dozen men with rifles and batons. A security van is parked by the side of the road. Wang asks me to give the name Hewitt. The guard talks on his walkie-talkie before waving us through. The security routine is almost identical to the one at General Chuma's farm.

In the main house, a butler leads us to a sprawling office, where two white men are poring over a map, drinking vodkas. They look like game hunters with their red, weather-beaten faces, their safari shirts and shorts and bushy beards. Old Africa hands. One of them is tall and skinny, has a no-nonsense look about him, a bit like Yu Shian. The other one is heavily built, with a thick neck, powerful, hairy arms, and huge potbelly, like a former rugby player gone to seed. A Pink Floyd track blares from a speaker in a corner.

The two men rise to welcome us.

"I'm Bruce," says the big man. "Bruce Hewitt. We've been expecting you, Mister Wang. It's wonderful to finally meet you. We really appreciate your cooperation. This is Jan van Louw. He'll be assisting us."

"Nice meet you, Bruce," says Wang, offering a handshake. "Me, too, I wait long time to meet you." He introduces us.

"Meeting went well in Jo'burg?"

"Very good. Everything ready. My contact coming soon."

"Excellent. Let's have lunch, what do you guys say? You must be starving."

Four other men are lounging on leather armchairs by the window, playing cards, their rifles lying on the brown carpet, within easy reach. They are wearing black suits and dark glasses, hair tied in ponytails. They remind me of East-European secret agents. They look bored, starved of action, waiting for a signal. There's a certain casualness about them that I find quite disconcerting, their deceptively calm demeanour, the way they smoke with a cultivated nonchalance, as if they're lying on a beach on holiday, unconcerned about anything going on around them, having complete faith in their weapons to neutralise any threat or danger.

Lunch is an assortment of roast beef, some game meat, boiled rice, salads, and South African wines, served by two docile domestic helpers. I can't enjoy the food with this company, especially the gunmen, who keep their sunglasses on and smoke throughout the meal. Chip and I maintain a guarded silence. Wang is doing just fine without us, although he turns to me occasionally when the language fails him. From their conversation, it becomes clear that Wang is organising the delivery of what they are calling "goods". That appears to be the reason they went to South Africa. And this mysterious contact we're waiting for is responsible for delivering these goods. The feeling that I shouldn't be here won't leave me. Silently, I battle feelings of foolishness and naivety. But as time goes by, it gets more and more difficult to demand answers, especially with all these guns and mean-looking guys around.

"Why all the guns, man?" whispers Chip. We're both aware Bruce probably understands Shona, so we have to be careful what we say. Luckily the loud rock music and noisy conversations around us provide sufficient cover.

"To protect themselves from war vets? Makes sense, but why would my man here be the one to help?"

"He's loaded. These guys have no foreign exchange, you know. Also, he has contacts."

"And what's there in it for him?"

"We'll know soon enough." The words are whispered with a chilling reminder of the superfluity of our presence here.

After lunch, we drive out in the direction of Chinhoyi Cavern with one of the gunmen. Hewitt and van Louw are now fully in charge, relegating Chip and I to mere observers. While Chip may still be required to scan and verify documents, my role has been reduced to that of an interpreter. Wang can get by with basic, conversational English until things get technical. My help comes grudgingly, as my loathing for him and his friends intensifies. They know I can't bail out that easily, not just yet, and certainly not so soon after pocketing what Chip described as a week's wages.

Five miles out of town, we turn off into a narrow dirt road that winds its way around a series of hills. The van kicks up a cloud of dust that settles on trees like a layer of melted brown sugar. Hewitt and van Louw converse in Afrikaans, in low tones. Jan van Louw keeps stealing glances at Chip and me, which I find disturbing. After fifteen minutes, we arrive at a clearance deep in the forest.

"So what happens here?" I ask Wang.

"We wait."

"For the mystery contact?"

"He'll be here soon, Eggman. Then everything will be fine." My heart sinks.

Soon enough, the sound of a car engine interrupts the cool afternoon air. A jeep roars into view and screeches to a halt just next to our van. Two men jump out, both carrying rifles. Wang gets out of the van to meet them. They hug and shake hands warmly, like long-lost friends. They're both wearing safari suits, their faces are partly obscured by dark glasses and baseball caps. Wang waves to us to come out.

The black guy goes silent on seeing me. Then he takes off his dark glasses, slings his rifle over his shoulder, and approaches me, mouth agape.

"Kabinga!" I tremble with shock, unable to believe my eyes. The last time I saw him, he was bandaged all over, walking on crutches. Now he's got the demeanour of General Chuma, the alertness, the confident, almost arrogant gait of a man who knows the meaning of power, the sharp, penetrating eyes that miss nothing.

We embrace. The smell of marijuana that envelops him is overwhelming.

"Yeah, man! Eggman, what the hell are you doing here?"

"It's my country, Chin Chin." He explodes with laughter. "I should be asking you what you're doing here. I'm confused, man." Very confused. A Kabinga and Wang reunion in Africa after the intrigue in Nanjing nine years ago leaves my mind reeling.

"Business, my friend. I'm here for business, small-small."

"Small-small, hey! You haven't stopped saying that."

"Eggman, does a leopard change its spots?"

"And what the hell is this business that needs rifles?"

"You need to protect your money, Eggman. I see you've never learned." He succumbs to another laughing fit, before introducing his friend. "This is Marc, from Brussels."

Out of the corner of my eye I notice Hewitt, van Louw, and their gunman leaning against the van, smoking, watching us keenly. Wang waves to them to join us.

"All right, gentlemen," says Hewitt. "Let's get down to business. You have what we need?"

"Right here," says Kabinga, pointing at the jeep. "You got my shit?"

Hewitt extracts from his pocket a small, velvet sachet, opens it slowly, keeping his eyes on Kabinga, and reveals a handful of small, glittery objects. Diamonds. Chip and I exchange glances. The blood is thumping so loudly in my head around my temples and ears I'm afraid they can hear it. I need to get as far away from these people as possible. Kabinga reaches for the diamonds, but Hewitt snatches his hand away, saying, "Not so fast, pal. Let's see what you've got."

"Sure, but I want to know what Wang's got for me, man."

Wang nods to Liu Ming, who opens his briefcase to expose thick wads of US dollar notes. A shiver runs down my spine. When I manage to steal a look at

Chip, I see his face creased with furrows, his eyes darting like those of a cornered thief searching for a way to escape from a mob that is closing in, wielding machetes.

Kabinga opens two large canvas bags in the jeep to reveal an assortment of weapons and other combat gear.

"Here's what you need, man," he announces. "AK47 assault rifles, Cesska pistols, drum magazines capable of holding a hundred rounds of ammunition, 600 rounds of live ammo, upholsters, jackets, hoods, jungle wear, VHF radios and handsets, CCTV, European passports. That should do nicely now, right?"

"Perfect," mutters Hewitt.

Jan van Louw picks up one of the rifles and inspects it.

"You'll see the firing pins are active," says Kabinga, lighting a joint. "Good and usable, small-small, you get? Top of the range."

Hewitt hands over the diamonds and he and van Louw pick up the canvas bags and load them into the van. Kabinga kisses the sachet and pockets it. Marc licks his lips as they exchange meaningful looks. Liu Ming is just handing over the money when a shot rings out. Everyone runs for cover. Shots and tear-gas canisters explode all around us, filling the air with gas, smoke, and dust. In an instant, the quiet forest turns into a war zone. Somehow, I manage to find my way to the van, grabbing Chip's hand. The drone of a helicopter engine fills the air, drowning the gunfire. In the noise and confusion, the driver races through the narrow forest road, screaming at us to get down. The helicopter is still following us, firing an incessant salvo of shots that ricochet off the vehicle and smash into the trees around us. I let out a scream as a shot sears through my shoulder.

The last thing I remember as I collapse and pass out on the floor of the van is Chip's bloodshot eyes beneath beads of sweat that look like a spray of spit on a worry-creased face.

The Fourth Chimurenga

THE WORLD IS CLOSING IN on me. I'm drifting through a dark tunnel, choking on smoke and dust and the smell of gunpowder, bouncing off oblong shapes with faces of chanting Chinese students. *Hei gui*! Some look like Chuck and the gang, others have turned into Wang, Yu Shian, and Liu Ming. Through all the confusion, Kabinga races down on his flying horse, which soon turns into a giant eagle, scattering diamonds as big as car wheels around me. I try to rise and flee, but the pain in my shoulder is unbearable. I turn my head and see Lai Ying lying on a white sheet, shrinking by the minute, holding out both hands so I can rescue her and stop her shrinking into nothingness. I reach out to hold her, but I can't clamber over the diamonds. Kabinga's eagle's beak stretches like a twisted spear towards the wound in my shoulder, and I know this time I'll surely die. I start to scream. Lai Ying is so small I can barely see her in the darkness. The eagle's beak fades away and then reappears with renewed vengeance. Deriving strength from the terrified look in Lai Ying's eyes, I grab it and squeeze until it shatters in my hand. Beakless, the bird utters a terrified scream and sinks into the darkness. I wake up shuddering.

I'm in a dark space, not quite a room, with no walls, no ceiling, just brown and silvery craggy rocks, water dripping down on my head. The terror is gone. In its place is a calm serenity, a deep silence. I'm drifting again, but this time, it feels as if I'm outside my body, floating through space, watching from a safe distance what looks like a war scene that could never be a part of my life again. The only thought on my mind is to run into Lai Ying's and Chacha's open arms. How could I ever have longed to be back here?

The air is dank, heavy with the miasmic smell of moss and tropical vegetation, like a rainforest. My left shoulder is stiff and immobile, numbed with pain, bandaged with a torn shirt. I can hear a stream trickling nearby, and the croaking of frogs. I try to turn and realise I am lying on a hard, wet rock. I've no idea how long I've lain unconscious for. Perhaps a few hours, a day, maybe longer. I try to rise but cannot. The hunger in my belly and the pain in my shoulder are like heavy weights that keep me pinned to the ground.

As my eyes get accustomed to the darkness, I become aware of human shapes spread out around me, some of them groaning with pain. In the semidarkness, I can just make out their bloodied clothes and faces.

But before I can determine who is who, three men in army fatigues appear, blinding us with torches, guns at the ready. They are soon followed by several others, like shadows, and before we can gasp in horror, they shower us with buckets of cold water.

"Are you ready to talk?" their leader barks. Then he takes off his dark glasses and pops them up on his clean-shaven head. Even in the gloom, his reddened eyes are glittering with a fierceness that leaves no doubt he'll use his gun without a moment's hesitation. Everyone sits up, wiping blood, sweat, water, and mud from their faces.

Shaven Head fires a shot and two men walk in, holding van Louw between them, revolvers to his head. Jan van Louw looks half-dead. His face is covered in blood. His safari suit is in shreds and covered with a mixture of mud and blood.

"If you don't answer my questions, he dies. I'll count to three." Shaven Head takes a deep breath and aims a gun at van Louw's head. "One, two—"

"Hold it!" cries Hewitt.

"You got something to say to me?"

"Just put your guns down, man."

Shaven Head fires a shot, inches above Hewitt's head.

"You don't tell me what to do with my gun. I ask again, what are the weapons for, eh?" He pulls out some passports from his pocket and reads out a name. "Bruce Hewitt. You'll talk, Mister Hewitt; otherwise, your friend dies, and all these others here."

"Look mister, we're just trying to protect ourselves."

"From what, eh?"

"ZANU thugs are screwing us, okay? What the fuck are we supposed to do?"

"And all that ambush and combat and surveillance equipment? Do I look stupid to you?"

"As I said, we're just protecting ourselves…"

A shot hits van Louw in the leg. The scream that follows is enough to strike terror into the frightened souls who gasp with terror as if they themselves had endured the bullet.

"Next time, the heart, Hewitt. Are you with me?"

"Go easy, all right?" pleads Hewitt, getting up on his feet with a supplicant gesture. The Chinese huddle together, not daring to move, watching the gunmen's every move.

"The weapons, Hewitt. What are they for?"

"As I said, protecting the farming community…and—"

"Struggle!" Kabinga blurts out, tightening a bloodied scarf around his arm. "You know *chimurenga*, right?"

Shaven Head turns to face him, seething with anger at the interruption.

"What the devil are you talking about?" demands Hewitt, before Shaven Head can find his voice.

"Let's be done with this whole shit, man," insists Kabinga, with a guttural laugh. "I want to go home."

"You have no idea—"

Shaven Head shoves Hewitt aside and turns to Kabinga, saying, "Somehow, I think he has some ideas. I rather want to know what he has to say. Hey, you, speak up!"

"It's always about bloody struggle in this country," says Kabinga, his voice dripping with sarcasm. "From the time the whites ruled it. You call it *chimurenga*, right? The third *chimurenga,* struggle for land, by…you lot." He points at the gunmen, lips curled in a sneer. The men train their weapons on him. "What, you're going to shoot me? If I don't get home, they'll come looking for me, and you won't have much time to regret your actions, 'cause you'll be fucking dead!"

"Keep to the point!"

"Very well, and what do I get in return?"

"You get your freedom. We have no use for bloody foreign devils. This is a domestic matter."

"Yeah, right. National sovereignty. Dictators say that all the time."

Shaven head fires a shot in the air.

"All right! My freedom, and that of my business partner and my brothers here, small-small. Do we have a deal?"

Shaven Head scowls and stomps his foot in anger. "Damn it!" He glares at Chip and I, pointing his gun at us. At this stage, it's frightening just to breathe. The silence in the cave is so intense that all I hear is the gunman's tortured breathing.

"Do we have a deal?" thunders Kabinga, shaking a clenched fist.

"All right!" Shaven Head grabs his sunglasses and smashes them against the craggy walls. "You have a deal. Now talk."

"It's like this. Everyone has their *chimurenga*, so why not the whites you're chucking out of this country?" Hewitt sinks to the ground, grabbing his head in his hands, as though someone has struck him in the face.

"They have a struggle, eh?" Shaven Head's voice is low, menacing, no louder than a stage whisper, more like a strangled hiss.

"White rebels, man. They call it the fourth *chimurenga*." On saying this, Kabinga explodes into laughter. Chip and I exchange glances. The shock of this revelation sends a shudder down my spine, intensifying the pain in my shoulder. Chip's jaw drops to his chest, and stays there.

"And what business do you have supplying them with arms?"

"You just said it, man. In a word, business. Small-small, you see? I don't give a shit about the bloody politics. We've got enough troubles in Rwanda, man."

"You deserve to be shot, selling your continent to these so-called white rebels." Shaven Head's face is contorted with pain as he chokes with a mixture of anger and disbelief.

"Hey, look! We have a deal. I've told you what you wanted to know. And as I said, this is just a business deal. The Chinese here don't give a damn about the politics either. They'll finance whatever deal is going as long as they get something in return. You can understand that, can't you?"

"And what exactly are the Chinese getting?"

"Ask them."

Shaven Head turns to Wang, raises him to his feet and sticks the gun in his ribs. Wang stoically doesn't even wince.

"What exactly do you want, eh? Speak up!"

"Business," murmurs Wang, unperturbed.

"Let me break it down," offers Kabinga. "Coltan, man. Ever heard of coltan? Coltan, diamonds, gold, copper. As the man says, it's called business, but you can't grasp that notion, can you? All you want is land you can't even bloody cultivate."

"One more rude word from you and you're dead." From the low tone and the fierce, narrowed eyes, the man means every word.

"Look, man, I've told you everything. Can we go now?" Kabinga rises to his feet and summons Marc, Chip, and I to follow suit. Chip and I stay rooted to the ground, until Shaven Head orders his men to take us away.

"Hey," Kabinga calls out over his shoulders. "What about the Chinese? They're just businessmen."

"Get out before I change my mind!"

They blindfold us and shove us into a truck. After a half-hour drive, they take the blindfolds off, and we find ourselves outside a large mansion on top of a hill. A tobacco plantation spreads into the far horizon. An assortment of rusting farm equipment and a wheel-less tractor resting on concrete slabs lie discarded along the driveway in front of a dilapidated warehouse. Two men lead us into the mansion and point out the bathrooms, where we take turns to freshen up.

The house looks neglected, and hasn't had a cleaning for some time. The wallpaper has been ripped off in places, and one whole side has been blackened by a fire. The sofas have been ripped apart, as if someone was looking for hidden treasure. Hooks that once held family pictures and paintings now stand bare and exposed. It is clear that people use the house as a hideaway but do not actually live here. There are voices coming from the direction of the kitchen and smells of cooking that caress the nose but torture the empty belly.

Half an hour later, a man in blue dungarees brings in a tray of roast chicken, loaves of bread, and a jug of water. He bows and waves us to the dining table.

"Strange," observes Chip. "One minute they're trying to kills us, the next minute they're laying on this rather nice spread. You reckon it's poisoned?"

"If I were you, I would just eat and stop complaining," says Kabinga.

After eating to my fill, I ask Kabinga how he got mixed up with the white rebels.

"You heard what I said to the man: I'm a businessman."

"It doesn't matter what the arms are for?"

"Eggman, I didn't realise you were so naïve."

"Kabinga, this is my country, in case you didn't realise."

"Marc and I are international financiers. If we were to factor politics into what we do, we wouldn't survive."

"You haven't changed much, have you?"

"You two are old friends or something?" asks Chip.

"College-mates. Nanjing. Kabinga was a serious businessman, even back then. You remember the White Card deals I told you about? No one did it better. But he lost it all. The Chinese took him to the cleaners, and nearly killed him, too."

"My goodness," murmurs Chip.

Kabinga is pacing up and down, furiously smoking a joint. The burnt-leaves smell leaves me nauseous. I move to the far end of the table to get away from Kabinga.

"You should have seen the state he was in when they found him – lying on the snow, like a dead goat, man." I massage my lower arm to ease the pain, but not even this minor respite can calm the anger welling up in me.

Kabinga smashes an empty glass into the fireplace.

"Everyone thinks the Chinese ripped him off, you know. But I guess it's because they realised *he* was ripping them off. They couldn't take it anymore." Chip glares at me, his crimson eyes warning me to be quiet. I ignore him, rise to my feet, and face Kabinga.

"You were ripping them off Kabinga, weren't you? That's why they screwed you."

"Easy, man," says Chip, rising to step between us. I brush him aside and point a finger at Kabinga. My whole body is on fire, a fire which emanates from my shoulder and is concentrated in my chest.

"You call yourself a businessman, but nobody can trust you. The Chinese turned out to be too smart for you, didn't they?"

"Listen here, man." He takes a step toward me. Marc holds his arm to restrain him. "I lost everything I had worked so hard for. I nearly got killed. Do you have any idea what that means? What they did to me, man, my life will never be the same again. I was going to be an engineer, man. They destroyed that dream. You don't know what you're talking about." He gnashes his teeth with an anguished sigh.

"Actually I do. What you did was business, not engineering, Chin Chin. No one stopped you from studying when you had a chance. And now I've no idea what's happened to you, but something tells me you're responsible for the mess we're in. You and Wang."

"I got you out, Eggman, didn't I?" he hisses.

"So what the hell are we still doing here, having a bloody party? They brought us here to amuse ourselves in a stolen house? What next, someone's going to bring a crate of wines, rolls of pot, music? And girls, perhaps? I mean if it's a party, for heaven's sake!"

"Danny boy, calm down."

"Look, Chip, I nearly died, man. They shot me. You're very lucky you didn't get shot—"

"I got beaten up, man. We all got beaten up."

"You didn't get shot! I could have fucking died, man. And for what – a few thousand dollars? Forget it. I'm getting out of here."

The effort of yelling sends a sharp pain through my shoulder. I slump into a sofa, seething with anger that almost smothers the pain away.

"If it's any consolation," says Chip. "The bullet went right through you. You'll live."

"Oh, thanks! I feel better already."

"You don't need to be rude."

"Absolutely," says Kabinga as he pulls a chair and sits facing me, smoking with slow deliberation, as if he's savouring the last joint before they hang him. "You heard the gunman: If you're rude, you could get shot." He laughs suddenly.

"I can see how being shot can be funny."

"Relax, Eggman…"

"To hell with you, Kabinga! What are you, some sort of warlord? Gangster? War criminal? Rwanda genocide, are you part of that? Tell me, how many people have you killed? No, forget it. I don't want to know."

"There are many things you don't know, Dan," he says, in a calm voice.

"Well, explain yourself."

"This whole thing wasn't supposed to end like this. It all goes back…it's a long story…"

"It doesn't look like we're going anywhere fast, does it? I mean, I don't see a helicopter outside waiting to whisk us back to Harare."

He chuckles with patient benevolence, like a school bully indulgently suffering one taunt after another from a regular victim who's emboldened by the presence of adults, waiting for a chance to exact revenge just as soon as the adults' backs are turned.

"Nanjing, my friend. That's where it all began. What you've talked about is only half the story. They took my money and tried to kill me, that part is true. I didn't rip them off. All right, maybe I overcharged them just a little. But remember, I was doing the White Card thing full-time. I gave up my studies for those people. I was available twenty-four hours a day. I could travel to Hong Kong or anywhere to shop for them at a moment's notice. Everyone else had to wait for weekends and holidays. I had to charge a premium small-small. It's as simple as that. But let me get to the point." He lowers his voice to a conspiratorial whisper. Marc starts to chuckle, and wanders away. He's heard all this before, whatever is coming. "What you don't know, my friend, but perhaps suspect, like most of the African students back in 1991, is that Wang was behind the whole thing, the beating, the attempted murder."

"What!" I reel back as if someone has punched me in the solar plexus.

"He was supposed to help me get my money out. Instead he stole it and tried to kill me to shut me up. Do you understand what I'm saying? He took my eighty thousand US dollars. That's how they started their business empire. He and his friends. This cop Yu Shian, and a bunch of others. I don't know this…what's his name?"

"Liu Ming?"

"Whatever. There were others. They owe their lives to me." He thumps his chest, King Kong-like.

"You're sure about this? Because that's not what I've heard."

"Heard from whom?" he demands, angrily.

"Well, Han Wei, for example."

"Oh, give me a break, man. The Whistle will say anything Wang pays him to say."

"He was paid to lie to me?"

"Han Wei has been their stooge all these years. Everything he owns, everything he's ever done, he owes it to them."

"Hang on. If Wang robbed you and tried to kill you, why are you still doing business with him? You've forgiven him, all in the name of doing business?"

"How can you forgive a man who tried to kill you? You revenge, small-small, yeah?"

I watch him, puzzled. Chip too is following the unfolding revelations as though they were a gripping courtroom drama, his eyes never once leaving Kabinga's face.

"Wang thinks I don't know he was part of it. The whole thing was beautifully choreographed, man. When I left Nanjing, I ended up in Belgium. That's where I went to complete my studies. My woman pulled strings. You remember Charlene? Tall American chick?"

"She never showed up after that first meeting at Wang's Den."

"Oh, man, she was into some deep-deep shit. Officially she was a journalist. Turned out she was a spy, an agent, CIA or something. I found out she was using me, getting information about foreign students, Chinese businessmen, students demanding democracy and all that stuff. Investigating China's motive for sponsoring African students. She spoke fluent Chinese, Eggman, but played dumb the whole time. Crazy! She helped me get to Belgium. Then we lost contact. Anyway, later I tracked Wang down through Han Wei, whom I've been working with, as it happens, from way back. Han Wei used to put me in touch with clients back in Nanjing. He was so connected, that boy, hey! Now we're into import-export. That's how I know they use him like a puppet. Han Wei has powerful relatives in Shanghai, top communists and what have you. Wang and company get protection that way. Han Wei's getting sick of this lot, and is sick, too, come to think of it. I got Wang interested in African coltan. He needs it desperately. Me and my people control tonnes of it in Congo."

"Jesus! You are truly a warlord."

"I'm a businessman, Eggman. Anyway, I arranged everything, lured Wang and his men to come down here. Ideally, I wanted them to come to Congo where they can get their arses kicked about small-small. But they're scared shitless of the fighting there."

"So why do they need me?"

"My meeting them was going to be a very small part of their itinerary. I don't live here. I fly in, get a job done, and fly out. They need a chaperone in Zim. And we all know you and he were bosom buddies."

"So what next?" I demand quickly, ignoring the jibe. "You were planning to kill them?"

He laughs. "That's too easy an option. I want my money back, with lots of interest, and diamonds. In the process, they get smacked on the wrist, just a little bit. Wang and company are more useful to me alive than dead."

"And the white rebels?" says Chip. "The gunmen really didn't know about that?"

"Of course not. But they needed to know, so they could get really pissed off. I've nothing to do with the white rebels. By associating with Wang, they too lose their deposit. Don't worry about them, man. They're no match for Mugabe's boys. They've brought in that South African former cop to advise them on how to fight for a white homeland. If you ask me, it's just bullshit. So you shouldn't believe that nonsense about me selling your beloved country to white rebels. I'm only selling a dream small-small. If they want arms, I'm the man. Of course, these particular arms will end up with the war vets. Hewitt is going nowhere. They might even kill him, if they're really pissed off. It's nothing to do with me, man."

His voice has a frightening hardness about it; it's hard to believe he's talking about real people taking each other's lives. I watch him closely, wondering how he acquired such callousness that allows him to talk about people's lives as though they were machines breaking down, needing to be replaced, or trashed. There's nothing about his demeanour that reveals what demons have penetrated his soul in the name of business.

Something else still bothers me.

"This attack we went through, you orchestrated that? Supposing we got killed? It doesn't make sense."

"I know. I'm owed an explanation. I think someone tried to double-cross that loudmouthed Makuni. Typical. They were supposed to fire rubber bullets just to cause a panic. I didn't see that helicopter clearly. It could well have been cops, getting in on the act. Good thing we lost them. No one was supposed to get hurt, Danny boy."

I watch his face closely. For a brief moment, I see the funny young guy in the first engineering class, bewildered by Professor Sheng's promise to feed us knowledge as though it were steamed rice. But the face quickly takes on the stern hardness of someone constipated by an indigestible diet of lies and betrayal and ends up grasping only the language of violence.

"Bizarre," mutters Chip. "If you were putting on a show for the Chinese, how about the beating – they were acting, too? They must be very bad actors. Those kicks and blows felt damn real to me, mister businessman."

"Like I said, it was either a double-cross or cops gate-crashed the party. It's not unusual in this line of work."

"All in a day's work, eh?" snorts Chip. "How reassuring."

I ask what the gunmen are planning next.

"They've got the guns. The Chinese will pay for their freedom. These guys will finance anything if there's a quick profit to be made, even a rebel movement, if it leads them to diamonds and coltan."

"Bloody hell!" mutters Chip. "You're talking about a war here, man. Can we just get out of here?"

Kabinga sits back, staring into space, lost in thought. Then he speaks in a voice so low we have to lean forward to hear him.

"You mention Rwanda, warlords, genocide. You have no idea what the hell happened in Rwanda. To you it's just stories about Hutus killing Tutsis, tribes forced to hate each other by the Belgians, their old colonial masters. You've no idea what it was like having Interahamwe gangs of hoodlums murder your family. Your own neighbours turning against you, raping your women, then murdering them. People who grew up with you, went to school with you, played football with you on the streets, chased girls with you small-small. You've no idea what 1994 was like. And all along, you're far away in Belgium, trying to survive. Your people are being slaughtered, and you have no idea because no one is fucking talking about it, not the papers, not the TV. The world just ignored us, man, our fellow African countries looked the other way, claiming it's an internal matter. The rest of the world didn't give a shit either. Most couldn't even place tiny Rwanda on a map. They only started to care when refugees showed up in Belgium, France, England, starving, bleeding, half-dead. Like dead fish washing up on their precious white beaches. Only then did they take notice. They couldn't ignore the smell and blood. You have no idea, Eggman. And you just come here from your air-conditioned, protected life in Asia calling us warlords. Man!"

My throat goes dry. I see Kabinga walking into our old hostel in an ill-fitting suit, his fortune gone, his pride injured beyond repair. I want to console him, to ask for more details, to apologise. But words elude me. His revelations make me yearn for the fragile innocence of our past, before the spectre of my mother's eagle started to haunt me, when all we cared about was to find somewhere to have a quiet drink and decent foreign newspapers to open a window into the world beyond China. But all that is now behind us, never to be retrieved, never to be relived.

"But why this kind of business, Chin Chin?" I ask, after a long silence, my voice barely louder than an apologetic croak.

"I tried to find justice for my people," he declares, eyes ablaze. "I went to Congo because I no longer had a home in Rwanda." He scans my face for a reaction, then, almost as an afterthought, says, "And I have to make a living, don't I?"

The sound of approaching vehicles brings the conversation to a close. A few minutes later, an armed man comes in with Liu Ming's briefcase. Kabinga opens it expectantly.

"Bastards!" he mutters, and turning to Marc, says, "They couldn't keep their filthy hands away from our cash."

"Let's see." Marc walks over to take a look. "Still looks good."

"I should have known. Come on, guys, let's get out of here."

Two jeeps are waiting outside. Kabinga and Marc jump into the first one.

"This is goodbye, then, my friends," says Kabinga, offering his hand, grinning from ear to ear.

"Sure," says Chip, wryly. "We must do this again sometime."

"Don't take it so hard, old boy, all right? End of the day, you get paid, don't you? No pain, no gain, eh? And as for you, Danny boy, get that shoulder looked at, all right? Look, guys, I'm sorry you went through all this shit. It wasn't supposed to go this way. If there's anything I can do, if you ever want a piece of the action, let me know. Wang and Han Wei know how to reach me. Don't be shy, Eggman, I owe you one."

"You've caused me enough trouble, Chin Chin. You don't owe me anything."

"I do." He assumes a faraway look as he puffs on a joint. "You covered my arse when the university tried to screw me. That was brave of you, man. They could easily have deported both of us small-small. I promised to take you and your girlfriend on a trip. It didn't happen, but I never forget a favour."

"Yeah, as Wang is finding out. Oh, sorry, I forgot – he's never going to find out."

"Relax, man," he says, laughing with unrestrained mirth. "Take her on a holiday, man, whoever she is now."

He throws a wad of notes at me, and before I can say anything, their jeep speeds off, shooting a burst of dust and rubble at our feet.

I'm All Ears

IT IS COLD AND WET in Chinhoyi town. Our driver intends to drop us off at the bus terminal, but we pay him to drive us all the way back to Harare. When we get to Harare, we ask him to drop us off at Unity Square, on Nelson Mandela Avenue. He doesn't need to know where I'm staying. But before taking a taxi to the hotel, I need to find a clinic to have my shoulder wound attended to and buy a new shirt. Chip knows a doctor who can treat gunshot wounds with no questions asked. On the way there, I try to call Wang on Chip's phone but his phone is switched off, which can only mean they haven't been released yet.

"You believe Kabinga?" I ask Chip. "That they wouldn't harm the Chinese?"

"They're not stupid enough to risk an international incident. Not while China's getting so interested in African raw materials and bringing money in. They'll hassle them a bit, rob them, maybe keep them a while to extort more money. But if they're going to kill anyone, it's the alleged white rebels. You feel sort of responsible?"

"I brought them here, man, remember? And I don't want them thinking I led them into some sort of trap. Did you see the look on Yu Shian's face when we were led away?"

"You shouldn't blame yourself. They set up the whole thing with Hewitt and Kabinga. I'm sure they swallowed Kabinga's act."

When we get to the hotel, a worried receptionist in a smart blue suit tells me they've been concerned that we've gone missing for two days. Perhaps she was afraid we had done a runner. But all our stuff is still in the rooms.

"You have some messages, sir," she says, handing me an envelope. "A General Chuma has been trying to reach you and your Chinese companions since yesterday. He sounded worried. Is everything all right, sir?"

"Yeah, everything is fine," I reply, hesitantly.

"If there's anything we can do, please, don't hesitate to contact us." She looks at me with sympathy. With the current security situation in the country, it is possible they've dealt with a disappearance or two.

I thank her and we head up to my room. The messages are all from General Chuma, wondering what has happened to us.

"All this hassle," mutters Chip, fetching a couple of beers from the minibar. "Why don't you check out of the hotel and stay with us? Why waste all this money? After everything that's happened, I can't imagine you still want that guy Wang covering you."

I've been thinking the very same thing.

"The stuff we've been through, Chip, I have very strong grounds for resigning from this assignment. And so do you."

"You're right," he murmurs, shrugging. "You got shot, after all. That can't be much fun. He wouldn't dare ask for the money back. As for me, I'm not about to give up another six grand for an extra week. I don't mind staying on as their lawyer, but I'm not getting into any more sticky situations. I'm not going to meet any more mystery contacts. And the minute I see weapons, I'm gone. I have one or two other contacts I can activate fairly easily for them. So I can basically run the show from now on."

I acknowledge the wisdom of Chip's words. Get out or stay on in a new capacity, where you can call the shots. After all, this is our country. First, I need to establish what happened to Wang and the gang.

"Are you going to call the general, or should I?" I ask Chip.

Before he can reply, the phone rings. It's the general. He goes straight to the point.

"Where are the Chinese?" he demands, in an agitated, gruff voice. "Our money has not been paid. What's going on?"

"We got into a little trouble, and—"

"What trouble?"

"We, er, we got attacked, beaten up, shot. But, we're fine. The Chinese haven't got away yet."

"Where did this happen?"

"Chinhoyi. The caves."

"Damn it! I knew it. I knew it."

"You knew?"

"Strictly confidential. We're on to it. We're having trouble with some hoodlums in that area. When you hear anything, call me right away."

While we wait for news, I call Lai Ying. She sounds anxious, and wonders why I haven't contacted her before. I tell her I was busy with family affairs and business.

"And how's this business going?" I detect a tinge of sarcasm.

"How's business going?" I pause. Chip is looking at me expectantly, waiting to see what lie I'll tell my wife. There's no need to worry her. "Hectic, crazy. How're my two lovely girls?"

"We're fine. Chacha has just gone to bed." There's a bleep. "Sorry, *lougong*, my battery is down. Let me charge it. Can you call me later?"

"Aren't you going to bed?"

"Tomorrow's Sunday, no need to work."

In the meantime, I call Alex. He's down at the Pirates' Rice Bowl.

"Glad you're still alive, man. Are you all right?"

"I got shot last night, actually. But apart from that, I'm fine."

"You got shot! Wang had anything to do with this?"

"Only indirectly. But, hey, I'm fine. We got caught in a crossfire between rival gangs. At least that's how it was explained to me. War vets, gunrunners, white rebels, diamond smugglers. It's nothing like getting beaten up in a dark alley in the Soho, man. It's wild!"

"That country's gone mad."

"It's nothing I can't handle, Alex. What was it you wanted to tell me?"

"I checked out your dudes. The news is not good. Wang's been running a massive smuggling ring. Petrol, wines, tobacco products, cars, white goods, steel. His companies are notorious for obtaining bank loans fraudulently, manipulating accounts, bribing officials. But no one has dared touch them. They've got the best protection money can buy."

"I know all that already, Alex."

"What you don't know, my friend, is that the ground is starting to shift."

"What are you saying?"

"There's talk of a reshuffle. If the top dog who's selling protection goes, heads will roll, my friend. I'm just saying be careful."

"All right. All parties come to an end, eventually. I know that."

"Yet you're still hanging out with these guys! Are you crazy?"

"I have a family to feed. Anyway, I'm not in on all this cloak-and-dagger stuff. I'm just a tour guide."

"You go on ahead, guide them to the nation's treasures. As you said, you've got a family to feed, right?"

Alex's words sting. Is that what I'm doing, helping sell my country to the highest bidder, just to make a bit of cash? I can find no words to answer him. After all, I did bring Wang and Co out here.

"They could just as well have come here without me, Alex."

"Of course. They're grown up, they can find their way around, I suppose. You just happened to be around. You can always tell Anticorruption you were on holiday, or looking up long-lost relatives, rescuing a country that has gone to the dogs. That's so fucking noble they'd give you a medal, man."

I feel a rush of heat in my face, as if I've passed by a blast of hot air from a heater in the winter. I hold the phone so tightly my fingers ache. Whatever happens now, there's no escaping the fact. The struggle for land is just about to enter a very bitter phase. For Father, it is looking increasingly like a pyrrhic victory, if it is a victory at all. The real winners are people like General Chuma. Wang and his gang are like vultures, hovering around menacingly, moving in to bite chunks off the land now that its soul is about to die. And my role in all this? Father looked up to me to bring agricultural knowledge and money. Has he let me off because of the futility of his own mission? And Mother? My misreading of her implicit expectations drove me close to the edge. But now I know better. And if the eagle stays with me, he'll be a friend, not a tormentor.

Suddenly my mouth fills up with bile. I take a big gulp of my Zambezi and swallow hard, gulping down a lump of shame in the process. Lai Ying's words come back to me in a mad rush, all those warnings to avoid the likes of Wang. Yet, here I am, leading him to the treasures of my land, paving the way for hundreds, maybe thousands, of other wannabe Admiral Zheng He opportunists like him. All in the name of business. All because of the need to fulfil a burning misplaced desire, to grasp opportunities that went begging in the past. Yet, like the dazed and miscalculating African fish eagle, all I end up with is an oversized tilapia.

"Alex, the arguments we had before, you were right to be concerned. What I've seen, it's just chaotic. The way things are going, soon there won't be any food to eat."

"I warned you, didn't I? That country will starve. If you had any sense you'd have seen it too."

"I know. So you won the argument, Alex."

"It's not about winning," he says coolly. "I lost my home, Dan. My roots, everything."

His loss is real. Yet my father would argue that Alex and his people were living on borrowed time, on stolen land. And my parents' home? I picture Father, proudly looking past the burning tobacco crop, as if hoping for salvation to come from beyond the hills, struggling to unite the people in the face of the arson and vandalism. Does *he* have a home? Can my parents call the workers' camp a home, or the farm itself for that matter?

"I don't have much of a home here either, Alex. Nor does my family. Where my father works, there's nothing left. Nothing works anymore."

"What a coincidence." He chuckles. "Nothing works for me in this job either. I'm quitting."

"Really! What are you going to do?"

"Start my own firm. I'm roping in two sharp locals who've also lost faith in the company. Half the staff's been laid off these last few weeks. Everyone's looking to move, afraid it's only a matter of time before they're let go. I've never seen Hong Kong this bad."

"Isn't it risky, venturing out on your own when the economy's so bad?"

"I've already tested the waters, Dan. I can do this."

"What do you mean? You've been moonlighting—" His breezy, guttural laughter interrupts me. "What's up with you, Alex? Why are you laughing like that?"

"Figure it out, dude! You're a smart guy."

"Are you saying…? Did you…?"

"Dan, we've both lost our country. We've got to look out for each other, my brother."

He hangs up before I can say anything. Chip is staring at me as if I've turned green.

We spend the rest of the afternoon drinking in the room, waiting for news. In the evening, Chip suggests we go to his house for dinner.

"Since you came back, all I eat is game meat," he complains. "Let my wife do some fine sadza with fried chicken for you, man. How often do you get that in China, eh?"

It's the best thing I've heard all day. It will be nice to meet his wife and two children again, after more than five years. Before I can answer, the phone rings. It's Wang. I find myself sighing with some relief that they're safe.

"Come to my room for drinks then we'll have dinner."

"We'll come and see you, Wang, but we have dinner plans."

"There's someone here who wants to meet you, Eggman."

"Not again, Wang," I snap. "The last time we went out to meet a mystery contact, I nearly ended up dead."

"It's all right, Eggman," he says, in a soft, placatory voice. "We nearly died, too. It has been terrible. We never expected things to turn out like that, and we lost a lot of money. It's different now. This is a true friend."

"I'm not sure, man," says Chip, wiping froth off his lips. "You never know with these guys."

"You're their lawyer. You've got to earn your money."

"I can quit, can't I?"

"And lose six grand? I don't think you have it in you, bro."

"There are limits to what one can take, Dan."

"So now it's your turn to get all soft?"

"Danny boy, you think just because you took a bullet you're some sort of hero now?"

"I don't know about hero, Chip, but after what we've been through, I can't imagine what could be worse now. Let's have a quick drink with them and then leave. I suggest you don't accept any commitments tomorrow so we can go see my sister in Mutare."

"Mutare might need two days, man. It's at least a three-hour drive."

In the end, I persuade him we're in the top hotel in the country. If it's not safe here, nowhere is.

Wang's room is a riot of aftershave lotions tinged with an infectious aura of celebration. The three of them are beaming, faces reddened by alcohol. On the coffee table, there is a half-empty bottle of brandy and a bottle of champagne in an ice bucket. General Chuma emerges from the balcony, holding a cigar and a glass of champagne.

"I've heard all about your troubles, gentlemen," says the general, with the contemplative air of a commander welcoming back a squad of special forces that has been tested to the limit in a commando raid, and have returned missing the odd limb, but nevertheless victorious.

Wang offers us champagne.

"Celebrate life, my friends," he says.

Gan be!

The room reverberates with laughter and excited chatter, and for the next half hour, we all forget our troubles and embark on celebrating being alive.

"I want to thank you, gentlemen," says the General, "for alerting us about our dear friends' whereabouts. Mister Wang has told me about the harassment and humiliation those worthless vagabonds put you through. The men have now been apprehended, including the farmer and foreign agent who staged the whole attack and were conspiring to engage in acts of high treason. Their farm has been seized forthwith, and our dear friends here have expressed a wish to purchase it and develop it. We are extremely pleased with this outcome, as you might well imagine. The economic saboteurs will face the full force of the law. My government thanks you for the role you've played in introducing our Chinese brothers to this country. Explain to them that our government will do everything in its power to make their stay here safe, comfortable, and fruitful. And for you two, get in touch with me next week so we can discuss how you will be rewarded for your patriotism and bravery."

General Chuma downs his glass and picks up a briefcase, which he caresses lovingly, as though it was the slim waist of his latest mistress.

Wang and the gang rise to shake our hands when I translate for them. They are looking at Chip and I in a new light, their faces beaming with gratitude and admiration. We've not only saved their lives, we have also helped realise the Zheng He dream. They stand in a semicircle beside General Chuma, each holding a glass of champagne like an award. The four of them are the new conquerors of Africa, working together, like a tightly knit team, united against what the general calls economic saboteurs, united against the interests of the people who will one day wake up to find their national assets mortgaged to men bearing briefcases full of US dollars.

When the general's gone, I can barely stand the triumphal grin on Wang's face. I try to picture him planning the attack on Kabinga. What did it cost back then to hire thugs to teach someone a lesson? I visualise him handing a wad of RMB to Han Wei to bribe the hospital staff after the gifts I gave them were deemed insufficient. And now he stands here, in the middle of Africa, grinning with a sense of accomplishment, swirling a glass of champagne in one hand, the other holding an enormous cigar. He keeps springing up these mystery contacts, but in my mind, he will always remain the biggest mystery. He puffs deeply on his cigar, eyes narrowed in concentration, as if he's trying to figure out what I'm thinking. I can't see myself sitting down with these people again, poking our chopsticks into the same bowls. By bringing him here, I've paid back that loan, many times over. That weight has been lifted off my shoulders.

As we get into a taxi, I suddenly remember I need to call my wife before she goes to bed. I borrow Chip's phone.

"I just got a call." She sounds agitated.

"What's the matter?"

"Minnie called me. Han Wei's wife. He was rushed into hospital yesterday. He was being operated on…"

"And? What happened?" Silence. "Darling, is he all right?"

"No, *lougong*. What can we do?…How can we help Minnie?"

The ground is starting to shift. I picture Minnie slurping her noodles, oblivious of the anti-corruption cops making their way up the stairs.

"Go and visit her tomorrow, darling. A visit, for now, please. And tell her she'd better sell everything and go away."

"I don't need to tell her that. It's always been her plan."

"Um…I know…Just tell her she has to do it urgently. She cannot delay. Can you do that?"

"Okay."

I want to say more, but my voice deserts me. An image of Han Wei with a frightened expression looms in my mind. His mouth is open as if he's about to whistle, wrinkles on his forehead squeezing his eyes shut. Lai Ying is waiting for me to say something. I glance at Chip, who's looking out the window, oblivious of the Chinese language. The taxi driver is trying to hide his perplexity.

I've no idea where the words come from.

"Lai Ying, come over, please. You and Chacha. Just one week, sweetheart, one week."

She starts to protest. "*Lougong*, be realistic…"

"I've never been more realistic." I think of Han Wei's pale, emaciated body, covered with a white, stained sheet. "Your company owes you leave. Chacha is not in school at the moment. Please, do this."

"It's too expensive, *lougong*. We can't afford it."

I chuckle as I remember Kabinga's travel allowance locked away in the hotel's safe deposit box, the American dollars that are appreciating in value by the minute as our currency goes into a tailspin.

"Please, darling. I need you to meet my people. Our families can't live like this forever. It's not right."

"Dan, you know I've wanted to meet them a long time."

"Then come, please?"

"Are we going to be safe?"

"A hundred percent. Apart from the occasional trouble at nightclubs, and fires in the countryside, everything's fine. No one's bothering ordinary people unless they're involved in politics, which we're not. Don't let the TV fool you. They show you a farm burning and the whole world thinks we're all dead or dying. I wouldn't bring you and Chacha here if I thought it was dangerous."

"Promise?"

"It will get worse in the coming months. All the signs are there. I want my wife and daughter to meet my parents and see the beauty of my country before our leaders destroy it."

"Oh, Dan. It sounds so bad."

"My cousin will help," I say in English, nudging Chip. "He knows people. Important people. He'll provide transport, and can arrange protection if we need it."

"Don't laugh. And your businessmen? I've no wish to meet them."

"You won't have to. I just feel so stupid. I should have trusted your instincts, darling."

"You never listen to me."

"I'm truly sorry, Lai Ying. From now on, I'm all ears. One more thing, darling: Don't quit your job yet, okay?"

"I wasn't planning to quit. Why do you say that?"

"It might take me a while to crack the Shanghai job market, in spite of what Julius says. What I saw in Shanghai, a China that is so different from what I remember. I know now, it will be home."

"Oh, *ban dan…*"

Another bleep. This time, it's Chip's phone. *You have less than one minute of airtime left.*

"What, *lougong?*"

"Tell Chacha not to nod and smile, but to laugh out loud. Tell her it's for real. It's not a secret anymore."

"Secret? What secret?"

"Africa. She'll know…"

You have no more credit. Bleep.

"What was that all about?" demands Chip.

"My wife and daughter are coming home."

"That's great." He shakes my hand as if I've won a prize. "But I thought you didn't want Chacha to see all the chaos?"

Chaos? What chaos? I let my eyes gaze upon the soothing green of Harare Gardens as we drive past. I'll bring Chacha and Lai Ying here for a picnic. They'll love the air, the bright green colours of the trees, grass and ferns, the songs of the birds building nests up in the trees. It is so peaceful here no one would believe there were any troubles in the country.

"They're not coming for the politics, but to meet family. We could be waiting forever if we want to see things get better, Chip. Anyway, with your connections to military generals, we'll be fine, right?"

He explodes into laughter, the first time I've seen him have a real good laugh in days. I desperately want to join him in the mirth. But I'm wondering who'll break the news to Wang. Or does he already know?

"Danny boy, you never cease to amaze me. But that's cool. I can't wait to see your girls."

Neither can I, and his family too, for that matter. I can almost sniff the delectable flavours of sadza and spicy fried chicken filling the corridor outside his flat.

∗∗∗